More praise for
THE LADY OF THE LABYRINTH

"Transports readers to strife-ridden Libya and romantic Sicily, blending the ancient with the modern in an action-packed tale of international intrigue . . . Brisk, captivating entertainment."

Booklist

"Llewellyn seems to have slipped easily into the Parthenon of Old Reliables in the realm of popular romantic suspense. This second novel, involv[es] an adventure in Sicily, marvelous scenery, cliff-edge dangers, and a myth of a fertility goddess."

The Kirkus Reviews

"Llewellyn skillfully weaves ancient and modern threads of greed and revenge into a richly atmospheric tale."

Publishers Weekly

D1253454

Also by Caroline Llewellyn
Published by Ivy Books:

THE MASKS OF ROME

THE LADY
OF THE
LABYRINTH

Caroline Llewellyn

IVY BOOKS • NEW YORK

Ivy Books
Published by Ballantine Books
Copyright © 1990 by Caroline Llewellyn Champlin

Library of Congress Catalog Card Number: 89–38135

ISBN 0–8041–0669–X

This edition published by arrangement with Charles Scribner's Sons, an Imprint of Macmillan Publishing Company.

Manufactured in the United States of America

First Ballantine Books Edition: June 1991

For my mother,
and to the memory of my father

"To the Lady of the Labyrinth, a jar of honey"
—*Inscription found at Knossos, Crete*

CHAPTER 1

Sicilia.

I have only to say the word, and the sirocco stirs again with a little shudder of dust, its hot breath whispering in my ear. On a bare mountainside, cicadas sing their tireless song, the pulse beat of the sun, while far below a man and a woman slowly sink together through the warm blue waters of the archaic sea. And as the last syllable of the ancient name dies away, I step once more into the labyrinth, lured back by the siren call of the past.

The heat, the fretful wind, and the sea were there when this story began, but the man and the woman appeared much later, some twenty-five hundred years later, on a wet May morning in Bonn. The morning that Hugo Raphael came back into my life. He sent no warning of course, no message or letter, nothing to prepare me. There had been no warning, either, when he disappeared three years before.

It seemed at first a day like all the others, with a thin rain thickening into a downpour as I drove to work along the Rhine. Umbrellas clustered at bus stops, the faces beneath them gray and cheerless in the watery light. Steam hung like a small cloud above a pretzel seller's cart as he pushed it hurriedly along the sidewalk to the shelter of a store awning. At a red light, I fished a handkerchief from my purse to wipe the condensation from inside the windshield, then switched on the radio, tuning in the American Forces station in time to catch the end of the news.

The last item was a call from the dead.

"Hugo Raphael, the controversial American architect, is reported to have fled from Libya, where he has lived for the past three years. Last month, after the American air strike of April fourteenth against Libya, Republican Congressman Jennings Hodge of Indiana called for a congressional investigation into

Raphael's purported close association with Libyan leader Colonel Muammar el-Qaddafi . . .''

An impatient blast from the horn of the car behind me drowned out the rest. The light had changed. For the next few minutes I drove without any sense of where I was going, blindly following the traffic ahead. When I realized that I had missed my turn, I pulled over to the curb and sat there with the motor running, watching the windshield wipers as they sluiced away the rain.

I had last heard from Hugo when I was twenty-three, before he passed out of my life and, in the eyes of many, beyond the pale, vanishing into Libya as thoroughly as a nomad into the desert. With one ruthless stroke, he had severed his past from a present he refused to explain or justify.

Hugo's past was glorious. He had first made a name for himself after the Second World War, not as an architect, but as a brilliant young British archaeologist whose most famous discovery, the spectacular beehive tombs at Capomonte in southern Italy, came about as the result of a dream—or so he claimed. When the twilight of archaeology's heroic age, the time of affluent, intuitive loners like himself, faded into myth, and the schools of technical archaeology took over, Hugo switched professions, and nationalities. At a point in life when most men are consolidating their careers, he started over—in architecture and in the United States, a profession and a country where there was still room, even encouragement, for the outsize ego of genius. There was little dispute about the size of Hugo's ego, somewhat more about the genius, but common consent eventually accorded him an international reputation. He made a specialty out of creating public buildings for governments and institutions the world over that wanted their cultural heritage to show to its best advantage, often incorporating ancient sites into the modern. The results were invariably beautiful, faithful in spirit to the past yet contemporary enough to please leaders who liked to be thought of as forward-looking.

Despite his equally international reputation as a hot-tempered, demanding autocrat, he was a man of considerable charm, famous for the number and beauty of the women he kept company with, a favorite of gossip columnists for many years. Handsome, wealthy, secure in his career, he had seemed to be someone on whom the gods smiled. Then, at the age of sixty-three, abruptly and without explanation, he had gone to Libya. Although rumor supplied reasons enough, some of them slanderous, he refused to explain why he had gone or what he was doing there. Some saw his puzzling decision to live in Libya as the act of a traitor, support for a leader whose stated purpose was to destroy American influence in the Middle East, and American lives along with it.

Now, it seemed, he was back.

And I was late. I was a very junior researcher with the Information Service of the American Embassy—a fact-grubber, as one of my colleagues inelegantly, if accurately, put it. Tomorrow I had a week's holiday, but today there was too much work and too little time for any calm consideration of what Hugo's return might mean. I would think about it in some sidewalk café in Madrid, with a glass of Spanish wine on the table and the hot Spanish sun shining down. It might be bearable like that.

A neat heap of assignments was waiting for me on my desk, along with a note from my supervisor telling me I was to complete them all before going off on my vacation. In Miss Shera's opinion, vacations were simply a dereliction of duty; she prided herself on never once using up all her own holiday time. I thought she would be happier in the Tokyo embassy, and tried to hint as much by posting articles about the amazing productivity and self-sacrifice of the Japanese worker on the office bulletin board.

After working my way through half the pile, I came on a request from Luke Kenniston, one of the political officers, for a biographical search. The subject was Hugo Raphael.

I sat staring at the memo for a long moment, then picked it up and went down two floors and along a corridor to Luke's office. He was at his desk, hunched over a stack of manilla folders. As he read, he ran his fingers through his dark hair until it stood up in quiffs all over his head, like the down of a newly hatched duckling. The inevitable rumpled tweed jacket, baggy at the elbows, hung over the back of his chair, and his garish tie—he was famous for his ties, this one was striped bright yellow and chartreuse—was loosened at the neck. Someone who had known Luke in his previous posting claimed that he had been a stylish dresser once. If that was so, Germany had cured him of it. But it really didn't matter what Luke wore—he was attractive in a way that had nothing to do with his clothes. I suspected, without ever having tested my theory, that, in his case, the fewer the better.

I stopped in the doorway. "Busy?"

He glanced up and smiled. He had hazel eyes and a smile of great charm, and a way of looking at you that implied there was no one half so interesting to him at that moment as you were. It could be devastating, that look, but it never seemed calculated. It was simply that Luke liked women. The feeling was mutual.

"I'm never too busy for you, Alison," he said. "You know that. Usually it's the other way around." With one foot he hooked a nearby chair and drew it closer to his desk. "What's up?"

I sat down, dropping his memo onto the desktop. "Why are we interested in Hugo Raphael? If it's not confidential."

"Have you heard the news yet?"

I nodded. "On the way to work. There wasn't much, just the fact that he'd left Libya."

"We don't know much more than that. Raphael appears to have parted ways with Qaddafi, and according to our people in Tunis, it doesn't look as though the divorce was friendly. Two days ago Raphael turned up there without warning, and apparently without possessions. A UPI reporter spotted him at the airport, but he refused to speak to her. According to her, he got on a flight to Palermo, but no one saw him get off, and so far no one has been able to trace him. Which is just as well if Qaddafi is after him."

Startled, I asked if that was likely.

"Who knows? At the moment it's pure speculation, based on the way Raphael left Libya and on the assumption that he might know too much for Qaddafi to let him slip the leash. You know he's been working on that new city of Qaddafi's, his desert Xanadu?"

"I thought that was just rumor."

Luke lit a Gauloise, his equivalent, he had told me once, of the bric-a-brac collected by other foreign service officers in their tours of duty. A Gauloise was a more effective way of reminding him of Paris, his posting before Bonn, than any number of miniature Eiffel towers. When I pointed out that miniature Eiffel towers weren't as hard on your health, he had given a very Gallic shrug and replied that it was difficult these days to find a healthy vice.

"We're inclined to think it's more than rumor," he said now, "although Qaddafi has been remarkably successful at keeping this city of his a secret. We knew he was up to something out there in the desert, but at first we thought it might be a missile base. We've been keeping an eye on military installations in Libya but this didn't seem to fit into that category. And it isn't near any major oil field, so we assumed it wasn't a new strike.

"Someone who knows a little Near East archaeology pointed out that it was the site of an ancient desert mosque, which used to be some sort of pilgrimage spot. There's always been an oasis there. Eventually we got satellite photos showing that whatever was going on was much larger than the archaeological site, and seemed to be laid out like a city plan. The theory is that Qaddafi is building himself a combination Brasília and Mecca, a city that will be both an instant holy city for believers and a political center for Arabs in the war against Israel.'' He flicked ash in the direction of the ashtray. ''A typical Qaddafi fantasy.''

''Will it work?''

''Probably not. But Qaddafi himself may be fanatical enough to think he can pull it off. If he can turn the place into a symbol for Arab Moslems, he may be hoping they'll take him seriously. He'd like to be the one to unite the Arab world, but so far he hasn't had much luck uniting Libya with anyone for very long.

''The odds are that the speculation about the city is true,'' he continued. ''Qaddafi's a Bedouin—he goes into the desert when he wants to hold secret meetings—so the desert is a logical choice for him. And he distrusts the cities on the coast because they're too vulnerable. Our bombing Tripoli proved him right, of course.''

''So you think that this city is the work Hugo Raphael has been doing for Qaddafi?''

''I don't think anyone has ever really been sure why a man like Raphael would stay in Libya all this time, but if the theory of the new city is right, it would explain a certain amount. After all, Raphael's combination of architecture and archaeology makes him the logical choice. Perhaps Qaddafi made him an offer too tempting to resist. There can't be many opportunities around on that sort of scale for a man of his talents. He's getting on, too—maybe he saw it as a kind of finale, the capstone to his career.''

He dropped his cigarette into the remains of some cold coffee, where it sizzled and stank, then leaned toward me, his eyes troubled. ''The question is, why has he left? He was never someone to let politics get in the way of his work, never seemed bothered by Qaddafi's anti-American activities, and he was willing to put up with considerable bad press because of his relations with the mad dog of the desert. Those can't be the reasons why he's pulling out now.''

I remembered a recent article I'd seen in the conservative *National Journal* that had lambasted the Americans, most of them in the oil industry, who had defied the government's order to leave Libya. ''Yankee Come Home'' was the title of the article, and in it the writer accused Hugo of being "an intellectual mercenary, selling his talents to friend and foe alike."

"Our air strike must have had something to do with it, don't you think?" I said.

He gave an ironical smile. "You mean, it might have occurred to him that there wasn't much point in building a city that might be flattened before it was finished?"

"That wasn't what I meant, but I guess it's possible." I knew that Hugo was a pragmatist where his work was concerned. Dreams were all very well as inspiration, I remembered his saying once, but they shouldn't blind you to reality. Reality was a set of circumstances; if you didn't like the circumstances you changed them, and if you couldn't change them you cut your losses. At the time, I had wondered if he included people in his definition of "circumstances."

Slowly, I added, "I was really thinking that if Raphael was in Libya against his will, the confusion after the attack might have given him the chance he needed to get away."

Luke was not convinced. "There's never been any hard evidence that he was forced to stay there. On the contrary, he seems to have been something of an honored guest."

I registered the first adjective. "Hard evidence? There's other evidence, then?"

"I only meant that unproven speculation is all we have. There's nothing concrete."

"The radio used the word 'fled.' Honored guests don't need to escape out the back door."

"And we're back where we started," he said equably. "But it should be interesting to see what he does next. He's someone who seems to take a certain pleasure from confounding expectations."

I could feel the stiffness of my smile. "Yes, I think he does."

Luke swung his long legs up onto the desktop and leaned back, arms folded across his chest. "Now it's your turn, Alison."

"What do you mean?"

"I've told you why we're interested. You tell me why you are."

I got up and shut his office door. As he watched me come back to the chair beside his desk, he opened a fresh pack of cigarettes, stripping away the wrapping. The crackle of the cellophane was the only sound in the room.

Conscious as I spoke that the words, and the closing of the

door, bordered on melodrama, I said, "This is just between you and me, all right?"

He nodded.

"Hugo Raphael is my father."

CHAPTER 2

Luke was lighting a second Gauloise as I spoke. He stared at me over the still-burning match, extinguished it with a flick of his wrist, and dropped it into the ashtray. There was a long moment when we simply looked at each other before he said quietly, "But your last name is Jordan."

"It's my aunt's name, my mother's half sister. She and my uncle adopted me when I was three years old."

"I didn't realize . . . What happened to your mother?"

"She wandered off when I was two, and that was the last I saw of her. The original hippie, my mother." Which was only a polite way of saying deadbeat, according to my uncle Harold. "My aunt was much older than my mother, and very different. Maybe that's why I ended up with her. Anyway, after my mother gave permission for the adoption, she lost touch with us. Later we heard she got married and settled in Australia. As far as I know, she's still living there."

"Didn't Raphael object to the adoption?"

"He didn't have much say in the matter. He and my mother never married. Not that he didn't acknowledge me as his child, he was always straight about that much."

"I see." Luke took his feet down off the desktop; his shoes left scuff marks behind on the glossy surface, which he rubbed at absentmindedly with one sleeve. "The little you've said about your family . . . well, I figured it wasn't a subject you enjoyed. I'm sorry."

I shrugged. "Don't be. I've come to terms with it."

There was a silence. I looked at the dripping branches of the chestnut tree outside the window; the bark was a sodden black, and the tips of the pale white candles drooped with the weight of the rain. It had been raining for days.

Luke turned the unlit Gauloise over between his fingers, con-

8

sidering it, then struck another match. "I take it from your questions that you don't know much more about Hugo Raphael right now than most people. Why is that?"

"Hugo wasn't what you'd call a doting father. I don't think there was much room in his life for a small child. He did visit me now and then, and sometimes I spent the school holidays with him. We had a friendly relationship on the whole, but not what you'd call close. Though when I was in college, things seemed to be getting better. . . . But then he went to Libya, and that was the last I heard from him." It was a bare-bones account in a bloodless voice; it might have been some other person talking, someone quite detached from it all.

"So he hasn't been in touch with you recently?"

"No."

"You must have been worried about him, with all that's been happening in Libya. Especially after the attack."

With a twist of pain, I recognized this as the simple truth. I had been frightened for Hugo, but I had never allowed room for the fear in my conscious thoughts. For some inexplicable reason, I had assumed that he was working somewhere in the desert, safely remote from the Tripoli bombings. And after all, Hugo was indestructible, as all parents are. He more than most. It was unthinkable that anything could happen to him. But now that I knew he was safe, I acknowledged the fear.

"You don't happen to have any idea where he might be holed up right now?" Luke asked me.

"Didn't you say he flew from Tunis to Palermo? Maybe he stayed in Sicily."

"Maybe." Through a small cloud of cigarette smoke, Luke stared at me as if I might know something he didn't. Suddenly I wished that I had said nothing to him about Hugo, and wondered why I had. Perhaps it was simply the impulse to tell someone who I really was, to say Hugo's name aloud, to make him real again. But did I want him real again?

I stood up. "I'd better get back. Miss Shera is determined to squeeze every last minute's worth of work out of me before my vacation. You're off too, aren't you? Paris?"

He nodded. "Still planning to go to Spain?"

"As long as there's sun."

"Don't tell me Germany's weather has got you down. Isn't rain supposed to be good for the skin?"

"Maybe. But five months of it is death on the spirit. For the first time I understand just what *Angst*, *Weltschmerz*, and *Scha-*

denfreude mean. I'd rather have a Spanish sunburn." Before I turned to leave, I added, "Or a Sicilian."

I was only halfway to the door when he grabbed my arm, not gently. "I don't think this would be the best time for a family reunion. Not if Qaddafi's men are looking for Raphael."

"I wasn't serious, Luke. Hugo hasn't shown more than a passing interest in me since I was born. Is it likely I'd go searching for him now?" I didn't mean to sound bad-tempered, simply matter-of-fact; I prided myself on a hard-earned detachment as far as Hugo Raphael was concerned. "Anyhow, aren't you being a little melodramatic? Why would an architect be such a threat to Qaddafi?"

"Qaddafi doesn't like defectors." He put his arm around my waist. "Why don't you come to Paris with me instead? I could show you sights the average tourist never gets to see. There's a club in Montmartre that has an amazing monkey act. These three monkeys and this incredibly beautiful woman—"

"My very own, very blue guide to Paris? Thanks, but I shock too easily. I think I'll stick to the pleasures of the Prado." I slipped out from the curve of his arm. "But I'm sure there are a lot of girls around who'd like your version of a Sentimental Education."

"It would be more fun to educate you, Alison."

"I'll remember that if I ever do postgraduate work."

The offer wasn't unappealing. I liked Luke's sense of humor; I also liked the harder edge that showed from time to time—with Luke, there was always a disturbing sense of other, more complicated layers below the easy-going surface. I found that exciting. But until recently I had been involved with someone else, a German I'd met when I first arrived in Bonn, while Luke had had a succession of someone elses. Our friendship, Luke's and mine, had evolved during a number of group dinners with colleagues and, lately, several casual lunches together. Friendship, I thought, was all I wanted from Luke.

"Sure you won't be lonely, all alone in Madrid?" he asked me.

"If you mean, am I going alone, yes I am, and no, I won't be lonely."

"The Herr Professor Doktor won't be along? Television commitments getting in the way, are they?" He grinned amiably. "You know, I've always wondered how he has any time left over for his students."

"That's unfair. Bernd is a good teacher."

"Who's your source—Bernd Renner? Though I will grant that if the PLO funded a chair in public relations at the Freie Universität, he'd be the obvious candidate."

"What makes you say that?" But I was being deliberately disingenuous; I knew very well why.

"Haven't you heard him on the subject? God knows he preaches on TV often enough."

"I haven't got a television. I know he's pro-Arab and left-wing, but to be frank, his ideas weren't what attracted me to him."

"I'm relieved to hear that. They're the least attractive thing about him." Luke was leaning back against the doorway, his arms folded across his chest. "So you're not seeing him anymore?"

"No."

"Good. Now I can tell you what I really think of him."

"You don't have to bother, it was always perfectly clear."

"Thank God. I was afraid I might have been too subtle."

I resisted the bait, asking mildly, "Not that I care, but what was it about Bernd that you objected to, apart from his politics?"

"You mean there's more to dislike about the man?" He mimicked thoughtfulness, brow furrowed. "Come to think of it, you're right. So let me give you a list. First off, I don't like people who make people I like miserable." I could feel myself flushing, and was about to protest, but he went on. "Or maybe I just don't like being lectured to, even by someone twice my age. Okay, okay, that's an exaggeration—he only *looks* twice my age. But I think the moment I knew I couldn't stand him was that evening we were all in the Königskeller together, when he took the time to educate me on our sins in the Middle East, El Salvador, Nicaragua, et cetera, et cetera. He was so goddamned reasonable about his prejudices, too."

I winced. "He can be a bit preachy, I admit. Idealists sometimes are. . . ."

"A bit? He makes Savonarola seem wishy-washy." Luke gave me an ironic look. "So when he found he couldn't convert you, he split?"

I tried for a dignified note. "Actually, I was the one who decided to end it."

"A wise decision." Luke turned to open the door with a flourish, and we went out into the hall together.

Luke was only partly right in his guess that Bernd and I had come to grief over politics, or rather my lack of any. But do many women really fall out of love over ideological differences? I don't think so. The real reason I broke up with Bernd was his infidelity—more accurately, infidelities. I didn't mind being preached at by a man whose passion for social justice coincided with a passion for me—but when I discovered that Bernd's passions also included a number of other women, I ended the sermons.

"I always figured Renner was an aberration," Luke said as we walked down the hall together. "Not Elinor's type at all."

Unwisely, I had once told Luke that one of my well-read and very dull cousins called me Elinor, after the sensible Dashwood sister in *Sense and Sensibility*. He imagined he was paying me a compliment—or perhaps it was a backhanded compliment to my aunt's upbringing. Aunt Constance had been determined that I, unlike my parents, would conform to the way "ordinary decent people" lived, and her training somehow stuck. In impatient moments, I imagined Aunt Constance leaning over my cradle and muttering, like the Emily Post of fairy godmothers, "Alison Jordan, you will always do the sensible thing."

I usually did. Sensibly, I accepted my mother's disappearance from my life, Hugo's intermittent, exciting appearances, and my aunt and uncle's undemonstrative, anxiously loving care. After their deaths, in a car accident when I was nineteen and in college, I pretty much looked after myself. On graduating, I went off to work in Europe, sensibly putting several thousand miles between my past and me. Apart from the spectacular lapse from common sense that Bernd Renner represented, I was careful, conservative, and, I realize now, a bit of a prig. And I was beginning to grow just a little bored with my life.

"Elinor Dashwood's type, if I remember the story rightly, was extremely dull," I told Luke. "And whatever Bernd's faults may have been, he was never that. Besides, I'm fed up with Elinor."

But Luke was no longer listening; he seemed to be thinking about something else. As I was on the point of leaving, he said abruptly, "Should I get someone else to do the search on Raphael?"

I shook my head. "I can manage."

"In that case, would you mind adding a paragraph or two of your own impressions? It might be helpful to have some sort of personal insight into the man."

But I balked at that. "There's no point, Luke. I don't know

any more about him than *Who's Who* does. Probably less." This wasn't true; but what I knew was such a mosaic of irreconcilable contradictions and intense, isolated moments, all of it colored by conflicting emotions, that the knowledge was virtually useless. "Anyway, I did say that what I've told you is just between us."

His eyes held mine a little too long, but he didn't force the issue. "Okay. Do what you can then. Promise me one thing, though . . ."

"What's that?"

"That you'll let me know if he gets in touch with you."

It seemed so unlikely that I would hear from Hugo before I left for Spain, that I agreed.

Later, when I was back at my desk, it occurred to me that Luke hadn't really answered my first question. Why did he want the information on Hugo? If Hugo was in Sicily, he was, after all, technically the Rome embassy's problem, not ours.

But my job was to supply answers, not ask the questions. Dutifully, I spent the rest of the morning compiling a brief dossier on Hugo Raphael. As an exercise in sifting fact from fiction, it was instructive; as the whole picture of the man, it was miserably inadequate.

For the most part, the sources managed to agree on the basic facts of his later life, but when it came to early details that were harder to verify, they differed considerably, even wildly. Meticulous in his work, Hugo was never very reliable when it came to the subject of his own life. He hated reporters, doing his best to confound them when they tried to interview him, and he loved a good story. Some people accused him of being his own mythmaker; others, those who knew him better perhaps, said that he was simply protecting his privacy with a labyrinth of misleading tales.

Contemporary Architects, for instance, got the professional details right for Hugo's careers—with the emphasis naturally on the second: the publications, the long list of works ranging from the fairy-tale villa of Nubar Haqqim, the fabulously wealthy arms dealer, in Beirut (since destroyed), to the Settecamine housing project at Rome, the awards, medals, societies, academies. But it gave him too many wives, and not enough children. As far as I knew, Hugo had married only twice. His first marriage, when I was nine, to a wealthy widow some years older than he, was so brief that I never met the woman. As for the extra wife, some relative or other had once let it slip in conversation when I was present that this early "marriage," to a Moroccan woman Hugo had met while digging in North Africa, had never been legally valid. My name, of course, did not appear; only the son by his last wife was mentioned, a half brother eleven years younger than I was, whom I barely knew.

Even his birth lent itself to a certain romanticizing independent of Hugo's own. At the tender age of twenty-one, fresh from Cambridge, Hugo's father, Richard, had met and fallen in love with an Italian opera singer who had come to London to pursue her career and a rich patron. By all accounts she was a very beautiful Sicilian, reputed to be at least ten years older than Richard Raphael. Richard, whose father was an associate of the Rothschilds, had vague musical leanings and the prospect of a lot of money. Despite his family's objections, he succumbed to the opera singer's charms and married her. But the opera singer, it seemed, was already married, and after Hugo's birth her legitimate husband put in an appearance. Surprisingly, Richard Raphael insisted on keeping his son. There was a brief and highly publicized skirmish in the courts, but Richard failed to persuade the judge that he was the father. Only the payment of a very large amount of Raphael money succeeded in retrieving Hugo from his mother. The opera singer and her husband went to Paris, where she died shortly afterward, some said of a broken heart. Richard did not outlive her for long. He drowned in a boating accident in 1922, when Hugo was two years old. After that, Hugo grew up in good, upper-class English fashion, raised by nannies in his grandparents' house until he was old enough for boarding school. From there, he had gone to Christ Church, Oxford, and then out into the world, a comparatively rich young man determined to make something of his gifts.

I found a 1950 article from *Life* magazine, written just after Hugo made his archaeological discoveries at Capomonte, when he was thirty. Accompanying it were pictures of Hugo taken in Libya, of all places, at a dig on the coast near Lepcis Magna. It was a dramatic setting, and in one photograph in particular Hugo made the most of it. He stood with one foot resting on a tumbled pillar, the tall, powerful body in three-quarter profile. His massive head with its great prow of a nose was thrust forward as he gazed out over the vast rubble of the ruins toward the sea.

But in the photograph, and in person, his eyes were what you noticed first. Not their color, which was a bright, piercing blue, for the photograph was in black and white, but what the eyes held. A restless, questing vitality that gave the handsome face its intense magnetism.

The journalist for *Life* noted that Hugo "walks over the ruins with the brisk, purposeful manner that distinguishes the archaeologist from the casual treasure-seeker. This young war hero has already made considerable discoveries in places where others believed there was nothing left to find. When asked to explain his success, he replies simply, 'Controlled imagination. It's worth more than any amount of technology.' "

Another, later clipping, from *Architecture* magazine, stated: "He matches ancient forms with modern materials to produce buildings endowed with extraordinary spiritual powers. . . ." There was a photograph of the refectory he had built for the monks of St. Bride's Island in the Orkneys. Outwardly it was a simple stone building in keeping with the rest of the austere fourteenth-century monastery, but inside the plainsong became paean in a harmony of glass and steel and light. The large abstract tapestry, representing the saint's vision, that hung above the high table had been designed by Hugo himself.

In 1982, the year before Hugo went to Libya, *Time* profiled his work as an architect. The article called Hugo "a worldly visionary who uses the past to build the future." He was quoted as saying: "Archaeology taught me that we build on sand. And yet, as an architect, I must build as if the sand were stone." And later: "When I was an archaeologist I was interested in digging up people, not things. The same principle still guides me. I build for people, not for some abstraction called the state or the corporation or the church."

And again: "All archaeologists dream of treasure. I know I did, still do. As an architect, I hope that I am building some future archaeologist's treasure. I should know better, of course."

When asked why he thought Hugo was so quickly successful in a profession he had come to relatively late in his life, another architect had replied, "He always has a private blueprint of action. He knows so clearly what he wants and he can make you see his vision. Moreover, you can see that he has the ability to carry out his vision."

The picture with the *Time* article showed a man still large and powerful, but with the signs now of age; the broad shoulders were slightly stooped, the nose seemed even more prominent, and his dark hair was thinner, graying. But the eyes, I thought, were still a young man's eyes. They were filled with the same questioning restlessness.

Other people talking, this time from my memory, not on record. First, my aunt Constance, wonderingly: "He has no sense of guilt, that man. Not an ounce of it."

Then a woman who was Hugo's lover briefly, and who had an extravagance to match his. At sixteen, I spent a magical weekend in New York with the two of them, when for some reason or other Hugo decided I was now an adult and should taste some of the adult pleasures of the city. I remember the woman, whose name I've long since forgotten, leaning toward me with a rustle of taffeta and saying, "In another age, Alison, your father would have been an epic hero. He deserves his own company of knights." When the affair was over she married a millionaire who had commissioned one of the private houses Hugo designed. Hugo had introduced them to each other.

Hugo himself this time: "All my mistresses make good marriages. I take care of that."

"He's a slave-driving s.o.b. who should have been neutered at birth. But the bastard can build." This from the owner of a large construction firm who had worked with Hugo on a project—the ex-husband of Hugo's second wife, Charlotte. Hugo, with a great yelp of laughter, recounting this story against himself.

So many facts, so many opinions. And in the end, they added up to a single man.

During my childhood, I had heard other stories about my father, many others. I tried to forget most of them. Told with passion, malice, envy, humor, admiration, filled with contradictions, they confused me. But because I saw my father so rarely, everything he said and did when I was present was stamped indelibly on my memory.

Like an evenhanded judge, I did not permit hearsay in my report. I merely listed important dates, proven facts, published work, and contented myself with pointing out the discrepancies in the sources. When I finished, I took the manilla folder along to Luke's office, which was empty, and placed it on his desk. I wasn't sure Luke would be able to keep his promise not to tell anyone I was Hugo's daughter, but at least I would be safely out of reach in Spain if my secret came out.

CHAPTER 3

At lunchtime, I went back to my apartment to do a little packing. I have never been able to fling a few belongings into a suitcase and take off. For me, part of the pleasure of a trip comes from the small preliminaries—leafing through guidebooks, buying sunscreen, new sunglasses, a novel for the beach, deliberating between the Marimekko with the yellow stripes and the blue cotton Laura Ashley—and I like to linger over them.

Footsteps came splashing up behind me as I walked through the embassy parking lot. Before I could turn around, Luke ducked his head under my umbrella. He'd forgotten his own umbrella, he said, and asked if I'd walk him to his car, which was parked not far from mine. With pleasure, I said, and as he was taller gave him the umbrella to hold.

"Did you know that there's a tribe in New Guinea that has over a hundred names for rain?" he told me as we navigated our way through the puddles. "My favorite is 'the lonely tears of the moon when she is waning in the sky.' Though sometimes I think I almost prefer 'Look out, the birds are pissing on our heads again.' They're loose translations, of course."

Luke and I sometimes played a game in which one of us produced some bizarre bit of information and claimed it as true. If the other challenged it and the "fact" was provable, the doubter paid a forfeit, usually in the form of a beer. We were fairly evenly matched, although because of my work I had a slight edge. But Luke was very good at making you believe him.

I called him on this one, however, and he confessed he'd made it up. "So I owe you a beer when you get back from Spain. When do you leave, by the way?"

"Tomorrow morning. Which reminds me, I'd better call Lufthansa and confirm the flight. How about you?"

"I was planning to take off for Paris late this afternoon, but

17

it turns out I've got to meet a couple of junketing congressmen. The odds are I won't get away until tomorrow, unless I can stuff them so full of bratwurst and beer at lunch that all they'll want to do is sleep this afternoon." With a sideways glance at me, he added, "Do you know what would console me for having to leave a day later?"

I remembered the club in Montmartre, and the lady with her animal act. "Monkey business when you get there?"

He was quick to catch the reference. In a mock-offended voice, he said, "I was never anything but an interested observer. The Foreign Service frowns on close fraternization with the locals. You know that."

I did, but doubted it was a rule much observed by Luke. "What would console you, then?"

We had reached his car. Before he turned to unlock the door of the driver's side, he said, "Dinner with you tonight."

I was startled. My first instinct was to resist this unexpected complication, to postpone any involvement with Luke until I had come to terms with the damage done by Bernd. "I don't know, Luke. I still have a lot left to do."

"Just an hour or two. You have to eat, after all." He stood very close to me under the umbrella, his face serious now.

It was such an appealing face, much more than the sum of its regular, handsome features, the hazel eyes with their dark lashes and the eyebrows that sloped slightly downward, which gave his smile a deceptively sleepy look. These were very satisfying in their way, but the appeal really came from a slight sense of tension created by apparent contradictions, the humor that failed to mask a fundamental seriousness, an intensity lightened by his willingness to poke fun at himself. And that seductive ability to make you feel somehow singled out, special.

Almost in spite of myself, I said I would have dinner with him. "But I need time after work to run a few errands."

"Eight o'clock okay? Good. I'll pick you up then." He smiled, and got into his car. And I was left with an unsettled feeling that told me I would have to be careful.

My apartment was on the second floor of a modern building on a hillside overlooking the Rhine, a characterless brick box redeemed by the view from my living room window. As it was still raining in a steady downpour that sent water swirling along the gutters, I parked the car in the underground garage rather than on the street. The slam of the door echoed in the dim silence; most of the other tenants' cars were gone for the day. The air was chilly, heavy with the smell of diesel exhaust and damp concrete. I set the car alarm, installed by a previous owner whose anxieties I had come to be grateful for—a number of my neighbors' cars had been broken into in the past month.

As I walked toward the entrance ramp I was looking down, carefully picking my way around the oil slicks and a few shallow pools of greasy water. I saw the man's shadow stretching down the ramp before I saw his face.

Startled, I jerked my head up. A tall, thin figure stood at the top of the ramp, silhouetted against the watery light. Behind him, the rain was falling like a curtain.

Before I could react, he took a few steps down the ramp toward me. It was a boy's face, I saw then, not a man's, the pale bony face of a boy in his middle teens, with a streak of dark hair pasted flat against his forehead. On his right cheek there was a long smear of dirt mixed with something that might have been blood. He was wearing a filthy windbreaker, ripped on one sleeve and soaking wet, and over one shoulder he held a backpack. He looked exhausted to the point of desperation.

His mouth was moving, but the rain drowned out his words. I shook my head, unwilling to go closer until I knew what he wanted. He didn't look like a thief—but, after all, what did I know about thieves? In German I shouted that I couldn't hear him, but he obviously didn't understand. Suddenly he said loudly in English, "Are you Alison?"

I nodded, and walked a few paces toward him. "Why?"

"I'm Jay."

With the flat of one hand he pushed the wet hair out of his eyes. The eyes were wary. They watched me without blinking while I took in what he'd told me.

And then I knew who he was. "Of course," I said, off balance. "Of course you are."

He was my brother, or rather my half brother, Hugo's son by his last marriage, Julius Andrew Yardley Raphael, to give him his proper name. I had seen him only twice before, the last time five years ago in Hugo's New York apartment, when he was ten years old, on the short side and plump. He had been a quiet child, shy with the half sister so much older than he was, uneasy perhaps under all the attention Hugo was paying him. I remembered feeling ashamed of a small twinge of jealousy at the fuss Hugo was making over this unknown little brother.

Slowly, I started up the ramp toward him. We stood there for a moment simply looking at each other, before I reached up awkwardly to kiss him, resting my hand on his shoulder. Through the wet cloth of the windbreaker I could feel him shivering. "Let's go inside," I said. As we went up the steps to the entrance, I asked him how he knew to find me in the garage.

"Luck. Your superintendent told me you wouldn't be back till tonight. I was just leaving when she saw your car turn into the driveway."

"Have you come all the way from England?" I knew he went to boarding school somewhere near Oxford. Although his mother, Charlotte, was American, she had sent Jay to school in England when he was thirteen. Some said it was to protect him from the increasingly bad press Hugo was getting in the States; those less kindly disposed toward Charlotte claimed she found it inconvenient to have such an obviously growing boy around to emphasize her own ripening years. I had never met Charlotte, but she figured frequently in the magazines that chart the lives of the flamboyant; her romantic past was easily a match for Hugo's. They had divorced shortly before he went to Libya, but it was common knowledge that the marriage had ended long before that.

He nodded. "I left yesterday. No one knows I'm here."

I glanced at him, but he did not explain. More questions, I decided, could wait until he was dry and fed.

Frau Gottschalk, the *Hausverwalterin*, was waiting for us in the hall. "You are back, Fräulein Jordan," she announced, settling her thick arms comfortably across her stomach. "I told the *Junge* it was your car." Her small eyes darted from Jay to me, bright with curiosity. I said that Jay was a relative whom I hadn't seen in a long time; the exact truth, I knew, would only launch her on questions I couldn't answer. While Jay waited for me in the hall, I went with Frau Gottschalk into her office to collect my mail.

"So, tomorrow you go to Spain," she said as she handed me a bundle of advertisements. There were no letters, there rarely were; I am a bad correspondent. "I will take good care of your plants," Frau Gottschalk went on, "as if they were my own. And I will do a little dusting. No, it would be a pleasure, Fräulein Jordan." This was the simple truth; the eradication of dirt in all its forms was Frau Gottschalk's mission in life. She glanced at Jay, who stood leaning wearily against the wall opposite her office, then whispered loudly, "Poor young man, he is tired. And so dirty that I think he must be very much wanting a bath."

Jay followed me down the hall, stumbling a little on the short flight of stairs that led up to my apartment. He stood just inside the front door, hugging the backpack to his chest, while I carried his dripping windbreaker into my tiny kitchen and draped it over a stool. "You look exhausted," I said. "Explanations can come after I've made us lunch. The bathroom's that way, if you're interested. Make yourself at home. I won't be long."

When I came back into the living room with a tray of hot soup and sandwiches, I could hear the sound of running water coming from the bathroom. I spread a yellow cloth over the round white table in one corner of the room and set out the food. After a few minutes Jay emerged, his hair slicked back from his forehead and the dirt gone from his cheek. He had changed into another pair of jeans. He looked even younger now, with the vulnerable quality a boy has when his body is growing too fast. Where the dirt had been, there was a jagged, nasty-looking cut. I fetched ointment and a bandage, insisting he use both, and then we sat down to lunch.

He looked around as he pulled his chair up to the table. "This is a nice place. Is all this stuff yours?"

"Unfortunately. I've lived in Europe for four years now, plenty of time to clutter up my life." But Jay was right; it was a nice place, a combination of functional white IKEA furniture warmed up with bright pillows and an apple-green rug, lots of plants, and an antique wedding chest painted blue that I had found in an open-air market in the Odenwald. "If I didn't have so much," I added, "I might find it easier to move."

"You don't like Bonn?"

"I've been here long enough. I'm ready for a change." I poured soup into his bowl and handed him the rolls.

Neither of us spoke while we ate. He concentrated on the food and I studied him surreptitiously, struck by his likeness to Hugo. The eyes were the same, a light, piercing blue, and the harsh line of the jaw, with its stubborn, almost arrogant, thrust. His nose, whose high-bridged arch was indisputably Hugo's, was still too big for his face, but he had the beginnings of what promised someday to be the same large-boned good looks; even his weariness, which had drained all color from his cheeks until his skin seemed sallow, and the strain visible in the thin line of his mouth, failed to disguise that.

Other, deeper similarities appeared later.

After swiftly and silently disposing of the soup, two pumpernickel rolls stuffed with liverwurst and Tilsit cheese, and a large slice of cherry strudel, he wiped his mouth with his napkin and sat back. "Thanks. For the food, which was great, and for letting me eat before you asked any questions."

"I'm afraid the questions start now. I take it this isn't just a fraternal visit. Has it got anything to do with Hugo?"

He nodded, then asked, "You call him Hugo?"

For the simple reason that he never struck me as anyone's dad, let alone mine. But I said only, "What name do you use?"

"When I was little I called him Daddy. Hugo makes sense, I guess." His voice cracked slightly and he cleared his throat. "Anyway, yes, that's why I'm here. Partly. To be honest, though I'm glad to be here, I wouldn't have come if I hadn't lost all my money. That was last night, near Paris. I remembered you lived in Bonn, and I figured it was sort of on the way. So I hitchhiked here."

"On the way to where?"

"To Sicily. That's where he is."

"You're going to Hugo? You mean he's waiting for you?"

"Well, not exactly." He played with some breadcrumbs on the table, rolling them into pellets.

"But you know where to find him?"

"Not that either, not really. It's more that I have a pretty good idea where he might be. Anyway, I have to find him. There are these men, you see, and I think they must be after him. . . ." The words tumbled out so quickly that he stuttered a little.

"Stop right there." I got up. "I'm going to make coffee. While I do that you get your thoughts organized, and when I come back I want the whole story, from the beginning. Okay?"

"Okay." He gave a wan smile.

In the kitchen, I concentrated on measuring out the coffee, and watched the water boil. I was finding it hard to get used to the idea that the boy in the other room was my brother; that he and Hugo had turned up on the same day seemed almost too much to deal with. When I returned, he was sitting on the sofa with his shoulders slumped forward, elbows resting on his knees and his chin on one fist. There was a rip in the left knee of his jeans. Whatever he was thinking, it was with a concentration that carved a furrow between his eyes.

"Are you still at Foxburghe?" I asked, handing him his mug of coffee. I brought one of the chairs from the table and sat down on the other side of the coffee table from Jay.

He nodded. "The place is the pits, but maybe they won't take me back after this. The headmaster doesn't like you to go AWOL.

It makes the school look bad." He sipped some coffee, lacing his long fingers around the mug. "That's where it all started, at the school two days ago. I'm a long-distance runner, and I usually go for a run every afternoon before dinner. I go about a quarter of a mile down the lane that runs past the school, then I switch to footpaths across the fields. On Wednesday, as I started my run, I noticed a couple of men in a parked car just past the school gate. When I passed them, the one in the driver's seat leaned out of his window and called my name. At first I figured they must be reporters. My mother warned me that reporters might try to ask me questions about Daddy . . . Hugo. She told me I shouldn't talk to anyone about him. She doesn't mind getting in the papers herself, but she hates questions about him."

"What did they look like, these two men?" I remembered Luke's warning that Qaddafi might send someone after Hugo.

"Not English. Though the English of the driver was pretty good. They might have been Italian, I guess, or Middle Eastern. It's hard to be sure. They were both dark-haired and dressed in suits, like businessmen. When I went over to the car, the driver said they came from Hugo. He told me that Hugo wanted to see me, that they would take me to him. I said I thought Hugo was still in Libya, but the driver said he'd left and was in London now, staying with friends. He wanted to avoid publicity, that's why he'd sent them instead of coming himself."

His voice dropped, and he looked down into the mug. "Of course, I was pretty excited. Just knowing he was safe. Ever since we bombed Libya, I've been wondering, you know, if he's okay. . . . And I wanted to see him. But something about them bothered me. They were ordinary-looking, I mean they weren't particularly creepy or anything, but the whole thing seemed a little weird. The other guy, the one in the back seat, didn't say a word the whole time, he just stared at me. When the driver told me to get in, he opened the rear door for me. But I told them I couldn't go without the school's permission. It was against the rules. The driver said there wasn't time, that I had to come right away if I wanted to see my father. Otherwise it might be too late.

"What did he mean, too late?"

"He didn't say. It was the way he said it that got to me. Like he meant permanently too late. It sounded like a threat. So I said no, I wouldn't come unless they talked to the headmaster first. The driver turned really smooth at that, he said all right, he'd do that. He told me to go for my run, and when I got back we would go. I said I'd rather go with them. I could see at first they weren't too keen on that idea. But the driver agreed. He said I should get in and show them where to park the car."

He gave a small, bitten-off grin. "Ever since I was a kid, I've been hearing you shouldn't get into cars with strange men. So I told them they could follow me in the car while I ran ahead. But I didn't get more than a few yards before somebody grabbed my arm. It was the guy in the back of the car. He must have moved like a barracuda, to get to me so fast. I was scared shitless." He blushed. "Sorry. Anyway, I don't know what he was going to do because just then Andrew Merton—one of the prefects— came running out of the school gate, shouting my name. He said I should come right away, that I had a long-distance call. I guess the man's grip wasn't so strong, or else he was startled, because I managed to pull free. I didn't wait around to see what was coming next. And neither did he. As I ran back to Andrew, I heard the car start up, and when I turned around it had disappeared down the lane.

"Andrew wanted to know who they were, of course. I told him I thought they must be reporters." Quietly, he added, "Andrew knew who my father was. Anyway, when I got back to the school it was my mother on the phone, calling from California. She said she wanted me to hear the news from her, not from the papers. Some friend of hers in the State Department had told her that Hugo had left Libya. He was in Sicily now, she said. Not London? I asked. She wanted to know why I thought that, but I told her there was no special reason, I was just hoping Hugo would come to see me."

"So you didn't tell your mother about the two men?"

"No," he said calmly. "I knew she couldn't handle it. She'd only have made a row and wanted to speak to Smelly, Mr. Smalley I mean, the headmaster. I could tell that the news about Hugo had already upset her. Besides, I wanted some time to think it all over."

I was struck by how cool Jay's reactions had been, and by the way he told his story, straightforwardly and undramatically, as though this sort of thing happened to him regularly. There was an odd combination, too, of protectiveness and wariness in his attitude toward Charlotte that told me something about their relationship. It was clear he was accustomed to keeping things to himself.

"You know," he said slowly, "everybody—my mother, the family, the papers—was saying Hugo was acting like some sort of traitor or something, because he was working for Qaddafi. I didn't believe them. I still don't. Maybe Hugo wasn't around much when I was little, but when he was, well, he was just there for me. I mean he really seemed . . ." He made an impatient movement. "I don't know how to explain—"

"I think I understand," I said. Jay had given Hugo the benefit of the doubt because he was sure his father loved him. It seemed to me that the conviction of that love had helped Jay deal with the last three years. He simply took it for granted that Hugo had good reasons for whatever he did, no matter how strange.

He leaned forward, clasping his hands between his knees, and stared at the floor. In a low voice he said, "I always thought Hugo might be in some sort of trouble. Maybe he didn't want to be in Libya, but they were forcing him to pretend he did. Of course, there wasn't anything I could do to help him." He raised his head and looked at me intently with those blue eyes. "Now maybe there is."

"What do you mean?"

"I'll bet those men were after me as a way of getting at Hugo. I've got to let him know. Besides, I want to see him again." This last was said quietly, but his voice roughened as he spoke. Abruptly, he got up and went over to the window. "That's the Rhine? I don't see any castles."

"Farther upstream." Through his T-shirt I could see the wings of his shoulderblades. He's much too thin, I thought, before I remembered that he was a long-distance runner.

As he came back to the sofa, he said, "I thought about it a lot that night. In the morning I got my stuff together and some money I'd saved, and took off. I left a letter saying that I wanted some time to be alone." With a wry shrug, he added, "They think I'm antisocial anyway, 'cause I run instead of playing cricket."

Hitchhiking to save money, he had made it to Dover with rides from friendly truckers. Some of his money went on the ferry ticket to France. But in the night near Paris, as he waited by the highway for a ride, he was mugged by a tramp who came out of a field, surprising him. "That's how I got this," he said, touching the bandage on his cheek. In the struggle, before a trucker stopped to help and the tramp ran off, he lost his wallet with all his money. Luckily, the tramp missed his backpack with his passport, which had fallen into the ditch beside the road. Briefly, he contemplated giving up, then remembered that I lived in Bonn. Each Christmas, in an attempt to keep up what little contact we had, I sent Jay a present and a Christmas letter. He always sent a thank-you letter back, as stilted as my own had doubtless been.

"So here I am," he said, almost aggressively, "a poor relation who's come to borrow money off you. If you could give me the train fare to Sicily and a little extra for food, I think I could manage okay. I'll pay you back."

"Of course I'll lend you money, whatever you need. But how on earth do you expect to find Hugo? Sicily's enormous. You can't just wander around looking for him."

Instead of answering, he bent over and rooted in his knapsack, spilling out underwear, T-shirts, a toothbrush onto the floor. "Read that," he said, and handed me a crumpled blue air letter.

It was from Hugo, dated June 10th, 1983, six weeks before he went to Libya. It was sent from Sicily, a long letter full of the kind of news a father might write to a twelve-year-old son whom he rarely saw, catching-up news recounted in a semihumorous, affectionate vein. In it, Hugo told Jay of a small and very dilapidated castle he owned near a village called Castell'-alto, and of his plans to rebuild it. "You must come for a visit soon," he wrote. "I won't spoil the surprise of the place with a description. Only to say that it has a puzzle, a kind of labyrinth without a resident minotaur. Local rumor tells of treasure buried hereabouts (the Sicilians are great treasure-seekers), a golden honeycomb fashioned by Daedalus in thanksgiving to Aphrodite for bringing him safely to Sicily. We'll search for it together."

Hugo loved puzzles of all kinds; complicated jigsaw puzzles were his invariable gift to me when I was small, and he was always willing to spend time with me putting them together. Luckily, I was good at puzzles.

"You see," Jay said, when I looked up again, "if he's in Sicily, then that place he mentions, Castell'alto, is most likely where he'll be. Anyway, I thought I'd go and find out. If he's not, maybe the people there will know where to find him. Before I left England I did try to call Castell'alto from a pay phone, to see if I could reach Hugo that way. But the overseas operator had no listing for the place. I couldn't even find it in an atlas at school. But I'm sure that once I'm in Sicily, it'll be easier."

His voice held all the optimism of youth; it made me feel suddenly much older, and depressingly realistic. But all I said, as I handed him back his letter, was, "I want to show you something of my own."

I went into my bedroom. From my desk drawer I took out a

small bundle of letters wrapped around with a thick gold chain. A medallion made from a gold coin the size of a quarter hung like a seal from the end of the chain. On one side of the coin was the standing figure of a woman in part profile, dressed in long, pleated draperies. Her right arm was lifted toward a small creature hovering in the air above her. It was difficult to be certain, but it seemed to be some sort of insect, perhaps a bee. Both the woman and the insect were beautifully made, finely modeled and delicate. There was an inscription, too, stamped along the edge of the coin, eight letters in what might have been ancient Greek: ΕΡΥΚΛΙΒ. On the reverse side there was only a tiny square pattern of lines repeated and interwoven.

Hugo had given me the medallion on my thirteenth birthday. He arrived without warning, in the middle of a blizzard, at the family gathering held in my honor, unapologetic, throwing the quiet supper party into an uproar with his presence. His cheek was cold, his dark hair wet with melted snow, and he smelled of faraway places, of the Turkish pipe tobacco he smoked, and the Oriental spice in the cologne he always wore. Interrupting the present-opening, Hugo had pulled the medallion from his pocket and put it over my head.

I thought it was the most beautiful thing I had ever seen, and when I told him so he looked pleased. But then I asked him who the lady on the coin was.

The Goddess of Love, he replied. Aunt Constance always provoked a certain malicious mischief in Hugo, and I suspect that what followed this was probably for her benefit. I don't remember precisely what he said, only that it was a frank description of the goddess's powers, which embarrassed me so much that I didn't listen to whatever else he might have said about the coin. I sat there wishing Hugo would shut up, while my cousins smirked and kicked me under the table.

But he must have sensed my feelings, for later, as I said good-bye to him in the doorway with the snow blowing in, he touched the medallion as it hung around my neck. "She's the Lady of the Labyrinth, Alison. A mystery. Like all women." His blue eyes looked past mine, as though they looked into a distance, and there was sadness in them.

Then, abruptly, he kissed me and left. I did not see him again for almost six months.

I wore the medallion only that once. It was too valuable, Aunt Constance told me, to have in the house; it belonged in the bank. And there it stayed until her death. I never thought of it until the lawyers handed it back to me. After that, the medallion went with me from move to move, like a talisman, proof that this man I had never really known was my father.

Now I unwound the chain from around the bundle of letters and slipped the medallion over my head, inside my blouse. It was not the medallion I wanted to show Jay, but a letter very much like his own.

There weren't many letters in the bundle, twenty at most, and few were longer than a page. Even as a child, I had seen that, as letters from a father to a daughter, they lacked something. Not affection, precisely; perhaps simply a sense of connection.

I removed the top letter, Hugo's last, from the pile, then went back into the living room and handed it to Jay.

"My dear Alison," Hugo had written.

Now that you have your degree, I hope you will see something of the world before you settle down in a job or marriage, to find out for yourself, after four years of received wisdom, what life is about. Perhaps my graduation present to you will make that somewhat easier.

You must make up your own mind, of course. I've never interfered in your life and I'm not about to start now. I doubt you would accept it if I did. But that's not to say that I don't care about you. Although I relinquished paternal rights long ago, I did keep a father's concern. Should you ever find yourself in difficulties, I hope you will tell me. I will help you in any way I can.

A number of years ago, I bought a rather romantic ruin here, a castle complete with tower and its own mystery, with the idea of making something of it. Erice is nearby, perched on its mountaintop above the sea. In the ancient world it was a famous shrine to the Goddess—Astarte, Aphrodite, Venus— the goddess of fertility, of ecstatic love. Her symbol was the queen bee, and the heather honey produced locally is still reputed to have an intoxicating effect. Daedalus himself dedicated a golden honeycomb of his own creation to Aphrodite of Eryx. Long since vanished, it was hidden hereabouts by her priestesses against the day when the goddess would return to her mountain. Or so legend claims. All this is by way of whetting any archaeological appetite you may have inherited (if the courses you took at college didn't spoil it)—in the hope that you will visit us here someday.

The local people say that Castell'alto is the village that God forgot, which may be why it suits me so well.

Your affectionate father, Hugo

At the time I had wondered why God's forgetfulness should make the village of Castell'alto so attractive to Hugo. I had wondered, too, about the "us" in the penultimate sentence of the letter.

Jay read the letter through, then looked up at me intently. "They're the same, these two letters. There isn't anything in them about abandoning everything for Libya. He had other plans. I just don't believe he went to Libya of his own free will."

"Look, Jay," I said, as gently as I could, "Hugo isn't a predictable man. He never stayed in one place—or with one person, for that matter—for very long. Castell'alto might have appealed to him for the moment, but that doesn't mean he didn't get tired of it just as quickly and decide to move on. That's his life story after all, isn't it?"

Clumsily, he got to his feet, sloshing coffee onto his jeans. "Don't you see? What you've said only goes to prove my point. If that's how he is, why did he stay in Libya such a long time?"

But I had no answer to that.

I looked at my wristwatch. Somewhat desperately, I said, "I think you ought to go back to school and wait for Hugo to get in touch with you. I'm sure he will, he may be trying to now. I can buy you a plane ticket back to London on my way home from work tonight. Or"—for I'd suddenly had what seemed like a brilliant idea—"you could take an extra few days and come to Spain with me. I'm off tomorrow on holiday. I'll treat you." It would just about wipe out my bank balance if he did, but it would be worth it, I thought. It was time we got to know each other.

"You mean you're on vacation?" Jay said, too eagerly, and at once I knew what was coming next. "Then you could go to Sicily with me, couldn't you?"

I stared at him. I might have said a flat no, but for the look in his eyes, the first defenseless pleading look I had seen there. Even when he asked me for money he seemed in control of himself, too much so perhaps. Now he looked vulnerable, and I remembered that, for all the talk of threats and warning Hugo, this was a boy in search of his father. My father, too, for that matter.

"I'm going anyway," he said quietly, the pleading look gone as completely as if it had never been. "Whatever you decide."

I turned away and stared out the window. Jay might have the faith of a Telemachus, but I had done my best to forget my father. Now that he had surfaced in my life again, I wasn't sure I liked it; I had grown used to his neglect.

Or so I told myself. I watched the long black barges on the river push their way upstream through the mist, like giant water snakes cresting the current, while the rain beat against my window in spattering sheets.

"Neglect," however, was too strong a word. Just before he went to Libya, Hugo had set up a trust fund for me—the graduation present he mentioned in his letter—the interest from which, while it didn't mean I could forget about working for a living, would prevent my ever starving to death. I would come into the principal at thirty-five. When there was no reply to my letter sent to his New York address, thanking him, I assumed that it was his way of telling me I was an adult now, and on my own as far as he was concerned, the tenuous link between us severed. He intended the money to sweeten the parting—or that's how I saw it. Some vestige of resentful adolescent pride tempted me to turn it down, to deny him this sop to his conscience, but I was too sensible for the grand romantic gesture. When I arrived in Bonn I spent part of the year's income from the trust on my car, a very secondhand BMW. It was eight years old, the smallest model BMW made, but it ran beautifully and I loved it. In his own way, Hugo had looked after me.

I was obscurely shamed by Jay's loyalty, and touched by his stubborn love for a father who had given so little time to him. And for once I ignored the small voice that warned me when I was tempted to do something foolish.

CHAPTER 4

I turned around. Jay was standing in the middle of the room, his head lowered, whistling tunelessly under his breath. With his fists dug into his jeans pockets and his elbows sticking out at right angles, he seemed all bony edges, graceless, and somehow, for all that he had shown both courage and resourcefulness, vulnerable.

"Jay?" He looked up at me, a guarded look. I said, "I'll go to Sicily with you."

Whatever tension had held him taut suddenly gave way and he let out a small sigh. "You mean it?" His voice sounded flat, not quite believing.

I nodded. "We can leave tonight. I've got to put in an afternoon's work first. In the meantime, you get some sleep on my bed. Or take a bath. Frau Gottschalk was sure you must be longing for one."

Only the sudden spark of life in the vivid blue eyes gave any sign of his feelings. I wondered who had taught him to hide them so well. He stooped to pick up his knapsack, and began to stuff his few belongings, scattered in his search for Hugo's letter, back into it.

Before I left the apartment, I called Lufthansa to cancel my flight to Madrid. I told Jay not to answer the phone or the door, "to avoid explanations. If I need to call you I'll ring twice, hang up, and ring again right away. Okay?" He nodded his head, accepting this without question; his adventures of the past two days must have taught him certain lessons, lessons that I was beginning to learn. "Help yourself to whatever you want if you're still hungry. We'll have the pork chops in the fridge for supper." I gave him some coins and told him there was a dryer in the basement for his wet clothes. "See you around five."

31

I collected my coat and umbrella and was just opening the door when he said quietly, "Alison?"

"Yes?"

"Thanks."

I smiled at him. "It's too soon for that."

On the way back to work I stopped in at a travel agency near the embassy to ask about car ferries to Palermo, the earliest possible. Jay and I would need a car in Sicily but I couldn't afford the combined cost of two plane fares, hotel rooms and meals, and a car rental. We would have to take the BMW. It would add at least a day to the journey, but that would give me time to get to know Jay a little better, time to think about Hugo, to prepare myself. Later, I acknowledged this reasoning as a form of procrastination, but now it seemed simply pragmatic.

The travel agent, a young Frenchwoman, looked up at me from the printed schedule. "There is a ferry leaving Genoa at three tomorrow afternoon," she said. "It arrives in Palermo at noon the following day. Can you make it?"

It meant driving all night, but I nodded and asked her to book us passage, as well as a hotel room for our first night in Sicily. After that, I thought, we would play it by ear.

"Where did you want to stay?"

I thought of the town near Castell'alto that Hugo had mentioned in his letter; we could use it as a base for our search. "A place called Erice. If it has a hotel."

The woman told me that Erice was something of a tourist draw, a mountaintop town on the coast, and added dryly that it had the curious distinction of being the cleanest town in Sicily. "Our German clients like to know these things," she said, grinning. She booked two single rooms at the Hotel Ginestra, a modestly priced hotel that rated a star for its view.

Back at work, I telephoned the Italian embassy. My counterpart there was pleasant but, after a search of their records, regretful; he could find no trace of any village in Sicily called Castell'alto. I thanked him and hung up, discouraged already at the prospect of the probable wild goose chase that was to replace my Spanish vacation.

Luke was out of his office all afternoon. At one point I went downstairs to consult with an information officer over some statistics she had requested; when I returned to my desk, one of my colleagues told me Luke had come by, looking for me. There was no message, and when I checked his office, he had gone again.

I worked quickly, tossed the completed pile of assignments on Miss Shera's desk, and escaped before she could present me with a new batch. Luke's office was still empty, so I left a note on his desk explaining that I would not be able to have dinner with him after all; something, I wrote, had come up. I said I hoped he would have a good holiday, and told him I would claim my forfeit when I got back. "P.S.," I added at the bottom of the page, "Did you know that in the Middle Ages a German warrior would demonstrate his passion by drawing a dagger across his forehead, letting the blood drip into his beer, then drinking a toast to his lady love?"

Shortly after four, I left the embassy, gaining an illicit extra hour to help with the long drive to Genoa. When I got back to the apartment, Jay was in the kitchen, peeling potatoes.

"What's this?"

He smiled shyly. "Dinner. My mom hates to cook, so I learned how. Do you like mashed potatoes with your pork chops? I could make a salad, too. . . ."

"You're hired." Self-reliant and helpful—it was, I reflected, a nice combination to find in a brother. "Any callers?"

"The phone rang just before you got here. I didn't answer it."

"Good. I'm going to have a shower now, and then I'll give you a hand with dinner."

When I came out of the shower I could smell the pork chops frying. I dressed and went into the kitchen, toweling off the wet ends of my hair. As I was telling Jay how pleasant it was to have someone else doing the cooking, the telephone rang.

"Alison?" It was Bernd Renner.

The connection was bad. His voice sounded distant, too remote to arouse any feeling but a dismay that I found oddly reassuring, for it told me that the affair was truly over. It was no effort to keep my own voice neutral.

"Hello, Bernd. Where are you calling from?"

"Berlin. I just heard the news about your father."

Bernd never wasted time on the conventions of polite speech; he always went straight to the heart of the matter, and for that much at least I was grateful now. But I was surprised that he knew about Hugo's defection from Libya. It was not an item likely to appear on German newscasts, and Bernd was the last person to listen to the American Forces station.

"How did you hear?"

When he answered, his voice held the familiar evasive note

that meant questions were useless. Forced, he would only lie. "Someone told me, a colleague." Bernd's "colleagues" were legion and not limited to his work, among them a ragtag assortment of radicals, leftists, and malcontents who supplied him with all kinds of information; it was a description that could cover a multitude of sinners.

"I wonder why your colleague thought you'd be interested."

But he didn't respond to this. "Has your father been in touch with you?"

"Why?"

"Only that it would be better to keep away from him. If he tries to contact you."

It was, I reflected, the second warning of its kind that I'd had that day. "What do you mean, better to keep away from him?"

"Safer," he said succinctly. "He's not a popular man now, with some elements. I hear things."

"Don't be coy, Bernd. What elements? Some of your students, Arab friends, who? And what sort of things?"

There was a silence, then he said, "There are rumors that Qaddafi wants him killed. I'm passing this on to you as a . . . friend." His voice dropped, so that I had to strain to hear. "That much at least we can remain, *nicht wahr*?"

"I don't think so. Friends trust each other."

This time the silence went on longer, and finally I was the one to break it. "Listen, Bernd, I have no idea where Hugo is and no expectation that he'll try to contact me. Thanks for the warning, but it doesn't help me much unless you can be more specific."

"I've told you all I know. I think you should take it seriously, but that's up to you. . . . You never liked my telling you what to think." There was a grain of humor in his voice, which disappeared with his next words. "Be careful, Alison."

Exasperated, I tried again. "Why would—" But it was too late, he had hung up.

I put the receiver down in its cradle, more angry than frightened. I believed that Bernd meant it when he said he wanted to warn me, but I knew how much he must have enjoyed the phone call, with its hints at danger, at secret knowledge, at love lost; it would have satisfied his sense of the dramatic on so many levels. In fairness to Bernd, I also acknowledged to myself that it was just this theatricality that had originally attracted me to him. Still, I knew I shouldn't discount the words themselves— Bernd's information was often accurate. The prick of worry for

Hugo's safety returned. I wished that I had never told Bernd about Hugo.

As I went back into the kitchen, Jay was slicing tomatoes, the expression on his face scrupulously incurious. I was still deciding how much to tell him; I didn't want to frighten him, but what Bernd had told me seemed a confirmation of his suspicions.

I stood beside Jay at the counter, shredding a head of lettuce. "That was an old boyfriend who teaches politics at the University of Berlin. He does some television commentary, too. The British have a name for someone like Bernd, don't they? For an academic who looks and sounds good on TV?"

"A telly don, you mean?"

"That's it. Bernd's the German version. Whenever they want something stronger than the Green point of view they call on Bernd. He's very left, not to mention anti-American. So of course our relationship was bound to end in disaster. I think it only lasted as long as it did because he hoped I might turn out to have the same sympathies as Hugo." I sprinkled basil on the lettuce. "What do you like on your salad? Oil and vinegar?"

"Fine." He dumped the tomatoes into the salad bowl. "What did you mean just now, the same sympathies as Hugo?"

"Well, pro-Arab among other things."

"But Hugo hated all that political stuff."

"He must have changed, then." I glanced sideways at Jay. "Working for Qaddafi for so long is a pretty strong political statement, wouldn't you say?"

He kept his eyes on his work, steadily chopping up a cucumber. "Maybe. If he had a choice. But even if he did, he's changed his mind."

"Well, maybe you're right. Bernd thinks Hugo's in danger, too—from Qaddafi." At this, Jay did look up, the knife poised above the cucumber. "That's why he called—to warn me." I told him what Bernd had said, explaining as best I could how he might get hold of that kind of information. "You know, Jay, it really might be better if we waited—"

But he didn't let me finish. "You can't change your mind now!" His face was flushed, agonized. "We've got to go—"

I put my hand on his arm. "Yes, all right. All right." I turned away to the stove, to give him time to deal with the tears I saw in his eyes.

We ate quickly, and while Jay, without being asked, did the

washing up, I filled a large thermos with coffee and packed a picnic. Afterward, I went downstairs to start loading the car.

The BMW was parked on the street, in front of the apartment building, facing downhill. The street, as always, seemed deserted, the garden gates shut, the neatly trimmed hedges enclosing tidy, middle-class houses, a neighborhood afflicted with the same orderly secretiveness that Bonn itself suffered from, the same sense of an invisible watchfulness. Although here it was a lace-curtain vigilance that made sure its neighbor's weeds were pulled, hardly the stuff of spies. But after I put the picnic basket and my suitcase into the trunk of the car, I noticed a man standing under the spreading branches of a linden tree farther up the street, half a block away, near the corner where it turned onto a larger road that ran along the crest of the hill. He was reading a newspaper. It struck me as odd that anyone would choose to read a newspaper in the rain, but I assumed he was waiting for someone. Still, mindful of the break-ins, I set the car alarm before I went back inside.

Jay was standing looking at something when I came into the apartment, his back to the door. He was wearing his by now dry but still disreputable windbreaker, with his knapsack over his shoulder. He turned around at my footsteps. In his hands, he had my photograph album.

"I hope you don't mind," he said, blushing slightly. "I was looking for a paperback to bring along, and saw this. I didn't mean to be nosy."

"You're welcome to look at it, though I warn you my photographs have been known to clear a room filled with people in under five minutes."

"Yes, well, I did notice that there are a lot of pictures of flowers and trees."

I laughed, a little ruefully. Too many trees, a friend had said once, halfway through some pictures of a walking tour of the Black Forest—and she was a German. On seeing some of my snaps, Luke, who took wonderful photographs, immediately offered to give me lessons.

As Jay closed the album, a photograph slipped out and floated to the floor, face down. He bent to pick it up, turning it over, and gave a mock wolf whistle. "Who's this?" he asked, handing it to me.

It was an old black-and-white picture that once had been torn in pieces; the pieces were held together now with yellowing Scotch tape. In it, a young woman stood in a garden, her hands on her hips, laughing, vamping a little for the camera; she looked confident, pleased with herself and with life. She was tall and, despite the slightly fuzzy focus, obviously pretty in the fifties fashion, round-cheeked, dark-haired, with a ponytail and a lot of dark lipstick. She was wearing a blouse and a bell-shaped skirt, and a wide belt that emphasized the narrowness of her waist and the fullness of her breasts. What came unmistakably through the camera, what had inspired Jay's whistle, was a sexuality that survived the bobby socks and the tightly curled bangs, and a vitality that stamped itself on the picture.

The picture had been in a shoe box filled with photographs that I'd found when I was sorting through my aunt's and uncle's belongings after they died. It was upside down, so that I first saw my mother's name, Amelia, written in my aunt's neat script, and the date, 1958, when she was eighteen. I was tempted to leave it lying there, undisturbed, but I had never seen a picture of my mother, and curiosity was stronger than any fear of what I might find. Pregnant, unmarried, throwing away a huge scholarship to have the baby, then rejecting the baby, my mother was the family disgrace. What photographs there might once have been had all disappeared long ago.

When I saw her face, I tore the photograph into pieces and threw them back into the shoe box. Later that night, I got out of bed and found the shoe box in the back of the closet where I'd shoved it; carefully, I taped the pieces together again. I put the photograph inside my album where I looked at it from time to time, never again with that same first instinct of rejection. But I didn't like the woman in the picture.

"That was my mother." I put the photograph back inside the front cover of the album. "Do you have everything?"

"It's all in here." He touched his knapsack.

"Good. Let me just give a last look around, and then we'll go."

Jay must have started downstairs to the car while I was in the bedroom checking for forgotten essentials, for when I came out of the bedroom my apartment door was open and he was nowhere in sight. I put on my coat, and was about to leave when I noticed that the living room window was slightly ajar. As I closed and latched it, I looked down into the street below. Jay was standing beside my car, his hand on the driver's door; it was locked, of course.

Someone was walking down the street toward him. It was the same man who had been reading the newspaper under the linden tree, but now the newspaper was folded over one arm and the arm held up against his stomach in an odd position, as though he had a stomachache. Farther up the sloping street, a green Opel was moving slowly in Jay's direction. In the same moment I registered all these things, and felt a first stab of unease, Jay turned to the rear door. I must have forgotten to lock it, for it opened—and the alarm's banshee wail broke loose.

Like a freeze-frame, there was an instant when the man, the Opel, and Jay were motionless, before Jay slammed the car door shut. The alarm continued its monotonous howling, the man with the newspaper stepped out into the street, and the Opel gathered speed. Suddenly frightened, I turned and ran from the apartment. There was no point in shouting to Jay; he would never have heard me.

In the stairwell, I thought I heard a siren's answering call, like an echo of the alarm, and by the time I reached the street, a police car was drawing up to the curb in front of the BMW. To my relief, Jay was still there. I looked for the Opel and the man with the newspaper, but they had vanished.

Clearly unsure of whether to come after me, or wait for the policeman, Jay was halfway between the apartment house and the car. He gave a grin of relief at the sight of me. I switched off the alarm—the silence was like the sudden absence of pain— then turned to deal with the policeman, who looked surprised, and slightly mollified, at the warmth of my thanks for his prompt response. Only in Germany, I thought gratefully, would he have bothered to come at the sound of a car's alarm. I showed him my papers, explained that it was all my fault, that I'd forgotten to lock the rear door, and apologized. Eventually, after giving Jay and me a short speech on the danger of false alarms, he drove off. You could almost hear the sound of lace curtains falling into place again.

"I'm sorry . . ." Jay began.

"Don't be. It gave my neighbors more excitement than they've had since a house down the way caught fire four months ago."

I did not add that the false alarm might also have saved him, and I said nothing about the man and the Opel. There might be an innocent explanation for what I had seen, or there might not—but there was no point in scaring Jay with vague possibilities when reality was frightening enough.

As we drove away, a sudden thought struck me: If the men

had been after Jay, how could they have known he was with me? And if they didn't know, that could only mean one thing—that they were after me.

CHAPTER 5

I took a roundabout route to the autobahn, using quiet back streets where I would know if a green Opel followed. I drove quickly, constantly checking the rearview mirror, but there was no Opel, and nothing stayed behind us long enough to worry me. Jay pored over a map of Sicily spread out on his lap, looking for clues to Castell'alto. I hoped he would put my nervousness down to the rush-hour traffic; the German driver intent on his dinner, I told him, was a force I had learned to respect.

I wondered if the remote chance that we would find Hugo in Sicily justified the risk we seemed to be running. But Jay was determined to go, with or without me—he had made that very clear—and I couldn't let him go alone. I reminded myself that everyone thought I was on vacation; if anyone asked questions, they would be told I was in Spain. It was some comfort, but not much.

When we were safely on the A61, Jay looked up from the map. "Mind if I turn on the radio? It's almost time for the news."

"Go ahead. The radio's already tuned in to the American Forces station. If there's anything new about Hugo they should have it."

Qaddafi was threatening Italy with further attacks if an American installation on the little island of Lampedusa, just off the coast of Sicily, were not removed—but there was nothing about Hugo, not even a repeat of the morning's item.

"So Hugo's still in Sicily?" Jay asked.

"Chi lo sa?"

"What does that mean?"

"Who knows? I mean, 'who knows?' is the translation. Do you speak any Italian?"

Jay shook his head. "Not really. Do you?"

"Enough to get by on. How did you think you'd manage in Sicily without it?"

"I didn't think about it. Hugo said if you spent too much time thinking about things you'd never do them."

"Oh yes? Then that explains why he's never written to us. He thinks about it all the time instead." It was meant to sound amused, but it didn't come out that way.

Jay turned away and stared out his window. Beside the autobahn, dripping trees fringed fields glazed with water. A thin mist wisped up to blend with the twilight. Finally, in a puzzled voice, he asked, "Don't you like him, Alison?"

A massive transport trailer thundered by, throwing off a blinding spray of water. I waited until the truck was past before I answered. "When I was little, Hugo was Sinbad and Ulysses and Jason and the Argonauts all rolled up in one. Someone magical and mysterious who had adventures in faraway places and brought back treasure, not a father who helped you with your homework and took you out for a Big Mac afterward." I glanced across at Jay. "You can't like or dislike someone from a fairy tale."

In this answer I recognized my own evasions, the half-truths laid out like a false scent to mislead everyone but myself, a way of dealing with questions I didn't want to answer as I came to understand that my father was no more magical than he was paternal. He would play at being Daddy for a while, then, growing bored with the role, would disappear, and I would be left with my head full of stories and dreams. As I grew older these sudden transitions from fairy tale to reality grew too painful; to protect myself, I judged him with the critical, unforgiving eye of adolescence. He must have felt the change and perhaps that, combined with the awkward age, dimmed his enthusiasm for those sudden swoops into my life, for during my middle teens I rarely saw him. Only when I entered college did I interest him again; tentatively, we began to forge a new relationship.

But the knowledge of who he really was eluded me.

Jay said nothing, and I tried again. "You're here because you know how you feel about him. I'm here because I don't. I never have. It's not so much that I don't like Hugo as that I simply don't know him." To change the subject, I began to sing along with the song on the radio. Jay joined in on the refrain. "You know 'Yellow Submarine'?" I asked him, surprised. He seemed too young.

"Sure. That's the Beatles, the group Paul McCartney had

before Wings." He saw the look I gave him. "Just kidding. I appreciate the classics, too." As I smiled back at him, I was struck by how quickly he had recovered. After a nap and dinner, the color was back in his face.

The radio crackled with static as the faint notes of an oom-pah-pah band came through the last verse of "Yellow Submarine." "We're losing the station," I said. "There are some tapes in the glove compartment. Why don't you pick out something you like?"

He chose an Elton John tape that a friend had given me, an album from one of his American tours. I was a fan, but I never listened to this particular tape; I had meant to throw it out or give it away. Elton John's voice spiraled out into the car, and with it the memory that tainted the music.

It was seven years ago. Hugo and I were at his club in New York. We had managed a relatively comfortable, almost affectionate dinner together, and were drinking coffee afterward in the club's library when a well-dressed woman, very blond, very sleek, came into the room. She had a slightly haggard beauty, the tall, thin body that wears clothes well but always looks undernourished, and she walked with a model's expertise, one foot directly in front of the other. When she saw Hugo, who was sitting at an angle with his back to the door, she came over and put her hand lightly on his shoulder. There was a certain possessive familiarity in the gesture that was clear even to me. I assumed she was one of Hugo's groupies, my name for the women who clustered about him.

"Jessica!" As he stood up, Hugo's face assumed the urbane, charming, ever-so-slightly wary expression he used sometimes with women, which told me something else. Whatever she might have been to him, she was no longer. Still, he seemed pleased to see her and, after introducing me, invited her to join us. She had the choice of two chairs, but the one closest to Hugo was under the fierce glare of a standing lamp and she chose the chair beside mine. Close up, her beauty seemed tight and brittle, it had a lacquered-on quality, and she moved as though afraid it might shatter at the least spontaneous gesture. She was a decade older than I had first thought, fifty rather than forty.

"I'm so glad this is Alison, Hugo darling. I have to admit I wondered. Though cradle robbing was never your style." She smoothed her skirt over her legs, which were long and beautiful and carefully crossed so that both facts were on display. I didn't like the way she spoke to Hugo, as though she knew him better than I, as perhaps she did, and I didn't like to be made to feel even younger than my nineteen years. Whatever the reason, I didn't like her, either.

A waiter came over. Hugo asked us what we would like. A cognac, Jessica replied. I said that I would have a cognac, too, half expecting some protest from Hugo because of my age. But he merely ordered the drinks. I sat silently drinking the cognac, which I didn't really want, and watched Hugo talk to Jessica. Hugo was never very paternal, but he was a distinctly different person when we were alone together; it was as though for my sake he deliberately damped down the stronger aspects of his personality, muted the easy sensual charm, his ironic sense of humor. So it was always a shock when he turned it all back on again and let the full force of one side of his character show, as he did now with Jessica. She clearly enjoyed it, flirted back, teased him, flattered him, did all the things I found so impossible.

Eventually, feeling perhaps that they were neglecting me, Jessica asked me about myself. Encouraged by some question or other about my studies, and desperately wanting to seem more sophisticated than I really was, I began to talk. Both of them listened politely at first, but then I saw Jessica smile slightly at Hugo. That smile deflated my pretensions, and I collapsed into embarrassed silence, miserably aware that under the influence of the cognac and on the basis of an introductory course in archaeology, I had just spent a good five minutes explaining precisely why Schliemann got it wrong at Troy. To an archaeologist.

Possibly Hugo took pity on me, for in the silence he announced that he had tickets for a concert that evening. Ungratefully, I assumed the concert would be classical and wondered if he had bought them so that he would be free to think; Hugo claimed he did his best thinking to Mozart. Instead, to my astonishment, he produced a pair of tickets to a sold-out Elton John concert. I had mentioned in a letter that I liked him, Hugo added.

I was touched that he'd remembered, amazed he would actually buy tickets and be willing to go with me, and I struggled to find words to tell him so. But my surprise must have shown more strongly on my face than my delight, and the pause was fatal. Hugo must have thought that I balked at going with him, for his face darkened. "Of course, if you'd rather go with a friend . . ." he began.

Before I could protest, Jessica spoke. "Much the wisest

course, Hugo love. Listening to the music kids like now requires real courage.'' She had a controlled, throaty laugh.

"It must seem that way, compared to the music you grew up with," I said in my politest tones. "Though the Charleston was pretty wild, wasn't it?" At nineteen the defenses we have against real adults are few, but they can be crudely effective.

Her laugh this time was a little less throaty. "I'm not quite so decrepit as all that, Alison."

Earnestly, I said, "Oh no, not at all. I think you're very well preserved for your age."

Hugo had listened with an amused smile to the first part of this exchange, but he wasn't pleased by my last retort. Deliberate rudeness was anathema to him—unless, of course, it was his own. Very smoothly, he said, "Jessica's right. You really ought to go with someone your own age." Before I could say anything, he turned to Jessica. "And perhaps we could spend the evening more suitably for people of our advanced years." He laid the tickets on the coffee table in front of me and stood up. I thought I saw a small smile of triumph on her face, but I may have done her an injustice. Hugo never lingered over goodbyes, and they were out of the room before I could do more than thank him for dinner.

After they had gone, I stared at the tickets on the table, then picked them up, went outside, and offered them to the first couple my age I met. Their delighted thanks failed to console me.

Hugo and I saw each other again soon after that evening. Things between us seemed much as before, that is to say, amicable but not intimate. He never asked about the concert and I never told him that I hadn't wanted to go without him.

Sometime around midnight Jay and I reached the Swiss border. After that the autobahn climbed steadily toward the Saint Gotthard tunnel; in valleys far below the lights from villages and farms twinkled like fallen stars. Jay was sleeping now, slumped against the door, a restless sleep that seemed full of dreams. Once his head came up and he looked around with wild unseeing eyes before sinking back into sleep again at the pressure of my hand on his shoulder. I never saw the Alps, although I felt their presence on either side of us, like watchers in the dark waiting for travelers of greater interest before they showed themselves. Switzerland passed by us like a ghost, pale and insubstantial, with the sound of cowbells through the dawn mist when we stopped for gas and breakfast.

Jay stumbled from the car, rubbing his arms. His face was pale, the blue eyes under the tousled hair confused. "Are we there?" he asked, looking around.

"Not yet. Not for hours yet." Shivering, I stretched and yawned, queasy from too much coffee and the long night's drive. The cold rain was still drizzling down.

"Schlechtes Wetter," the man behind the counter said as I paid, his pouched, bulldog face gray in the fluorescent light.

Yes, it was terrible weather, I agreed, but we were going south, leaving it behind.

How far?

All the way to Sicily.

He grunted and handed me my change. "Ah well, they always have sun there, don't they?" He made it sound like a well-known Sicilian weakness. As we turned to go, I saw the headlines of a German newspaper on the rack by the door: Qaddafi Threatens New Wave of Terror.

In Italy the weather brightened, along with my spirits. The Alps rolled down to wide plains through which meandered rivers lined with rustling poplars. Hill towns crowned the peaks of small mountains to the east, romantic, mysterious, made more desirable as the autostrada took us relentlessly past them. On our way back, I told Jay, we might have time for side roads and Italian hill towns.

From time to time during the long drive I thought of Luke. He seemed to me like one of the hill towns, alluring yet momentarily inaccessible; he was the promise of certain pleasures when I returned from our journey, if I was willing to explore.

When we drove onto the car ferry in Genoa at two in the afternoon it was clear and hot, allowing me the comfortable illusion that I really was on holiday. Exhausted, and reluctant to think about the real reason for the trip, I went straight to our cabin and slept until suppertime, while Jay explored the ship.

After dinner we sat in a seedy lounge filled with cigarette smoke where Jay and most of the male population of the ship watched a soccer game on television and I read up on Sicily from the guidebooks I'd bought in a rush before we left Bonn. There had been no time to search out the best—I simply scooped up what was available, along with a road map and a phrase book to help me brush up my rusty Italian.

All I knew about Sicily was what any ignorant foreigner knows about the place—its reputation as the breeding ground of the Mafia—but as I read I learned that some of the most beautiful

Greek temples aren't in Greece at all, they're in Sicily, along with Arab Norman cathedrals, Byzantine mosaics, and history and legend enough to satisfy the most romantic tourist. Not to mention stories to terrify the cowardly.

"Did you know that until just a few years ago, bandits still lived in caves in the mountains around Palermo?" I told Jay when there was a break in the game.

"I'd like to see them," he replied. "The caves, I mean."

"Why?"

"I'm a caver." This was said shyly, almost apologetically, with a slight shrug of his shoulders.

"Then you can't be related to me after all. Not if you actually enjoy exploring dark places filled with bats."

He smiled. "Bats aren't so bad, if you get to know them. You could get used to caves, too."

"I hope I never have to. How did you get started?"

"Hugo got me started. When I was eight he took me to Les Eyzies, in the Dordogne, to see the cave paintings. Afterwards I used to dream about the caves. When I wrote and told him that I wanted to live in a cave, he sent me all these books on troglodytes and caving. He was good about that sort of thing, taking an interest, I mean."

"As long as he was interested, too."

There was a silence. Awkwardly, Jay said, "Your relationship with him must have been different, you being a girl, I mean."

"Well," I said as lightly as I could, "as a rule Hugo was pretty fond of girls. I think it may have been daughters he found difficult. Sons were really more his thing."

"It's too bad he didn't have more, then. I always wanted a brother when I was little."

I smiled at him. "I'm discovering that brothers aren't so bad myself. But don't despair—who knows how many of Hugo's children there are in the world. A brother may turn up." Too late I remembered that for all his poise Jay was, after all, only fifteen.

"You think there might be more besides us?" He sounded curious rather than shocked.

"The *National Enquirer* would have discovered them if they existed. No, I'm afraid you're stuck with just a sister."

"That's okay. Sisters aren't so bad, either." He said it poker-faced and turned back to watch the game.

While Jay slept in the bunk above, I sat up late into the night in our hot, claustrophobic cabin reading about Daedalus, who took refuge in Sicily in his flight from King Minos, and about Odysseus, the first in a long line of tourists to come to grief on the island. Later I dreamed that I was chasing Hugo through a maze of temple ruins, as men with guns hunted minotaurs and Cyclopes for sport. Toward dawn I woke up sweating and afraid. Someone was standing by the cabin door. Startled, I reached out for the bedside light.

"Did I wake you?" It was Jay, his voice apologetic in the darkness.

"I had a nightmare. Too many bandit stories before bed." I switched on the light and tried to read the time on my wristwatch. "Good grief, it's not even six yet. Where are you off to so early?"

"Can't sleep," he muttered. "I thought I'd get some air."

"Well, please stay away from the railing."

Good-naturedly, he agreed that he would, disappearing through the door before it occurred to me that I must have sounded just like an older sister. I groaned, rolled over, and fell instantly asleep.

When I finally came on deck, the southern sun was glaring down with unfamiliar strength, a reminder that sometime in the night we had crossed the invisible border separating the north from the Mezzogiorno, the land of the mad-dog midday sun. Far to the west the long profile of a ship, the tanker of the new Phoenicians, went by like a shadow on the horizon. After a short search I found Jay in the prow of the upper deck, watching the water.

"It really is wine-dark," he said. "I thought that was just literary stuff. But Homer got it right after all."

"You've read Homer?"

"Foxburghe prides itself on giving its students an excellent classical education." He spoke in a plummy voice, the mock-headmaster persuading parents to invest their child. "Which means it has lousy science masters, and doesn't spend any more money than it has to on sports equipment. But," he added more cheerfully, "you can do pretty much as you please. As long as the bills are paid on time."

I was thinking that this cynical assessment of his school's shortcomings would probably horrify his mother, until I remembered Aunt Constance's sharp comments on Charlotte's maternal instincts. "She's no better than a cuckoo, letting someone else look after her chick." This, I knew, was an oblique thrust at my own mother; Aunt Constance never criticized her directly.

"Have you had anything to eat yet?" I asked Jay. He shook his head. "Well, I think the restaurant's about to close. Why don't you go get breakfast." I gave him some money, asking him to bring me back coffee and fruit. "While you do that, I'm going to sit here and soak up the sun. I'd almost forgotten what it looks like."

A warm wind was blowing from the Aeolian Islands, the same kind breeze that the King of the Winds gave Odysseus. I found a bench in the lee of a lifeboat and put on my sunglasses. With a pencil and notebook in my hands and the guidebooks on the bench beside me, I tried to concentrate on planning some sort of itinerary, determined to squeeze a holiday of sorts out of this quixotic quest. My faith in our ability to find Hugo was considerably less than Jay's. Even if we did manage to track him down, I wasn't at all sure of our welcome. Sentiment had never been Hugo's strong suit and he might easily see us as distractions at best, and at worst as unwelcome nuisances. If he did, I intended to salvage what I could from the wreckage of my vacation.

But it was no use. Hugo waited at the end of every road I went down. I was fooling myself if I thought I could remain detached, nothing more than a guide to Jay's search. A dry sense of duty and the stirrings of affection for Jay were not the only emotions that had brought me on this journey. No matter how I might try to disguise it, I was worried about Hugo. I didn't examine the source of the worry; I only knew that once I had made sure he was safe it would be easier to put him out of my mind again.

I looked up from the guidebooks. Across from me an old woman dressed in the inevitable mourning was sitting in a patch of shade with her black-stockinged legs planted on a battered suitcase. Dark eyes gazed out of a face wrinkled like a walnut shell, a face with the fierce handsome features of some Arab ancestor. She was chewing slowly on a roll, pausing every now and then to brush the crumbs off her dress. On her lap she held a small box cradled in one arm. Our eyes met, and she inclined her head politely.

At that moment two little boys ran past us. One threw a ball to the other, who missed it, and the ball struck the old woman's arm, jostling the box. Good-humoredly, she scolded the children before allowing them to retrieve the ball, which had rolled under her bench. As they ran off, forgiven, she lifted the box and held it to her ear. After a moment she put it down again, glanced up, and saw me looking at her. She smiled, a smile that creased her face into a thousand lines, and said something that I could have sworn was "Ave Regina." Hail to the Queen. When I looked puzzled she repeated the words slowly. *"E un'ape regina."* It's a queen bee.

"You're a beekeeper," I said, suddenly understanding. I remembered Hugo's description in his letter of the intoxicating power of the honey of Erice, and I wondered if this elderly lady made honey that drove men mad. The thought made me smile.

But she shook her head. "It is for my neighbor. My son in Milan, he sends it to her." She had been visiting her son, who worked at an agricultural institute as a researcher into bee-breeding methods, and was bringing the queen, the result of one of his experiments, back to a neighbor of hers who raised bees. For my sake she spoke in Italian rather than Sicilian, but with an accent almost as impenetrable as the heat haze on the horizon. By the time I had managed to decipher this much Jay was back with my breakfast.

Politely, he greeted the old woman, then handed me a paper cup of coffee and an orange. "Sorry, but apart from some plastic rolls in plastic packages this is all there was in the cafeteria. Dinner last night must have worn out the cooks."

"You're in Italy now," I told him, setting the coffee down beside the guidebooks on the bench. "England is the country where people eat breakfast. Italians dine." The coffee was cold but the orange was enormous and very sweet. "I could have sworn you ate enough last night to keep you going for days. Two platefuls of pasta, chicken, roast potatoes and green beans, salad, bread, an apple. Have I forgotten anything? Oh yes, and that poisonous-looking thing with the green icing."

When I offered part of the orange to the old woman, she shook her head, reaching into the shopping bag on the seat beside her for a small packet of pastries, which she held out, urging us each to accept one. As Jay bit into his, she told me that they were honey cakes made by her daughter-in-law from the honey produced by her son's bees. They were delicious, like an Italian version of baklava. I told Jay that the *signora* had a queen bee with her in the little box on her lap. Swallowing down a large mouthful of cake, he said, "Ask her if the queen has worker bees with her." When I translated this back to the *signora*, she nodded her head vigorously. "But of course," she replied. "She must have her court. Otherwise she would die. She can do nothing for herself."

"Nothing but mate, breed, and murder her rivals," Jay said wryly. "I guess that's why we call her a queen bee."

"The Germans say 'mother bee,' " I told him.

"Then they must have a pretty weird notion of motherhood. A queen bee loses interest in her kids as soon as she's had them. It's the children who look after their mom in a hive."

I laughed. "How come you know so much about bees?"

"I don't, not really. But sometimes on the weekends I help out on a farm near the school. The farmer has some hives, and he's taught me a bit. Plus I've done some reading. Bees are fantastic. Did you know that a queen bee mates only once in her life, up in the air, with maybe four or five drones? Mating kills the drones because when they pull away they leave part of themselves inside her. That's the future hive she's carrying, maybe over a million bees if she lives for a few years."

Warming to his theme, and perhaps mistaking the look on my face for fascination, he was about to go on when one of the men standing by the railing gave a shout. Ahead, rising through the haze that lay across the surface of the sea, bulked the gray outline of a rocky headland. *"Sicilia!"* the old *signora* informed us happily, in a voice that said it was the promised land.

Gradually the bare humpbacked mountains that rimmed the coast receded inland to curve around the Conca d'Oro, the plain where Palermo lay facing the sea, backed by a crescent of orange and lemon groves. A tide of urban sprawl washed through the lush green of the valley and lapped at the stony flanks of the surrounding mountains. Bristling with antennas, modern apartment buildings jutted up like concrete slabs against the skyline. In the harbor, where the world's great fleets had sheltered, rusting freighters anchored next to fishing boats with brightly painted hulls. Apart from the loveliness of the setting, nothing of the city's once-famous beauty showed from the ferry's deck.

"That," I told Jay, on the strength of my reading, as we leaned against the railing, "was the most brilliant city in Europe once upon a time."

Jay was silent, considering the scene before him. Musingly, he said, "It reminds me of something Hugo used to quote. That poem by Byron—or was it Shelley? You know the one I mean. 'Look on my works, ye mighty, and despair.' Something like that, anyway." He seemed vaguely ashamed of himself for remembering it so well.

" 'Ozymandias.' A depressing poem if you happen to be a tyrant or an architect. I remember Hugo saying that it should be required reading for anyone who has the illusion he's building for posterity.''

The ship's loudspeaker warned those who had cars in the hold to prepare for debarkation. I turned to Jay, but he wasn't listening. He was staring inland at the mountains to the west, and his face was somber. Somewhere beyond that barrier of sun-baked rock, perhaps, lay Castell'alto.

When I touched Jay's arm he looked at me blankly for an instant, as if he'd forgotten who I was. We said good-bye to the old lady and went below, into a hot din of revving motors, stevedores' shouts, and the stink of diesel fuel. Now that the moment had come, I had a brief failure of nerve. Distracted, I tried to back the car out of its space, forgetting the chocks wedged behind the wheels to keep it from moving during the voyage. Sweat trickled down my neck while Jay and I got out and kicked away the chocks, and I gave a moment's regretful thought to Spanish cafés and cool Moorish cloisters.

But it was much too late to turn back. Behind me, the driver of the following car was already honking his impatience. I said a silent prayer to Hermes, the god of travelers, and drove down the ramp to the concrete pier, out into the hard Sicilian sunlight. Beside me, Jay sat with the map spread across his knees, the route to Erice marked in red.

As the line of cars slowly snaked its way between the foot passengers toward the gate and the city street beyond, I saw the old lady walking in front of a small three-wheeler van, indifferent to the honking horns, her scarred brown suitcase perfectly balanced on her head and the little box with its queen tucked under her arm. As I watched, a young woman came running up to her. She took the suitcase and the two of them embraced before walking away together.

Something of the old woman's calm dignity reached me. Uncramping my hands from the steering wheel, I sat back. We would find Castell'alto, I promised myself. We would find Hugo.

Men in worn gray suits and white shirts lounged by the entrance to the docks, watching the daily ritual of the ferry's arrival with impassive faces, meeting friends and relatives, reading newspapers, or simply sleeping in the sun, their heads thrown back against the railing of the fence. Obvious foreigners, we were the objects of a certain amount of interest, but only the stare of a skinny little man with a thick black mustache lingered long enough to disturb me.

He was standing behind the car, off to one side, as we waited in the line of cars leaving the docks. I happened to glance in the rearview mirror at a moment when it was clear he was looking at our license plate. As I watched from behind my dark glasses, he walked casually past and stood near the gate, smoothing his mustache with one hand and occasionally glancing our way. Shorter than most of the men around him, he was also more expensively dressed, in a flashy peach-colored shirt and white cotton pants with a matching white jacket draped across his shoulders. A pair of sunglasses was perched on top of his head.

I hoped his interest was nothing more than curiosity. In the north my little BMW was outclassed by a whole range of more distinguished cars, but I was dismayed to realize that in Sicily it acquired a certain glamour by default. The competition was minimal, at least in the area of the docks, where most of the cars were impressive only for their age or the size of the dents in their bodies. And of course my car had foreign plates, which made it much more attractive.

To my relief, however, the man with the mustache turned away and walked over to a gray van with a crumpled antenna parked just outside the dock gates, on the main avenue. He climbed into the driver's seat and with a noisy acceleration drove off. Then there was a break in traffic, and the line of debarking cars surged out of the dockyard onto the avenue.

"Careful!" Jay pointed to the car on my left, whose driver seemed determined to make a right turn despite the fact that we were squarely in his way. As I jammed on the brakes, a young boy on a motor scooter wove around us with the panache of a champion slalom skier, a crate of chickens riding pillion behind him. The chickens' terrified squawking was barely audible over the blare of the transistor radio that dangled from the Vespa's handlebars.

For the next half hour we threaded our way through the maze of city streets in search of the autostrada that would take us to Erice. With a growing sense of fatalism, I fought both the anarchy that passed for traffic flow and the urge to turn back to the safety of the ferry.

Palermo was one vast chaotic bazaar. A hot wind spiced with the smell of drains whipped dust and noise into the car, carrying with it the rhythm of a city where life was lived in the street to the beat of engines that idled, drove, drilled, and blasted in frantic counterpoint to the ceaseless sound of the human voice. Handcart vendors shouted out their sales pitch from the shade of dusty palms, their voices rising and falling like the swarms of flies that eddied over garbage in the gutters; bus drivers hailed each other hoarsely across the traffic; women leaned from open windows to scream at children playing in the street below. The clamor carried us in a wave to the city's farthest edge and deposited us on the autostrada to the west. Gradually the tumult washed back on itself, the city receded, and we found ourselves on a silent highway fringed with eucalyptus that threaded through the mountains beside the flat, glittering sea.

CHAPTER 6

Apart from the occasional truck or battered, dusty Fiat, and once a white Mercedes with four men in it that cruised past us at eighty, there were few other cars on the highway, a wide ribbon of fresh black asphalt almost painfully new in a landscape as old as the gods. A solitary square farmhouse on a bare hilltop, the occasional patchwork of vineyards and hayfields, sheep grazing in a field of brown thistles, these testified to villages hidden somewhere in the hills. But for the most part it was wild and lonely countryside.

The sirocco was blowing, the hot southern wind that whirls up out of the deserts of North Africa. It funneled through the valleys that breached the stony barricade of mountains beside the sea, hammering the car with sudden violent gusts. I could feel its power as I gripped the steering wheel to keep the car from veering. The treeless rolling hills rippled with the shadows of low, scudding clouds and the movement of the wind in the long grass.

Jay pointed to a distant cluster of dusty-white houses, like a handful of dice thrown down beside a wide bay. "That should be Castellammare del Golfo," he said, carefully pronouncing each syllable of the name. "So we're about halfway to Erice." Stony mountains whose lower flanks were terraced with olive groves loomed above the little town; fishing boats rocked at anchor on a sea in iridescent shades of blue and green. It was a tourist picture postcard town, from a distance. Up close, I had read, the truth was otherwise.

Soon after this the autostrada turned south for a few miles. It was a particularly desolate stretch of road; no cars approached, no cars passed, the only signs of life the gulls that flecked a freshly plowed field like chips of white paint. Then, around a curve, we came upon a small red Fiat parked on the verge ahead, its hood raised.

"What a lousy place to have a breakdown," said Jay.

I glimpsed a dark head on the far side of the car, bent over the engine. "I'd like to be a Good Samaritan, but there's no point taking risks."

"What do you mean?"

"That town back there, Castellammare del Golfo? In one guidebook it was described as a 'picturesque Mafia stronghold.' More murders per capita than Palermo. Besides, these are the mountains where bandits used to lurk, remember?"

At the sound of our car the dark head came up from its study of the motor. A girl with a familiar face stared at our car. Perhaps she thought that we weren't going to stop, for she bent over the open engine once more, stretching her arm down inside it to remove something. But even before I saw the white-haired old woman in black beyond her, sitting on a suitcase in the shade of a eucalyptus, I was lifting my foot off the accelerator. "It's the old lady from the ferry," I told Jay. "The one with the queen bee. I thought I'd seen the girl before." I braked and pulled over to the side of the road, a hundred yards or so beyond the Fiat.

"You don't think she's got a gun in her suitcase?" Jay asked as we got out of the car, eyes wide and voice exaggeratedly serious.

"Do you know what the emperor Domitian said?"

He looked surprised. "No, what?"

"That only his assassination would convince people that the conspiracies he believed in were real."

"Meaning?"

"Meaning paranoia gets no respect until it's too late. After what happened to you at Foxburghe, we should be careful." Not to mention the ambiguous incident with the Opel in Bonn. Or, to indulge my paranoia thoroughly, the man with the mustache I'd seen at the Palermo docks.

"What happened to Domitian?"

"He was assassinated."

Jay's grin was mischievous. "Too bad. He never even got the chance to say I told you so."

The girl, it seemed, was just as suspicious as I had been. Scowling at our approach, she walked over to stand beside the old woman. She was twenty or so, short and sturdy-looking, with a determined mouth and a curly aureole of thick black hair springing out around her head. Her features had the same chiseled cast as the old woman's, but less sharply defined. The skirt of her yellow dress blew in the wind, a splash of mustard against the backdrop of green fields, billowing out until she was forced to hold it against her bare legs with one hand. In the other hand she held a narrow strip of rubber.

When she recognized us, the skin of the old woman's face pleated into its wide smile and she reached one hand up to the girl for help in rising. As she struggled to her feet she must have explained who we were, for the girl's scowl faded, replaced by curiosity.

I greeted the old woman in Italian, and asked if we could help in any way.

She thanked us for stopping but shook her head. No, they couldn't think of troubling us; her granddaughter would look after her. The granddaughter was silent, her face blank, but I sensed from the way she turned the broken piece of rubber over in her hands that she was less confident of her power.

Jay said, "We can't leave them here. That must be the fan belt she's got. They'll need a new one."

I tried again. "We're going to Erice, Signora. Perhaps we could take you that far. Or at least to the nearest garage."

At this the girl turned and spoke to the old woman in rapid incomprehensible Sicilian, beating time in the air with the piece of rubber. From the tone of her voice, which was low and urgent, I guessed that she was encouraging her grandmother to accept our offer. Finally, after a moment's silent reflection, the old woman nodded.

The girl swung back to face us. When she spoke it was in English, oddly phrased, with a strange, almost musical accent, but far easier to understand than the old woman's Italian. "My grandmother is one who helps others, but will not ask for help herself," she said. "I am not so modest." Her smile was challenging, tart where the old woman's was sweet. "My grandmother lives in San Teodoro. It is not far from Erice. If I explain you the direction, can you take us there?"

"Yes, of course. My name is Alison Jordan, and this is my brother, Jay."

"And I am Rosalia Solina. My grandmother you have already met on the ferry?"

I nodded. "With her queen bee." Signora Solina was clutching the small brown package against her chest, protecting it from the wind that threatened to carry it off. The girl slammed down the hood of the car, brushing the dirt from her hands as she said,

"I will be glad when we are rid of that one. She makes me nervous, and I know that bees do not like you to be nervous. It makes them want to sting you."

After some persuading on Jay's part, Signora Solina allowed him to carry her suitcase, and together the four of us walked slowly to the BMW. When the girl had helped her grandmother into the back seat, she straightened and said, "One moment please. I must fetch something from my car." She ran back to the Fiat and leaned inside it, over the dashboard. A few minutes later she emerged with the car radio under one arm. After locking the Fiat's doors she returned, explaining as she climbed into the back seat beside her grandmother, "I must take the radio with me, or it would be stolen. There is nothing else of value in my car. And it cannot be run without this." She held up the piece of rubber.

Rosalia leaned over the front seat and pointed to a spot on the map that Jay had opened up. "There, that is San Teodoro, a few kilometers before Erice. It is off the autostrada only a little way. You will not lose much time." As she sank back again she added, barely pausing for breath, "I thought at first you are German, because of this car. But you speak English, although you do not speak it in the same way. Yet you are brother and sister?"

"We are Americans," I told her, "but we live in Europe. We have the same father but different mothers."

"A typical American family," Jay said tonelessly. He was turned away from me, looking out the window at the hills that rose up around us, striped with ancient terracing and the narrow lines of low, crumbling stone walls.

"Americans are always marrying," Rosalia said, "and moving. They must be hard to please."

"And Sicilians," I asked her, nettled by the note of contempt in the girl's voice, "are they different?"

"Sicilians are too easily pleased," she returned promptly. "As long as we are left alone, we are content to accept things as they are. And so things change very slowly here, too slowly."

"Jay and I have a little Sicilian blood," I told her. "Our father's mother was from Sicily."

After Rosalia translated this for her grandmother, the old lady clapped her hands together. And where did our grandmother come from in Sicily, she wanted to know? I had no idea of the actual place, but on an impulse I replied, "A village called Castell'alto." There was a silence from the back seat. When I checked the rearview mirror I saw an unreadable look pass between Signora Solina and her granddaughter. "Have you heard of it?"

Slowly, almost reluctantly, Rosalia said, "It's not far from San Teodoro, but in the mountains. The real name is Castello di Torracchione Alto, but it is known as Castell'alto." That would explain, I thought, why the Italian embassy in Bonn had no record of it. "There is a saying," she continued. "The local people call it—"

"The village that God forgot," Jay said, making the grim words sound almost lighthearted. He was staring straight ahead, to hide the excitement on his face from the two women in the back seat. For the first time, Castell'alto was more than a name on a piece of paper.

"Ah, you know it." Rosalia seemed surprised. "Then perhaps you will understand me if I say this is not a place for foreigners." The girl fell silent, as though this were explanation enough.

Jay turned to look at her, resting his left arm along the back of the seat. "Even if we had family there?"

"It's true, in many other places that would be enough. But Castell'alto . . ." Her voice trailed off. "It's not like other places."

"If we do decide to go to Castell'alto," Jay persisted, "could you tell us how to get there?"

She did not answer immediately; instead, she spoke in Sicilian to her grandmother. Despite the rapid flow of words her voice sounded tentative, and when Signora Solina replied the old lady seemed to be protesting, arguing about something. "My grandmother is old-fashioned," Rosalia said at last. "She does not want even to talk about this place."

Firmly, in slow Italian, Signora Solina told me, "It is no place for such as you and your brother, Signorina."

When I translated this for Jay, he said to Rosalia, "Can you ask your grandmother why?"

"I know why," the girl replied. "Castell'alto belongs to a man who was once very powerful in our part of Sicily. Now he is old, but people do not forget what he was. He prefers to keep his village to himself, and they respect that."

"Who is he?" I asked.

"His name is Don Calogero Coccalo." The name provoked another flood of Sicilian from Signora Solina. She was scolding Rosalia, that much was clear, and the girl shifted uncomfortably in her seat while she listened. Finally she shrugged, and I thought I understood her to say that, after all, it was none of their business what Jay and I did.

"Signora Solina," I said, speaking slowly so that the old lady could understand my Italian, "it's very important that my brother and I talk to someone from Castell'alto. Can you tell us if that would be possible without actually going to the village?"

She considered this for a moment and then let loose another torrent of Sicilian. Rosalia interpreted for us. "She says that she has a neighbor who might help you. Like you, she is an American. My grandmother is taking the queen bee to her. This woman knows Castell'alto."

I looked at Jay. He was trying hard, but the hand that lay along the seat back was trembling. He put it in his lap. "How long has this American woman lived in San Teodoro?" he asked. "Perhaps three or four years now," Rosalia replied. Long enough, perhaps, to have known Hugo when he was in Castell'-alto; there was a good chance she might even know if he had returned there. I asked Rosalia if her grandmother would be willing to introduce us to her neighbor. "Of course," the girl said. "The *signora* lives not far from my grandmother's house. She is—*come si dice? Un'originale*, we say."

"An eccentric?"

"Perhaps a little. But all the same *simpatica*, you understand."

"What's odd about her?" I asked.

Rosalia shrugged. "Perhaps only that such a woman would choose to live alone in San Teodoro. Ah, look," she said suddenly, pointing ahead. "There, that is Segesta."

There was a vivid, fleeting vision of golden harmony against a wild green hillside, a Greek temple lightly hovering in the landscape as though blown there by the wind from the sea. And then it was gone. The road dipped and turned, descending into a long dark tunnel that ran under a range of hills. Jay was quiet, but I had heard the intake of his breath. "We'll come back," I promised him, "no matter what happens." He smiled at me. The road emerged from the tunnel onto the broad plain of Trapani, the nearest coastal city. Far off in the distance a solitary mountain reared into the sky; it was Monte San Giuliano, Rosalia told us, and at its peak was Erice.

Jay was asking Rosalia where she had learned to speak English. "In a convent in Palermo," she replied, and laughed at the expression on Jay's face. "No, I was not myself a nun. The sisters taught me, the Little Sisters of the Holy Cross. It is an order from Ireland." That would explain her accent, I thought. "When you are in Palermo, you must buy marzipan from the sisters. They make very beautiful flowers of marzipan. When I gave a rose made by the sisters to my mother, she screamed. The sisters had put a marzipan bee in the center." Now, Rosalia continued, she was studying agriculture at the university in Palermo. Someday, she told us, she hoped to teach her countrymen modern farming methods. "My mother says I must be crazy to think I can ever succeed. No one will listen to me, she says."

"Why not?" Jay asked her.

"First, because I am a woman. And then because each Sicilian thinks his own way is the best. We don't like to work together with others, we don't trust each other enough for that. In Sicily we say, 'You play alone, you never lose.' " Rosalia's voice was somber. But when Jay mentioned that he worked on a farm in England, she brightened and began questioning him about English farming. The two of them were in the midst of an animated discussion of fertilizers as we turned off the highway toward San Teodoro, passing on the verge a boy leading a donkey so heaped with hay that it looked like a moving haystack. He stared at us impassively, a timeless image that made the modern Agip gas station across the way seem even uglier.

Surrounded by vineyards and olive groves, the little town lay like a cubist painting on the gently rolling plain, its houses all squares and angles and color-washed walls bleached by the harsh sun, with long green shutters closed against the heat. On the second stories, bright waistcoats of laundry stretched haphazardly across big-bellied balconies, somewhat spoiling the painterly effect but adding another kind of charm.

The house of her grandmother's neighbor was at the other end of the road, Rosalia said. "The village is not large. Three thousand people, not more." Following her directions, I steered the car slowly through the narrow streets, weaving around playing children, motor scooters, and piles of trash. The whine of a power saw echoed a woman's voice shrilling passionately from some alleyway. "Pepiii-no," she called in a long, dying fall to the last syllable of the name.

We crossed a dusty piazza where dark-faced men lounged in the doorway of a barbershop, while others watched the barbering through the plate-glass window. A silent group of men played cards at a little table set up beside the fountain in the middle of the square. Almost without exception, the men wore dark caps pulled low on their foreheads.

Soon the houses thinned as the land tilted gently up toward Monte San Giuliano, some three or four miles distant as the crow flies. We passed the local cemetery, where tall slabs in neat rows housed the dead, a town in miniature shaded by a few scrawny cypresses; it seemed tidier and better cared for than San Teodoro itself.

Rosalia and Jay were still caught up with obscure agrarian matters when I noticed an odd sight to my left in the distance, the figure of a woman dressed all in white walking slowly through a scrubby field dotted with bushes of yellow broom, one arm lifted above her head. Enveloping her and trailing behind her like a thin dark mist was a cloud of what could only be insects. Yet the woman seemed unconcerned; her pace was slow and stately, her manner calm. I had only a glimpse, no more, before she disappeared from view behind a house. It was a disturbing image, like something from a dream.

"There," said Rosalia suddenly, "that is the *signora's* house." It was the last house in the village, a square, two-story whitewashed house with a sloping red tile roof, separated from its neighbors by a field of wildflowers and an acacia grove. Abutting one side of the house was a flat-topped concrete garage; through its open door we could see a Land Rover parked inside. The front yard was neatly cultivated in rows of beans, peppers, tomato vines, and a melon patch; in one corner were several orange trees heavy with green fruit and a gnarled olive with clusters of pale flowers on its branches. On either side of the front door, two yellow-painted metal oil drums spilled bright orange nasturtiums over their edges. On one drum, in the middle of the nasturtiums, sat a large stone bee.

Signora Solina rapped on the front door and then, when there was no response, tried the handle. The door was opened at her touch. "Signora," she called out. But there was no answer. She disappeared inside for a moment and we could hear her calling again, before she returned, shaking her head.

"Perhaps Signora Hunt is with her bees," Rosalia said. "Behind the house there are *bugni*, how do you say in English—"

"Beehives?" I hazarded.

"*Sì*, beehives. She may be there."

But before we could move, a dog came rushing around the corner of the house, barking furiously, a huge German shepherd with black markings on its face like a mask. It got between us and the front door and stood there, with its four feet planted wide apart, barking its outrage at the trespassers. When Signora Solina spoke to it, the barking died away, but the dog continued to protest in a low rumbling growl, one corner of its upper lip lifted to expose sharp pointed teeth.

"It is my neighbor's dog," Signora Solina said calmly. "He will not hurt us."

In a firm, quiet voice Jay spoke to the animal. "It's okay, boy, we're friends." He repeated this rhythmically until the animal stopped snarling and watched him, assessing the overture with intelligent eyes and a partly cocked left ear. He let Jay approach, then lifted his muzzle and sniffed Jay's outstretched hand. Finally he allowed Jay to stroke his head. "That's a good fellow," said Jay.

I heard a movement behind me and turned around. A woman was standing at the corner of the house, watching us, a slim, handsome woman wearing a black cotton shirt and trousers. Our eyes met, and in hers I clearly saw a distress that seemed somehow more than a simple dislike of strangers, of privacy invaded. The look faded almost at once, and she came forward.

CHAPTER 7

"It isn't often that Argo lets anyone but me do that. You're honored."

She spoke in English, American English with an odd inflection that I could not place, and her voice was strong and assured, almost masculine in intonation. Although she could have passed for Italian—the skin tones so close to olive, the dark hair and eyebrows—there was something more than the language that confirmed her as American—an athletic ranginess, perhaps, in the way she moved as she came toward us, and the frankness of her gray-eyed gaze.

She was, as the French say, of a certain age; in other words, a woman who wore her middle years well, the sifting of gray through her short dark hair and the rayed lines in the skin next to her eyes the only clues that she was well over forty. She wore no makeup, her clothes were baggy and utilitarian, and the only deliberate touch of femininity was a necklace of small green stones joined to each other by tiny gold discs, half hidden in the neck of her shirt.

She greeted Signora Solina and Rosalia in fluent Sicilian, addressing the old lady as Donna Anna. When Signora Solina handed her the little package with its queen, she received it with obvious delight, asking questions and listening intently to the answers. At last Signora Solina explained why Jay and I had come. I was able to follow very little of the rapid Sicilian, only enough to know that they were discussing Castell'alto. The American woman's face was grave, and she looked at me for a long moment, an odd look, though not unfriendly. Finally she held out her hand to me. "I'm Clio Hunt." Her slender, muscular hand was callused, with the grip of someone used to manual labor. I was surprised to feel the hand tremble slightly in mine.

63

When Jay and I introduced ourselves, she gave a peculiar little nod of her head, and it was as if she had suddenly relaxed—there was no other way to explain the sudden easing of the tension in her face. "Donna Anna thinks I might be able to help you in some way," she said to me. "I gather you and your brother want to go to Castell'alto."

"Signora Solina suggested we should talk to you about the place first, before making up our minds. She thinks it's a bad idea."

"She may be right." Clio Hunt gave a small smile. "Come inside, why don't you, and we'll discuss it."

But Signora Solina said that she must get home, otherwise the daughter who lived with her would worry, and they must see to her granddaughter's car. When I offered to drive them, Rosalia replied that her grandmother's house was only a short distance away, back down the road we had come along; they could easily walk. I tried to insist, only to be told firmly by the old lady that I must stay and talk to Signora Hunt. In that case, I replied, Jay would carry her suitcase for her. But Rosalia looked almost offended by the idea. "I am strong," she said, "almost as strong as my grandmother, who walks two miles to her fields and back every day." She thanked us for bringing them to San Teodoro, inviting us to visit her at her parents' house in Palermo before we left the island. We promised to take her up on her offer of a tour of the city if there was time. As we watched the two women go off down the road, the yellow dress beside the black, Clio Hunt said, "I like to see those two together. Donna Anna is the old Sicily, Rosalia's the new, but they have the same strengths." She closed the garden gate and turned to us. "Shall we go inside?"

When Jay and I entered the house behind her, we came into a large, cool room whose white walls were lined with bookshelves. Any space on the shelves not filled by books was occupied by pieces of pottery, antique tiles, and small figures of clay or bronze, interspersed with great bunches of wildflowers stuck in jam jars and empty olive oil tins. The scent of jasmine filled the room. There was not much furniture—a daybed scattered with cushions, a small desk, and a large and elaborately decorated copper brazier that sat on a low platform of tiles at the opposite end of the room. Beside a window was a wooden table covered with books and papers, with three wooden chairs, whose flat backs were painted with red and yellow flowers, drawn up to it.

It was a simple, almost ascetic room—the flowers were the only notes of color—yet somehow attractive. There were no framed photographs, however, nothing to reveal whether its occupant was married, had children or family, and this struck me as odd for an expatriate—although she might very well keep family memorabilia in her bedroom. Donna Anna had called her Signora, but that might be only a term of respect, no proof that she was or had ever been married. I wished that I had thought to ask Rosalia more about the woman.

"I must unwrap my new queen first, and give her some water," Clio Hunt said. "She's had a long journey. And what about you two? You must be thirsty as well. What would you like, lemonade, coffee . . . ?"

Jay and I both asked for lemonade. She disappeared through curtains that divided the living room from a small kitchen; in a moment we heard water running and the clatter of plates. While we waited, I browsed along the bookshelves. There was an entire shelf of books devoted to the subject of bees and beekeeping, some with beautiful old leather bindings. I looked at a few of the titles: Varro, De re rustica; Virgil, Opera; Columella; Aristotle, Historia Animalium; Fraser, Beekeeping in Antiquity; Ransome, The Sacred Bee. Among the other books were histories of religion, an eclectic mix of poets, and Sicilian folklore and history. But the majority, as far as I could tell, had to do with archaeology.

"Alison," Jay suddenly whispered from across the room, "look at these." He was pointing to some books lying on a hassock beside the brazier. When I went over, I saw Hugo's name on the covers of two of them. One, the published results of his discovery of the tombs at Capomonte, was his first, the other his last as an archaeologist, written more than twenty-five years ago. I opened the second to the flyleaf and there, in Hugo's characteristic oversized handwriting, were the words "To Clio, the muse." There was no date.

"She must have known—" Jay began excitedly, but I motioned him to be quiet as Clio Hunt came back into the room carrying a tray. Pushing aside the clutter of papers, she set the tray down on the table by the window.

"Are you an archaeologist, Miss Hunt?" I asked as Jay and I went over to join her. "I couldn't help noticing you have a lot of books on the subject." If she were, it might explain her knowing Hugo.

"Please call me Clio," she said. "I'm a beekeeper who happens to be curious about the past.'' She poured lemonade into three glasses from a green earthenware pitcher painted with lemons. ''I think any foreigner living in Sicily must find its past irresistible. I certainly do.''

As she leaned across the table to hand me my glass, the necklace of green stones came loose from her shirt and swung forward. A small gold medallion hung suspended from it. Before she tucked it out of sight again, I saw, on the side facing outward, the figure of a standing woman, one arm upraised. I had only the briefest of glimpses, but it was enough. The medallion was, I was certain, if not identical then amazingly similar to my own.

''Excuse me a moment.'' Abruptly, she left the room before I could ask her about it. When she came back, bringing a loaf of bread and a honeycomb in a bowl, she was no longer wearing the necklace. Bewildered, I wondered if she had taken it off because she had seen me looking at it. Did she distrust us?

She cut chunks from the square of honeycomb and spread them on large slices of bread, which she passed to Jay and me. ''A neighbor brought me the bread this morning from Erice. The bakers in Erice burn orange wood in their ovens and some of the flavor comes through in the bread. The honey comes from the orange blossoms in my garden.'' The combination was delicious. ''Will you be visiting Erice, by the way?''

When I said that we would, she asked us what we knew of the place. ''Nothing, really,'' I replied, ''other than that it's supposed to have a wonderful view.''

''If you can see it for the fogs, which can be ferocious. They come up very suddenly, too, so take advantage of good weather if you get it. It can be perfectly clear down below in Trapani and a pea souper in Erice.'' She smiled, and the effect was startling, breaking up the severe planes of her face, making her seem younger, more feminine. ''But there's more to Erice than the view. It's the site of one of the oldest shrines in the classical world, one that goes back to the Mother Goddess herself. Astarte, Aphrodite, Venus, they were all worshiped there.''

Jay accepted a second slice of bread and honey. ''Is there a temple? We saw a fabulous one on the way here.''

''Segesta? I'm afraid there's nothing like that now. Until the Romans conquered Erice, the goddess was probably worshiped at an open-air altar. The Romans built a temple, but apart from some fragments that you can still see set into the walls of the castle, it's gone. What's left is mostly medieval. No, classical

Erice demands a leap of the imagination back several thousand years, and further. Even Daedalus was supposed to have been a pilgrim to the shrine.''

Jay must have been thinking of Hugo's letters, as I was, for he asked, "Didn't he make some sort of golden honeycomb, and isn't it supposed to be buried around here somewhere?"

"The story's probably apocryphal," Clio replied, "but I rather like it. It fits the place. The Sicilian peasant has always been convinced that the countryside is full of buried treasure, if only he knew where to look for it. Or if the Ladies of the Outside would condescend to show him."

"Ladies of the Outside?"

"The Eumenides, the Furies. We give them a gentler name, so as not to offend them. They're the ones who guard buried treasure here."

"Do you mean that people here still believe in them?" Jay said. "I thought they were just myths?"

Clio smiled. "Stories to study for school tests? You should spend some time in this country. Myths change, and many of them are all mixed up now with Christianity, but the fundamental ones have remarkable staying power. Especially the ones to do with the chthonic gods—the earliest gods, the one who lived underground, in caves. Look, as long as you're going to be in Erice . . ." She got up and went over to the desk, rummaging through the top drawer. When she came back she had a thin, buff-colored pamphlet in her hand.

"You can take this with you, if you like. I have other copies. It's something I wrote several years ago about the cult at Erice. It might make the place clearer when you're there." Her voice was suddenly diffident, almost shy, and she changed the subject abruptly. "Signora Solina mentioned something about your grandmother coming from Castell'alto. That's why you want to go there?"

"Yes. She was our father's mother." I hurried on, eager to gloss over these half-truths. "Signora Solina advised us to talk to you before we go. She gave the impression that it's a strange sort of place. Why is that?"

"It had an evil reputation once. It takes a long time to recover from that here. And the Castell'altesi don't exactly welcome outsiders. Though of course if your grandmother . . ." She did not finish whatever it was she had been about to say, and I wondered if I had imagined a faintly ironic note in her voice.

I forged on. "Signora Solina also mentioned a man who's a power in the town—"

"Don Calogero Coccalo." She took a sip of her lemonade. "A Sicilian success story. He emigrated to the States when he was a young man, made a lot of money, and came back to spend it in Castell'alto. He's responsible for Castell'alto's change for the better."

"She made him sound a bit sinister," Jay said.

"An image carefully cultivated by Don Calo. Unfortunately, fear is often what gets things done here." She set her glass down. "Is it important that you go to Castell'alto?"

"Yes," said Jay, "it is." He must have realized that he'd said it with too much emphasis, for he glanced at me and flushed.

She kept her eyes on him. "Why? If that's not too nosy a question."

"You know how Americans are about tracking down their roots," I said lightly, answering for Jay. "Especially when they're rootless."

"Are you?" The unsettling gray stare was turned on me.

"I suppose we are," I replied. "Maybe that's what happens when you live abroad too long." I explained that neither of us had lived in the United States for a number of years. "How long have you lived in Sicily, Miss Hunt—Clio?" She might consider the question presumptuous, but I wanted to deflect the conversation away from Jay and me.

"More than four years now. But my own roots never mattered much to me." She said it almost harshly, and I wondered where she had come from and why she had chosen to settle alone in this small town in a country so different from her own. She pushed back her chair and stood up. "It's time I introduced my new queen to her hive. I'll get her."

"What's the matter?" Jay asked quietly while she was gone from the room.

"Is it that obvious?"

"You just seem jumpy, that's all."

I pulled the medallion out from under my shirt, and showed it to him. "Hugo gave me this. Clio was wearing one like it. But she took it off just now." Jay was about to speak when we heard Clio returning. Quickly, I tucked the medallion back out of sight.

Clio came back into the room carrying the package Donna Anna had brought to her, which, now unwrapped, proved to be a small wooden box about the size of a child's pencil holder.

Two interlocking circles in roughly the shape of a figure eight were cut into the wood and the holes covered with fine mesh. Through the mesh we could easily pick out the queen, much larger than the half-dozen worker bees surrounding her.

"Why don't you come with me? Then we can talk as I work." She took a newspaper from a stack in a basket by the brazier, glancing at the front page. "Another I haven't read. I don't know why I bother to buy the newspaper, I never seem to have the time for it. And on the whole it's very pleasant to know nothing of what's going on in the world."

Tucking the paper under one arm, she picked up the little cage with the queen bee and led the way outside. The dog Argo rose from the middle of the path where he'd been sleeping in the dust and followed us as we went around to the back of the house. The air smelled of thyme and meadow grass, and the faint salty tang of the windborne sea. Argo trotted over to an almond tree and lay down in the shade.

Directly behind the house was a concrete terrace facing onto a large garden longer than it was wide, about an acre in size, filled with fruit trees and bushes and another vegetable plot. In the southwest, to our left as we stood on the terrace, rose the great bulk of Monte San Giuliano, Erice's mountain, but directly beyond the garden were fields and vineyards, and beyond them the plain, which ended in a range of mountains to the northeast. "There," Clio Hunt said, shielding her eyes against the sun as she pointed to the mountains, "that's where you'll have to go. Castell'alto is on the seaward side of the first mountain, Monte Castello. It's the one that looks like the hump of a camel. It's about half an hour from here by car. If the road is passable."

"Why wouldn't it be?" Jay asked her.

"There were heavy rains this spring. Sometimes mud and rock slides block off the mountain roads. A number of times in the past I've had to leave the car and walk." She turned her attention to the queen bee. "Now I must get you settled, little one." Her voice was low and caressing, almost loving. "I have some extra veils in the honey house—you two should wear them while we're near the hives. The bees don't like the sirocco any more than humans do; it makes them just as irritable." She opened the door of a small shed that abutted onto the back of the house. Through the doorway we could see gleaming metal machinery and shelves stacked with jars of honey.

While she was gone, Jay said in a low voice, "Why don't we ask her straight out if she knows Hugo?"

But I was hesitant. "We'd have to explain who we are and why we're here. If Hugo is hiding in Castell'alto, the fewer people who know about it the better."

"Then let's just get directions and go up there now."

"I don't know, Jay—it might be better to see what we can find out about the place first. And maybe she'll give us some sort of introduction to this Don Calogero. He sounds formidable."

Jay looked only half convinced, but at that moment Clio came out of the honey house carrying canvas hats with wide stiff brims, from which hung long veils. She was already wearing one herself, as well as white coveralls that clothed her from neck to ankles. Reminded of the curious figure I had seen earlier in the field, I asked her about it.

She smiled, and said that it was she. "I was hiving a wild swarm that had settled in a neighbor's tree. I should have expected you," she added, surprisingly. "A visit from strangers, I mean. The ancients believed that a swarm heralds the arrival of a stranger."

"It was a remarkable sight." I thought of the courage it must take to let yourself be so completely surrounded by bees, and said as much to her. "At least the Pied Piper didn't have the rats buzzing around his head."

"It isn't courage so much as the absence of fear. Nothing frightens me anymore." The words might have been arrogant but for the way she said them, with a sudden frank seriousness, and something oddly close to regret in her voice. "When I was young I spent too much time being frightened, running away. I've stopped now. Maybe it's one of the rewards of middle age." Then, more lightly, "Besides, it doesn't take that much courage when you're protected with veils and gloves. Swarming bees are gorged with honey, and that makes them good-tempered, unless you provoke them."

While we put on the hats, she asked if either of us was allergic to bee stings. When Jay replied that he had been stung so often he was immune, she asked him if he kept bees himself. He blushed. "I wish I could. Maybe someday. I have worked with bees, though."

"Good. Then you'll be relaxed around them. That's the main thing when you're dealing with bees," she told me, "to be completely calm and methodical in your movements. They don't like surprises." She handed me a small tin pot shaped like a pitcher with a tiny bellows attached. It was a smoker, she told me, and asked me to carry it for her. "Smoke quietens bees. Nobody knows why exactly."

Carrying the small box containing the queen and her workers, she led us through a cluster of fruit trees to the back of the garden, toward a group of hives. As we approached the hives, I noticed a small marble statue half hidden by the pendent branch of a lemon tree. No bigger than a foot in height, it stood on a stone pedestal overgrown with jasmine, a tiny goatish man with upflung hands and a wild satyric grin on his bearded face. In one hand he held a small sickle. What drew the eye first and inevitably, however, was lower down—a phallus so enormous that it could only be described as intimidating.

Clio saw where I was looking. "That's Priapus. He has no sense of shame, I'm afraid." She walked over to the statue and rearranged a tendril of jasmine. "I'm all out of fig leaves, so this will have to do for now." The effect was, if anything, even more startling.

I glanced at Jay. "Don't mind me," he said, with a half-embarrassed grin, "I've seen one before. In the British Museum," he explained, at the sight of my raised eyebrow.

A friend had given her the statue, a copy of a fourth-century B.C. original, Clio said, when she started keeping bees. She pointed out some words in ancient Greek hand-painted on the stone, translating them for us. " 'I abide here to guard the hives, on the watch for him who steals the bees.' Bees were under Priapus' protection in the ancient world because they were associated with fertility. I generally cover him up when Sicilian friends visit. Not because of outraged sensibilities, but because some people think he's making the evil eye at them. That's fine with me—it keeps trespassers away. That and Argo."

There were two dozen or so hives scattered in front of a hawthorn hedge that separated her garden from the fields beyond. Each hive rested on a stone foundation and was divided into horizontal sections, a small tower of three or four white boxes, like a miniature apartment house. Bees flew in and out of the hives; the air thrummed with their buzzing. One hive was shorter than its neighbors, only two sections high, with a third section, a white box whose open top was covered with fine wire mesh, resting on the ground beside it. A small opening was cut in one side. Clio removed a piece of wood that blocked one end of the little queen cage and then, tilting up the large white box, gently shook the contents of the cage through the opening of the box. Swiftly, she plugged up the opening with a wad of newspaper.

Then, very carefully, she lifted the hive from its base and set it down on the grass. A few bees buzzed around the hive but didn't seem much disturbed by what was happening. We wouldn't need the smoker after all, Clio told us. She took the box with the queen and set it down on the stone base, covering the wire-mesh top with a single sheet of newspaper.

"Why do you do that?" I asked her.

Jay said, "To protect the queen, right?"

"Yes, exactly. You see," she explained to me as she put the rest of the hive back on top, "if you put the queen right in with the hive, there's a chance the bees will attack her because she's unfamiliar. This way, by the time they've eaten through the newspaper to get to her, she has absorbed the scent of the hive and they'll accept her." After a pause she added, "It's the same in Sicily. If you just barge in, you won't be accepted, people might even turn on you. But if you're patient—or, better yet, have a sponsor, so to speak—then you have a better chance of succeeding. That's why Donna Anna advised you to come to me. And why I tell you that there's no point going to Castell'alto unless Don Calogero approves. You'd get nowhere without his permission. No one would speak to you, no one would tell you anything." Calmly, she closed up the beehive again.

"What about you," Jay asked, "what if you 'sponsored' us?"

"Oh, I have no influence with the people there." This was said over her shoulder as she strode on ahead of us, back toward the house.

"Not even with Don Calogero?" he persisted, catching up with her.

She stopped to look at him. "Well, perhaps a little. But there would have to be a very good reason for me to use it. Nothing comes for free here, you understand. Perhaps if you were frank with me . . ."

Jay and I glanced at each other. "What do you mean?" I asked as I lifted the veil up onto the brim of my hat.

"I mean that such determination to go to a place that several people have warned you away from makes me think there's more than ancestor hunting involved."

I had never considered the possibility that Jay and I might have to have a story manufactured to explain our presence in Sicily, apart from simple vacationing. Caught unprepared, I managed an explanation that sounded feeble even to me. "There really isn't anything especially mysterious about our wanting to see Castell'alto. Someday I'd like to write a book about our family, and I think it's important to actually see the places where our relatives came from. Surely Don Calogero can't object to that?''

She did not answer. She took Jay's hat and held out her hand for mine. "Will your father be in this book of yours?" She let a beat go by. "You are Hugo's children, aren't you?''

CHAPTER 8

The silence was filled with the sound of bees and the rustling of the wind. Above the yellow fields a flock of birds broke and scattered at a hawk's spiraling descent from the mountain. As though he sensed a tension in the air, Argo raised his head from his paws, then got to his feet and moved out from the shade of the almond tree toward us. Jay was whistling tunelessly under his breath. The dog settled down by his side on the concrete.

"You know Hugo?" I said at last.

"Yes, I knew him."

"What makes you think we're his children?" I wondered why she had said nothing until now.

"You mean apart from the evidence standing before me?" Her smile was amused, ironical. "I knew that he had a daughter Alison and a son Jay. Fairly conclusive, I think."

While Jay and I hesitated, she went on, "Hugo's mother came from Syracuse, not Castell'alto. So let's stop all this talk of grandmothers, shall we? I take it you've come here because of him?" When I nodded, she said, "But he's in Libya." It was as much a question as a statement.

"Not any longer," Jay told her. He was squatting beside the dog, stroking its head. "He got out four or five days ago."

"I didn't know," she said simply.

Only the American news would carry the story, I thought, so it was not surprising she hadn't heard, unless she and Hugo were more than acquaintances. If that was so—and both the inscription in the book and her medallion hinted at something beyond friendship—and if Hugo was in Castell'alto, then why hadn't he contacted her? Because he was not in Castell'alto, after all? I felt an odd pang of disappointment—for Jay's sake, I told myself.

But what Clio said next made me think Jay might still be right.

74

She wasn't looking at us now; her eyes were fixed on the range of mountains to the north, where Castell'alto lay, a dark and undulating wave beating up against the fierce blue sky. A line deepened in the flesh beside her mouth. Almost to herself, she said, "That must be why Don Calo won't talk to me. . . ."

I waited. When the pause lengthened, I asked her what she meant.

Speaking slowly, as if she were beginning to understand something that only now seemed odd, she said, "I've been trying to reach Don Calogero these past few days. To get his permission to visit some hives I keep on land of his just outside Castell'alto. From courtesy I always call before I go. There's never been a problem before, but this time he put me off. Or rather, he had his housekeeper put me off. I haven't been able to reach Don Calo himself."

"And you think that's because Hugo's there, in Castell'alto?" Jay's upturned face was strained, the blue eyes intent.

Clio furrowed her brow. "But isn't that why you want to go there? Because you know he's there?"

As Jay got to his feet, he glanced at me for guidance. I said, "We're hoping. That's all."

The canvas hats were tucked under her arm. She was pulling the veiling of one through her fingers as we talked; suddenly she turned away, letting the veil stream out behind her. "I really must get on with my work. I have an order to fill by tomorrow. But we can talk in the honey house as I work." She went into the shed at the back of the house, hanging the hats on pegs by the door.

The honey house was a single room with a screened window facing the mountains. Jars full of honey in shades of gold from palest yellow to a dark rich amber lined the shelves against two walls. A dozen or so wide-mouthed jars, each with a chunk of honeycomb inside, stood on a scarred wooden trestle table next to three of the white wooden boxes that went to make up a hive. A pile of white paper labels sat beside them. I glanced at the top label—MIELE D'ERICE read the inscription printed across it. But what made me catch my breath was the drawing above the words. It showed a standing woman, her hand reaching up to what was clearly, more clearly than on the coin in my medallion, a bee.

Clio noticed my glance. "It's stretching it a bit to say it's honey from Erice. But bees will forage for more than three miles, and in a beeline, Monte Giuliano just makes it."

Jay stood leaning against the closed door, his hands shoved into his jeans pockets. Clio told me to sit on a tall three-legged stool pushed up to the table. "I have to extract honey to pour over the combs in those jars," she said as she tied a white apron on over her clothes. "You're welcome to watch, but please stay put. It's a messy job, and there's no point in your getting honey all over yourselves."

At one end of the table was a large cheesecloth-lined bowl with a strip of wood placed across it. Next to the table stood a drum-shaped stainless-steel tank, an odd metal contraption with a wood handle resting on its top. It looked a little like an old-fashioned crank-handled washing machine. Clio explained that it was an extractor. "You put the honeycomb in, turn the handle, and the honey spins out of the comb. Centrifugal force."

She picked up a broad-bladed electric knife from the counter beneath the window and plugged the cord into an outlet on the wall. Then she lifted the top wooden box from the stack of three and set it beside her on the table. It was called a super, she explained. "Each super holds nine frames vertically side by side. And each frame holds the comb." As she spoke she took a frame from the super. A rectangle of thin wood strips roughly a foot and half long by nine inches deep enclosed almost perfect, crinkle-surfaced honeycomb capped with white wax.

Abruptly, she asked, "So you've come to find your father?" Her voice had a harsh edge to it, as if she had to force herself to ask the question, and it occurred to me that she might have deliberately chosen to work while we talked—a distraction for her, and for us.

"Hoping to find him." Less candidly, I added, "But we have nothing more to go on than the news report. We aren't even sure if he's still in Sicily."

"He hasn't been in touch with you?"

"No."

If she found that odd or surprising, she gave no sign. The impulse of most men returning from some sort of exile might be to see their families, but perhaps she knew that Hugo had never pretended to be like most men.

Resting the frame of honeycomb on the strip of wood above the bowl, she picked up the heated knife. With a steady, fluid upward movement of one arm, she sliced thin layers of wax off the top of the comb. The wide curls of wax capping fell into the bowl. When she finished she reversed the honeycomb and re-peated the process on the other side. Then she placed the uncapped comb, now a sheet of liquid gold, in the extractor. All her movements were graceful, deft, with the practised ease of an expert.

"What makes you think Hugo's in Castell'alto?" she asked as she took another frame from the super.

"Jay and I knew about Castell'alto from letters he wrote to us. It's the only clue we have."

Jay said, "We were wondering about one thing . . ."

"What's that?"

"Why Hugo chose Castell'alto. There's that saying, 'the village that God forgot.' It doesn't make it sound very attractive."

She smiled. "The people of Castell'alto have a reply. 'God may forget, but Don Calo remembers.' Meaning that things aren't so bad now as outsiders once believed they were. True, it has an unfriendly reputation, but I think perhaps it's slightly exaggerated. To keep strangers out. And a stranger is anyone who lives more than twenty kilometers away. When you first see it you think it's like any other mountain village, still fairly primitive. But inside it's another story. Most houses have electricity, plumbing, new furniture. The farming is subsistence, but unlike most such places in Sicily the men haven't all gone off to jobs in Germany. Don Calo has a great deal to do with whatever prosperity Castell'alto enjoys. And I think he also had something to do with your father's decision to stay, though that's only a guess. All I know is that he's in Hugo's debt for some reason. That, of course, would smooth Hugo's way in settling in Castell'alto."

"But why would someone like Hugo want to live there? I mean someone who had the whole world to choose from," Jay asked her.

"Well, for a start it is very beautiful, if your taste runs to the wild and dramatic, which Hugo's does. And it combines both of his passions, architecture and archaeology." She looked up at us from her work. "You know about the castle, do you?"

"In a letter he wrote that he'd bought a romantic ruin," I said. "He talked about fixing it up."

"It needs quite a bit of that. There isn't much of it left, apart from the keep, some of the walls, and a magnificent tower with a wonderful view over the sea. And the dead town."

"The dead town?" I thought of the cemetery we had passed as we drove into San Teodoro.

"The old Castell'alto. Casteddu—that's what the local people call it. No one lives there now. They've all moved a little way down the mountain to the new town." Dryly, she explained, "It's new only in contrast, you have to understand. Fifteenth century as opposed to the Neolithic origins of Casteddu.

"It was one of Hugo's dreams, to restore Casteddu." Her voice dropped. The knife paused for a moment in its upward sweep of the comb, then went on slicing away the wax capping. "The castle itself is a Norman ruin that was once a Saracen stronghold and before that a sort of primitive fortified rock in the Bronze Age. The cult of the goddess at Erice that I told you about? Well, Hugo thought he'd found traces of a similar cult at Casteddu." She finished off the second frame and added it to the extractor.

"What were the others?" I asked.

"Others?"

"Other dreams. You said the castle was one of them, as though he had others."

But perhaps she felt that she had said too much, for she only gave an indifferent shrug of her shoulders. "Hugo was always planning. I couldn't possibly remember all his schemes." She paused in her work to scrape off some wax stuck to the handle of the knife.

In the silence we heard Argo barking. "Someone's come," Clio said, wiping her hands on the apron. She opened the honey house door. Together, we went around to the front of the house. Argo was by the gate, barking at a man sitting in a black Alfa Romeo.

"Damn," Clio muttered under her breath. "Look, don't say anything about who you are or why you're here, all right?" Then she went forward to grab Argo by the collar. "I've got him, Giudico," she called out in Italian.

A short middle-aged man in a well-cut suit and mirror-lensed sunglasses got out of the car, careful to stay half shielded by the open door. He was slightly built, with thinning dark hair neatly combed over a narrow skull. He looked insignificant, apart from the expensive suit—or so it seemed from a distance.

"I expected you tomorrow," Clio replied as he called out a greeting. *"Basta, basta."* This last was spoken to the dog, who was still growling.

The little man came toward us, smoothing down the jacket of his suit. "If you had a telephone, Clio, you would not be troubled by surprise visits. I could arrange it for you." His smile gave an unexpected charm to his nondescript face.

Clio's own smile was cool. "You arrange so much for me

already, Giudico. I mustn't abuse your kindness." In English, she said, "This is Alison Jordan and her brother, Jay. Giudico Coccalo. Giudico and his partner are the distributors for my honey."

Coccalo. Whatever the relationship of this man to Don Calogero Coccalo, it was clear he was no peasant from the mountains; he looked more like a banker or an accountant.

"A pleasure." His sunglasses reflected back my own image as we shook hands. Despite his size, he had a powerful physical presence, almost as strong as the cologne he was wearing. I resisted the urge to step back, away from him. "You are Americans, like Clio?"

"I'm sure they're better Americans than I am," Clio said, before Jay or I could reply. "And they're in something of a hurry, so if it's business . . . I take it that it is business you want to see me about?" Her voice was brusque. In some way, it was clear, Giudico Coccalo's presence made her as nervous as it made Argo.

He appeared to take her tone in stride, however, merely agreeing that yes, it was business, but managing to hint at a certain regret that this should be so. "I came to tell you that the order is larger than we expected. Elliot and I need perhaps half as much again. Can you manage that by tomorrow?"

"I think so. I'd put up extra for the hotel, but they can wait."

"Good." The sunglasses turned my way. In English, he said, "You are visitors to Sicily, Signorina Jordan?"

"Yes. This is our first time here."

"You are lucky, then, to know Clio. She can tell you much about Sicily. More of our past, perhaps, than we Sicilians can tell you." One eyebrow lifted above the sunglasses. "Or want to know."

Clio gave a faint smile. "Giudico has no patience with my interest in Sicily's past."

"It's true, the past bores me. And you live too much there." It was said to her with the same pleasant smile, but there was a hint of an impatience that implied this was an old argument. And something more, a subtle threat. Perhaps it was simply that the sunglasses made everything he said seem somehow menacing. I found myself wishing he'd take them off.

As if he read my mind, he did just that—and I saw why he wore them. Without them the nondescript face was suddenly hideous. Something had torn his left eye askew, pulling the flesh and the eyeball down and away to the side. The eye was opaque;

it looked blind. The skin that surrounded the eye was almost artificially smooth and pink, in shocking contrast to the dark olive tones of the rest of his face. The terrible squint intensified the impact of his presence; you were doubly aware of him, only more uncomfortably so. That he knew this was plain from the slight flourish with which he had pulled off the glasses and carefully folded them, watching us all the while. Jay turned away to pat Argo. I tried to meet his stare, failed, and said, for lack of anything better, "Clio's been telling us about Erice. It sounds fascinating."

"Did she tell you that the women there have always been the most beautiful in Sicily? The Arabs asked Allah to deliver the women of Erice into their hands." Giudico smiled at Jay. "You will have something more than the view to enjoy." He seemed amused by Jay's blush. To Clio, he added, "I will come tomorrow, early, for the honey."

"Fine. If I'm not here, it'll be in the honey house, in crates by the door."

He gave her an odd look, in which anger and some sort of appeal were mingled. In Sicilian, very quickly, he said something that sounded like "It would be better if you were here. Not only because of the dog . . ."

She nodded, her face unreadable. "I'll try."

"I will come very early, then. To make certain you are here."

As he put his sunglasses back on, he said to me, "If you come to Palermo, I would be happy to show you and your brother around." Then he wished Jay and me a pleasant time in Sicily. With an unstated mutual sense of relief, we watched him get back into the Alfa Romeo and drive off. There was a short silence while the dust settled in the car's wake. Argo scratched himself, then trotted back to the front door of Clio's house and lay down on the stoop.

Jay was tracing patterns in the dust of the path with a long stalk of grass. When the roar of the Alfa Romeo's engine died away he raised his head and asked Clio if Giudico was Don Calogero's son. His nephew, she replied. "But Don Calo and his wife pretty much raised him after his parents died when he was a teenager."

"Then," Jay said, "why did you tell us not to mention why we're here? If he's Don Calogero's nephew, couldn't he help us?"

"Giudico was never Hugo's friend. He wouldn't be much

help.'' She stooped and pulled a weed from among the marigolds growing by the gate.

When she did not elaborate on this, Jay muttered, ''It doesn't seem that we're going to get much help from anyone.'' With an effort at politeness, he asked Clio if she would tell us how to get to Castell'alto.

''Of course,'' she replied equably. ''Unfortunately, the road up to it is bad. This discourages tourists and casual visitors.'' She gave a small smile. ''I think that probably had something to do with Castell'alto's appeal for Hugo. It's such a difficult place to drop in on. He was never someone who had much tolerance for unexpected visitors. Friends and family included.'' There was a pause, then a sideways look at us from intelligent gray eyes. ''What I'm trying to say is, don't you think Hugo would contact you when he was ready to see you?''

Although I resented her assumptions, this was so much what I had already wondered myself that I had no answer for her. But Jay was equal to it. With quiet force he said, ''I've waited three years for my father to contact me. I'm tired of waiting.''

When she looked at me, I shrugged. ''This is Jay's trip. I provide the transportation.''

A flicker of her eyelids was the only sign that she might have found this a cool response compared to my brother's. ''You seem prepared to go quite a distance.''

''As far as we have to. We know Hugo isn't someone who meets you halfway.''

Politely but firmly, Jay said, ''We are going to Castell'alto, whatever its reputation. But it would help us if you'd be willing to call ahead.'' His eyes looked straight into hers.

She shrugged her shoulders, as though conceding defeat. ''Very well. I can't promise it will do much good, but Don Calogero may at least agree to talk to you.''

''That's all we're asking,'' I said.

''I don't think you realize what you're asking, Alison,'' she replied in a quiet voice. She turned to open the gate. ''There's a bar in the piazza with a public phone that's not too public. It's only a few minutes' walk. Shall we go?''

We walked along in silence. The late afternoon sun spilled across the mountains, gilding the wheat and fuzzing distant outlines with a soft golden haze. Bright colors splashed against the boulders littering the roadside, thick bushes of yellow broom, scarlet geraniums, daisies, and morning glory. Over garden walls bougainvillaea foamed in a gaudy purple wave. But sharp on the breeze came the ever-present smell of drains, the drone of flies that hovered over a slime of rotting garbage heaped by the pitted concrete road. And once, out of the corner of my eye, I saw a gray, humped rat disappearing down a sewer grate.

Jay was the first the speak. His voice was hesitant, as though he knew that what he asked Clio might not be welcome. "You never really told us how you met our father. Was it here in Sicily?"

She nodded. "It was four years ago, at a party in Palermo given by the American cultural affairs officer, if that's the right title. I knew he'd been an archaeologist once, and I mentioned that I was interested in the cult of Aphrodite at Erice. We got to talking. Gradually we became friends. Your father has a gift for friendship. Other kinds of relationships with him can be more complicated." The gray eyes looked away, and the expression in them seemed almost wistful.

"We talked of working together at Casteddu," she said. "I have a theory about the cult there, that it was some sort of bee cult. I'm afraid I have a tendency to let my theories influence my life." She gave a small, self-mocking smile, then added, "But Hugo went to Libya before we did much more than talk." As she spoke, I had the feeling she was choosing each word deliberately. It made me wonder about the words she was leaving out.

"Were you already living in San Teodoro when you met Hugo?" I asked her.

She shook her head. "In fact, I'd just arrived in Sicily when we met. Eventually I decided to stay here more or less permanently. Someone here in San Teodoro was willing to sell their house, so I bought it. That doesn't happen very often—despite the poverty, people are reluctant to let go of their land. Even Sicilians who leave and settle in other countries hang on to their houses, hoping they'll be able to come back someday. Don Calogero helped me with the purchase."

Don Calogero again. The man, it seemed, had played a part in both Hugo's and Clio's settling in the area, if only in smoothing the way. Or was there more to it than that? And how large a part, I wondered, had Hugo played in Clio's decision to stay?

We were nearing the center of San Teodoro, walking between a wall of old houses on either side. Every now and then I had the distinct impression that someone was watching us, but when I turned around I saw only a child holding a ball, or a cat in an open window, eyes half closed, observing the strangers. Once an old woman leaned over her balcony and shouted down a greeting to Clio. Beside her, suspended from the wrought-iron balcony railing, was a pair of pink running shoes, dangling like fruit from a metalwork vine.

The small main square was thronged now with cars and children and women shopping. On the opposite side of the piazza was a bar, a plain room with fly-blown posters peeling from the walls and a long wooden counter at which a small group of men stood talking with the barman. Jay and I ordered *spremuta d'arancia*, freshly squeezed orange juice, while Clio went to use the pay telephone at the other end of the room. There were occasional glances our way, the scrutiny veiled but still palpable.

"Is it just because I'm a woman," I asked Jay, "or do you have the feeling that we're being watched?"

"A bit. But we are strangers, after all."

"Yes, but it's more than that somehow." I half hesitated, then plunged. "I suppose I should have told you before now, but there was someone at the docks who made me nervous." I went on to describe the man with the mustache.

Jay seemed unfazed. "I think Clio's friend Giudico is the one to worry about, not some creep trying to pick up female tourists off the boat." Closing one eye, he twisted his face into a leer and whispered, in a wildly exaggerated imitation of Giudico Coccalo's accent, "May Allah deliver you into my hands, beautiful Signorina." Immediately he blushed.

I had to laugh, which may have been what he wanted, for he looked almost relieved. This trip with all its dangers was an adventure for Jay, that much was clear—but an adventure with a streak of the night terrors. I would be wise to keep my misgivings to myself.

When Clio came back she ordered a mineral water. She waited until the barman had set the drink down and returned to the men at the far end of the bar to tell us that she still had not been able to reach Don Calogero himself. "I gave your message to Assunta, his housekeeper. She said she would tell Don Calo when he returns. I'm to call again later tonight." She drank some of her mineral water, blotting the moisture on the side of the glass with the scalloped triangle of paper napkin. "By the way, did you plan to spend the night in Erice?"

I nodded. "We have reservations at the Hotel Ginestra. Do you know it?"

"Yes, it's fine. I'd invite you both to stay with me but I'm really not set up for guests. You'll be much more comfortable at the hotel.'' This may have been true, but I had the impression she was relieved to have the issue already resolved. ''I'll telephone the hotel as soon as I've talked to Don Calogero. If he agrees to see you, I'll take you to Castell'alto in the morning.''

I was surprised—she hadn't seemed that eager to become involved in our search. ''If it's any trouble, I'm sure Jay and I could find our way there.''

''It's no trouble. And it'll give me a chance to visit those hives I mentioned.''

When we came out of the bar, San Teodoro's main square was transformed, entirely filled with cars and dark-suited men, the women and children all vanished. The men stood talking in groups, gesticulating, slapping a car hood to make some point, rarely laughing. Their voices rose on the air like a thick pungent smoke. Boys on motor scooters cruised among them, then shot off down side streets with great explosions of exhaust in a loud assertion of their own manhood.

''Where have all the women gone?'' I asked Clio as we skirted the square.

''Gone to their kitchens. San Teodoro is still very much a traditional Sicilian village. Though I'm told the girls are more liberated than their mothers were—or more degenerate, depending on who's telling you.''

In the narrow back streets female voices called through open doorways where old women sat on kitchen chairs, peeling vegetables and gossiping. Faces peered out at us from windows that gave glimpses of dark rooms below the level of the street, or down from balconies bright with geraniums. The air was filled with that delectable smell of a summertime meal in the south, the smell of basil, of onions and garlic frying in olive oil, of vegetables freshly picked and cooked.

Once, Clio stopped briefly to chat with a teenaged girl who stood outside a house holding a puppy in her arms. As we walked away, she said, ''Not so long ago a girl that age would be sitting with her back to the street, as a sign of her modesty. A remnant of the Islamic occupation.''

''Like the Lady of Shalott,'' Jay said, ''watching the world go by in a mirror.''

''Exactly. Maybe the same fate, too, if she peeked at the wrong man.'' Clio's voice was grave. ''Newborn baby girls used to be washed in water or wine, which was then thrown into the ashes of the hearth. To show that home was their proper place.''

"And boy babies?" I asked.

"The liquid went into the street." She smiled. "The symbolism's not subtle at all."

"They had the right to go where they wanted?" Jay guessed. When Clio nodded, he looked thoughtful. "Not very fair." A hopeful sign for whomever he married, I reflected, that note of indignation in his voice.

"Fairness is a British concept, not Sicilian," Clio said. "But men paid in other ways. They still do. Just this year I heard of a six-year-old boy taken secretly by his mother to England from a village near here. To escape a vendetta. He was the only male left in his family."

I shivered. "No wonder you see so many women in black."

"Black is a useful color in this country," she agreed, touching the sleeve of her shirt. "When I first came here, dealing with men had its difficult moments. Unlikely as that sounds at my age . . ." Her voice was dry. Not unlikely at all, I thought, watching the beautiful, grave face. "Then a friend—well, your father actually—told me that if I really wanted to be left alone I should cut my hair, which was long in those days, and wear black. I took his advice, and found he was right."

By this time we had reached her front gate and were standing by the BMW. "Now, you know the way up to Erice?" she asked us.

I took this as a hint that our visit was up, and unlocked the driver's door. "We do, but while I think of it, could you show us exactly where Castell'alto is on the map?"

"Of course."

Jay reached into the BMW for the map and spread it out across the hood. With one finger Clio traced a wiggling white thread that wound away from a thicker yellow line leading off the autostrada. Where the white road ended the topography showed a mountain peak next to the coast. "That's Monte Castello. The village isn't marked, but that's where it is. Here's the way you go. . . ." Her finger moved along the white line. "The road's an improved *mulattiere*, an old mule track. Hard on a nice car like this."

As Jay and I got into the BMW, I remembered the pamphlet, which I had left lying on her table. She said she would get it for me, and returned bearing both the pamphlet and a jar of her honey. "For the rolls at breakfast. All you'll get otherwise are those awful little plastic cups of jam." She added that she would call us later on in the evening at the Hotel Ginestra. "Probably sometime around nine or so."

When we tried to thank her, she said simply, "I'm glad to meet Hugo's children at last. He was right." Before I could ask her what she meant, she was explaining how to find our way back to the main road. Then she grabbed Argo by the collar and went back inside her gate.

As we drove away, Jay turned to look at Castell'alto's camelback mountain. "I wish we could go straight there."

"I know. But what Clio said is true—Hugo never liked surprises." Unless, I thought, he was on the giving end. "If he's there now he'll be there tomorrow, and we'll be surer of our welcome. If we went now, and found he wasn't there, we'd just have to come back down that mountain road in the dark. And by then our reservation at the hotel might be gone."

"All right. But it seems weird to make an appointment to see our own father." He paused, looking at me. "You know what else is weird?"

"Yes, but you start."

"Well, I know I've never seen her before—Clio, I mean—but she reminds me of someone. There's something about her. . . . That sounds feeble, I know."

"No, it doesn't. She seems familiar to me, too. Maybe it's just the type."

"What type?"

"The frontier spirit turned expatriate. Someone out of sync with her country but somehow still very American. I've met people like her ever since I've lived abroad, though they're generally younger and usually men. What was it Rosalia called her? *Un'originale*—not really eccentric, just out of the ordinary."

"So how does someone like her end up raising bees in a place like this? Do you think it has anything to do with Hugo?"

"I don't know. There are a lot of questions I'd like to ask her. But I don't think I'd get any answers—at least, not honest ones."

"She's hiding things," Jay said. It wasn't a question.

"Yes, I think she is."

I wanted very much to know what they were.

CHAPTER 9

After consulting the map, we decided not to return to the autostrada, which would have meant retracing our steps. Instead, we took the two-lane road out of San Teodoro west toward Erice. At the edge of the village there was a slight delay. Rush hour in San Teodoro consisted of three dozen black-faced sheep, most of whom lacked a healthy fear of cars. A young shepherd prodded at them with his staff, staring at us all the while from under the flat cap pulled low on his forehead, while a small black-and-white dog worried the sheep's hindquarters, persuading the flock toward the safer attractions of the meadow grass on the side of the road.

"Can I have a look at that pamphlet Clio gave you?" Jay asked me.

"Help yourself. It's in my purse on the back seat, with the jar of honey." I steered the car around a last recalcitrant sheep. "Archaeological interest?"

"Partly. But I thought it also might tell us something about her."

During the next little while, we drove in silence as Jay read Clio's article. The road meandered through the plain in a leisurely fashion not revealed on the map. One moment it approached Monte San Giuliano, the next it veered teasingly away again. We passed between fields patchworked brown and green and yellow, dotted with bundles of bamboo canes, and drove through modern hamlets of square, flat-roofed concrete houses. Each house seemed mysteriously to be in a state of flux, with a doorless garage, an unfinished second floor, or the crumbling remains of a half-built wall. Rusting metal rods jutted at crazy angles from plaster and masonry, like monitory fingers wagging at work undone, while honeysuckle and morning glory curled softly around piles of builders' rubble. This was a country, I was to learn, where nothing was ever finished—not even at death.

Perhaps Jay was glad of the distraction from his thoughts. Now that we had such a clear lead to Hugo, the wait for Clio's call would be hard for him. As for myself, I was grateful for the delay; I needed time to prepare myself to face Hugo again. Until now he had seemed safely remote, nothing more tangible than a shadow in the far distance, a mirage. I had never really expected that Jay and I would find him. But Clio Hunt changed that; she brought him closer.

The enigma of Clio herself disturbed me. That she was linked to Hugo beyond the common interest in the cult of Aphrodite she had mentioned seemed almost certain. Given Hugo's reputation and her own attractions, there was surely an element of the romantic to their relationship. And a shared past? The inscription in Hugo's book hinted at something beyond the physical, although with a woman like Clio Hunt I suspected there would always be more than the physical.

"Educate me," I said when Jay came to the end of Clio's pamphlet. From his concentration I assumed that he had found it interesting.

"Do you want to know the naughty bits as well?" He laughed at the expression on my face. "That's how the English describe anything about sex."

"Well, of course—the naughty bits most of all."

"Then you're going to have to read them yourself. Sorry, but it's not the kind of thing a brother can read to an older sister. Here, I'll give you an idea of what I mean." He riffled through the pages, then cleared his throat ostentatiously. " 'The bee cult at Erice had a darker side. During the earliest rites, Aphrodite's priestesses took consorts in the name of the goddess. But the king's reign was short-lived, like the drone's, and he suffered the same terrible fate. Just as the queen bee destroys the drone in the act of love, so the priestesses killed the king by tearing out his—' Ugh." He made a face. "Anyway, things got better later. If a man brought the right gift, he could have a good time with a priestess, and get away with everything still intact."

"Fascinating. And here I was wishing I'd brought a novel to read at bedtime. Please go on."

"She talks a lot about the prehistoric cults around here, the ones to the Great Goddess that preceded Aphrodite's cult. She says the earliest worship took place in caves, and that whenever the main shrine at Erice was threatened the priestesses probably retreated back to those caves. She thinks the lost treasures of Aphrodite at Erice could still be in one of the caves around here." He looked at the mountains in the distance and said, a little wistfully, "Maybe when this is all over we can come back and do some caving."

"What do you mean 'we'? I'm flattered you include me, but even Daedalus' golden honeycomb wouldn't get me into a Sicilian cave." I slowed for a tractor that was crossing the road, hauling a load of artichokes in a wagon behind it. The traffic was heavier now, and while we waited for the tractor a small train of cars collected behind us. "Did you learn anything about Clio herself from the article?"

"Nothing more than we know already. She's smart and she sounds like she knows what she's talking about, but she's obviously got a thing about bees."

The hieratic image of Clio crossing the field, one arm upraised, surrounded by the wild swarm, passed through my memory in separate frames of movement, like some old, flickering film. Once again I saw the chain around her neck swing forward, the gold medallion flashing in the shaft of light from the window. Had Hugo given it to her?

Jay's thoughts must have paralleled my own, for he asked, "Do you think she and Hugo were . . . well, more than friends?"

"Probably. But whatever their relationship was, it must have ended badly, or been over by the time he went to Libya. Otherwise he would have been in touch with her now." The tractor turned off into another field and we picked up speed again.

In a quiet voice, Jay said, "He didn't get in touch with us, either."

"You never gave him time to, Jay. I'm sure he would have, eventually."

"I couldn't wait for eventually. Things happen, things that might mean there would never be an eventually. By looking for him I'm doing something, not just sitting around waiting. At least I don't feel helpless, the way I have these past three years." His head was bent over Clio's pamphlet and he turned the pages at random, as if he wasn't really seeing them.

We were approaching Monte San Giuliano again. To the right of the winding road, the land tilted up to meet the mountain's flanks. By the roadside a skinny dog nosed at an ad hoc garbage dump, raising his head warily at the approach of two young boys with sticks in their hands. I glanced back at the pregnant little scene in the rearview mirror.

But the dog's fate remained a mystery. For at this point the highway curved again, and in the bend of the road, just behind the dusty blue Fiat following us, I saw a gray van with a crumpled antenna. The same one, I was willing to swear, that I had seen at the docks. It was too far back for me to make out the driver, but I felt sure he would have a peach-colored shirt and a thick mustache.

There was a simple way to confirm my suspicions.

With a sudden spurt of speed, I pulled out to pass the car ahead. Back in my lane again, I checked the rearview mirror. As I watched, the van swung out and whipped around the Fiat. I passed another car, and a third. Each time, after a moment's pause, the van followed suit. But it always kept a car between us.

It had to be the man from the Palermo docks. Mustache.

He was tracking us like a wary hunter careful to stay downwind from his prey, using the car between us as a blind. If I hadn't chanced to notice him before, it would never occur to me now that he was following us. But he was always there, a persistent, undeniable presence.

"What's wrong?" Jay was watching me.

"Look in your side mirror, but don't turn around. See that gray van?"

"The one that's about to be flattened by the truck?"

Startled, I glanced back again. A double-axle big-rig trailing two empty flatbeds was gaining on the van, throwing off a small dust cloud as it stormed up the highway. A spiral of oily black smoke from its funnel smeared the sky in its wake.

"That would solve our problems."

"What do you mean?"

"Remember the man I told you about, the one who was watching us as we got off the ferry? He had a gray van like that one."

"The same one? Are you sure?"

"Fairly sure." I described my experiment. I tried to sound calm, and managed a rueful smile as I glanced at Jay. "I'm afraid that those Sicilian bandit stories I read last night are coming back to haunt me."

"Well," said Jay reasonably, "if he really is a bandit or a car thief, there's not much he can do to us with the other cars around. The main thing is to make sure he doesn't follow us when we leave the highway. We'll just have to lose him.'' I needn't have worried about frightening Jay—he was clearly enjoying the drama.

Amused despite myself by his confident tone, I told him to let me know as soon as he had a plan. But in fact, when I glanced in the rearview mirror again, I saw the glimmerings of a plan of my own. By now the truck had caught up to the van. Like some enormous leech it hung on the van's tail, plainly impatient to pass. The combination of the winding highway and occasional oncoming traffic meant that the truck could not risk passing three cars at once. The driver leaned on his horn, but Mustache was giving no ground—if the truck got ahead of him, he wouldn't be able to see us for the dust. So he tailgated the car in front, a little green mini, and refused to let the truck by.

''There's a road sign coming up, ahead at that crossroads,'' Jay said. ''I can't read it yet, but it must be the turn for Erice.''

Ahead the highway ran straight and momentarily empty. It was a chance, the only one we might get.

''Hold on,'' I told Jay, as I stamped down on the accelerator. The BMW shot forward, opening up a wide gap between the green mini and us. The truck driver saw his own chance, swerved out from behind the van and charged up the road. He cut sharply back into his lane in front of the mini, which slowed at once to give way to him, forcing the van to do the same.

Over the noise of our own engine I heard the warning blast from the truck's horn, the clatter of its empty flatbeds as they bounced along behind the tractor. At each bump in the road the trailers swung wide on their axles, whipping out from side to side like the tail of a rattlesnake. Every few seconds, when the off-side wheels hit the dry dirt verge, dust devils swirled in the air, merging with diesel exhaust and smoke into a blinding smog. Mustache couldn't possibly see us now.

Jay twisted around in his seat to look out the back window. ''He's coming up fast!''

Maybe the truck driver thought I'd given him some sort of challenge, maybe he simple enjoyed terrorizing tourists—whatever the reason, he roared up behind us and hung there, a few yards from the rear bumper, both of us doing fifty.

The sign at the junction was visible now. Jay leaned forward in his seat. ''There's the road to Erice,'' he cried. Beyond it, a small road forked off the the right, rising rapidly as it began its climb around the mountain. The turn was almost upon us—there was no time to think, no time for a choice.

"Put your head down," I shouted to Jay.

I signaled, took my foot off the accelerator, and touched the brakes, to warn the truck off. We slowed, not a lot, but enough, and then I wrenched the wheel to the right. With a squealing protest of tires, the car skidded into the turn to Erice. For a heart-stopping moment it shimmied, fighting a patch of loose gravel, then grabbed at the road and held it. Simultaneously the truck thundered past and on up the highway, its horn blaring furiously.

When I had the car under control I slowed to a stop and looked out my window. A quarter of a mile down the highway, just visible through the dust cloud, was the van. Had the dust screened us? Was the driver too busy watching for his chance to pass to see us take the turn, or had he wondered why the truck had suddenly braked, and looked back? It all happened so quickly we might have got away with the ruse, but as soon as he got past the truck he was bound to realize what we had done. By then, however, we should be in Erice.

At the turn, Jay had bent down with his arms over his head without asking why. Now he raised his head, looked around, then stared at me with a flattering if misplaced admiration. "You did it!"

I laughed shakily. "Amazing, isn't it? You'd never guess I failed my driver's test twice." We started up the winding road. "Now for the Hotel Ginestra. You keep a watch out for the van."

Despite Jay's enthusiasm, I knew that it had been a singularly stupid thing to do. I was a competent enough driver to recognize that we had come dangerously close to an accident. What had possessed me to react so unthinkingly? If a stranger's intimidation could shake me so easily, I must be more frightened by Luke's warning and Jay's story of the two men than I had allowed myself to acknowledge. Was Mustache really after the car, as I had suspected when I first saw him, or was he following us because he hoped we might lead him to Hugo? He had clearly been on the watch at the docks—but for us in particular, or simply for any vulnerable tourist? And if for us, where had he been while we were in San Teodoro with Clio?

No one knew we were coming to Sicily, no one knew we were looking for Hugo; I recited this like a mantra as we climbed steadily upward. Still, I decided to register Jay under my name at the hotel, and to avoid mentioning the name Raphael. As for

Mustache, he had no way of knowing we were spending the night in Erice. With luck we had lost him for good.

The road looped up the mountain in a series of switchbacks, with the occasional glimpse of blue sea through clearings in the pine woods that girdled the slopes near the crest. Far below us, creamy villages spotted the plain, San Teodoro somewhere among them.

Jay watched the road behind us but saw no following car, not even the telltale dust in the air that might mean the van had doubled back and was on the scent again. It seemed we had been lucky after all.

At the next turn in the road we saw the massive ramparts of the town wall rising sheer above us. There was a gate in the wall with a parking lot outside it, scattered with a few cars and a tour bus, but Jay caught sight of an almost illegible sign painted on one of the huge stones of the wall, which read TO THE HOTEL GINESTRA. Like a promise of safety, a fading red arrow pointed to the narrow lane that curved around a corner, between the town wall's outside face and a short but impressive drop to a small meadow starred with giant yellow daisies. There was barely enough space for our car, none at all for anything coming from the other direction, and nothing to indicate that the lane was one way.

I hesitated to leave the car in the parking lot, immediately visible to anyone coming up the road and a giveaway to our presence in Erice, so I shifted into first and gingerly inched my way forward around the bend. Almost at once the lane widened into a small piazza, which fronted a three-story building of pale blue concrete. The Hotel Ginestra sat on a tiny plateau with the city wall at its back and a pine woods beyond, on its northern side. In front of the piazza's own low boundary wall was a steep drop to more pine woods, the tips of the trees like green-gold waves breaking against the mountainside. Far below, the salt flats and the sea glittered in the late afternoon sun.

The hotel itself was insignificant, almost ugly, but to me it had all the beauty of a safe harbor after a storm. In front there was a postage-stamp terrace and a little fountain where water dribbled rustily into a stew of rotting plants. I parked beside the fountain and we got out.

There wasn't a soul around, no sound but the trickle of the fountain, the inevitable crickets, and the wind in the pines. Not the slightest rumbling of a pursuing van's engine. Still, I hoped there would be somewhere else I could park the car; I would feet better when it wasn't so plainly in sight.

We took our belongings out of the trunk and walked up the steps into the hotel. An old man with a flattened boxer's face and closed eyes was sitting on a bench by the door, snoring gently. His hands were folded in the lap of his trousers. Behind the reception desk that ran along one side of the small lobby another man in a crumpled blue suit was slumped back in a chair, his head bowed over the newspaper spread across his stomach. Flies buzzed lazily above the dregs of two espresso cups on the desktop. Apart from this, and the rhythmical snores of the old man, the silence was absolute.

I set my suitcase down with a thud. "Signori?" I said tentatively. In response, the old man by the door gave a low reproachful grunt and increased the volume of his snoring. Jay loudly cleared his throat, to no avail. Longing for a bath, I watched the motes of dust drifting along a shaft of light from a window behind the reception desk. I felt half hypnotized by the silence, suspended between inertia and a growing sense of unreality, as though I'd come too far too fast.

Reading my thoughts, Jay said with quiet menace, "This is the land of the Lotus Eaters, where no one ever wakes up." He hummed the theme to "The Twilight Zone."

I laughed, and the spell was broken. With a rustling of newspaper, the man behind the counter sat suddenly up, blinking and open-mouthed. Plump as an olive, he had sleek black hair and large, mournful eyes, like a seal's. Then he came completely awake and stood up, pushing the newspaper onto the chair. "Signora, forgive me. I am Signor Indelicato. How can I help you? But of course," he added when I explained who we were, producing a pen and a registration card, which he set down on the counter with a brisk little slap, as though to compensate for the yawn that he was trying to suppress.

As I filled out the card, I mentioned that we'd parked our car in front. "Is there somewhere else I could put it?" I meant somewhere out of sight, where Mustache could not see it.

"When the hotel is full, we ask our guests to leave their cars at the Porta Trapani, where there is a car park. But as you can see, now it is very quiet. Too many people have been frightened away this year." Frowning slightly, he added, "It is a pity. Sicily is very safe."

"Qaddafi doesn't make you nervous?" Jay asked him. Qaddafi and terrorism combined had certainly made tourists nervous; this was the year when, for most people, a holiday in Europe had all the allure of a stroll alone in Central Park after midnight. First the hijacking of the *Achille Lauro*, then the various terrorist attacks in major cities, and finally our retaliatory air strike on Libya for the West Berlin disco bombing that had killed an American serviceman. And Qaddafi threatening worse to follow. It was no wonder, I thought, that business at the Hotel Ginestra was poor.

"That madman." Signor Indelicato's voice was contemptuous, and I had the feeling that if we had been outside, he might have spat. "When there is trouble he hides in the desert like a rat in his hole." As though to dispose of an unpleasant subject, he tapped a bell to summon the old man, who had wakened and was watching us through half-opened eyes from his bench. "Salvatore will take you to your rooms. We have given you a room with a private bath, Signora, as you requested. Your brother's has a shower."

Before we followed Salvatore, I pushed the issue of the car, playing the insecure tourist. "I'd really feel better if I could park my car behind the hotel. It's so conspicuous where it is. We've heard so many stories. . . . Is there room?"

He looked mildly offended and declared that Erice was perfectly safe. "It is not like other towns in Sicily, you understand. However, as you are anxious, there is a place for one car behind the hotel, next to the trash cans. It is for the owner's car, but he is away at the moment. If you wish, you may use that."

"Thank you. That's very good of you." I told Jay to go ahead with Salvatore while I moved the car.

"We will wait, Signora," the old man said, settling down on the bench again. "We have time." When I returned, his eyelids were drooping once more. The somnolent air of the Hotel Ginestra must have been contagious, for Jay, too, was yawning as Salvatore turned the key in the lock of his room. I told him to take a nap, that we would meet afterward for supper. He nodded and vanished through his door.

My own room was next door to Jay's. It was shuttered against the sun and airless, but the old man raised the shutters to reveal wide windows and opened the glassed-in door that led out to a small balcony. A breeze drifted in, bringing with it the tireless rasp of the cicadas and the occasional drone of a motor scooter or airplane in the distance. Light and high-ceilinged, the room was a combination of the decrepitly picturesque and the functional, or barely functional. There was a small chandelier of colored glass, ornate and very dusty, a bedside lamp in the shape of a shepherdess who had lost one arm as well as most of her sheep, and a pretty writing desk in gilded wood. A large wardrobe and a bed with a carved headboard stood against one wall. Later I was to discover that the chandelier and lamp together gave an unsteady light insufficient to read by and the desk wobbled so badly it was almost unusable. The bed, at least, was reassuringly firm.

After I tipped Salvatore, I ran water for a bath and lay soaking in it while I read Clio's pamphlet. As Jay had said, it was interesting and intelligent, but there was also the faintest hint of an idiosyncrasy that explained why it had been published in a popular archaeological magazine and not a scholarly journal.

"The earliest cult at Erice," I read,

undoubtedly worshiped the Earth Goddess, or Great Mother, who presided over agriculture and fertility. In archaic times, Mother Earth evolved variously into Demeter, goddess of agriculture, Artemis, goddess of wildlife, and Aphrodite, goddess of human fertility, and although Erice's goddess was worshiped as Astarte by the Phoenicians and as Aphrodite by the Greeks, She was always an amalgam of these three aspects.

Bees and honey were intimately bound up with the cult, both as symbol and as a part of the ritual. Aphrodite's lover was Butes, the beekeeper. Daedalus himself was reputed to have made a golden honeycomb in the goddess's honor. The Goddess at Erice, like Her sister Artemis at Ephesus, might well be called the Bee Goddess, for the bee represented the triune Goddess in all Her aspects: agriculture, wildlife, and fertility. . . .

A ritual dance performed by the priestesses may have been part of the rites. The evidence of several pieces of incised pottery (fig. 1) dating from the seventh century leads us to believe that this was a Bee dance, imitating the complex dance of the bees themselves. (Of course, we know now that bees really do dance in order to transmit information to one another.) This dance may be compared to the Crane dance performed on Delos by Theseus and his companions to celebrate their escape from the labyrinth. Like the Crane dance, the Bee dance may also have been danced in a labyrinth or maze. Such maze dances are occasionally still performed in modern Italy.

Early rites connected with the cult were probably savage, resembling in some ways those of the worship of Cybele.

Then followed the bit Jay had read to me in the car.

We have evidence for this in a graffito found in the last century in a cave on Monte Castello (fig. 2). Tragically, this sketch, which was scratched onto the cave wall, has been almost completely destroyed by vandals. However, Professor Paolo Tebaldi made a drawing of it in 1897 when it was still clear; opinion holds that the graffito may be late Bronze Age. The sketch shows four figures, three upright standing around a fourth lying on his back; his arms are not visible and may have been bound behind him. The three upright figures are clearly women, the fourth appears to be male. One figure, larger than the rest, is holding something in her upraised hand. A crude outline in the shape of a bee hovers above this. Ritual castration may be the explanation.

There was a lot more along these lines, explaining how the cult developed and what it represented to the ancients. So potent was Erice's myth that the Romans simply adopted it in its entirety and built a temple to Venus Erycina in Rome. There was a disconcertingly modern piece by the Greek historian Diodorus; he described Roman politicians' junkets to the shrine at Erice, and the high times they had with Venus's priestesses.

Modern feminists may take inspiration from this cult, which was never quite suppressed and ultimately evolved locally into the modern-day worship of Mary and, peripherally, her Son. At Erice, unlike many other shrines in the ancient world, no god ever supplanted the Goddess.

Today, the Goddess's shrine at Erice is empty, her altar has crumbled into dust. Nothing remains. But somewhere, in some cave underground perhaps, a lamp stands waiting for the sacred oil, a treasure for discovery.

I found the article fascinating. It was eccentric but appealing; it had something in common, I thought, with Samuel Butler's half-serious theory that the *Odyssey* was written by a woman who had lived just below Erice, in Trapani. I wondered what Hugo had made of it.

After I dressed, I went over to the open glass door. I was about to step outside when I heard the low rumble of an engine. In a moment, the gray van drove into the piazza. I moved back into my room and partly closed the shutter doors, leaving a wide crack through which I was able to see the van. It made a slow circuit of the small piazza, then drove away again, back around the bend. Once or twice, through the pine woods, I caught sight of it winding down the road toward Trapani before it vanished.

CHAPTER 10

My right hand gripped the door frame so tightly that the fingers were starting to cramp. I relaxed it, thinking, He's too persistent, a car thief would have given up and gone off in search of easier prey.

But we were safe. Mustache must have scouted Erice, checked the hotel's piazza on the way back, and perhaps assumed that we had taken another road down. For the time being, at least, we had foxed him.

I stood there, wondering what to do next. Too shaken to follow Jay's example and nap, I wanted exercise, some sort of distraction from all the questions that nagged at me. I went out onto the little balcony with its crumbling concrete floor, eaten away at the corners as though by mice with a taste for mortar. The distant sea shimmered like a vision of water in the desert, elusive and remote, almost invisible in its shroud of opalescent mist.

The wind was a gentle breeze now, and carried with it the scent of the pine forest. In the west, the sun wheeled gradually over toward the horizon, its course nearly spent. But an hour of light remained to the day—enough for a visit to Aphrodite's shrine, or what was left of it. Mustache was gone; it would be safe to take a walk, and it might be my only chance to see Erice and its shrine. Even modern pilgrims, I thought, should pay their respects, acknowledge the ancient goddess of the place. And who knows, I told myself as I collected my purse and guidebook, she might have a little of her old power left to help the supplicant.

When I tapped on Jay's door there was no answer; he must have fallen asleep almost at once. On a piece of paper I scribbled a note explaining where I was going, slipped it under the door, and went downstairs. Outside, the tensions of the drive seemed miraculously to dissolve in the limpid, peaceful air. The seething streets of Palermo, the irritable, dusty wind, the throbbing of the car's engine, all these had been left behind down on the plain; on this height there was only the soft sound of the wind in the pines, the childlike cry of swallows skimming insects from the air.

The walls around Erice were an enormous palimpsest, layer upon layer of history. The base of huge, rough-hewn stones was so ancient, my guidebook said, that a race of giant Cyclopes was supposed to have built them. Repaired through the centuries by Carthaginians, Greeks, and Romans, they were topped by medieval towers. Above the gate was a remarkable inscription, remarkable for Sicily at any rate: CLEANLINESS AND SILENCE ARE THE SIGNS OF CIVILIZATION.

Inside the walls was a city of stone. Stone houses rose sheer from the stony streets in unbroken lines, pierced by narrow windows and arching wooden doors that opened onto shared courtyards, their stark, square facades decorated only by elaborate wrought-iron balconies on the second stories. The cobbled streets, too narrow for any but the smallest car, were patterned in lozenges of gray and white, beautiful for their perfect symmetry. In these austere and tranquil back streets there was nothing of San Teodoro's noisy fellowship, let alone any trace of Erice's own promiscuous past. Immaculate, trimmed in white marble, the gray stone cloaked the town like a nun's habit, hiding it from the curious eye.

Through the occasional open gate I caught glimpses of the small, flower-filled courtyards where the Ericini lived their lives, cloistered and apart. Once a little girl with a thick fringe of dark hair stared solemnly up at me as she led a white dove slowly along on a string, and once two men came suddenly out of a doorway, talking intently; otherwise the town seemed deserted. Like a great medieval monastery on its peak, Erice observed the hour of vespers with silence and retreat.

The site of the shrine lay on a high spur of rock in the ruins of a Norman castle, a few minutes' walk to the easternmost end of the town. To reach it, I climbed up through the mounting levels of terraced public gardens, which, in contrast with the stonily geometrical streets, were a lush thicket of trees and bushes threaded by meandering walks. The gardens seemed chiefly to be populated by thin brown lizards, who scuttled under the boxwood hedges at the sound of my footsteps, and a few townspeople out for their evening stroll.

The temple of the goddess in all her incarnations had stood on the highest pinnacle of the mountain, isolated by a ravine. A bridge reputed to be the work of Daedalus once spanned the gap, but that cleft was filled now and a steep stone stairway led from the gardens into the ruins of the Norman castle that had been constructed over the temple site. Inside the crumbling shell of the old castle was a great courtyard filled with tumbledown stone overgrown with grass and wildflowers. Several pairs of lovers wandered hand in hand through the grounds, but otherwise the Castle of Venus was empty. I searched for the spot described in my guidebook as Venus' Well, the place where her altar supposedly stood. The guidebook stated unromantically that it was probably only a granary where the priestesses stored the pilgrims' gifts of grain.

Whatever it might have been, nothing seemed left of it now. It was simply a dent in the ground, that was all—as though, when they neatened the castle grounds, the Ericini had tidied up the spiritual detritus of three thousand years as well. The view alone remained, evocative, sublime. As I leaned against the sun-warmed stone, gazing down at the classical sea, it was easy enough to imagine Aphrodite rising through the windblown spume, or Aeneas' ship beached on the salt flats to unload the forlorn refugees from Troy.

For a thousand years before Christ, Trapani's harbor had welcomed voyagers from the lands that ringed the Mediterranean, come to pay homage to the goddess. Laden with wine jars and offerings, the pilgrims had climbed the mountain to the goddess' aerie. It wasn't quite as easy to imagine that after that half-mile perpendicular climb they would have had energy for anything more strenuous than sedate conversation with her priestesses. But perhaps ancient man was made of sterner stuff.

I wondered if Castell'alto on its own mountain was anything like Erice. Had Hugo dreamed of a life lived at the top of the world, remote from the modern, the past that he loved a constant haunting presence to inspire him with dreams of new discoveries, new visions? An antidote, perhaps, to the old age he might fear.

As I turned away from the view, modern man made his own appearance on the scene. Dressed in an elegant cream-colored suit and panama hat, with a large camera hanging over his shoulder, he was standing near the entrance, looking about. Then his head turned my way. The brim of the hat was tilted forward, partly hiding his face, and he was wearing sunglasses, so that I sensed rather than saw his hesitation, his disappointment perhaps at not having the place to himself, and I felt a mild sympathy. If that was in fact how he felt, he overcame it, moving away to the other side of the garden to photograph the view from a small embrasure of stone. I strolled slowly along the little path in the opposite direction until I found a bench in the lee of a hummock of grass thickly covered in buttercups. This corner of the courtyard was deserted, and as the bench seat was hard and the little hill so invitingly soft, I stretched out on the grass to watch the sky recede above me.

But the nearby sound of a woman's voice startled me to my feet again almost at once. "Why, look there, Martin," she said. "It's a century plant."

I was smoothing down my skirt as an elderly couple, arm in arm, came into view along the path. Gray-haired, with the identical expression of benign goodwill on their faces, they looked like Jack Sprat and his wife, he tall and thin, towering over his plump wife, whose arm was hooked onto his like an umbrella. Even if she hadn't spoken, I would have known them at once as American by the way they were dressed—her dress was that shade of lime green that only Americans wear, and his trousers were plaid. They stopped in front of a giant plant that looked like nothing so much as a huge stalk of broccoli gone to seed, surrounded by sharp pointed leaves.

"You know, I do believe it's about to bloom," the old lady said. "Imagine that." She caught sight of me, and added in friendly explanation, "People used to think it only blossomed every hundred years. That's how it got its name. But I'm probably telling you something you already know."

I shook my head. "I thought it was an agave."

"That's its other name. I'm Emmeline Barlow, by the way, and this is my husband, Martin." When I introduced myself in turn, Mrs. Barlow said, "I saw you were American right away, that's why I spoke to you in English."

Amused that I had been identified as easily in my turn, I asked her how she had known. She just smiled. "I can always tell." Then she considered me, her head cocked on one side. "I'll tell you something else. You have high principles, are serious-minded and discriminating, though perhaps a little too cautious and inclined to shy away from whatever you feel might affect you too deeply. But I see a romantic streak there, too."

Perhaps I gaped a little, for she continued tranquilly, "I don't mean to show off, but it's my business to know these things.

You're dark-haired, and dark-haired people are generally conservative. You have a high forehead, and that indicates principles. Your eyes are gray and deeply set—so you are probably cautious and tend to avoid deep emotions.''

"And the romantic," I asked her, fascinated despite myself, "where do you see that?"

"In the shape of your face, dear. People with triangular-shaped faces often are romantics."

"My wife is a physiognomist," Martin Barlow explained proudly. With a hint of reproof, perhaps at my smile, which was more instinctive than polite, he added, "It's a profession like any other, you know."

"Oh, I'm sure. I didn't realize . . . ?" I began, hoping I hadn't wounded her feelings, at the same time wondering why I wasn't offended by her summary of my character. Perhaps simply because she seemed so inoffensive herself.

"That's all right, my dear," Mrs. Barlow said kindly. "Most people don't. They confuse it with palmistry. But of course reading palms doesn't tell you nearly so much about someone as you can learn from studying their face. Back in Bakersfield—that's where we live—people come to me instead of a psychiatrist. My rates are so much more reasonable, you see. And if they bring a photograph with them, I can tell them about anyone else they like. Boyfriends and girlfriends, for instance. Mind you, it has to be a good likeness. Why, I've saved any number of people from making a bad mistake. You're too polite to look skeptical, my dear, but I'm sure you must be wondering, and I don't blame you. If only there were more people here. . . . But then there was someone a moment ago. Now where did he go?" She looked around, then exclaimed, "There he is. Now let me show you what I mean. . . ."

She bustled over to the man in the panama hat, who was now standing with his back to us, looking at the view. When Mrs. Barlow came up behind him and spoke, he whipped around, clearly surprised. Whatever it was she said to him caused him to shake his head curtly and at once hurry away toward the exit. I had a momentary sense of déjà vu, the feeling that something about the scene was disconcertingly familiar. But what?

Mrs. Barlow came slowly back to us. "Did you ever? I only asked him if he would mind taking off those sunglasses of his to help me with a little experiment. You'd think I'd asked him to undress. I should have been more tactful about it, I suppose. Well, he couldn't have been Italian, at any rate. We've found they're usually so friendly, at least they were up north. We've just come down from Rome, and the people there were lovely. They're the best talkers, aren't they, Martin?''

"It's true." He smiled at me. "Emmeline finally met her match." But it was said with affection.

"Where are you from, my dear?" Mrs. Barlow asked me. When I told her that I was living in Germany, she said, "So you're here on holiday? But surely not alone?" I replied that I was traveling with my brother. "I'm relieved for your sake. We've heard such stories, haven't we, Martin? Why, we hardly dared come up here from the ship by ourselves except that we wanted to see this wonderful town. And we have the nicest driver. He's waiting for us outside. We're on a cruise, you see. People at home told us we were crazy to come after all that's happened, but we figured we might not get another chance. And it does seem a lot quieter now, doesn't it?" She paused for breath. "Well, I suppose you're like us, then, aren't you? Taking a risk, I mean. Except that you're younger, of course. But I do hope you'll be careful when you're not with your brother. A girl alone has to be on her guard." Although there was no one nearby, she lowered her voice. "That man just now, the one who was so rude? Why, when we came in he was just standing there staring at you. You couldn't see it, of course, but I think if we hadn't arrived you might have been bothered by him."

Her husband said dryly, "How you knew he was staring at Miss Jordan is beyond me, Emmeline. The man had sunglasses on."

"Physiognomy, dear. The whole face, not just the eyes. Sometimes a glimpse is enough, you know. His chin, for instance. With a chin like that, he's probably aggressive. Besides," she went on, "a woman knows these things. Anyway, you look after yourself." She patted my arm. "And now we'd better get back to the ship or they'll leave without us."

After I had said good-bye to the Barlows, promising to look them up if I ever found myself in Bakersfield, I watched the sun sink down into the Mediterranean. Its watermelon glow spread across the sky, painting Trapani a pale luminous pink. Far out on the horizon a ship shone like a star in a sea that was all soft blue mist. Idly, I wondered what Emmeline Barlow would have made of Hugo's face.

While I speculated, a cold wind sprang up. It swirled the mist up from the sea to envelop the lower flanks of the mountain. The mist rolled upward, scaling the mountain with ease, snuffing out the first city lights that had blinked on with the twilight in the plain below; gradually Trapani vanished from sight. It was eerie to stand in the clear blue of the evening sky and see night advance like a tide at my feet, but wonderful, too, and I found myself lingering while the others in the courtyard took themselves off for their dinners. In a few moments, I was alone. I turned away from the edge and wandered back to Venus' Well.

Perhaps it was the silence, combined with the first traces of mist wisping up over the parapet, which suddenly gave me that missing sense of what the shrine must have been like in its golden age. A place of mystery, numinous, holy. The mist that crept over the grass changed the mounds of rock and earth into moving forms. In the twilight, the pale shades of priestesses and pilgrims took shape and gathered at Aphrodite's altar, sailors praying for an omen to guide them safely home, farmers for good harvests, barren women for children, while the goddess hidden in her sanctuary chose to hear or ignore according to her will, or the size or beauty of the suppliant's offering. Had Daedalus' gift of the golden honeycomb saved him from Minos, an offering so pleasing to the goddess with its reminder of her beekeeper lover that she allowed the murder of the Cretan king?

I stared at the dimple in the ground. On an impulse I took Clio's jar of honey from my shoulder bag, and as I poured the traditional libation into the well I muttered the sailor's prayer, a safe journey and a safe return. For an instant afterward I almost expected some sort of sign. But the only sound was the sighing of the cypresses as the rising wind stirred their branches. Feeling foolish, I wrapped the sticky bottle in a tissue, put it back in my purse, and turned to go, grateful that no one had witnessed the proceedings.

But I was wrong. There was someone standing on the stone stairs that led into the courtyard. A dim figure rising like a ghost from the mist.

After the first chill touch of fear had faded, I recognized the man in the panama hat, ghostly in his white suit. He seemed to float toward me as the mist swirled around his feet, and I thought of Mrs. Barlow's warning. Before I could react, however, he suddenly turned and vanished. Almost at once the custodian appeared in his place, calling politely to me that the castle grounds were closing now.

When I emerged from the gardens, the mist had already closed in on the lower level of the town, blotting it from view. I had my guidebook with its map of Erice, but the map would be virtually useless in the fog. I turned to ask the gatekeeper for directions back to the hotel, but the gate was shut now and he was nowhere in sight. Well, I told myself, there was only one way to go and that was downhill; if I kept to the left I would find the city wall and I had only to follow that to the Porta Trapani. From there it would be easy enough to find the way back to the hotel.

I set off with the uneasy sensation of descending into a well. The only light remaining to the day was above and behind me, fading fast, and the cold and damp thickened with every downward step. Worse, the wind was rising. It whipped my hair into my eyes and tried to tear the sweater off my back. Half blinded, shivering, I stopped to button up the sweater, and pulled my shoulder bag across my chest as a kind of windbreak, before I struggled on.

After five minutes of battling the wind and fog, I was chilled and confused. By now I should have reached the wide street that ran beside the town ramparts. Instead, I could see the dark stone of house walls rising up on either side and the dim outline of balconies jutting out above me. A faint yellowish light glowed palely from shuttered windows, barely penetrating the mist, which had clotted here, stirred and swirled by the wind whistling in the narrow street. A stronger light shone out above the arch of a closed courtyard door and I went over to it, standing in the semi-shelter of the doorway while I looked at the map and tried to puzzle out where I was. I decided that where the street forked I must have turned by mistake onto a little street that ran parallel to the one I was looking for. In the mist, I had gone straight on instead of bearing to the left.

It was then, as I paused to get my bearings, that I heard footsteps softly padding on the cobblestones.

If not for the fog and the unnatural quiet of the town, I wouldn't have thought twice about it. After all, it was still quite early, only shortly after eight, and this was a street where, for all their cloistered lives, people went about their daily business. Still, perhaps because my senses were tuned by the fog to a sharper pitch or because I had never really ceased to think about the possibility that Jay and I might be followed, I listened now to those steps in the fog with a nervous interest. They paused, but I did not hear the reassuring sound of a door opening or a voice calling out to say they were home. The fog seemed dense with silence.

But the longer I stood in the cranny of the rock, the more the cold and damp penetrated my clothes and the more tired I grew.

Forcing myself out of my shelter, I started down the street again, keeping one hand on the cold stone of the walls beside me. Once or twice I paused to listen for following footsteps, and caught what might have been only an echo of my own. When I looked behind, I saw nothing more than mist and streetlight. Gradually, I relaxed. Too much adventure, I thought, and I don't have Jay's taste for it. I wanted a hot dinner and the dubious comforts of the Hotel Ginestra.

Then I heard the footsteps again. At the same instant I passed by an alleyway, hardly more than a crack in the wall. Without pausing to think, I squeezed into it and waited. In a moment the shape of a man went past, walking quickly, but softly on his feet, like someone who would prefer not to be heard. It was the man in the panama hat.

I gave him twenty seconds or so, then slipped out of the alleyway after him, curious to know if he was merely a tourist, or someone more dangerous.

He did not go far. After a few hundred yards he paused in the light from an open doorway. It must have been a bar, for I heard men's voices and dimly made out a neon sign. The man took something from his jacket pocket and then bent his head, hunching his shoulders slightly. I guessed that he had stopped to light a cigarette, and in a moment the wind carried the smoke to me. It had a pungent, familiar smell, the smell of a Gauloise.

CHAPTER 11

I meant to take him by surprise, a small revenge for my own fright, but he was already turning around, a wry smile on his face. He dropped the cigarette to the ground and crushed it out underfoot. The white suit shone in the light from the streetlamp.

"Hello, Alison." His voice was deadpan, unruffled.

I mimicked his tone. "Hello, Luke." For some reason not quite clear to me, I felt I had to meet Luke's unflappable calm with a sangfroid of my own; it would be a loss of face to let him see that he had frightened me.

We were as cool as a pair of former lovers who had just bumped into each other at some tedious embassy party, relieved to see each other, but wary. "I didn't recognize you in the castle gardens. Amazing what a transformation a new suit can make. These must be your Paris clothes." I touched the lapel of his jacket, then let my hand drop. "But haven't you taken a wrong turn somewhere?"

"We both seem to have changed direction at the last minute," he observed mildly.

"Such a coincidence."

He ignored the sarcasm, taking my arm and linking it through his. "You're shivering. Come on, I'll walk you back to your hotel. We can talk about wrong turns and coincidences as we go."

"And skulking. I have quite a lot to say on the subject of skulking, not to mention minding your own business."

Before I could expand on this, however, I heard what I thought was singing. The sound seemed to pour toward us in a thin bubbling stream through the mist, growing stronger, until suddenly a throng of children appeared at the far end of the narrow, sloping street. There must have been twenty or thirty of them, all of an age, perhaps eight or nine years old, and they were accompanied by a small group of adults who were holding lanterns to light their way. The children were singing in rounds as they trooped up the street, one group singing a line, another responding, their clear voices fizzing in the night air.

Halfway down the street, a bright yellow light flowed out from the open gate of a tiny medieval palazzo. The wind teased the edges of the mist where it glistened in the light, whisking it out like spun sugar over the heads of the children, who turned and marched inside the gate, still singing. Curious, Luke and I paused to look in as we passed by.

The small square courtyard was brightly lit, but much of the light was focused on a makeshift stage set up opposite the gate; everything else was shadowy and indistinct. Behind the stage, stone stairs led up to a gallery running along three sides of the courtyard on the second story, where a dozen or so people stood looking down on the scene below. Everything seemed on a child's scale, the stage, the small trees that grew like a tiny grove in one corner of the courtyard, the ancient building itself, and the combined effect of scale and shadowy light was somehow wonderful and mysterious, as though the little palace was the setting for a fairy tale. Outside the gate were the dark, misty streets; inside was enchantment.

The children must have felt the spell, for they were almost unnaturally well behaved, speaking to one another in whispers or laughing softly as they filed into rows of wooden benches set up in front of the stage. A young woman who was shepherding the last of the children to their seats noticed the strangers standing by the gate. Unerringly, she marked us down as tourists, and in heavily accented English said with a smile, "Come in, come in. Don't be afraid. You are welcome." She explained that a puppet show would be performed; it would tell the story of Orlando Furioso, Charlemagne's heroic paladin Roland, and his last battle against the Saracens. "Once such puppet shows were everywhere. Now they have almost disappeared. Tonight is something special."

The invitation was somehow irresistible. "Shall we stay and watch the beginning at least?" Luke asked.

I nodded. "For a few minutes anyway." Jay would begin to worry if I stayed away too long.

We thanked the young woman and said we would stand at the back, near the gate. While we waited for the performance to start, I said in a low voice to Luke, "So what were you doing just now, lurking in the fog like Jack the Ripper?"

"Lurking and skulking both—and not very good at either, it seems," Luke said as he leaned against the smooth stone of the courtyard wall. "Here I thought I was being so discreet. What gave me away?"

"One of your bad habits. You should switch to a more anonymous brand of cigarette."

Luke, who had been about to light another, put the packet back in his jacket pocket. "I thought you must have guessed who I was in the castle grounds. When that woman asked me to take off my sunglasses. Why on earth did she do that?"

I was amused by the look on his face as I explained Emmeline Barlow's profession. Perhaps it was the effect of the surroundings, perhaps it was feeling safe again, but suddenly I wasn't angry with him anymore, I was simply glad to see him. It was impossible to stay mad at Luke for long, anyway. "She warned me about you, you know. She said a chin like yours was a sign of aggression. She thought you were going to pester me."

He fingered the offending chin thoughtfully. "Aggressive? Me?" His smile faded. "Well, maybe she was right. Because I am going to pester you, Alison, until you give me some answers. You can begin by telling me why you're in Sicily."

"Is that a rhetorical question?"

"You promised no family reunions."

"Promised? That's taking quite a lot for granted." I gave him a long look, but he only shrugged. "As for why *you're* in Sicily—at the risk of sounding immodest, I assume it's because of me."

"Partly."

While I digested this, I stared at the lopsided curtain hung on a rope across the stage, which was painted with a florid scene of battling knights. From time to time, this curtain bulged with a life of its own. Delighted by the phenomenon, the children giggled, and a little boy on the front bench ran up and wriggled up onto the stage, to lift the bottom of the curtain and peek under it. One of the grownups grabbed his legs, planted him firmly on his feet again, and led him back to his seat.

After a moment I said, "What other reason is there?" I knew, however, there could only be one other reason: to find Hugo.

But Luke's answer took me by surprise. "Well, for a start, your brother is missing. You wouldn't happen to have any idea where he is, would you?" Something in his manner made it plain that Luke had a very good idea where Jay was.

I was careful to meet his eyes. "And if I did?"

"Then perhaps you'll let him know his mother is worried about him. To put it mildly."

I ought to have made Jay call Charlotte before we left, I told myself with a pang of guilt; she might not be a perfect mother but I had no right to assume she wouldn't worry about him. I was twenty-six after all, not fifteen, and should have known better. "I'll get him to call her tonight," I said.

"Fine. And I'll put him on a plane from Palermo tomorrow."

"I wish you luck. This expedition was his idea, not mine, and he's pretty set on seeing it through." I reflected that Luke would have his work cut out for him if he thought he could persuade Jay to go back to England. Some people might mistake Jay's determination for adolescent willfulness, but it wasn't that at all—it was simply that he was Hugo's true child. Once he knew what he wanted he could not be deflected from its pursuit. "How do you know about Jay, anyway? And how did you know where to find us?"

"I asked questions." He was holding his hat in his hands, fingering the crease that ran along the crown. "I got your message but I wanted to talk to you anyway, so I went over to your place. The superintendent said you'd taken your car and gone off with a relative, a teenaged boy who'd arrived that day to see you. Because you had your suitcase with you, she figured at first that you'd gone to Spain early. But when she checked your apartment she found you'd left your plane ticket and all your Spanish guidebooks behind on the coffee table, so unless you'd forgotten them you must have decided to go somewhere else. The FBI could use talent like Frau Gottschalk's." He grinned, but I didn't smile back. "Next I called Lufthansa. They said you'd canceled your flight and hadn't rebooked, so I checked travel agents in your neighborhood and near the embassy. I got lucky with the tenth or so that I tried. She told me about the ferry to Sicily and your hotel reservations in Erice."

I raised an eyebrow. "So many helpful ladies eager to tell you what you want to know."

"Don't hold it against them. I showed them my ID and said that relatives in the States were trying to track you down because there'd been a death in the family."

"And how did you figure out who Jay was?"

"When he disappeared, the school naturally notified his mother. She got on to our people in London and made a fuss—it seems she knows the ambassador or someone fairly influential there. The description Frau Gottschalk gave me of your teen-aged companion fitted with the one we got of Raphael's son.''

The grownups were shushing the children now; the performance was about to begin. The curtain rose slowly until it was halfway up, revealing a backdrop crudely painted with a forest scene. Suddenly, an overamplified voice boomed out into the courtyard. Like the bellowing of an angry bull penned in a stall, it bounced off the four walls, echoing in the night. I jumped, and several children cried out with fear. Then the voice softened, and began to recite what must have been the prologue to the tale; it was in Sicilian, and incomprehensible. After a minute or two, the voice paused. With a loud clashing and thumping, a huge wooden puppet gave a mighty leap from the wings onto the stage.

The puppet was at least three feet tall, dressed in royal-blue satin covered by shining gold armor, with a tall red plume waving from the top of his visored helmet. His dark eyes were large and expressive, his cheeks were rosy, and he had a luxuriant black mustache. Altogether he was a magnificent sight, and the children cheered their approval. "Orlando! Orlando!" they called out, delighted. The puppet gave an elaborate bow.

After that it was nonstop action for at least fifteen minutes. Orlando was joined by other knights, all lovingly painted and gaudily armored; together they fought giants, a moth-eaten green dragon, and their enemies, the Saracens. The puppets took great leaping strides across the stage, banging their shields and swords, crashing their armor, landing with great thumps of their wooden legs, and groaning loudly as they died. It was deafeningly noisy and outrageously, enthusiastically violent. As lopped-off heads fell onto the stage, great gouts of red blood spurted out from the severed necks, and the children roared with joy.

The little puppet show had all the violence of a Grimm fairy tale, the potent stuff of children's nightmares, translated for a southern sensibility. Intense, extravagant, it conjured up passions as pure and powerful as the blazing colors worn by the knights: loyalty, love, hatred, grief. As the puppets played out their drama of friendship, betrayal, and revenge, there were no shades of gray, no ambiguities to confuse. And for all its hyperbolic unreality, for all its absurdity, some essence of the story fell like a tiny drop of distilled terror, pure and cold, onto the surface of my mind. This is Sicily, it seemed to tell me; bloody deeds happened here once upon a time. Still happened now.

Eventually, the knights were betrayed. Orlando found his

friend Oliver dead on a heap of bodies and went mad, furiously fighting the Saracens alone. Dismembered arms and legs went flying across the stage in the final battle, until Orlando collapsed, mortally wounded. A collective hush settled on the audience.

Orlando had breath enough for a last soliloquy, but as his dying words seemed to be turning into long paragraphs, nothing of which Luke and I could understand, I made a sign to him that it was time to leave. Quietly, we turned and went out of the gate.

"Well, that should guarantee some poor parents a few sleepless nights," Luke said as we walked along the street. "I'm glad I'm not on the cleanup committee. All that blood on the stage, and I think some kid was being sick in the back row." His voice was amused, reducing the little spectacle to its proper proportions. We passed a restaurant, and the smell of frying meat, together with the clatter of dishes and the sound of voices raised in passionate conversation, transformed the silent, stony street. A man walking his dog nodded good evening to us, an uncurtained window revealed a woman feeding a baby. Erice became any town at suppertime, and the world of puppets and goddesses retreated back into legend.

Luke seemed to know the way back to the Hotel Ginestra, and as I let him plot our course I thought about all he had told me. Someone, probably the London embassy, had passed on to Bonn the fact that Jay had gone missing, which reminded me that Luke had not answered my original question to him, back in his office in Bonn. "You never did explain why our embassy is so interested in Hugo's doings," I said now. "I could understand London's or Rome's involvement, but why Bonn?"

"Because a few days ago the Germans dug out a Libyan terrorist cell in a West Berlin apartment. Literally. What there was left of it, anyway. Someone was making a bomb and blew himself up. A successful terrorist really should start with those small motor skills." He gave a grim smile. "When the police sifted through the debris, one of the things they found was a scrap of paper with the information that your father had escaped from Libya and was now a 'people's enemy.' Probably nothing more than a standard circular that goes out when Qaddafi is pissed off with someone. But there's always the possibility that it was a directive to an assassination squad based in Berlin. Have you ever heard of al-Burkan?"

I shook my head. "Is it a man or a thing?"

"A group. The name means 'the volcano' in Arabic. It's an

underground faction of the Libyan People's Committees. Its mission is the elimination of Qaddafi's opponents living abroad.''

But I wasn't listening to Luke's answer. I was thinking of Bernd. Of his sympathies, his "colleagues." Could they include terrorists?

They could, and I knew it. But for all his inflammatory eloquence, Bernd was no murderer himself. I was equally certain of that.

Luke ran the fingers of one hand through his hair, pushing it off his forehead. With an edge to his voice, he added, "There wasn't much point in alarming you before, but since you seem determined to get yourself and your brother into trouble, you might as well know the risk you're both running."

If he meant to frighten me, the slightly bullying manner with which he said this undermined the message. I bristled. "So Bonn sent you here to track us down."

"Nope. I'm on holiday." He held up the camera that was hanging from his shoulder. "This trip is strictly unofficial. For now, anyway. I decided that since you wouldn't come to Paris with me . . . You know, if it's excitement you're after, you really should have tried that club in Paris I told you about. It's a safer way to get rid of Elinor."

"What are you talking about?" Then I remembered our last conversation together. "Do you think that's the reason I'm here, just because I got tired of being sensible? Don't you think there might be more to it than that?"

"Such as?"

"Concern for my family, for a start."

He smiled pleasantly. "I had the distinct impression your only concern for your family was to stay as far away from them as possible."

"Wouldn't a stroll along the Seine with your acrobatic friend and her monkeys be a better way to spend your vacation?"

Luke took my hand. "Alison," he said in a deliberately patient voice, "doesn't the fact that I'm here tell you something?"

"Sure. It tells me that you're probably CIA and that I should have kept my mouth shut." But I left my hand where it was; it felt comfortable in his, and was certainly warmer there. The wind had dropped and the worst of the mist was gone now, but the night air was chilly.

"It should tell you that if I've given up Paris, it has to be for a damn good reason." His hand tightened slightly on mine, whether from passion or exasperation it was impossible to say. "Besides, if I were CIA you and your brother would still be in Bonn."

Cynically, I wondered if he would find me half as appealing if I were safely in Bonn. An unpleasant speculation was taking shape in my mind: Hugo would more than likely know a lot about certain secret Libyan affairs, and a junior diplomat who produced Hugo and managed to persuade him to spill the beans would score a minor coup. How ambitious was Luke?

Tentatively, I raised the issue, following up his last remark. "Unless you needed to find out where Hugo is," I said. "Which you could only do by following us." Immediately, I was half ashamed of myself for my suspicions.

"As it happens, I have a fairly good idea where Raphael is, or at least where you think he is. A message came for you from the Italian embassy. I saw it on your message pad at your desk when I went to look for you after I got your note. It said they'd found Castell'alto. I called them and they were very helpful. I thanked them on your behalf."

I stopped walking and turned to face him. We were passing under the Porta Trapani; the wide square beyond was almost empty now of cars, and I was more than ever thankful mine was parked behind the hotel. "If you aren't CIA, you ought to be. So tell me, what comes next?"

He seemed relieved. "I'd like to talk to your brother. And if I can't persuade the pair of you to go home, then I'll stay with you from now on."

"Do we have a choice?"

"Sure you have a choice. You can go back to Bonn or I can turn this whole thing over to our consulate at Palermo. Which I'm tempted to do anyway."

I wasn't going to make it easy for Luke—he deserved some punishment for frightening me—but now that I'd had time to get used to the idea, I acknowledged to myself that I would be glad to have Luke along on our expedition. He could deal with men like Mustache.

"All right," I said at last, gazing pointedly at Luke's suit, "I'll admit that my very own white knight might not be such a bad thing. There may be a dragon or two to slay. . . ." I told him about the van driver's behavior at the Palermo docks, and the subsequent chase on the highway.

But to my surprise he only looked chagrined. "I had the feel ing Nardo was too enthusiastic to do a good job. He kept telling

me he was the best ghost in Sicily. I think he meant shadow—
the word's the same in Italian. He reads thrillers to improve his
English.''

I wasn't amused. "Do you mean to say that you had him
follow us?''

"Keep an eye on you at any rate.''

"I don't see the difference.''

"Only of motive. To make sure you were safe. And to make
sure you came straight here, which it seems you didn't. What's
in a place called San Teodoro?''

But I ignored his question. Now that the threat from Mustache
had vanished, I could afford to indulge a certain retrospective
bitterness. "Your Nardo was so busy seeing we were safe that
he almost caused a wreck. Next time please find someone who's
less conscientious about his work.'' Despite my tone, I was so
relieved to find out Mustache was innocent after all that I silently
forgave Luke the deception. "Where did you get him, anyway?''

"He does odd jobs for the Palermo consulate. I checked in
there when I arrived yesterday.''

"Oh yes? And told them you were just here on holiday but
that someone like Nardo might be useful? They didn't ask any
questions, of course.''

"There are ways to get things done without making people
curious.''

"Is that the professional speaking, or just the enthusiastic
amateur?''

But Luke simply smiled. "Your imagination's running away
with you again.''

"My imagination isn't the one hiring ghosts.'' Just the one
turning them into car thieves or killers. Luke was right; my
otherwise unexceptionable imagination seemed to have grown
as rampant and convoluted as any of the vines that writhed across
the stone wall beside us. The effect of the Sicilian sun, perhaps,
a head unused to heights, or too many stories with too many
questions and not enough answers—or the wrong answers.

"What's in San Teodoro, Alison?'' Luke repeated.

If he was going to be traveling with us, Luke would have to
know about Clio Hunt; but I planned to tell him once we were
on our way to Castell'alto, when it would be too late for him to
tell anyone else. I believed Luke when he said he wanted to
make sure Jay and I came to no harm, but I didn't trust him not
to pass on information about Hugo to the Palermo consulate. At

least not yet. So I said only, "Nothing really. We played Good Samaritan, and picked up an old lady we'd met on the ferry whose car had broken down. She lives in San Teodoro." The hotel lights shone out now across the dark piazza, warm and welcoming. I quickened my steps.

"You spent over an hour there, according to Nardo."

"Sicilian hospitality," I said shortly. "It wasn't easy to get away."

Whether or not he believed me, Luke let it drop. As we went into the hotel, I told him that since he had elected himself our traveling companion, he might as well have dinner with us. "While you find us a table in the dining room, I'll go and get Jay."

I started to turn away, but he touched my arm. "I'm curious about one thing, Alison. . . ."

"Surely you mean one more thing."

"One more thing, then," he said equably. "What were you doing back there in the castle grounds, when you were kneeling down?"

"Oh, that." I could feel myself flushing as I explained. "Call it an atavistic impulse," I finished lamely.

He lifted one eyebrow. "But look at the results."

"What do you mean?"

"Well, here I am, aren't I? Heaven-sent, and by the Goddess of Love no less." The hazel eyes were amused as he considered me. "What more do you want?"

CHAPTER 12

Upstairs, I knocked on the door of Jay's room. After a moment, I heard footsteps cross the room and then Jay opened the door, looking groggy. One cheek was pink and creased from the pillow, and he checked a yawn. "Alison, hi. Come on in. Is it dinnertime?" He looked at his wristwatch. "Man, I didn't realize it was so late. You should have woken me up."

"I went for a walk—I left you a note." It was still lying on the rug near the door and I went over to retrieve it. As Jay struggled into a sweater, I added, "I met someone, a friend from the embassy. A man named Luke Kenniston." His face was startled when it emerged from the neck of the pullover. "He knows everything, why we're here, who you are, about Castell'alto. He's downstairs now, waiting for us. He wants us to go back to Bonn because he thinks it's too dangerous for us here."

I had decided that the time for shielding Jay from things that might frighten him was over; I told him about the Libyan terrorists in Berlin.

"Those two men, the ones in the car outside Foxburghe, do you think . . . ?" he asked, when I finished.

I nodded. "I want you to tell Luke about them. Do you remember them well enough to give him a description?"

"Sure, no problem."

"Good. One other thing . . . Your mother's very upset about your disappearance. She's contacted the American embassy in London about you."

For a moment Jay looked stricken, and as guilty as I had felt. He bent to pick up a pillow that had fallen beside the bed. "I guess I'd better call her. But"—and his voice was defiant as he threw the pillow onto the bed—"I'm not telling her where I am. And I'm not going back until I've seen Hugo."

118

"Talk to Luke first, okay? Before you decide."

"Okay," he said grudgingly. "But I won't change my mind." He took a comb out of his backpack, watching me in the oval mirror above the bureau as he made a halfhearted effort to tidy his hair. "Who is this Luke, anyway? I mean why would he come here after us?" Suddenly his eyes widened and he turned around to face me. "Is he from the CIA?"

I had to laugh. "You ask him that. Maybe you'll have better luck than I did in getting a straight answer. As far as I know he's simply a political officer at the embassy, but that's a fairly vague title. Come on, let's go downstairs." We were through the door before I thought of Clio Hunt. I put my hand on Jay's arm. "Maybe we should stay off the topic of Clio Hunt. It's not that I don't trust Luke, but it might be better not to give everything away."

"Okay. What about Don Calogero? Should we keep quiet about him, too?"

"I don't know. . . . Yes, maybe so. He might not be quite so helpful with Luke along, too. Let me think about it for a while."

As we went down the hallway to the stairs, I added that Mustache was harmless, after all, and explained why. Before we joined Luke, we stopped by the front desk and I mentioned that I was expecting a telephone call, and that we would be in the dining room.

Luke was waiting for us at a table near tall French windows. He got to his feet as we approached. Jay was polite when I introduced him, carefully meeting Luke's eyes as they shook hands, but he held himself stiffly and his own eyes were wary. And for once Luke's easy manner seemed to have deserted him; he looked uncomfortable. The awkward moment of their meeting was bridged by the young waiter who came over to hand us menus and describe the antipasti.

"Caponata should be good," I told Jay. "It's a Sicilian specialty, a kind of casserole of eggplant, tomatoes, and olives. I'm going to have it." The waiter agreed that it was very good.

"Okay," said Jay, "I'll try it, too."

"Make that three," Luke added.

After the waiter left, there was a silence. I glanced out the window beside me, but saw only my own reflection and the light from the elaborate chandelier of colored glass that hung in the center of the room, pink and blue flowers glowing dustily among pale green leaves. "There must be a wonderful view when the mist goes," I said, for lack of anything better.

Ignoring this, Jay and Luke began to speak at the same time. "Go ahead," Luke told him. When Jay shook his head, Luke said, "All right, then. Alison told you why I'm here?"

"Yes, sir."

"Then you know that I think you both ought to leave Sicily, for safety's sake?"

"Yes, sir." Jay was suddenly the very model of the polite English public-school boy. "But if you'll excuse me, I don't see that it's anyone's business but ours."

"When you're eighteen, you can tell me to go to hell a dozen different ways," Luke replied, unruffled. "Until then, I'm afraid that it is my business. Unless, of course, your mother decides otherwise. If you'd like, we could call and ask her?" He unfolded his napkin and spread it across his lap as the waiter set a plate of caponata down in front of each of us and wished us *"Buon appetito."*

"Let's eat dinner first," I said, picking up my fork, "before we all lose our appetites. Jay, why don't you tell Luke about what happened to you in England? Tell him why you think it's important to see Hugo."

Around mouthfuls of eggplant, Jay described his encounter with the two men outside the school. Luke listened, interrupting only to ask Jay to repeat his description of the men. "Do you know who they are?" Jay asked him. "I mean, other than being Libyans."

"I can make an educated guess," Luke replied, "but I don't know for sure. Go on, please." When Jay finished, Luke said, "I take it you've come to warn your father about these men. Am I right?"

"It's one of the reasons I'm here," Jay replied quietly.

As he removed our plates, the waiter told us that the grilled swordfish was superb, worth the king's ransom penciled in beside it on the menu. Too expensive, Jay and I agreed with regret, but Luke said to go ahead and have it; dinner was his treat. I looked at Jay, and could see quite plainly in his eyes that swordfish was not going to compensate him for having to put up with Luke's company. We ordered it anyway.

"And I'll have the grilled tuna," Luke added, oblivious. Or maybe not.

"Do you two work together?" Jay asked when the waiter had gone.

"Well, we're both at the embassy," I said. "But Luke's a

career foreign service officer. I'm fairly low on the embassy totem pole."

"What kind of work do you do?" he asked Luke.

"Political stuff. Mostly smoothing the way when our diplomats get together with their diplomats. Making sure ours are properly briefed. Handling information."

"And disinformation?"

Luke looked startled. "Sometimes. If it's necessary."

"So why should we trust you?" Jay sounded genuinely troubled, rather than rude. "I mean, Alison says you're here to protect us, but it sounds to me more like you're here to find out where Hugo is."

"Would that be so terrible? Haven't you gathered from all I've told you that he may need protection, too?" When Jay didn't answer, Luke turned to me, and for the first time his carefully judicious tone changed, became intense. "Damn it, I'm trying to make you understand the risk you're running."

Jay glanced sharply at him, then at me. He must suddenly have intuited that there was something more than simply our work between Luke and me, amorphous as that something was, for he flushed and dropped his eyes to his plate. "This trip isn't Alison's fault," he said. "She didn't want to come at first, but I persuaded her. I'm to blame." Then, naively, "Couldn't you just give us a phone number where we can reach you? If we need you . . ."

He must have realized as he said it how foolish it sounded, for his voice trailed off and he bit his lip. For a moment he looked so very young and beleaguered that I touched his hand under the table for reassurance. But he refused to meet my eyes, as though I were somehow responsible for Luke's being here. As I suppose I was.

"You know," Luke said to Jay, "there isn't a whole lot that even the American government could do to help you if you get into trouble in a place like Castell'alto. There probably wouldn't be much the police here could do either, for that matter. If you do get mixed up in something you're not able to handle, I'd like to be around. The people who are after your father aren't particular about innocent victims who get in their way. The same day your father turns up in Tunis, those two go after you. Someone fairly important must have contacted Libyan agents in London as soon as Hugo's defection was discovered. That suggests a certain eagerness to persuade your father to return, wouldn't you say?"

"The Libyans have no idea where we are now," I replied defensively.

"Oh yes? You don't think that if I found you so easily someone else couldn't, too? The Libyans have a small network in Sicily. They're undoubtedly involved in drug smuggling here."

"But no one else knows about Castell'alto," I said, and then thought of Clio Hunt. "For that matter, does anyone here even know that Hugo's supposed to be in Sicily?"

"Well, no," Luke replied slowly. "It hasn't been reported by the Italian press, but—"

I said, "Jay and I just feel that as we've come this far, we want to go on."

"Then you'll have company," he said firmly. I shrugged and said that was fine with me, but Jay was silent. He was fiddling with a piece of fish, pushing it around his plate with his fork. Abruptly, he shoved his plate away and stood up. "Excuse me." Before I could stop him, he had left the room.

I turned back to Luke. "Weren't you rather hard on him? He's only fifteen, after all. Not really in your league."

"He's old enough to have learned the facts of life some time ago. It's time he learned the facts of death, too. But you're right, he's still a kid. It's understandable that he feels invulnerable, all teenagers do. You're the one who's grown up and should know better."

I had to acknowledge the justice of this; I might resent Luke's manner, but that didn't alter the truth of what he said. I got up. "Let me go talk to him. Maybe I'll have better luck persuading him."

As I came into the hallway, Signor Indelicato called to me. "Signora, your telephone call. Shall I put it through to your room?"

"Yes, thanks. I'll go straight up."

Jay was coming down the stairs, his knapsack over his shoulder. When he saw me, his face grew defiant, and he started to speak. "Alison, I just can't—"

But I interrupted whatever he was about to say, grabbing his arm and turning him around. "Come on back upstairs. Clio Hunt's on the phone."

At my hello, Clio said she had good news, of a sort. "Don Calogero has invited you to lunch with him tomorrow. I spoke with him myself this time, but he wasn't giving much away. He expressed interest in meeting Hugo's children, but was fairly cagey about Hugo himself. I had the impression he won't commit himself to anything until he's met you. Now look, why don't you come here tomorrow morning and I'll take you up there in my Land Rover. I'm going to visit those hives of mine anyway, and you might be glad of someone who knows the place.''

With mixed emotions, I accepted her offer. ''We'll arrive at your place soon after breakfast. Will that be all right?''

''Fine. See you then.''

Deliberately, I hadn't said anything to Clio about Luke. It was going to be difficult to explain his presence, and I needed time to think about how to do it.

''Don Calogero has asked us to lunch,'' I said to Jay. ''He wouldn't tell Clio whether Hugo was there or not. I guess we'll be checked out before he tells us what he knows. Now,'' I continued, pointing to the knapsack, ''what's all this about?''

Jay looked stubborn. ''Your friend Luke is right. I shouldn't drag you into something that's so dangerous. You didn't want to come anyway, and I made you. I'm glad you did because . . . well, you've been great about everything. But now, maybe it's better if I do this on my own.''

''How are you going to do it on your own, for heaven's sake?''

''I'll hitchhike to Castell'alto. I couldn't care less about this Don Calogero guy's permission, or meeting his approval. I'll find Hugo whether he likes it or not.''

Mildly, I said, ''I think it would be hard to find a ride at this time of night, Jay. And even if you did, the odds against your finding anyone going to Castell'alto would probably be astronomical.'' I did not want to seem scornful of Jay's plan, yet at the same time I wanted him to realize its impracticality.

Jay lowered his head, studying something on the carpet. When he spoke, his voice was mulish. ''I can hike it from the autostrada. I remember the road that Clio pointed out on the map. If I need to, I can sleep in a cave somewhere.''

''So you're just going to abandon me,'' I said lightly, ''without giving me any choice. I don't think that's very fair.''

''You have him,'' Jay replied, still not meeting my eyes. He shifted the backpack to the other shoulder. ''You don't need me.''

All at once I thought I understood. I touched Jay's arm. ''Look, we began this thing together and I think we ought to see it through together. Besides, you haven't dragged me here against my will. I want to find Hugo as much as you do. And I want to do it with you.'' As I said this, I realized how much I meant it.

Perhaps Jay did, too, for the set line of his jaw softened and he lifted his eyes to meet mine. "But can't you see, Alison, that if Luke really is here to track down Hugo, and we lead him to him, then Hugo will think we betrayed him? It's bad enough that we have to go with Clio, but at least he knows her."

He was right. Meeting Hugo again was going to be difficult enough as it was, without the added complication of Luke. Hugo would find it hard to forgive our exposing his refuge to a stranger whose motives for searching for him were so unclear. The argument that we had done it in his best interest wouldn't appease him, either. I thought I knew him well enough to feel certain of that.

Still, did it really matter if Hugo were angry with me, so long as Jay was safe? Luke had made the risk he thought we were running abundantly clear; what right did I have to ignore his warning from fear of some hypothetical reaction of Hugo's?

I tried again. "Hugo won't blame you, Jay. I'll tell him the truth, that I insisted on bringing Luke with us. Hugo and I— Well, anger isn't going to spoil our relationship." There was so little left, after all, to spoil. "And it does make sense, you know, to have Luke's help."

But Jay was stubborn. "We've done fine so far without it. Besides, you did say that Don Calogero might not be so helpful if Mr. Kenniston was there. I'd rather go back to England," he added, his face pinched and white, "than take him with us."

And that would be the end, I thought, of the fragile alliance that brother and sister had forged between them. Jay would never trust me again. It was too high a price to pay for the nebulous possibility that we might encounter Hugo's enemies, a possibility that seemed remote now that the threat from Mustache was gone. And I suspected that no matter what he agreed to, Jay would find a way to search for Hugo alone. I couldn't let that happen.

Reluctantly, against my better judgment, I told Jay that he would not have to return to England. "I have an idea. Do you remember the story of the three little pigs and the big bad wolf?"

Jay looked startled. "Sure, but why—"

"Remember where the clever little pig agrees to go with the wolf to the orchard, but sets off early, ahead of him?"

He understood. "Of course. Brilliant."

Not, I thought, if there were wolves in the orchard, too, waiting for us; but the transformation in Jay's face made me forge on, ignoring my own misgivings. "We'll agree to meet him at ten, here at the hotel, but you and I will be off at seven. Luke knows about Castell'alto. If he wants to, he can follow us. But we won't be responsible for bringing him there. At least, not directly. Now let's go down to Luke and say we've thought it over and agree to his proposition. Do you have an alarm clock?" He shook his head. "Then I'll knock on your door around seven. All right?"

"Great." His eyes were sparkling.

"You've got to do one thing," I told him.

"Sure. What is it?"

"Call your mother and tell her you're okay. I ought to have made you do it long before now."

"All right. I'll say I just needed time alone, that I'm fine and will call again in a couple of days."

"Whatever. So long as you reassure her. Why don't you do it now and then come down and have some dessert?"

But Jay's face shuttered again. "I will call, but I don't think I'll come down again. I've had enough to eat."

"You're sure? In that case, I'll see you at seven tomorrow. Sleep well."

Before I could move, Jay put his arms around me and gave me a hug. "I'm glad you're my sister." Then he turned and disappeared into his room. What chance did better judgment have against the sudden surge of gratitude and love that his words stirred up in me? For good or ill, I told myself, I had made the right choice.

When I returned to the dining room, Luke was drinking coffee. He stood up. "I let the waiter clear away. Did you want anything else?"

I shook my head. "Jay's tired. He's going to call his mother, then go to bed. I persuaded him to let you come along with us tomorrow—but he's not happy about it."

"I upset him."

"Yes, but he'll get over it. We agreed that we'd meet you here around ten. Does that suit you?"

"Fine." Luke motioned the waiter over and settled the bill. As we walked out of the dining room, he asked, "What do you intend to do then, go straight to Castell'alto?"

"Yes." I paused at the bottom of the stairs, not quite able to meet his eyes. The lies I was telling Luke had drained away some of the elation I had felt at Jay's declaration; suddenly, I

was very weary. "Good night, Luke," I said abruptly, and
started up the stairs.

"Alison."

His voice made me turn around.

"The main reason I'm here has nothing to do with Hugo
Raphael. That's the simple truth." He paused, then said quietly,
"I'll see you in the morning."

I watched him leave, tempted to call him back. Perhaps, if he
understood how important it was to us, I could convince him to
let Jay and me go on alone. But it was too late—he was already
out the door while I hesitated.

CHAPTER 13

The next morning, before I roused Jay, I sat down at the rickety desk to write a letter to Luke. In it, I tried to explain why Jay and I were going on without him. I struggled with excuses and justifications, but they looked false on the page. Finally, I simply put down the truth.

"Dear Luke," I wrote.

Jay is afraid that your being with us might jeopardize his chance of seeing Hugo, or might make Hugo angry with us. He refuses to agree to your coming to Castell'alto and threatens to go off on his own if I insist. So I've promised him that as we began this journey alone together, we'll go on alone.

Here I remembered Clio.

Well, not quite all the way alone. Someone who knew Hugo here in Sicily is taking us to meet a man who's a power in Castell'alto, and also a friend of Hugo's. His name is Don Calogero Coccalo. He has agreed to talk to us. So you see, we aren't just wandering off haphazardly into the wilderness. Maybe this will make you feel a little better about what we're doing.

Please give us at least today to try to find Hugo on our own. We'll come back to Erice for the night and tell you what happened. After that, if you still think you should be with us, I'll try to persuade Jay to see reason.

I'm sorry, Luke—it's a mean trick to play on you, but I hope you'll understand. I never really had a brother before.

The letter was clumsy, and I avoided responding to Luke's final words to me the night before. That would have to wait for

127

a time when I could think about their implications. At least, I told myself, I was honest with Luke about our plans.

Jay was ready to go, dressed in his jeans and T-shirt, when he opened his door. He gave a joking, exaggeratedly conspiratorial smile as he picked up his knapsack, and went down the corridor beside me whistling "We're off to see the wizard" under his breath. Some of the insouciance of the day before seemed to have come back to him, inspired perhaps by getting the better of Luke. I couldn't blame him for gloating a little; Luke had been surprisingly tactless with Jay, treating him like a child. It was no wonder if Jay's fragile manhood wanted to reassert itself.

Although I was lighter-hearted myself now that Mustache was no longer a threat, I still felt uneasy. I knew that, in some ways, I was responsible for Jay; if anything happened to him, I would be partly to blame.

Nonsense, the devil's advocate inside me replied. Jay is determined to find Hugo with or without you. Short of locking him up, you couldn't stop him and neither could Luke. He's less likely to get into trouble with you along, and if he does, you'll be there to help him. Anyway, why expect the worst? In a few hours, you'll be in Castell'alto, with a very good chance of finding Hugo. Once you've delivered Jay safely to him, your duty is done, and you can go home again. If Don Calogero Coccalo is half as formidable as he's made out to be, he's quite capable of protecting the pair of them from Libyan thugs.

So I told myself. But I was only too well aware of the argument's weaknesses.

As we passed by the front desk, I stopped to leave the letter for Luke with the young desk clerk on duty, asking him to give it to Signor Kenniston when he called for us at ten o'clock. For the benefit of anyone who might ask questions about us, I added casually that we were going to see the ruins at Selinunte. Selinunte was on the south coast, in the opposite direction from Castell'alto.

Outside, the mountain air had the thin, exhilarating quality of all high places, almost effervescent, with a cool, piney tang to it. Above a flat blue sea the sun was rising into a cloudless sky. It promised to be hot. "If you're hungry," I told Jay as we got into the car, "there are some apples left in the picnic bag on the back seat. When we get to San Teodoro we'll get something to eat. Clio won't expect to see us quite so early as this."

Glimpses of the plain and the sea swung by as the road looped downward through the silent pine forest. Huge yellow daisies trailed in thick swaths across sunlit clearings where magpies and robins sang and quarreled. Gradually, Erice disappeared above us, its walls and towers screened by the palisade of trees. Through bites of apple, Jay asked me if I thought Luke would follow us.

I replied that I didn't know Luke well enough to be sure. "But in the letter I left for him, I asked him to give us a day on our own. I half promised him we'd include him after this. You know, I think he means it when he says he really isn't here to spy on Hugo." I glanced sideways at Jay; in profile, with the thrust of the stubborn chin emphasized as he chewed on the apple, he looked more than ever like Hugo.

Jay grunted noncommittally and crunched up his apple core. "Are you going to tell Clio about him? I mean, what if he turns up in Castell'alto after all?"

"We can't control everything, Jay. We'll just have to deal with things as they happen. Luke is free to do as he likes, and he can do his own explaining." To change the subject, I asked him if he had managed to reach his mother the night before.

"Yes. She wasn't too happy with me, but she was glad I called. So was I. But she read the riot act. You know how mothers are. . . ." He glanced at me, his face apologetic. "I'm sorry."

"You don't need to be," I said matter-of-factly. "Aunt Constance was a good mother to me in a lot of ways. We never argued, and when my friends told me about the fights they had with their mothers, I realized I was pretty well off."

A little shyly, he asked, "Would you like to meet her someday? Your real mother, I mean."

It was a question I had asked myself. "Once I would have said no, not at all. But I think . . . Well, I suppose now I don't know what I think. So much would depend on the kind of person she is."

"You have some of her genes, so I know she's got to be at least partly okay." Jay blushed.

I smiled at him. "I feel the same way about Charlotte, now that I know you."

I began to tell Jay about the puppet show Luke and I had seen, and soon afterward we drove into San Teodoro's main square. We had coffee and rolls in the same little bar that we had visited with Clio the day before. I bought a newspaper and sat reading at one of the outside tables while Jay prowled the square, ex-

ploring the few small shops that were open. Although I searched
the paper carefully from front to back, there was nothing in it
about Hugo. The Italian and Sicilian press hadn't reported Hugo's defection from Libya, according to Luke; after all, it would
hardly interest their readers. Although I hadn't really expected
to find anything, I was relieved nonetheless.

Jay came back with a paper parcel under one arm, looking
pleased with himself. "Look what I found, Alison." He took a
large flashlight with a pack of batteries out of the paper wrapping
and set about loading the batteries into their casing in the flashlight. "I usually carry a flashlight in my backpack, but I forgot
it when I left the school."

I folded up the newspaper. "Why do you need it now?"

"Oh, you never know. They're useful things to have, in case
you run into trouble. Like a Swiss army knife and a chocolate
bar." Suddenly he looked more like ten than fifteen, the little
boy still visible in the teenager. Then he grinned. "Or an Uzi."

I made a face at him. "Let's hope we don't need any of them."

It was just after nine when we set off for Clio's. As we drove
up to her house, we saw a pickup truck parked beside the Land
Rover. A man was leaning against the driver's door, smoking.
He looked up to stare at us as we got out of the car, acknowledging our *"buon giorno"* with an almost invisible nod of his
head. Clio's door was open, but no Argo rushed out to greet us.
Jay suggested we try the honey house.

We went around the back, and as we crossed the terrace we
could hear a man's voice raised in anger coming through the
open window of the honey house. He was speaking in a mixture
of Italian and Sicilian. I could pick out some of the words, but
not enough to make any sense of what he was saying, or, rather,
shouting. Clio's voice interrupted the furious torrent; although
she spoke more quietly, she sounded in her way as angry as he
did.

Jay and I looked at each other. "Maybe we should—" I began. Before I could finish, Giudico Coccalo came out of the
honey house. Rage twisted the already skewed features of his
face so that it was even more hideous. As soon as he saw us, he
made an effort to hide his anger with a smile that was somehow
more unnerving than his fury had been. Anger looked at home
on his face, the smile did not.

"Sightseeing so early? You Americans always have such energy." He managed to make this sound like an insult.

"You're up early, too, Signor Coccalo," I observed mildly.

"I'm a businessman. It pays to be early."

Clio appeared behind him, holding a growling Argo by the collar. "Good morning," she said calmly to us. Then, to Giudico, "We'll talk about this another time."

He said, "Perhaps your friends will be able to persuade you to change your mind."

"You know me well enough, Giudico, to know that I won't change my mind. Until you give me answers to my questions."

Giudico put his sunglasses on, and metamorphosed back into the nondescript accountant. Only his quietly menacing voice, tight with suppressed anger, gave any sign of what he was feeling. "You talk like an American, Clio. A Sicilian would know there are questions it is better not to ask."

"Then perhaps I should ask another American," she replied evenly. "Elliot may not have your aversion to questions."

"Elliot has nothing to do with export, only with the honey we sell here." Giudico hesitated, then added with deliberate emphasis, "You won't find it easy to sell your honey without us."

Clio did not respond to this; instead, she let Argo strain forward in her gasp, within snapping range of Giudico's leg. To his credit, the Sicilian stood his ground. "You'd better go, Giudico. I don't know how much longer I can hold him."

Giudico seemed about to speak, then looked at Argo and perhaps thought better of it. Abruptly, he turned and strode away, disappearing around the corner of the house. In a moment we heard the truck's motor start up.

Clio patted Argo's head and released him; at once, he ambled over and pushed his nose into Jay's hand. Clio smiled at me, somewhat wanly. "I'm sorry you had to be part of that."

"Was that a threat, what he said about not being able to sell your honey?"

She shrugged with apparent unconcern. "More like masculine bluster. Besides, I doubt if Don Calo would let him drive me out of business. Elliot will calm Giudico down." She went on to explain that Elliot Carter was a young American who was living in the *castello* tower, looking after it for Hugo. An architecture student touring Sicily on his own, he had turned up at the tower one day in the spring of 1983 to pay homage to Hugo. Hugo had invited him to stay on, and he was still there three months later, when Hugo went to Libya.

"Elliot has a gift for making himself indispensable. He's a bit of a fixer, someone who knows how to get all kinds of things done. At any rate, he made himself useful to Hugo, and to me. He's Giudico's partner in a number of things, including the marketing of my honey. You'll probably meet him today. Don't let his looks fool you, by the way. Elliot is more than the sum of his physical parts.'' Briskly, she asked us if we had eaten breakfast. "Then if you'll give me a hand loading the Land Rover, we can get started.''

As we followed her into the honey house, I wondered what had happened in the short time since we had last seen Clio to make her so angry with Giudico Coccalo. Despite her disclaimer, Giudico's warning had sounded very much like a threat—perhaps his response to a threat of her own to give her business to someone else. I was very curious, too, to meet Elliot Carter, a man who had obviously managed with ease to become part of Hugo's life here.

Crates filled with jars of honey were stacked inside the screen door. Next to them was a single open-topped crate that Clio told us held frames of comb foundation, sheets of wax embossed with the base of honeycomb cells. "The bees will build their comb onto it," she said. "Buying commercially prepared foundation saves time and money. Especially when the honey is flowing heavily, the way it is right now. When I remove the filled combs, I replace them with these. Some beekeepers even use plastic foundation, because it won't sag or break apart in the extractor, the way wax foundation sometimes does. But I just don't like the idea of it.''

She asked Jay to take the top crate of honey jars to the Land Rover, then gathered up her equipment, handing me the smoker and one of the veiled hats. "I generally take some honey to Don Calo, to thank him for letting me keep bees on his land. I didn't think I'd have enough this time because Giudico said he needed my whole production. But now . . .''

Boldly, I asked her if she had broken with Giudico because he was cheating her. She was stooping over to pick up her overall, which had fallen onto the concrete floor, and as she straightened, I half expected her to tell me to mind my own business. Instead, pushing the hair off her forehead with the back of her hand, she replied, almost distractedly, "That's the confusing part. I'm sure he wasn't, not financially anyway. If anything, the profits were often more than I'd reckoned on.''

"Then why—''

"Because he hasn't been honest with me in other ways. After you left yesterday, I spoke with a Sicilian friend just back from a vacation in New York. I had asked her to visit the stores that were selling my honey, to check on their displays. But she couldn't find my honey in any of the stores, and when she asked she was told that they hadn't had a shipment in more than six months. When I questioned Giudico about it, he would only say that he needed the honey here. Which is ridiculous, because he's always said the real money lies in the export side of the business, not the local. So, until Giudico gives me a better explanation than he has, I've told him I won't let him have any more of my honey.'' She picked up one of the white boxes called supers, adding, "Hugo may have been right after all. He never liked my working with Giudico.''

"Why not?"

She handed me the empty super. "Have you had a chance to read my article yet?''

I thought she was changing the subject, and replied that I had. "I enjoyed it. And reading it made the site itself so much more powerful.''

"I'm glad. But I wasn't fishing. Do you remember the graffito I mentioned, the one in the cave on Monte Castello that was vandalized?'' I nodded. "Hugo always suspected Giudico of being the vandal, when he was a teenager.'' As Jay came back through the door with Argo trotting at his heels, Clio smiled. "You know, I'd almost swear that Argo somehow knows you're Hugo's son. He shadowed Hugo in exactly the same way. Hugo found him in Palermo, beaten half to death and abandoned by the road. After Argo recovered, Hugo gave him to me—he said that, living alone as I do, I should have a dog. And besides, he was always traveling. Argo accepts me, but in his heart he's Hugo's dog.''

Her smile seemed warmer today, less guarded, and despite the run-in with Giudico, she was clearly more relaxed with us, even approachable. Perhaps Jay sensed this, too, for as we finished loading the Land Rover with Clio's equipment, he asked her what had happened to Giudico's eye. She was lifting the last empty super into the back of the Land Rover. There was a moment's silence before she responded. "An accident when he was sixteen.'' Perhaps she heard the curtness in her voice, for she added, "He and another boy were hit by a rock fall in a cave on Monte Castello. The boy with him was killed, and by the time Giudico was found, it was too late to save his eye. The doctor botched the job and an infection set in, which made it worse. I suppose nowadays he could have some sort of plastic surgery to make it less noticeable, but I have the feeling he rather likes the effect it has on people.''

Quietly, she added, ''Hugo thought Giudico was lucky to get away with his life. He had already profaned the cave once before.'' She threw her white coveralls in on top of the supers. ''Now, why don't you climb into the back, Jay? That seat on the side pulls down. Alison, you sit up front with me.'' She told Argo to stay and guard the house. Reluctantly, he trotted back to the front door and lay down on the stoop, gazing sadly after us as we drove away.

''Don Calo won't expect us till midday. I hope you don't mind if we visit my hives first. It won't take too long. Afterward, if you like, I'll show you something interesting.'' She spoke loudly over the noise of the engine, which was considerable, a kind of aural counterpoint to the jolting ride. ''There's a cave very close to the hives that was probably used as a religious site for as long as there have been people living in this part of Sicily. The cave I mentioned in my article.''

''Fantastic!'' Jay leaned forward from the back seat. His enthusiasm made Clio glance around at him.

''Jay's a caver,'' I explained.

''Really?'' Clio sounded pleased. ''I'll be interested to know what you think of this one, then. It may not be as large as others you've seen, but it is a remarkable place. It has a spirit of its own. It has . . . well, a supernatural quality.''

''Supernatural?'' There was a trace of polite skepticism in Jay's voice.

''In the best sense of the word. Spiritual. It was a place of worship for several thousand years, right into the last century. Now, though, the local people won't go near it.''

''Why not?''

''Superstition. There were several accidents in it, including Giudico's, and so they say that the cave is cursed. It's just as well, because otherwise it might be used to stable goats or sheep, like many of the caves around here. That would be a pity, in my opinion. Sacrilegious somehow.''

''What kind of worship went on there?'' I asked her.

''In the earliest times, offerings to the underworld divinities, the chthonic gods. Later, I'm positive it was consecrated to the Mother Goddess, a local offshoot of the cult at Erice. I'm convinced it was some sort of bee cult. I was beginning to persuade your father, too.''

''But you said that the cave was sacred in the last century,'' I pointed out. "Surely they weren't worshiping the Mother Goddess then?"

"In a sense, they were." Clio smiled at my reaction. "In another form. The Virgin Mary is far more popular in Sicily than her Son, and always has been. It was easy, almost natural, to graft her cult onto the Mother Goddess'. It happened all over the Mediterranean world, and the Mater Dolorosa is an especially potent myth here. Demeter weeping for Persephone, for instance. This is her country."

"One of my least favorite myths," I said idly, watching a bird with black-and-white wings swoop low over a rolling hayfield. Through my open window came a vegetable smell, like celery.

Clio glanced at me. "Why is that?"

"Maybe because when I was young I somehow got it into my head that Demeter must have been a neglectful mother. She was off somewhere being worshiped, having a good time, while her daughter played alone. No wonder Hades was able to kidnap Persephone."

There was a silence while Clio steered carefully around a large pothole. After a moment, she said, "I don't think I've ever heard quite that construction put on it before. But, you know, she was well punished for her neglect. She suffered. And she did her best to get her daughter back again. Myself, I've always found the story very moving, full of hope. A paradigm of what, in a sense, happens to most parents and children. Separation and reconciliation."

Before I could ask her if she had children herself, Jay began to question her about the cave, clearly eager to bring the subject back to what was for him its more interesting aspect, the purely physical.

"It's a limestone cave," Clio told him. "Part of a system of tunnels that runs under Monte Castello, carved out by some sort of underground river eons ago. But I've explored only a small part of it. Really only the main cave itself, which is where we found the archaeological evidence for our theory. Some niches carved into the rock where lamps were placed or the offerings left, pottery shards, and a remarkable bowl that I'll show you. Hugo could tell you much more about the whole system. At one time or another, he explored most of it."

I slid my window back as far as it would go, resting my arm on the sun-warmed metal of the door. We were on the coast now, driving northeast, and the road ran between flat fields that bordered the sea and a ridge of bare, yellow-gray hills rippled with the terracing of the low, ruinous stone walls that seemed to be everywhere. On a hilltop, a solitary goat stood in profile against the sky. Clio pointed out Monte Castello to us, its peak rising to the north, virtually out of the sea.

"It must have been difficult for you," I said eventually, "when he went off to Libya so suddenly. For your research, I mean."

She inclined her head slightly. "Yes, it was." Seen from the side, her face had the clean, chiseled outline of a classical female head, all its features strong and smooth and severely beautiful.

"Did you have any warning? Jay and I didn't." I hoped my own admission would make her more forthcoming.

"How terrible for you." Her voice was low, intense, and the knuckles of her hands on the steering wheel stood out whitely against the tanned skin, as if she was holding on to some sort of life preserver.

I let a moment go by. "And for you?"

"Yes, Alison. It was terrible for me, too." She turned her head and gave me a long look, and for an instant we were connected by something more than her admission of pain. Then her eyes went back to the road. "So, you see, I do understand."

"Are you angry with him?"

Jay stirred a little in the back, but if Clio resented this inquisition she gave no sign of it. "There's no point being angry with someone like Hugo. It's a waste of time, like being mad at a thunderstorm. You might as well just get on with your life." I wondered if she meant this as some sort of warning, though the tone of her voice was fatalistic rather than pointed. But a sharpness etched her next words. "If you're wondering if I'm feeling like a woman scorned, or vindictive, or liable to give his hiding place away, the answer is no. That is what you wanted to know, isn't it?"

Jay leaned forward before I could answer her. "It's just that we have to be sure."

"Of course." In the rearview mirror her eyes met his in a quick, sympathetic glance. Then she went on. "You see, I wasn't angry with Hugo because . . . well, because I knew his reasons for going." She paused, and even the engine's roar seemed to fade in the weight of the silence. "He wanted to undo the past."

CHAPTER 14

Startled, I stared at her. "What do you mean?"

But having given so much away, she suddenly drew back into her shell. "Hugo should explain. He has to be the one to tell you." She raised one hand from the steering wheel and pointed to the crossroads ahead. "There. That's the road to Castell'-alto."

There was no signpost, nothing to indicate where the winding tarmac road led after it disappeared into the uplands. When I asked Clio why not, she replied that the signpost never lasted long. "The Castell'altesi like their privacy." It was just as well, I reflected, that she was with us; on our own, we might never have found our way.

As the road twisted away from the plain, the countryside grew wilder, with jagged boulders and stubby, wind-bent trees that sprouted from steeply tilting fields yellow with thick clumps of broom. Flat-topped bluffs of bare rock reared up in the distance, Monte Castello's outposts; behind them, the mountain rose like a black sun. In the harsh blue sky, gulls soared and circled above an invisible sea.

Every now and then a dirt lane lined with brambled hedgerows forked off from the road, leading to nowhere, or so it seemed. Once we passed a herd of hump-backed black cattle walking single file, each cow with a massive wooden halter around its neck from which dangled a bell. The dull clanging of the wooden clappers as the herd moved slowly along had a curiously melancholy sound in the empty landscape. The herdsman followed, the ubiquitous cloth cap shading his eyes; he raised his hand to us, but did not smile. After that, we saw no one.

The road seemed in good repair, crumbling into dirt only at its edges, but when Monte Castello with its limestone cliffs crowded in on our right we could see where rock slides had tumbled across it, the scars still visible in the form of potholes and heaps of rock that had been bulldozed or shoveled onto the verge on either side. Clio had to weave the Land Rover around huge potholes that would have sunk my car. The winter rains, she said, had done a lot of damage, loosening earth already unstable from earthquakes.

Here the only traces of man were the tall telephone poles that marched along the road, and the road itself. And once a metal sign warning of rock and mud slides.

We were all three silent, each of us occupied with our own thoughts. Mine—and doubtless Jay's, as well—were turning restlessly around Clio's revelation. Hugo had gone to Libya because he wanted to undo the past, she had said. But whose past—his own, or someone else's? And why did that past lie in Libya? Violently, I wished that I could somehow push Clio to give more than gnomic responses to our questions. But I knew that it was useless; she was so plainly someone who was not to be forced beyond her own will to respond.

We were in a labyrinth, Jay and I, with Hugo at the center. Each question, each answer, might take us closer to him—or lead us off into a blind alley. And, in the end, after all, the center might be empty.

Clio's voice broke the silence. "Don Calogero's house isn't much farther now. Less than a mile. But we'll stop here first." She turned off onto a rutted path, a set of tire tracks barely visible in the long grass, that ran between enormous boulders and then opened into a small upland meadow. Scarcely bigger than a baseball diamond, it lay like a natural amphitheater, cradled by the mountain that curved protectively around it to the north and east. To the southwest, the sea and sky lay blended in a blue harmony.

"The Castell'altesi call this the *prato di Venere*," Clio said. "Venus' meadow. They say it's had that name since people first lived here because Venus was born from the sea below the cliffs. Sicily is traditionally one of her birthplaces."

We got out of the Land Rover and stood for a moment just looking around. A gentle breeze brought the scent of crushed mint and the sea. Wildflowers starred the grass like some medieval tapestry, purple thistles, clover, a sort of mauve-and-cream broom like a sweet pea, pale pink cistus, and, when I knelt down to get a better look, a tiny wild iris with a streak of orange-yellow on each miniature petal. At the far end of the meadow, nestled up against the cliff face, stood a cluster of white beehives, a dozen or more, each protected from the fierce Sicilian sun by a kind of canopy made from bamboo poles covered with dried palm branches.

Clio told us that she had other "outyards," as she called the places where she kept hives that were not on her own property. "But this is my favorite. It's certainly the most beautiful. And the bees here produce the best honey."

As Clio stepped into her white coveralls, Jay asked her if she wanted our help. "Not yet. But later, when it's time to carry the supers to the Land Rover, I'd be glad of it. Full supers are very heavy. In the meantime, why don't you have a look around and see if you can find the entrance to the cave? It's not far off, but it is fairly well hidden. Don't go in it, though, until I'm with you. And watch your step over there, where the meadow ends."

While Jay searched and Clio worked with her bees, I walked to the edge of the meadow and, mindful of Clio's warning, peered over. Instead of the sheer drop I half expected, there was an outward slant to the cliff face, with a scree of large boulders. Still, the height was considerable. Five hundred feet below, a small sickle-shaped bay with what looked like a sand beach lay in the embrace of the cliffs, with giant stalagmites of rock thrusting up out of the water at either end, like watchtowers guarding the bay. Beyond, the sea moved lazily in peacock shades of blue and green, shimmering, translucent. Searching for a way down to the beach, I walked along the cliff edge and discovered a stony path winding down the sloping cliff face through the boulders. To judge from a pile of dried droppings near the top of the path, it was used by some sort of animal, donkeys or mules, perhaps. Holding on to the rocks, I cautiously clambered down a little way, until I had a better view of the route that the track took. As far as I could tell, it seemed to go all the way down to the beach. The day was hot and the water looked seductively cool, but it was a long way down and would inevitably seem, I knew, even longer back up again. As I turned to retrace my steps, I noticed a pack of matches lying in a crevice. So man used the track, too. It seemed a shame, this tiny bit of garbage in so beautiful a place; almost without thinking, I picked it up and slipped it into my pocket.

When I reached the top again, Clio waved at me. She was standing by the full supers she had taken from the hives. Bees were flying all around her, but she seemed oblivious to them. "Can you help me with these now, Alison? There are some gloves and a veil in the Land Rover.'' Bunches of bees clung to each box but she gently brushed them away, with a few puffs from the smoker for the persistent, which drove them off long enough for us to pick up the box. The super was surprisingly heavy, a good forty pounds, at least. As we carried it to the Land Rover, Jay reappeared.

''Any luck?'' Clio asked him.

''I think so. Let me give you a hand, then I'll show you.''

While we worked, I asked Clio if her hives were ever robbed. ''They're so isolated here. Anyone could come by and take the honey.''

She shook her head. ''The people around here have too much respect for bees. They think that bees are insects of good luck and so it would be very bad luck to disturb them. Besides, a stolen swarm won't thrive, they say. The cult of bees that I described in my article survived until quite recently. In different forms. An old woman from Castell'alto once told me that only a woman could keep bees properly because they didn't like men. It's hard not to see that as a direct link with the time when bees were sacred to the Great Goddess, and cared for by her priestesses.

''In Sicilian Christianity, bees were singled out by God because they'd renounced sexual love out of respect for Him and His saints. Some of that reputation still lingers, the feeling that bees are somehow divine. Like caves. Bees and caves are often linked.''

I was remembering something Hugo had once said: Myth is somebody else's religion.

Jay gently blew a bee off his arm. ''Weren't caves sacred because people thought they were entrances to the Underworld?''

''That's right. And because bees so often built their nests in caves, the ancient world believed they were the souls of the dead.'' Clio used what looked like a miniature crowbar to prize loose each frame from the super that was sitting on a large rock near the Land Rover. She wanted to make sure, she told us, that the bees had filled and capped the honeycomb all the way to the edges of the frame.

''But didn't you say that this cave was cursed, or something?'' Jay persisted. ''What do the people here think when you go into it?''

She shrugged. ''Perhaps that I'm spared bad luck because of my bees. Or perhaps because I observe the rituals.'' She said it matter-of-factly, casually, but the look that accompanied the words was almost shy.

"Rituals?" I asked.

"Well, for instance, when I take the honey, I say a prayer to Saint John that beekeepers here have always said, a prayer to keep the bees free from infection, and grant a good harvest of honey and wax in the hive. There are other, older prayers as well. And good luck charms of all kinds for bees. Did you notice that stone bee by the front door of my house? Hugo gave it to me. He said it was supposed to keep the evil eye from my door."

When we had loaded all the supers into the Land rover, shutting the windows against marauding bees, we followed Jay across the meadow toward the mountain's north flank, which rose from the meadow at a gentle angle. Jagged crags of pale limestone towered above us, lying in serrated ranks against one another, bare rock gleaming hotly in the sun.

Before Jay could reveal the entrance to the cave, Clio raised her arm, pointing to the northwest. "Look up there."

With my hand shielding my eyes against the sun, I followed the line of her arm up to a spur of stone thrust out in profile against the sky, visible through a narrow gulley in the mountainside where the rock face seemed to have collapsed in on itself, forming a shallow trough. Squinting through the bright white glare off the limestone, I made out what looked to be battlements rising into the air. I blinked, and the image quivered for an instant in the heat, like a mirage. When it stilled and took solid shape again, I saw a manmade curve of stone crowned with crenellations.

"That's the top of Hugo's tower," Clio said. "This is the only place it can be seen from the meadow."

Was that, I wondered as I gazed up at it, the center of the labyrinth? Suddenly, I felt almost dizzy, the effect perhaps of the blinding glare from the stone, the thick, sweet scent of heather and broom, and the tiny insect voices that drilled through the heat.

Clio went on to explain that the *castello* sat on a promontory that had split off from the mountain thousands of years ago. "The sea almost surrounds it. It's a remarkable site. There's a local legend that claims it was the Cyclops' lair, though of course this is the wrong coast. I heard an odd theory once," she added with a laugh, "that argued that the Cyclops was a mythical explanation for a childhood fear. The memory of a parent leaning down at us when we were small until the two eyes merged into one, and saying, the way parents do, 'You're delicious. I'm going to eat you up.''

"Not my parents," I said without thinking. "Hugo was the least devouring father imaginable. And my mother didn't want even a nibble." The words were out before I realized how they sounded. Clio stared at me, and I could feel myself blushing.

Jay, however, seemed not to have heard. He was studying the distant fragment of tower, twisting a long stalk of bearded grass in his hands. "Can you reach it from here?" he asked Clio.

She nodded, and pointed up the mountainside. "There's a track up there, an old sheep route, which leads around the mountain to Casteddu. But it's a hike, and you have to have a head for heights." We could just make out a thin white line that wriggled like a dusty snake up the mountainside to disappear among the rocks.

"Come on," Jay said at last. "This way." He moved forward, and as we followed him the tower top disappeared from sight, blotted out by the wall of stone. We followed the curve of the mountain around the meadow to a cluster of large rocks tumbled together at the foot of a stony outcropping, some fifty feet from the meadow's edge, where in prehistoric times, Clio told us, a slab of the mountainside had split off and crashed onto the meadow. We threaded our way among the rocks until we came to an enormous boulder, at least seven or eight feet high and twice that across. Jay pointed out a narrow fissure in the cliff face above and behind the boulder. "When I saw that, I knew," he said.

Behind the boulder there was a small corrie, a circular hollow some ten feet in diameter strewn with fallen stones, where the fissure widened to an opening that was clearly the entrance of a cave. At the bottom it split the rock to a width of five feet, and was high enough for a man to enter without bending. Above it the cliff face canted back, with a lot of loose shale and rock clinging to it, barely held together by clumps of wild grasses and feathery white heather. Clio followed my gaze. "Someday a rock slide will bury this entrance forever. There have been one or two in the past that came close."

"Was it one of them that injured Giudico Coccalo?" I asked her.

She shook her head. "Not here. Quite a way inside the cave. He and the boy that was killed were treasure hunting, or so I've heard."

"What sort of treasure?" Jay's voice was eager.

She smiled, not in any patronizing way, more as if she shared his excitement, and I remembered that she was by inclination an archaeologist, in a sense the ultimate treasure-seeker. "The golden honeycomb, fairy gold, bandits' loot, you name it. The stories get mixed up together. Or maybe Giudico and his friend were just trying to find out if the legends were true. When Zeus defeated the Giants, the Titans, he buried them underground in Sicily—under Mount Etna, according to one myth, in caves along this coast according to another. The local people used to say that you could hear them bellowing sometimes if you put your ear to the ground. In the last century some huge human bones were found in a cave under Erice, and that was fuel for the legend. Caves here are rarely simply caves. Though you're more likely to find a goat in one than a giant. Now, if you're ready . . ."

Jay opened his knapsack and took out the flashlight. I grinned at him, acknowledging the prescience of the purchase earlier in San Teodoro. When Clio saw it, however, she said. "I never use one of those. It just doesn't suit the atmosphere of the cave. Anyway, I couldn't leave one in the cave because, eventually, the damp corrodes the batteries. A lantern is better. I have two of them just inside. I'll go in first, and light them."

Jay put the flashlight away and we followed her into the cave. The air was cool, almost cold after the heat of the sun, and smelled of damp earth. Although the breeze in the meadow had been gentle enough, here in the cave, channeled perhaps by the rock, it blew chilly against the skin. While my eyes adjusted to the sudden gloom, Clio lit the lanterns. She handed one to Jay. By their flickering apricot glow, we saw a chamber shaped roughly like an inverted bowl, fifteen or so feet in diameter, its roof shadowy and indistinct some ten feet above our heads.

With a caver's instincts, Jay found the tunnel almost at once, a black hole about four feet wide and just higher than he was, which led off into darkness. "Where does this go?" he asked Clio.

"Right down under the mountain, according to Hugo. He explored it a number of times, but he never really talked about what he'd found. I . . . I think it made him angry for some reason. Maybe frustrated is a better word."

Jay, who had been peering down the tunnel, the other lantern in his hand, straightened up again. "You haven't gone down it yourself?"

"A couple of times, but only as far as the ruined graffito I described in my article. Hugo said it wasn't safe to go farther."

Clio set her lantern into a niche carved into the stone wall of the chamber; other niches were spaced around the curve of the cave. In the center, on the cave floor, which was hard-packed dirt worn smooth by the centuries, there was a low, flat stone, almost perfectly circular, on which sat a small bowl. Clio went over to the stone and picked up the bowl. She held it out to me.

"Hugo found this here, or, rather, the original of this. Hidden far back in the tunnel. It's too valuable to keep in the cave, so he had an exact copy made. He reckoned that the original is late sixth century B.C." The little bowl was scarcely bigger than the palm of my hand, and was made of a dull metal, bronze perhaps. "Hold it up to the light," Clio commanded. When I did, I noticed markings, small shapes, scratched onto the surface in a band around the neck. As I looked closer, I saw that each was in the crude shape of what looked very like a bee. Inside the bowl, incised on the bottom, were three figures with upraised arms. They seemed to be female. "We think those three might be priestesses. Bee priestesses for this cult I've told you about. The bowl may have been used to hold a sort of honey drink, like mead."

Clio took the bowl from me and set it back on the central stone. Then, with actions eerily recalling my own at Erice, she unwrapped a small piece of honeycomb from a scrap of newspaper, placing it in the bowl, and stood silently for a moment, her eyes closed.

The flesh prickled at the back of my neck. Like Erice, the cave inspired the same mystical impulse, had the same unearthliness embedded in the massive rock. I remembered a theory that the past lives on in another dimension, parallel to the three we know, and that certain objects hold within them the power to evoke a specific instant of the past, replaying it over and over for as long as some magical current lasts. As I stood with my hands clasping my arms to warm them, it struck me that Clio's cave held that current, like the echo of the beating of some ancient pulse, a long-dead moment trapped in stone. The silence hummed, seemed almost alive.

Jay must have felt something of this, too, for his face was somber, with no trace of embarrassment or amusement as he watched Clio's actions.

When Clio stepped back from the stone, she said, quite matter-of-factly, "It's never a bad idea to observe the customs of the country, especially here. The Castell'altesi used to leave a cup of honey, among other things, at the entrance to the cave, as a sort of votive offering to placate the spirits of the dead. The honeycomb is always gone by my next visit. Mice may have eaten it, of course." I couldn't tell from the tone of her voice whether she found this explanation satisfactory or not.

Then, as I glanced around the cave, I saw a very earthy explanation for the humming sound. A bee shot past my face and vanished into the shadows on the opposite side of the cave. Clio must have seen it, too, or another, for she suddenly fetched one of the lanterns from its niche and walked over to that part of the cave, holding the lantern up to something. When Jay and I joined her, we could see a small mass of bees swarming over an irregularly shaped piece of honeycomb suspended from the rock, just at eye level.

"This wasn't here the last time I was in the cave," Clio said, "a few weeks ago. A swarm must have gone out from one of the hives and decided to build here."

"Maybe they're the souls of the dead," Jay said cheerfully. "Lost treasure-seekers. I'm glad you made that offering just now. I'd hate to get them angry at us."

Clio lowered the lantern until the bees were in darkness again. "I'll come back sometime, and hive them again. They won't bother us now if we leave them alone."

All the same, I moved a good distance away, to make sure of it, while Clio held out her hand for Jay's lantern. She carried both lanterns back to the mouth of the cave where she hung them on a pair of metal hooks that were screwed into the stone on either side of the entrance. She waited until Jay and I were in the entrance before extinguishing them.

Outside, the light was blinding, the blue of the sky much sharper after the blacks and browns of the cave. I was delighted to be back in the open again, but Jay, I could tell, would have liked longer in the cave. He had an almost dreamy look on his face. I shivered a little, grateful for the heat of the sun on my skin.

As Jay started around the enormous boulder, something crackled under his foot. It was an empty cigarette packet. It looked fresh, as though it hadn't been lying there that long. He picked up the packet. "People must come here, after all."

Clio made no response; she was standing with her dark eyebrows knitted together, clearly puzzled.

"I found these on the path that leads down to the beach." I

gave her the book of matches. "Maybe the same person dropped them."

Clio took them, turning them over in her hand. "Maybe. You can find these brands everywhere."

"Perhaps it was picnickers," I suggested. "Can you swim from the beach?"

"Yes, though almost no one does. It's just too difficult to get to. You can only reach it by water, or by the track. And it's quite a climb back up again." We started walking back to the Land Rover. "Not so long ago, smugglers used the cove. But there are easier ways and places nowadays, so they don't bother any more. Don Calo may know who's been in the meadow." She stepped out of her coveralls and threw them into the back of the Land Rover, adding, as an afterthought, "Matteo smokes that brand. Maybe it was he. He's helped me with the hives a couple of times. He might have been checking them for me." In explanation, she added, "Matteo worked for Hugo, a sort of general factotum. He still helps Elliot out at the *castello*."

"The *castello* is beginning to sound quite populous," I said. "Elliot Carter, and now Matteo . . ."

Clio smiled. "Only those two. But Matteo doesn't live there anymore. After Hugo left, he moved down to Castell'alto." Dryly, she added, "Matteo also considers himself something of a caretaker for the *castello*, but he and Elliot don't always see eye to eye. Matteo was devoted to Hugo. Hugo took him in six or seven years ago, when an earthquake killed his family and destroyed his home—he literally found Matteo in the hills, living in a cave. God knows how he'd managed. Anyway, Hugo brought him back to the *castello* and gave him board and lodging in exchange for work around the place. Hugo always claimed that sentiment had nothing to do with his helping Matteo—he reasoned that a twelve-year-old who had survived a winter in the mountains on his own must be clever and as strong as an ox, useful to have around. Hugo's very keen on resourcefulness and independence. But you know that." She slammed her door shut and started up the motor. "Now I'll take you to Don Calo."

CHAPTER 15

Don Calogero's house lay in the middle of a gently rolling plain, a shallow bowl of land scooped out of the high hills, with Monte Castello rising in a great wing of jagged stone at its back. A grove of olive trees close by the house blew silver gray, the twisted trunks and branches forever reaching to the east; beyond them, a windbreak stand of Aleppo pine flowed in a dark river of green toward the mountain.

The house stood foursquare and solid, a small, gated fortress built of a light gray stone, with roofs of rippling terra-cotta tile. It had been a *masserìa* originally, Clio told us, a primitive cluster of farm buildings grouped around a courtyard where the landowner or, more usually, the overseer and his workers stayed only during the harvest. Don Calogero had modernized and added to it. "When Don Calo bought it, he went against the grain. As a rule, Sicilians don't like to live in such isolation. That's why you see so many abandoned farmhouses in the country-side. The Rome government built them in the fifties in a vain attempt at land reform, but the Sicilians refused to use them. They're just too vulnerable and lonely. I think Don Calo's wife probably would have preferred to live in Castell'alto itself, but as he gave up the States to come back here for her sake, perhaps this was her concession."

"Why did she want to come back here?" I rooted through my shoulder bag in search of a comb for my hair, in an effort to tidy up a bit before we arrived.

"She had some sort of heart condition, and wanted to die where she had been born. After her death, some people thought Don Calo might go back to the States, but he told me that he was too old to adapt a third time. And I think by then he enjoyed being a very large frog in a small pond too much to give it up."

"He doesn't mind the isolation?"

"Apparently not. He's not a vulnerable man, and he prefers to live away from the town itself. He said once that it gives him the freedom to do as he pleases, without bothering about what others might think. Perhaps he also likes it because visitors can come and go without being seen." With this elliptical remark, she turned the Land Rover off onto the stony lane that led to the house. The main road to Castell'alto meandered on in a leisurely fashion across the plain, then slithered around the mountain's flank and disappeared from sight. "The house is called Lupaia, the wolf's lair. There were wolves once in the hills here." She gave a wry smile. "I sometimes wonder if Don Calo didn't buy it as much for its name as anything else.

"It's an odd sort of house inside. Half Don Calo's taste, half his wife's. There's an addition that you can't see from this side. Hugo designed it—it's exactly what Don Calo wanted, but very un-Sicilian." As we approached, we could see the massive double doors of the gate standing open. She drove through into the large cobblestone courtyard and parked next to a green tractor. Beyond the tractor were two Mercedes, one white, one black, both gleaming under a light coating of dust and looking slightly incongruous in front of an open-fronted building housing farm equipment, oil drums, and stacks of orange crates that formed one side of the *masserìa*; two of the three other sides were long, low buildings with few windows, while the third was clearly the main house. It was two stories high and partially covered with vines, with large, green-shuttered windows and lemon trees in clay tubs by the front door. As we got out of the Land Rover, the door opened and a woman stepped into the sunlight, as strikingly out of place in the farmhouse setting as the Mercedes.

"That's Giudico's wife, Benedetta," Clio said. "I'm surprised to see her here. She told me once, quite seriously, that the country is only fit for donkeys and peasants. She made it very obvious that she thinks I'm crazy to live in San Teodoro when I could live in Palermo or, better yet, New York."

"Do you think Giudico will be here, too?" I asked her, somewhat nervously.

"Let's hope not."

Benedetta Coccalo was a small, plumply pretty woman, snub-nosed and sloe-eyed, with curly dark hair trailing tendrils down the creamy skin of her neck. She was wearing an overly ruffled pink dress and a pair of bright green, spaghetti-thin sandals with very high heels. Around her wrists hung heavy gold bracelets, and a small gold bell dangled from each earlobe. Her smile as she came toward us was charming, decorated with deep dimples in each cheek, but it was somehow artificial, as though she had put it on with her perfume, and it did not reach her eyes. She reminded me of the elaborately confected Sicilian cakes I'd seen, all sugar and cream and thick, brightly colored icing. Men must have found her as deliciously tempting to look at as one of those cakes. But I suspected that too much of Benedetta might have the same uncomfortable results.

She brushed a kiss past each of Clio's cheeks, then shook hands with Jay and me. Her hand was tiny and soft, like a baby's. "Welcome," she said in slow, careful English. "Please come in."

Clio looked surprised. "Benedetta, I didn't know you spoke English."

"I am taking lessons now for six months. There is an English lady in Palermo who learns . . . who teaches me. I can understand, but to speak is more difficult." With a small pout, which deepened the dimples, she added in Italian, "It's a terrible language, but I want to learn it. Giudico has promised that we will go to live in America someday, when Don Calo dies."

Clio's voice was carefully neutral, but there was amusement in her eyes. "I expect you'll be bilingual by that time. Don Calo strikes me as fairly healthy."

"I am in no hurry," Benedetta replied tranquilly.

Clio paused on the stone steps. "Is Giudico here, too?"

To my relief, Benedetta shook her head; the little gold bells hanging from her ears tinkled among the tendrils of hair. "I haven't seen him since yesterday. I came up from Palermo last night."

"For the mountain air?" Clio's voice was teasing.

Benedetta made a face, but did not reply.

Inside, the tiled hallway was cool and dark, with a flight of stone stairs to the right. An old woman in black with a shawl over her head was coming downstairs, carrying a basket of clothes in her arms. Benedetta asked her to make coffee, then opened a door on the left and stood aside to let us pass through. We entered a large, high-ceilinged room where everything seemed oversized and from some more generously upholstered era, chandeliers and candelabra, dark, highly polished wood, standing lamps with huge fringed lampshades that towered over large stuffed armchairs and sofas covered in velvet. Thick Oriental rugs covered the marble floor, and the windows were obscured by yards of lace and red brocade. On one wall hung a

large, highly tinted color photograph of a middle-aged woman
that was surrounded by a wreath of dried laurel leaves and lit
from below by an electric candle. Knickknacks covered every
available surface and filled several wire-mesh-fronted cabinets.
There was so much of everything that at first I didn't notice the
man standing with folded hands by a window. Once seen, however, he riveted the eye.

He was a short, balding, powerfully built old man, with a
massive head set on broad, stooping shoulders. His nose and
thin-lipped mouth curved down, bracketed on either side by a
deep furrow that scored the olive flesh and gave his face a caus-
tic, almost contemptuous, expression. Dark eyes, barely visible
beneath their wrinkled lids, stared unblinkingly at us; they held
a piercing, unsettling intelligence. He looked like an ancient sea
turtle, shrewd and inscrutable, with a very tough shell.

He came toward us. Although his movements were slow and
deliberate, they suggested power, not weakness, and when at
last he spoke, his voice was harshly forceful. You knew at once
that this was a man accustomed to command.

"Welcome to my house." Don Calogero's gaze settled heavily on my face, but if he felt any emotion other than simple
pleasure at meeting the children of a friend, I couldn't read it in
those dark eyes. "So, you are Alison. Your father hoped we
would meet someday. Although I think he would have preferred
to be with us." This was said with a certain dryness, with a
touch of what might have been disapproval, but before I could
respond, he turned to Jay. "You have the look of Hugo when he
was a young man. I would know you were his son." He pro-
nounced the name in the Italian way, without the H—"Ugo."
He gestured to a group of velvet-covered chairs around a low
table. "Come, sit down."

As I turned, I found Benedetta staring at me, gaping almost,
and it struck me that perhaps she hadn't known who Jay and I
were; she looked as if she was hearing it now for the first time.

"Benedetta, coffee for our guests."

Although Don Calogero spoke quietly enough, Benedetta
jumped. "Assunta is bringing it. It will only be a moment."
Her voice was submissive, almost apologetic.

But Don Calogero had not waited for her answer; he was
already asking Clio about the hives on his land. "Giudico tells
me that the honey this year is particularly fine. If that's so, I
must take my tithe." The dark eyes held a gleam of humor.

"I brought it with me. Though I thought at first I wouldn't

have enough. It seems as if the orders get larger each time, and I only have a little left for my friends.''

"Then business flourishes?''

"Almost too well. I'm not sure my bees will be able to keep up with the demand.'' Clio paused, and when she spoke again it was clear that she was not going to mention her break with Giudico—not yet, at least. "Elliot and Giudico keep finding new customers for me. The American base at Comiso is the newest. The soldiers there seem to have a taste for honey. There's a complication, though. Perhaps, another time, you would give me your advice?''

"Of course. Whenever you wish.'' Don Calogero's gaze shifted to Jay and me, studying us. "I had not expected such a pleasure as this. As always, Clio, you surprise me.'' He spoke a curiously hybrid Sicilian-accented English with an intonation that hinted at Brooklyn.

"We're both surprised, you and I.'' She said it without accusation, simply as a statement of fact, smiling a little.

Don Calogero gave a small smile in return, ironical, conceding her point. The old woman came into the room with the coffee, and Benedetta rose and took the tray from her, carrying it over and placing it on the table in front of Don Calogero; when he asked her to pour the coffee, she inclined her head in an Oriental acquiescence, moving her hands gracefully among the cups, her long, pink-enameled nails clicking on the porcelain. She served Don Calogero first, stirring the sugar into his coffee for him, watching as he sipped it. His broad hands, which looked as if they might crush the fragile cup, held the tiny handle with a surprising grace. When he nodded his approval, she gave us ours, then sat forward at the edge of her chair to drink her own. Although she must have been over thirty, there was something curiously childlike about her, eager to please. She seemed nervous, too, playing with her bracelets after she set her cup back down, glancing anxiously at Don Calogero. It was almost as though she was afraid of him.

In silence, we drank our coffee. Don Calogero offered us pistachio nuts from a silver bowl on the table. He took a handful himself and cracked and ate them, placing the shells one by one in a little pile on his saucer. Jay sat still, his eyes on the floor, but one finger tapped out an impatient rhythm on his knee. Apart from Don Calogero himself, only Clio seemed at ease, slowly drinking her coffee. At last, when the final pistachio nut was cracked and eaten, Don Calogero turned to me. He went straight to the point. "You have come to Sicily to find your father, Clio tells me. And you think that he may be here, in Castell'alto?"

"It seemed the best place to start."

Don Calogero nodded. "You are right. Your father was here."

The admission came so much more easily and quickly than I had expected that for a moment I was at a loss for words. But not Jay. "Was?" He sounded wary, almost openly skeptical. "You mean he isn't anymore? Where did he go?"

"That I can't tell you. But he will come back. Perhaps tomorrow, perhaps the day after. It's impossible to know." He leaned slightly toward Clio. "Forgive me, I couldn't tell you until now. It was Hugo's wish."

"Yes, of course." Clio placed her cup carefully in its saucer. As she raised her head, she glanced at Benedetta, who had been watching her with a curious, almost avid, look on her face. I wondered how much of the conversation, which had been in English, Benedetta was able to understand. Caught staring, she flushed and made a show of adjusting the bracelets on her wrist.

"How is he?" Jay's voice was strained and the furrow was back between his eyes. He sat forward, his cup and saucer perched precariously on the edge of the sofa beside him. I reached over and put it on the table.

Don Calogero paused, then said judiciously, "I think well, on the whole. But tired. It has been difficult for him, this period. He needs to rest. But my sons are with him. Gaetano and Tommaso will look after him."

"Why do you think he'll come back to Castell'alto?" I asked.

"Because he told me that he would. And I have never yet known Hugo to fail in his word."

Jay looked straight at the old man, a challenging look. "Then we'll wait for him."

"Naturally you want to see your father," Don Calogero replied, inclining his head. I was afraid, however, that he might take exception to Jay's tone, and while he turned away to set his coffee cup down, I motioned to Jay to be careful. Placing his hands on his knees, Don Calogero rose heavily to his feet. "Let me show you something of your father's that you may find interesting."

He was speaking directly to Jay, as if the invitation was for him alone, so I stayed with Clio and Benedetta as he led Jay over to a far corner of the room where there was a large oak desk. He took a roll of papers from one of the desk drawers and spread it out across the desktop, weighting the corners down with books.

"Those will probably be Hugo's plans for the addition," Clio said. "The addition was unfinished when Hugo went away, but Don Calo hired an architect from Palermo to complete it. Don Calo has always said that anyone with a feeling for architecture would know where Hugo's design leaves off and the other architect's begins. He says the work of a great architect like Hugo is seamless, but the stitches of the other man are visible."

After a few minutes, Don Calogero left Jay still poring over the plans and came back to us. "He has Hugo's gift, that boy. With one look, he understands." At that moment we heard the sound of a car's engine in the courtyard. "That will be Elliot. I invited him to join us for lunch." Quietly, he added something in Sicilian to Benedetta, who had risen from her chair. She sat down again, biting her lip.

"Elliot does not know that Hugo has left Libya," Don Calogero continued. Clio raised one eyebrow, but if she found this surprising, that was the only sign of it. "He was away from Castell'alto during the short time Hugo was with me. I thought it best to wait for Hugo's return to tell him, but now . . ." He looked at me, and spread his hands wide.

A man of about my own age came into the room with Assunta. He was smoothly handsome in the blond California fashion that seems slightly unnatural in its very naturalness, tanned, fit, the teeth flawless and white, a product of twenty-five years' worth of sports and orthodontics. He was wearing an open-necked white shirt with the sleeves rolled up and wheat-colored cotton trousers over white espadrilles.

I remembered a name we had for the type in college—Wonder Bread man, all air and no taste—although this, I knew, must be unfair. The very fact that he had made himself "indispensable" to Hugo, and useful to Clio, told me there must be more to Elliot Carter than his bland good looks. Clio herself had warned me not be misled by his appearance.

He had an almost enviable self-possession, an air of being completely at his ease, which was made inoffensive by his pleasant smile as he greeted Clio and Don Calogero. There was nothing in his attitude to Clio to indicate whether he already knew what had passed between her and his partner, Giudico. Benedetta, who was pouring herself a second cup of coffee, seemed unaffected by his arrival; she hardly bothered to look up at him when he approached her, and her cool hello was almost rude. But Elliot Carter's good-natured smile never faltered.

Don Calogero took his arm. "Assunta will bring you something to drink before lunch, Elliot. Only *acqua minerale*? Are you sure? Then let me introduce you to my charming guest. Perhaps, now that you see her, you have already guessed who she is?" His tone was mild enough, but he watched the younger man with an almost clinical interest.

Elliot Carter gave a puzzled shake of his head. "I'm sorry, Don Calo. But I'm looking forward to finding out." He had a slight stutter on the *f*, a hint of vulnerability that made him suddenly more appealing, and I found it easy to answer his smile. The eyes that looked down into mine were a pale olive-green, as cool as spring water and disconcertingly shrewd. The mellow, easygoing manner coated a tougher core.

Don Calogero looked from him to me, and with a certain dramatic emphasis said, "Then let me present Alison Jordan. Hugo's daughter."

The green eyes widened as Elliot Carter did a classic double-take; then he grinned and held out his hand. "Don Calo's absolutely right, I should have guessed. Hugo showed me a ph . . . a ph . . . a picture of you once, but it must have been taken when you were about thirteen and it didn't do you justice."

I shook his hand; it was smooth and hard. "Almost any age is bound to be an improvement over thirteen."

"And this," Don Calo continued, turning Elliot slightly with the pressure of his hand on the younger man's arm, "is our other guest."

Half hidden by the large desk and almost invisible in the shadowy corner, Jay had been out of Elliot Carter's line of vision as he came into the room. With a smile of polite surprise, Elliot Carter turned to face this second stranger. The smile remained, but I thought I saw him almost imperceptibly stiffen as Jay came out from behind the desk toward him. But Don Calo's hand on his arm urged him forward.

"I think you recognize him, don't you, Elliot?"

"I can't believe it. . . . It's Jay, isn't it?"

Jay nodded, smiling shyly at the impact he'd made on the other man. "How did you know?"

"Are you kidding? Take a look at yourself in the mirror sometime. It's amazing you're actually here at last. Hugo said he wanted to get you to Castell'alto someday, but it's such lousy luck that he's not here when you f . . . finally make it."

Jay made a noncommittal noise in reply, but Don Calogero, whose dark inscrutable gaze had never left Elliot Carter, said, "That is my second surprise." He held out to him the glass of mineral water brought by Assunta. "You see, Hugo has returned."

This time there was something more complicated than simple astonishment on the perfect features. He looked stunned, caught badly off balance, and I thought for a moment that he was going to drop the glass. But the shock passed away almost at once, replaced by an excited eagerness. "Fantastic! Is he staying with you?"

The explanation Don Calogero gave was the one that he had made to us, brief and far from satisfying. Elliot Carter turned the untouched drink slowly around in his hands as he listened. He interrupted only once, to ask if Don Calogero were sure Hugo would not return sooner. When Don Calogero finished, he said quietly, "After the attack on Tripoli, I was af . . . f . . . I was worried something might have happened to him. I should have known better. Hugo's indestructible, of course." The smile that went with the words was affectionate. He took a long swallow of water, draining the glass. "So now we just go on doing what we've been doing all along, waiting for Hugo? Is that what he wants, Don Calo?"

But Don Calogero only shrugged.

Clio crossed her legs impatiently. "You've been doing more than waiting, Elliot, and I imagine Jay and Alison have, too."

Much of the conversation had been in English, but Benedetta must have followed some of it, for she interrupted now, in Italian. "I don't understand. Hugo goes off, he comes back, he goes away again. All without saying a word to any of you. What way is that to treat people? But instead of getting angry, you worry about when you're going to see him again." She examined her long sugar-pink nails with a critical eye. "Myself, I think you're crazy."

Suddenly Elliot laughed with genuine amusement, his head thrown back. "You're right, Benedetta. That must be the explanation. If we were in California, we'd all be in analysis. What do you think, Don Calo, are we crazy to put up with Hugo?"

Don Calogero refused to be drawn. "I think we should go in to lunch. Whenever the conversation becomes analytical I begin to feel hungry. No doubt there is a theory to explain this phenomenon, but for the moment I prefer to satisfy my stomach rather than my curiosity."

He led us through a closed door and down a passage to another room, a room stunningly different from the one we had just left. In a few steps we walked out of the nineteenth century and into the late twentieth, into a room of glass and stone that verged on the elemental in its simplicity. It was an austerely modern room, yet completely in harmony with the natural world beyond its walls. An opulent rug, worked in shades of green, that lay across the stone floor was the only luxurious touch. There was very little furniture: a single dark leather sofa, a pair of unusual bentwood chairs with curving arms, a huge armoire, and several floor-to-ceiling bookshelves against a stone wall. Two walls, facing north and east, were glass, tinted against the glare of the fierce summer sun. Through the expanse of glass directly ahead of the door that led into the room, there was a panorama to the east, where the country rolled away inland, rising and falling in sage-green waves toward a distant line of mountains, a wild landscape that seemed close-cropped by generations of goats and sheep, bitten down to the stony nub, then rubbed smooth by the wind. At the southern end of the room, at a lower level reached by two steps, was a semicircular apse-shaped alcove, completely empty of furniture apart from an elaborate copper brazier, far larger than the one we had seen at Clio's. The space seemed out of keeping with the rest of the room, the proportions somehow not quite right, and I wondered if this was the section unfinished in Hugo's plans.

Don Calogero answered my unspoken question. He walked over to the steps that led down into the apse. "Hugo had an idea for this area—it was to be a proper *lupaia*, he told me, the very den of the wolf. He sketched his idea in words to me, but he had no time to draw them up before he went away. I told the other architect what he said, and he came close, but to me it is not yet perfect. Someday, I am sure, Hugo will fix it.

"When Hugo designed this room for me, I told him that I was tired of cities, of feeling surrounded by people and their wants. I asked him to make me a room where only nature intruded." The thin mouth curved upward. "This is not very Sicilian, you understand."

Open sliding glass doors that led onto a stone terrace gave a view of Monte Castello and the gently rolling plain that lay between the *masseria* and the mountain; a winding road, the one along which we had driven, crossed the plain and vanished around the mountain's flank. In front of the glass doors was a long table, a single slab of pale green marble resting so lightly

on thin stainless-steel legs that it seemed to float above the floor.
It was set with brightly painted plates. Don Calogero showed us
to our places; Clio and I were on his left and right, Jay beside
Clio, with Elliot Carter directly across from him, beside me.
Benedetta sat in the hostess's chair, at the end opposite Don
Calogero. Assunta came in, bringing a large bowl of soup, which
she set down in front of Benedetta. It seemed to be some sort
of fish soup, with white chunks of fish and chopped-up vegetables floating on the surface. The smell coming from it was wonderful, a mixture of wine and herbs and seafood. As Benedetta
ladled the soup into bowls, Elliot Carter asked me where Jay
and I were staying.

"In Erice."

Jay leaned forward across the table. "But we'd like to be
closer. Is there a hotel in Castell'alto?"

"Castell'alto is too insignificant for that," Don Calo replied.
"But it's no matter. You will be my guests."

This was awkward. The last thing I wanted was to be Don
Calo's guest, to have our comings and goings scrutinized and
perhaps controlled by a man so ambiguous. Now that I had met
him, I found him less frightening than the image conjured up
by Rosalia and her grandmother; but still . . . Luke would worry,
too, if we failed to reappear. So I thanked him, but explained
that our luggage was in Erice. "And we told them at the hotel
that we'd be back this evening. Really, Jay, I think it's better if
we stay there tonight."

"I will send someone for your belongings. You won't need
to leave." Don Calo's voice was calmly matter-of-fact, and in-
flexibly firm; it was clear he expected submission.

As I hesitated, searching for words of polite refusal, Jay said
quietly, "Thank you, sir, but we'd like to stay in our father's
house, in the tower." His face had the stubborn set I had learned
to know, and his voice was a match for Don Calogero's.

Don Calogero made a dismissive movement of one hand.
"You will be more comfortable here. Isn't that so, Elliot?"

With an apologetic smile, Elliot said, "Don Calo's right. I
don't want to be inhospitable, but in fact the generator's been
giving me trouble. So there's a certain amount of inconvenience—"

"We don't mind," Jay replied. "And I think my father would
like us to stay in his house." He laid the faintest emphasis on
the last two words. I tried to catch his eye, but he wouldn't look
at me.

Don Calo must have recognized that Jay was not going to be easily dissuaded, for instead of insisting he merely glanced at Elliot. "Well, it is not for me to say. It is Elliot's home, too."

Elliot's good-humored smile was a shade forced perhaps, but to his credit he acquiesced with good grace. "Then of course you can stay in the tower. I warn you, though, it's pretty rustic."

"That's okay. We don't mind," Jay said again. Now he looked at me, and in his eyes I saw an appeal. "Do we, Alison?"

I wondered what "rustic" meant, but I said only, "Not for a night or two anyway. It's very kind of you, Mr. Carter. You're sure we won't be in your way?"

"Please call me Elliot. No really, it'll be good to have company. I've been like a hermit up there since Hugo took off."

"That's settled then," Don Calogero said. He turned to Clio and Jay, and conversation became general.

I asked Elliot how he had come to work for Hugo.

"Dumb luck. I was over here in the summer three years ago, bumming around. I liked to think of it as research." He gave a self-deprecating smile. "I was in architecture, had just finished my second year, and wanted to see the classical stuff. I heard from a contact in Palermo that Hugo was living up here, so I hitchhiked up to pay my respects. He invited me to use the tower as a base for a couple of days, and somehow those days turned into weeks and then months. I kept quiet and made myself useful. Once Hugo saw I wasn't going to be a pain to have around, he let me stay. And then I guess he just forgot to tell me my time was up."

"What about your classes? Didn't you have to go back to the States in the fall?"

"I figured I was going to learn a hell of a lot more from Hugo than any course could teach me. And I kind of got involved with Giudico Coccalo, in his business. Did Clio tell you?"

"She says you've expanded her sales."

"Yeah, well, I found I was a pretty good businessman. Or at least, I liked it. And generally whatever I do, I throw myself into. Giudico and I make the business contacts for Clio around the island. I let Giudico collect the honey from her. Bees aren't my favorite insect. I'm allergic to them, so I keep out of their way. A couple of stings, and that could be the end of me. Anaphylactic shock, it's called." Elliot made a face. "Not nice . . .

"Anyway, after Hugo went to Libya, I stayed on. I only knew your father for a couple of months before he disappeared, but I feel like I've gone on learning more about him while he's been away. I've been putting his papers in order. He was thinking of writing his memoirs. Maybe you knew that.''

"No, I had no idea.'' I spooned up the last of my soup.

"He'd only just started. I was going through material here in the tower—he's got stuff scattered all over the globe, of course— trying to organize it for him. Just before he went to Libya he asked me to keep on with it. And to be a kind of house sitter for the tower.''

"That doesn't sound as if he meant to be away for very long.''

"That was my impression, too. I thought a couple of months at most. But Hugo's unpredictable. You know that.''

I caught an oddly sour look on Benedetta's face as she watched this exchange between Elliot and me. She had said very little during the meal, either because much of the conversation was in English or for some other, more obscure reason, and whenever Don Calo glanced her way, her eyes went down to her plate.

"What about you, Alison?'' Elliot asked me. "I think I remember Hugo saying that you work in Germany?''

After that we talked a little about my job and life in Germany, casual small talk, but I sensed Elliot Carter wasn't that interested. Something else seemed to be on his mind. And I was wondering what it really was that kept him in Castell'alto; somehow, selling Clio's honey seemed an inadequate motive for giving up his architectural studies. At one point, when Clio was telling Don Calogero about the trespasser in the meadow, Elliot stopped in the middle of what he had been saying to listen. Don Calogero replied that he knew of no one locally who might pay visits to the meadow. Abruptly, he turned to Elliot. "Do you, Elliot?''

Elliot looked startled. " 'F . . . 'fraid not.''

"There are no tourists here,'' Don Calogero continued, "so perhaps it was simply someone from Castell'alto meeting a woman away from her husband's jealous eye. I will make inquiries, Clio. I don't want the bees disturbed—I enjoy their honey too much.''

During the main course—braised veal with anchovies and black olives—Don Calo told stories of Giuliano, the last great bandit of Sicily, and his exploits. He gestured with his wineglass toward the mountain. "Up there are caves where Giuliano and his men would hide while the *carabinieri* hunted for them. Many here knew this, but no one went to the police. He was a hero in Castell'alto. When I was a young man, I myself saw him ride like a king through the streets with the children running after him.''

"We're talking about a Sicilian Robin Hood," Elliot told Jay. "A man as handsome as a god, who robbed the rich to give to the poor, and was only twenty-eight when he was betrayed by a friend and killed. A very romantic figure."

"Who managed to murder four hundred and thirty people in his short, romantic career," Clio observed dryly. "A good number of them the poor."

Don Calo wiped the juice from his plate with a piece of bread. "Murderer, martyr, god, or devil, what is interesting about Giuliano is that no one can decide which he was. In the end, however, it did not matter. It only mattered that he was trouble and had to be destroyed. It was his destiny." He swallowed the sodden crust of bread, then looked around the table, his dark eyes coming to rest on Elliot. "There is no room for trouble-makers in Sicily."

I felt my napkin about to slide off my lap and glanced down to retrieve it. Below the table, to my right, a bright green sandal rested on a white espadrille. The sandal withdrew, but it had stayed there just long enough to make me certain that it was no accidental encounter.

CHAPTER 16

After Assunta had cleared away the lunch, Don Calo poured Marsala into thimble-sized tumblers of red glass webbed with gold tracery. Jay had drunk a little wine mixed with water during the meal, and now he took the glass that Don Calo handed him with a querying glance at me. There was so little in the glass I couldn't imagine it would do him any harm, and so I nodded, pleased and a little surprised by this appeal to an older sister's authority. Then I remembered that Hugo, too, was always careful to defer to people in the little things, knowing that it would make it easier to have his way in the important ones. For all that he was only fifteen, Jay was as skillful in his fashion as Hugo. He had persuaded me, against my better judgment, to come to Sicily with him; he had got Clio to intercede for us with Don Calo; he had evaded Luke, with my complicity; and now he had forced Elliot Carter, albeit politely, to let us stay in the tower. I looked at him with a new respect.

"Clio told us that you first met our father when he was here during the Second World War," Jay was saying now to Don Calo.

"Your father and I met before that," Don Calo replied. "He came to Castell'alto the summer before the war, in 1938. He was a young student of archaeology in those days, and he was traveling around the island with a pack on his back. Like Elliot, when he first arrived in Castell'alto."

"Why did he come here?" I asked.

"He knew of the excavations at Casteddu," Don Calo replied. "The *castello* is very old, but I am told that what lies under it is ancient. Casteddu was once a holy place, and when you see it you will understand why that should be so." He paused to refill Elliot's glass, then leaned back in his chair, which creaked a little under his weight.

161

"You must imagine a great tower of rock rising from the sea in the shadow of Monte Castello. As though it was the child, and the mountain the mother. Casteddu was born in an earthquake many thousands of years ago, when the rock that bound it to Monte Castello collapsed. Now a chasm separates the two. The top of Casteddu is flat. There is a word in English to describe it . . ."

"A plateau," Clio said. The long, elegant fingers of her right-hand, tanned and bare of rings, rested without moving on the cool marble of the tabletop. She was looking down as Don Calo talked, her eyes invisible.

"A plateau, exactly. And so man was able to build on it easily enough. There is a bridge, of course—there has been a bridge for hundreds of years—but no one knows how man came there before there were such things as bridges.

"Some British archaeologists once tried to find out by digging under the *castello*. That was in the twenties, when the old Duke of Caltabella's father was alive. He admired all things British and he gave his consent for the excavations. But they found very little, and later their money ran out. After that, the place was forgotten. Until Hugo came."

A faint smile of reminiscence lifted one corner of Don Calo's mouth, and the dark eyes stared down the table, beyond us, at the mountain that rose stark and massive in the distance and the winding, dusty road that crossed the little plain toward it. Don Calo raised his hand and pointed to the road. "I met your father for the first time on that road. He was riding a motorcycle. This to us was a very exciting way to travel in those days. He was covered with dust, from head to foot, so that all I could see were his blue eyes. And of course that nose of his.

"He asked me the way to Castell'alto. He said he wanted to look at the work of the British archaeologists. I told him he must speak to the mayor of Castell'alto, Don Ciccio Fallucca, to seek his permission. Don Ciccio was the duke's *gabellotto* in Castell'alto, his manager. This duke, the son, never came to Castell'alto. He lived in Paris, and I think he never again set foot in Sicily after he left it when he was a child. The mayor gave his permission, and this, you must know, was an achievement, for we do not often welcome strangers here. Even at so young an age, Hugo understood that with a man such as Don Ciccio much can be achieved by the right proportions of flattery, respect, and cash. But Don Ciccio also liked your father. In Sicily, when we like a man, we say he is a piece of bread. Hugo was a piece of bread.'' With a small smile, Don Calo added, ''In English, it sounds not so wonderful, but bread to Sicilians, who have little . . .

''For the first few days, we were curious about this stranger. The children especially were always with him. They swarmed around him like little flies, but if he minded them, he gave no sign of it. He took them for rides on the motorcycle. After a while, however, what he was doing seemed not so interesting— walking around the ruins, sitting, studying plans. And to reach Casteddu from Castell'alto you must walk a half mile up the mountain. When we grew used to him, the walk began to seem long again. He lived in a tent at the *castello*, and he came down to Castell'alto for supplies, so we saw him from time to time. He would sit in the café, and listen to the old men's stories.

''The tower and the *castello* ruins lie at the western end of the plateau. But there are also houses on Casteddu, near the bridge, and in those days, there were still a few villagers living there, old people for the most part. They said Hugo worked at night, for they saw his light moving about the ruins. They thought he was crazy. After dark, no one went near the *castello*. That was when the lady walked. A castle must have its ghost, you see.'' Don Calo gave an ironic smile. ''I think that was why Hugo chose to sleep there. Perhaps the spirit respected his privacy more than we did.

''He stayed for a few weeks, always working in the ruins, and then he went away and we thought no more about him.'' Don Calo was sitting hunched forward now, with his elbows on the armrests of the chair, his chin sunk down onto the steepled fingers of his clasped hands. His slow breathing seemed loud in the silence.

''The war came,'' Don Calo continued after some moments. ''I confess that I was glad, for I was very eager to get away from my village and see more of the world. I was young and ignorant. But a land mine ended my adventures long after I had grown sick of them, and I was sent back to Castell'alto because my right arm was slow to heal. That was in 1943. And that was when I met Hugo for the second time.

''By now there were only women, children, and old men left in the village, and a few young men such as myself who had returned wounded from the war. And the Germans.

''The Germans were our friends, of course, in the beginning. Although the friendship perhaps existed only in the minds of Hitler and Mussolini.'' There was a sardonic edge to Don Calo's voice. He took a sip of his Marsala. "But by 1943 in Castell'alto even the pretense of friendship was gone. The Germans made no secret of the contempt they had for us. In the beginning they were merely hard, but when they saw the war slipping away from them they blamed us. They became brutal. They treated us as subjects, not allies.

"The German soldiers did not want to be in Castell'alto. They had nothing to do here but watch the coast from the tower. And so they were bored, and they resented us. There were not many of them, but for all that their commander, a certain Lieutenant Kappel, might have been the leader of a large battalion. He was a pompous, self-important man. And a man without humanity.

"Nevertheless, we lived together, the Germans and the Castell'altesi. Until the day a German soldier raped a young woman from Castell'alto. Afterward, he boasted of what he had done. The girl's brother, Luzzu, was thirteen, too young to go as a soldier, but old enough to avenge his sister's honor. The next day the body of the German was found lying beside the road outside the village, trussed up and butchered like the pig he was.

"An older man might have known it would be wiser to hide the body, but Luzzu was hotblooded, and he wanted to leave a sign of his vengeance. In so doing, he gave himself no time to escape. Of course, Kappel was quick to find out who had killed the soldier, and he ordered a search for the boy.

"We hid Luzzu in Casteddu, in the roof of one of the houses. They turned Castell'alto upside down looking for the boy but could not find him. They burned his house, and still he remained hidden. Then they searched Casteddu and the *castello* ruins. With no greater success. Kappel then gathered the people together in the piazza, in front of the church.

" 'Tell me where we can find Luzzu Pisciotta,' he said, 'and you may all go home. I will punish only the boy. But if you continue to shelter him, you share in his crime.'

"Kappel waited. No one spoke. Then he tried to persuade one of the children, a little boy of perhaps five or six, to tell him. He squatted down beside the boy, who was standing at the front of the crowd, holding his mother's hand. One of his soldiers spoke a little Sicilian, and he got the soldier to tell the child that he would give him candy if he showed him where Luzzu was.

"But all the children thought Kappel was the devil himself. Their mothers had told them so. He was very thin, with a long thin nose and yellow teeth, and his eyes were like cold stones.

He terrified the children. When Kappel put his hand on this boy's shoulder, the boy threw up. The vomit went all over Kappel's boots. We were too frightened to laugh, but one of the soldiers must have, for we heard stifled laughter from behind Kappel.

"He grew very angry then. 'You will stand here until you tell me,' he said to us. And he left us there—old people, pregnant women, babies—in the hot sun, with no water, nothing to eat. . . . An old woman collapsed and fell to the ground, but we were not permitted to help her. The youngest children cried. Still, we would not speak. The Germans had trampled on our pride for so long, they thought we had none left. But they were wrong.

"When darkness came, the women and young children were told to go home and gather their belongings. That night they were put on trucks and sent away. Later we learned they were taken to Trapani, where they were set free. But they were forbidden to return to Castell'alto. The men—every boy over the age of ten, the old men, and the few men such as I who could no longer fight—stood in the piazza until morning. There were perhaps twenty of us. At daylight, the Germans drove us like sheep up the mountain to Casteddu. We were not allowed to take anything with us, and they had confiscated whatever food and water they had found in the old town.

"Before we crossed the bridge, Kappel addressed us. He was a short man, and he stood on a rock to make himself heard above the wind. The sirocco was blowing. If it starts on a Friday, we say, it will blow for five days. It had begun three days before, on a Friday. The sirocco sometimes drives men mad. I think it had driven Kappel mad.

"He said, 'Give me the boy or starve to death. It is your choice. And when you are dead, I will string up your bodies by the feet, and let the flies eat them.' I still can remember his eyes as he looked at us. I knew that he was not seeing human beings in front of him, but only beasts to be broken to his will. A crow came down and settled on a rock above his head. The crow is the devil's creature.

"Then they forced us across the bridge into Casteddu.

"There were two soldiers already stationed in the tower of the *castello* who kept watch on the coast. Kappel placed two more at the mountain side of the bridge. They all had guns. He told us that they would shoot anyone who tried to come back across the bridge.

"This happened in the first week of July. We did not know then that the Allies would soon invade Sicily, although the Germans were preparing themselves for such an event. Hugo landed secretly on this coast to scout the countryside before the invasion. He knew the language, and of course he knew the area well. He got to know of what was happening in Castell'alto. The Germans made no secret of what they were doing to us—we would be an example to others. When Hugo heard that we were being held in Casteddu, he laughed and said that he could crack it open like a safe. Then he vanished. No one knew where he had gone. That same night a German officer in Trapani also vanished.

"By now we had been prisoners in the old village for three days. No one had yet died, but some of us were very weak. Above all, we needed water. Luzzu was hidden in the roof of one of the houses, and late at night one of us would visit him. But we stayed only a few minutes with him each time, for we were afraid that the Germans might take us by surprise.

"On the night of the third day, those of us who were stronger sat talking together while the others slept. We were by now so desperate with thirst that we talked of attacking the guards. It would have been suicidal, of course. No one spoke of giving up the boy. Luzzu himself offered to go to the Germans, but we would not let him. We knew very well what the Germans would do to him.

"We sat outdoors, near the gate of the *castello*, where the German guards could not see us. Because it was summer, the night was warm. If it had been wintertime . . . well, things would have happened differently.

"I don't remember which one of us noticed him first. Only that suddenly he was there. A man dressed all in black, standing a few paces from us. We were struck dumb. We could only stare at him, as if he had sprung from the stone itself. I was the first to recognize the boy from four years ago. Hugo. A grown man now."

Don Calo paused to pour some water from a pitcher into a glass. The silence in the room was profound; no one moved. When he had swallowed a little, he spoke again.

"At last, when we found words, we asked him how he had got past the soldiers. But he would not say. He only asked if we were all there, was anyone missing? A few of the younger boys and the old men who were weakest were sleeping in one of the houses. He told us to wake them. And then, when we were all gathered together, Hugo asked us to bring him Luzzu.

"There were those of us who were afraid to tell him where the boy was. They were not sure of him. But he said that without the boy we would not escape. He said we must trust him. And so we brought Luzzu to him. As I have said, Hugo is a very persuasive man.

"He had—what is the word—a canteen of water with him, and some dried fruit that he gave to us. There was just enough for a mouthful each. While we shared these, he opened the pack on his back. In the pack were two guns and the uniform of a German officer. He put on the uniform. Then, holding Luzzu by the arm, he went into the courtyard of the *castello*, where they could be seen by the two soldiers on duty in the tower, and called out in German. He was a scholar and he knew the language.

" 'Come down,' he shouted to them. 'We have found the boy.'

"The two soldiers looked down from the tower roof, saw Hugo in their uniform, saw Luzzu, and at once disappeared. In their eagerness, they never thought it might be a trap. The soldier Luzzu had killed was their friend, and I think they wanted to have some time with the boy before they handed him over to Kappel. Also, they had such contempt for us, they thought of us as weak and ignorant, incapable of tricking them.

"When they came out of the tower door, we were waiting. It was a simple matter to knock them out. Although some of us very much wanted to kill them, Hugo would not permit it. When a few argued with him, he said we would not leave Casteddu alive if we did. And such was his authority that we obeyed him.

"First we took off the soldiers' uniforms, then we tied them up. The two of us who were most like the Germans in size—Santuccio and myself—put on their uniforms. When we were ready, Hugo explained to us the rest of his plan.

"We did as we were told. We left him there, by the tower, and we crept through Casteddu to the houses that were at the end of the middle street, which led to the bridge. We hid ourselves inside the two at the end of the street, on either side.

"Now we had to wait.

"I remember how everything was clear, like day. It was very easy to see the two German guards on the other side of the bridge. Their rifles were shining in the moonlight.

"For two hours, we waited. There is a *trazzera*, an old sheep route, across Monte Castello from Casteddu to the *prato di Ve-*

nere. While the two guards were talking to each other, with their backs to the *trazzera*, Hugo came quietly down from the mountain. He had to get behind the guards, to make it seem as if he was coming up the path from Castell'alto. He was still wearing the German uniform.

"At last he succeeded. He ran toward the two guards as they stood by the bridge with their backs to him, shouting in German that the prisoners had escaped. At the same moment, Santuccio and I stepped out into the open street where we could be easily seen, and waved our pistols. We shouted the two words in German that Hugo had taught us to say. *"Komm! Schnell!"* And then we turned and ran up the street.

"Of course the guards thought we were the men from the tower. They ran across the bridge, and when they reached the houses the others who were hidden fell on them. There were no shots fired. Hugo was very pleased at this. The sound of gunfire would have warned the Germans in Castell'alto, of course.

"We dragged the Germans to the *castello* tower, where we had left the other two. Again, some of us wanted to kill them, but Hugo said we must not. He told us it would be very bad luck, and we needed our luck. Then he said something very strange. I have never forgotten it.

"He said, 'The lady of the labyrinth would be angry.' "

I had been listening, rapt, to Don Calo's story. But at these words I felt a shock of recognition running like a current through me, carrying me back to that long-ago birthday. I saw Hugo's face, the blue eyes that seemed to search past mine for something lost, and once again heard his voice as he touched the figure on my medallion: "Call her the lady of the labyrinth, Alison. She is a mystery. . . ."

"His face was in a shadow," Don Calo was saying, "so we could not see it, but his voice was very serious. He had taken off the uniform, and was wearing black again. He seemed at that moment almost like a priest. Someone set apart. I think we all felt it, for we did not argue with him.

"Then he told us to leave the Germans with him. He knew another way to punish them. He said we must go, at once, along the *trazzera* across Monte Castello to the *prato di Venere*. Then down to the bay. There would be a fishing boat waiting there for us. But we must hurry, and go silently. If he did not come within the quarter hour after we had boarded the boat, we were to leave without him.

"It was difficult, that climb, for we were very weak. But we made it, all of us together. And at last we came down into the bay. And the boat was waiting for us, as Hugo had said it would be. It was only a few minutes after that Hugo came himself.

"Later we heard the Germans were so angry we had escaped that they blew up the bridge. But within two days the Germans had no more time to think of us. On the tenth of July, the English and the Americans landed in Sicily. By the middle of August, the Germans were gone from our island."

The low, guttural, mesmerizing voice stopped and Don Calo picked up his glass of Marsala again. He turned it slowly around between his fingers, then drank off the remaining drops.

Jay was the first to speak. "Did anyone ever find out what happened to those four German soldiers?"

Don Calo leaned back in his chair and half closed his eyes, as though exhausted by his story. "Many years after the war, two boys from the village went into the cave in the *prato di Venere*. They became lost themselves, and after much time stumbled on two skeletons. The bones were lying on their sides, curled up, as if to protect themselves from something. Around the wrist of one was a watch. It was of German manufacture. Did the skeletons belong to two of the German soldiers? If so, how did they come to be in the cave? And what happened to the other two? These questions have never been answered. For myself, I have to confess I do not much care.

"One of the boys was no luckier than the Germans. The cave killed him. The other escaped."

Guidico, I thought. I glanced at Clio, who gave an almost imperceptible nod of her head, guessing and confirming my thought.

"As for your father," Don Calo continued, "he was naturally a hero to this village. To many, his appearance that night was a miracle, something that was not to be explained by any natural means. He had called upon the Madonna and she had saved us. That is who they thought he meant by the lady of the labyrinth. I myself was not so sure.

"Others thought that he had scaled the cliffs or dropped from the sky. Later we learned that the British had used gliders to land some troops in Sicily. As for me, I always wondered if he knew a way in through the cave. But he never told anyone how he had done it. Not even when he bought the *castello* from the Duke of Caltabella, and came to live in Castell'alto."

Don Calo's voice faded into silence. Through the hooded, opaque eyes, he looked at Jay and me in turn. "So long ago, it was, yet it is all still here.'' He tapped his forehead. ''I have not forgotten what your father did for us. Castell'alto will be forever in his debt.''

I didn't doubt him, but I wondered if at times that debt might become too heavy. It was a lot to owe to one man, your existence.

CHAPTER 17

Immediately after lunch, Elliot Carter tried to excuse himself in order to go ahead of us to the tower. "It'll give me a chance to get rid of the worst of the mess before you arrive."

Curiously, Don Calo would not allow this. "I am sure there is no need, Elliot. You are too much the perfectionist in such matters. And I imagine," he added, turning to Jay and me, "that you are eager to see the tower."

It might have been awkward, but he gave us no time to reply as he rose to his feet, dropping his heavy linen napkin onto the table. We all took this as a signal that our lunch with Don Calo had come to an end. Elliot seemed to accept Don Calo's interference in his domestic life with the same good temper that he had shown to Jay's proposal that we stay with him. He was remarkably unruffled for someone not only landed with unwanted guests but prevented from preparing for them. In an easygoing voice, he asked Clio if she would bring Jay and me with her to Castell'alto. "I've got the Jeep outside, but it's full of supplies, so Alison and Jay would have an uncomfortable ride with me. I'll wait for you in front of the church and we can go up to Casteddu together."

Clio frowned, and for a moment it seemed as though she was about to refuse. But instead she nodded, adding quietly, "It would be interesting to see Casteddu again. I haven't been there since Hugo left."

"Nothing's changed," Elliot said. "Matteo sees to that. Hugo's going to find everything just like he left it." He thanked Don Calo for lunch, said a cordial good-bye to Benedetta, who once again avoided his eyes, fiddling with one of her earrings, and left the room.

"I'm afraid we're putting Elliot to a lot of trouble," I said when he had gone. "I hope he doesn't think we care if the tower's untidy."

"I doubt that it is," Clio replied, as we all walked together through the house to the courtyard. "Hugo once told me that Elliot was the best cook-housekeeper he'd ever had. I think that might have been partly why he let Elliot stay on at the tower. Elliot has a gift for organization of all kinds." The expression on her face was innocuous enough, but there was an astringent note to her voice that implied more than the words alone.

Don Calo ushered us through the front door. "What Clio is too discreet to tell you is that Elliot's tidying may only be in a manner of speaking. A romantic housecleaning, if you like. There have been rumors of a female visitor to the *castello*."

"But if that's true," I protested, "Jay and I really will be in the way."

Don Calo only shrugged. "Perhaps your visit will be timely. I hear he tires of the liaison and may be looking for a way to end it. Elliot, you must understand, is a young man who has many valuable qualities, but fidelity is not among them."

This remarkably blunt statement seemed almost a warning, but to whom was unclear, for Don Calo looked at all of us as he spoke.

"Whatever the truth of the matter is, Alison, I wouldn't worry about it," Clio said evenly. "Elliot is very good at finding ways to do what he wants, despite the obstacles. In fact, he thrives on obstacles. Wouldn't you agree, Don Calo?"

Don Calo's smile was ironic. "I am afraid that you are right. He has not yet learned that some obstacles are there for his protection, and are better left alone."

There was a sudden movement of bright color as Benedetta stepped forward into the sunlight. She put her small hand on her uncle-in-law's sleeve. She had a headache, she said, and wanted to lie down. She looked at Don Calo almost beseechingly, as though for permission.

The old man inclined his head. "It would be well to be rested before you drive back to Palermo."

"But you—" Benedetta began, then seemed to think better of whatever she had been about to say. In a subdued voice, she said good-bye to us and went back into the house, her sandals clicking on the stone steps.

We made our own farewells. As Jay and I thanked him for his hospitality, Don Calo told us that if we changed our minds about staying in the tower, we would be welcome at Lupaia. Once again, we told him how grateful we were for the invitation, while privately I swore that nothing would induce me to accept it. More than once during lunch the old man had seemed disturbingly like a puppet master, twitching invisible strings while he watched the way we all moved. There was nothing specific I could point to, only my impression that at times we danced to a complicated pattern of his devising. He observed Elliot, especially, with what struck me as more than a host's concern for his guest's comfort. Don Calo had never been anything other than friendly to the younger man, but it was as though Elliot's reactions interested him in the way an insect fascinates a small boy. You couldn't help feeling that the benign curiosity might shift at any moment into something dangerous for the bug.

The explanation might lie, I reflected, in that little scene I had observed under the table. I was certain that Benedetta's coldness to Elliot had been a charade performed to disguise her true feelings from the rest of us, and from her formidable uncle-in-law in particular. But judging by Don Calo's treatment of her, and by what he had said about Elliot's romantic entanglement, it seemed reasonable to conclude that he already had some idea of what his nephew's wife was up to with his nephew's partner. If so, that might explain why he had not resisted Jay's insistence that we stay in the tower. Jay and I would be Elliot's unwitting duennas.

Just before we drove away, Don Calo rested his hand on my open window. The impenetrable eyes looked at Jay and me in turn. "Your father is not a man to be frightened for himself," he said gravely. "And you must not fear for him. You will see him again." He nodded once to Clio, turned, and walked slowly back to the open door of his house.

It was a ten minutes' drive from Lupaia to Castell'alto. When the main road left the plain, it began to climb the mountain, circling to the northeast around a small valley, a landslip of stone and dirt that in places came perilously close to eating away the road itself. Great tufts of red valerian grew out of the rock like tongues of flame; an eagle swept down from a distant pinnacle, circled, and disappeared into the blue; a huge tortoise, perhaps the eagle's intended prey, crawled across the road while Clio kept her foot on the brake. And then, as it emerged from between two heaps of rock, we saw Castell'alto at last.

I'm not sure what I had expected a place "forgotten by God" to look like. Desolate and bleak, at the very least. But although the setting was undeniably dramatic—an unbroken line of narrow houses curving along the crest of a ridge with the mountain peak at its back—the domestic touch of laundry strung out to dry, flapping like multicolored banners from balcony railings, made the little town seem reassuringly ordinary. Ragged strips of sunlight and shadow moved slowly across tiled rooftops the color of burnt earth.

Up close, Castell'alto had the harsh, rugged quality of the countryside surrounding it, stony, all angles and rectangular slabs. It tumbled down its steep main street like a rock slide off the mountain, the two-story houses of concrete and stone slammed tight against each other, fissured by dark, crevicelike alleys that led to the upper reaches of the town, where there were streets too narrow, Clio said, for a car. At two-thirty in the afternoon, the town lay silent and seemingly deserted, its citizens all indoors observing siesta. We passed a butcher's, where a spindly lamb's carcass hung from an iron hook in the window, a bank, several grocery stores, all closed. In front of a bar, some old men were playing cards at a table in the shade of a tattered blue awning. They turned to stare, and as we drove slowly past one of them hawked and spat into the dust.

But although it lacked Erice's air of well-being, there was nothing squalid about Castell'alto's simplicity, no sign of the terrible poverty we had glimpsed in Palermo. Some of the houses had new additions, many looked freshly painted, most had television antennas. Jay said, "It doesn't look as bad as I thought it was going to."

Clio shifted down as the gradient changed to a terrifying one in four. "Don Calo's money and influence have made a difference. There are proper drains now, and glass in the windows. Casteddu will give you some idea of what it was once like."

The upper end of the main street ended in an oblong piazza dominated by a monumental building of yellow stone that was decorated with delicate iron balconies supported by carved stone grotesques. It seemed far too grand for so elemental a place as Castell'alto. Clio explained that the palace had been built by the Bolognese noblemen who were the feudal overlords of Castell'-alto during the Spanish occupation. Opposite was an equally elaborate baroque church, porticoed and pillared and pitted with scars where the plaster had fallen away in large chunks, revealing the coarse stone underneath. Weeds grew in the cracks of the steps leading up to it. These two buildings loomed over the little town below, dwarfed in their turn by the mountain above.

Elliot was waiting for us beside the Jeep, which was parked

in front of the church. He made a striking picture, all blond good looks and smiling affability, and he seemed as out of place in Castell'alto as the palace and the church.

"The Jeep can squeeze up that alleyway," Clio said as we got out, "but not the Land Rover. Either we'll ride with Elliot the rest of the way, or go on foot."

On foot as it turned out, for the Jeep was crammed with boxes. "I'll send Matteo down for it later," Elliot told us. "Casteddu's only about a fifteen-minute walk from here."

The church and palace marked the limit of the town. Beyond them the cobblestone street degenerated into a stony dirt lane rutted with wheel tracks, which curved up and around the mountain, running alongside terraced gardens of an acre or two carved out of the steep slope. Each plot of ground had a little hut built of bamboo, several fruit trees, vines, a vegetable garden. But we soon left these behind and came out onto the open mountainside, where the yellow heads of giant buttercups and marguerites waved in the coarse, windblown mountain grass that grew between huge boulders, tangled up with tendrils of purple vetch. Beside the track thick clumps of prickly pear were a hazard for the unwary—Jay let out a yelp when his bare arm brushed by a spiny ear. To our right, the mountain shelved away in a series of narrow ledges to the hilly plain below. At this height, the hills looked like so many bumps on the ground, and the roads that wound between them like skinny, dusty worms.

"You know," Elliot said as we walked along, "I'd never heard that story of Don Calo's before. What about you, Clio?"

She shook her head. "But it explains why Hugo can do no wrong in Castell'alto. I thought it was just because he enjoyed Don Calo's protection."

"Did you know why that was?" I asked her. "I mean, why Don Calo had given Hugo his protection?"

"Only that they had known each other when Don Calo lived in New York. Don Calo had a tile works, and apparently Hugo saw to it that Don Calo's tiles ended up in buildings he designed. I always assumed that was the reason Don Calo looked after him here in Sicily. I never realized it went deeper."

The track rounded a bend and suddenly widened into a flat expanse of stony, dusty ground. Clio and Elliot gave us no warning, and Jay's gasp of surprise echoed mine. Ahead of us, on a solitary spit of rock, framed by the sea and the sky, was Casteddu. The "dead town."

It was hardly a village, let alone anything so grand as a town, simply a small cluster of red-roofed gray cubes perched on a plateau high above the sea, utterly silent, apart from the wind and the sound of the sea, and utterly empty. It was as if a race of giant children, playing with building blocks, had constructed a miniature village, then abandoned it for some other amusement, forgetting to clean up after themselves.

Casteddu sat on a flat-topped promontory, which was separated from the mountain itself by a gorge roughly twenty yards wide and perhaps ten times as deep. The side of the mountain had bulged out in a small mesa, which seemed to rise from the sea, as though some volcanic pressure had pushed against the mountain's skin, forcing a spur of stone from its flank. Three sides of the mesa were sheer walls of rock that fell away to the cobalt-blue sea, a thousand feet below. On the eastern side, the side we were facing, the rock face sloped down to the bottom of the gorge and was thinly coated with scrub. But only a particularly agile goat or mountain climber could scale that cliff, and would finally be stopped by the smooth, windowless house walls, inseparable from the rock on which they were built, which formed the battlements of the dead town. There was just one way into Casteddu, across the modern metal footbridge that spanned the chasm, guarded by a single, wind-tormented pine.

Off to our left, the track that we had followed from Castell'-alto mounted steeply through the boulders to curve and disappear around the mountainside above us. It was the *trazzera*, Elliot told us, the path that led to Don Calo's meadow. The path down which Hugo had crept in the darkness to take the German soldiers by surprise.

No man is a hero to his children, they say; but as I turned to follow Elliot across the footbridge into Casteddu, I was remembering the long-ago words of Hugo's extravagant, taffeta-clad lover. "In another age, Alison, your father would have been an epic hero. . . ."

I had a moment's vertigo when I looked down at the boulder-filled chasm below; the bridge seemed so flimsy, creaking a little at our weight. "How did they do it," I said over my shoulder to Clio, who was following behind me, "the people who built the castle and the village? How did they get the materials across?"

"Well, of course there was a much better bridge once, a real stone bridge. I suppose it was the one the Germans blew up." She pointed down into the gulley. "It's down there, in pieces. Hugo had this bridge built when he bought the place."

Casteddu itself was merely three lines of tiny houses joined wall to wall that fanned out from the bridge, trisected by two short and narrow streets, alleys really. There were only three dozen or so buildings, simple one-story row houses of plastered stone, some with just a gaping door as their only source of air and light. Where there were windows there was no glass, only a wooden shutter to keep the wind out. We looked into several of the houses as we walked down the center street, but they were all the same, a single dirt-floored room with a ceiling so low that you wondered if the inhabitants had been able to stand upright. Most were littered with debris and smelled of damp. One house, close to the bridge end of the street, looked in better shape than its neighbors; its padlocked door and wooden shutter were each painted a bright, oily blue.

It was impossible to enter Casteddu and not think of the drama played out on this desolate plateau forty years before. In one of these houses a young boy had hidden, terrified and alone. Starving, tortured with thirst, Don Calo and the others had lain down on these stones, waiting for death. Men with guns had stood watch over them. And then Hugo had appeared, risen out of the rock itself to save them.

A half-ruined arch tufted with miniature wildflowers framed the remains of the castle. It stood at the western end of the dead town, poised above the sea at the very limit of the rock. The round Saracen tower, three stories tall, rose like a massive pillar of gray stone into the blue sky, softened by the flowering vines and small green bushes that sprouted from chinks and crannies in the stone. Its crenellated battlements brooded over a wide, dusty courtyard patterned with the low lines of grass-covered stone that marked the remains of what once had been the castle's mighty walls. After the great castle was demolished, Elliot told us, its stone had been quarried to build the houses of the dead town or carried down to Castell'alto. Apart from the tower, all that endured were the crumbling ramparts that enclosed this end of the plateau, two small outbuildings used now as storehouses, and a grassy mound next to the tower with a half-ruined flight of stone steps going down to a bolted wooden door. "That leads to the arsenal, an armaments room, where weapons were stored," Elliot said. "Or so Hugo told me. I've never been in it. It's locked, and I've never found a key for it."

As we walked over the place, Elliot quickly sketched its history. "The castle was really a fortified monastery built in the twelfth century, in the remains of a Saracen fortress. In the fourteenth century, some minor warlord attacked and pretty much destroyed it. Time and the locals did the rest. Hugo bought it in the fifties from that absentee duke Don Calo told us about. Apparently the guy had blown all his money at Monte Carlo. But Hugo never had the time to do anything with this place until a few years ago. He talked about rebuilding some of it, making it into a sort of Taliesin West transplanted to Sicily—you know, Frank Lloyd Wright's community of disciples in Arizona. He planned to fix up the abandoned houses, make them livable, turn some into studios. That's why a couple of them are pad-locked. We keep construction materials in them.

"When he's got it fixed up the way he wants it, Hugo plans to invite a few choice students to study with him in the early summer." Elliot paused, and laughed. "I always thought this was the perfect place to dispose of up-and-coming rivals. Invite them for a seminar, then heave-ho over the edge."

"Like Daedalus and his nephew," I said.

"How do you mean?"

"Daedalus was supposed to have killed his nephew by push-ing him off the Acropolis. He was afraid that the boy was going to be better than he was. The Athenians condemned him to death, but he escaped to Crete."

"It's strange that you should mention him," Elliot said. "Hugo had a theory about Daedalus and this place. Most of the time it was pretty clear that he realized Daedalus never existed, was just a way of explaining how technology or certain arts came to Sicily. But every now and then Hugo would talk about him as though Daedalus was real to him."

"What was the theory?" asked Jay.

Clio answered for Elliot. "In a way, the golden honeycomb is a symbol of it. He thought that if there had ever been anything like the honeycomb, some remarkable work of art that inspired the legend, then this is where it might have ended up when the priestesses hid Erice's treasure."

Elliot turned away, but for an instant before he did, I saw the oddest smile on his face. I interpreted it as the patronizing smile of the realist for the dreams of the imagination, and at that mo-ment I felt an almost instinctive dislike of him. I put the dislike down to a simple jealousy of someone who had been on such easy terms with Hugo that he knew his dreams.

I wondered why I didn't also feel jealous of Clio, who after all had a relationship with Hugo that must have been far more complicated than Hugo's was with Elliot. Perhaps because, despite her strength, she struck me as a woman who had lost something, a woman who for all her independence was lonely.

Elliot led us across the courtyard to its western end next to the tower, where there was a gap in the walls with a tumble of stones beside it. He pointed to the horizon. "Africa's over there. You can see it on a very clear day."

Jay was leaning over the edge of the wall, straining forward to get a good look down at the sea. It was all I could do to keep myself from reaching forward to take a firm grip on his belt. To my relief, he straightened up again, wiping the dust from his hands onto his jeans. In a dreamy voice, he said, "I'll bet the Romans watched the Carthaginian fleet set sail from here. Maybe even—"

Before he could finish, a harsh bray shattered the silence. We all jumped, except for Elliot, who laughed and apologized for the racket. "That's Orlando. The donkey. We use one of the abandoned houses as his stall."

"Orlando? As in the puppet hero?" I asked, amused.

"The very same. Orlando Furioso, to give him his full and proper name. Hugo called him that because it's so inappropriate. Orlando's the polar opposite of the original, absolutely passive and unexcitable. And normally very silent. He must have seen Matteo. Like calling to like."

Clio gave him a stern look. "That's not very kind, Elliot."

"Maybe not. But true. Have you ever known anyone as silent and as stubborn as Matteo, except Orlando? And don't they look just a tiny bit alike, with those big brown not very intelligent eyes, and that long face?"

But Clio refused to smile. "I don't think you give Matteo enough credit. And I'm fond of him."

"I am, too. Don't get me wrong." Elliot was suddenly serious. "I don't know what I'd do without Matteo and Orlando. Between them, they keep this place going."

"Why do you need a donkey?" Jay asked him.

"That track we came up here on is a mess of mud in the winter and early spring. Even the Jeep can't handle it. So we use Orlando to carry groceries and supplies. He's useful in a lot of ways."

As he spoke, a young man appeared under the ruinous arch, leading a donkey by the halter. He was wearing blue jeans and a violently magenta T-shirt with the words PARTY ANIMAL printed in black across the front.

"Matteo!" Elliot waved at him to come over to us. "Matteo

understands English. He can even speak it, when he speaks at all, but it's a brand all his own, a mixture of what he learned from Hugo and what he's learned from comic books. He's addicted to G.I. Joe.''

"Where does he get those around here?" I asked.

"I'm afraid I'm his supplier. I have a source in the PX at Comiso, the American base."

"I'll bet you're to blame for the T-shirt, too," Clio said. "That's not Matteo's usual style."

With a wink to Jay, Elliot said blandly, "I like to think that in my own small way I'm continuing a long and honorable tradition of American goodwill in Sicily. We've given so much to this island. I realize that comic books and T-shirts can't compare to Lucky Luciano and Cruise missiles, but I've got plans for bigger things."

"I know about Cruise missiles," Jay said, "but who's Lucky Luciano?"

"He was a famous American gangster in the thirties, born in Sicily. When the Americans invaded Sicily in 1943, they released Lucky Luciano from prison in the States and flew him back over here. They thought they could use his contacts with the Mafia to control the island. Under the Fascists, a lot of Mafiosi were thrown into prison, but the Americans set most of them free again." He gave a cynical smile. "So you see, the Sicilians have a lot to thank us for."

Clio sat down on one of the large stones to remove a pebble from one of her sandals. "You know, Elliot, I'm always amazed at how well you've done here, for someone who doesn't speak Sicilian. Matteo's English is fluent in comparison."

"I've never found the language a barrier. Maybe because I grew up in California, where you do most of your talking with your body anyway. Besides, there's Giudico to translate."

Clio refastened her sandal and looked up at him, her gray eyes intent. "We've got to have a talk about Giudico, you and I. Can you come and see me tomorrow morning?"

Elliot's surprise was obvious. "Sure. Around ten?"

"Fine."

Matteo was slowly crossing the courtyard toward us, with his head bowed and a sullen look on his face, as if he was sorry we had noticed him. He looked about twenty, stockily built, with thick, dark hair falling over his forehead. There was some justice to Elliot's comparison with the donkey. The two of them plodded along together with their heads down, shaggy, stolid, and sturdy-looking.

But when he lifted his head and saw Clio, Matteo gave a shy smile, which lightened the long, lugubrious face. The smile broadened into a touchingly transparent pleasure as Elliot explained who Jay and I were. A strong smell of donkey and sweat filled the air as he shook our hands enthusiastically.

Elliot went on to say that we had just been with Don Calo, who had told us that Hugo was coming back to Castell'alto sometime in the next few days. As he listened, Matteo's expression, or rather lack of expression, never changed. When Elliot finished, Matteo glanced at Clio, as though for confirmation; she gave a quick nod of her head, smiling. He made a curious sound, like a small sigh, but whether of pleasure or relief or astonishment wasn't easily discernible.

"It's great news, isn't it, Matteo?" Elliot prompted him.

There was a glint of surprise in Matteo's eyes as he nodded, as if that went without saying. He looked uncomfortable, shifting slightly from one foot to the other, but he stood there as patiently as Orlando. In a faintly exasperated tone of voice, Elliot asked him to fetch the Jeep from Castell'alto and bring the supplies in it to the tower. Matteo nodded again, gave Jay and me his shy smile, and turned to go.

"That should give him time to control his excitement," Elliot said. "You wouldn't believe it from the dumb-Sicilian-peasant act just now, but he worshiped Hugo. He used to follow him around like a puppy. I think he would have slept outside Hugo's door, if he'd let him. He was pretty broken up when Hugo left. Now, let me show you inside the tower. You ready, Clio?"

At first she didn't seem to hear him. She was standing apart from the rest of us, with her hand shading her eyes, looking at the sea. The wind ruffled the dark hair around her face, softening the hard line of her jaw; at that moment she looked very beautiful, but almost painfully remote, a solitary isolated by boundaries of her own making. In that, she was like Hugo. Perhaps that had been what attracted them to each other, the recognition of a kindred spirit.

"Clio?"

When she did respond, it was as if Elliot had roused her from a daydream. Her voice sounded abstracted, at a distance. "I've got to leave, Elliot. Perhaps the rest of the tour could wait until later. Jay and Alison will have to come with me—their car is at my place."

Jay cleared his throat. "If it's all the same, I'd like to stay here. I've got all my stuff with me—I didn't leave anything back at the hotel. I sort of figured we might end up staying here. Do you mind going without me, Alison?"

"No . . . no, of course not." Although I was dubious about leaving Jay behind, I realized that, after all, he was probably safer in Castell'alto than anywhere else. And now that he was finally here, he wanted to stay. "What will you do?"

"I'll put him to work," Elliot said. "Like I said, the generator is giving me trouble. We've got no electricity and no hot water. You could give me a hand with the repairs, if you'd like, Jay."

"Great."

As Elliot seemed amenable to the idea and Jay enthusiastic about helping him, I agreed, somewhat reluctantly. "All right, then. I should be back in a couple of hours."

They went off in search of tools, and Clio and I walked back through the silent houses of Casteddu. If Elliot had seemed out of place in Castell'alto, I thought, he was even more so up here. I asked Clio how he managed to make a living. "I mean, what sort of work could someone like that do here?"

"Elliot's an entrepreneur," she replied. "He has a dozen different irons in the fire at once. Selling my honey is only one of them. I don't know that any of them brings him in much money, but it doesn't cost him that much to stay in the tower. Hugo wanted it lived in, and he left money behind in an account to pay basic expenses like upkeep. If you're asking me what keeps him here, I've no idea."

I had, however—Benedetta Coccalo.

We lapsed into silence, and after a moment heard the approach of the Jeep. Matteo raised his hand to us as we stood to the side of the path, to let the Jeep pass. As we continued down the track, Clio seemed abstracted. Perhaps the visit to Casteddu had been difficult for her, perhaps that was why she refused to enter the tower. Some of the ambivalence toward me I'd sensed in her the day before seemed to have returned, too, and I wondered why. I was also trying to find reasons that weren't sinister for Hugo's inexplicable failure to contact her, a person who presumably had been close to him. We had only Don Calo's word that Hugo intended to return to Castell'alto, Don Calo was the only one who had seen him, had talked to him, who knew something of his plans. There was too much secrecy to give me any sense of comfort from Don Calo's purported friendship for Hugo.

Suddenly, I found I was very glad that Luke was waiting in Erice. I wanted to talk it all over with someone who had no connection to Castell'alto and was not in Don Calogero's debt. Both Clio and Elliot owed too much to the man.

As we drove out of Castell'alto, Clio asked me what my impression of Don Calo had been. I was careful as I answered her. "That he's a very complex man. Not easy to know. I hope he's right about Hugo coming back soon."

"Like Hugo, Don Calo's a man of his word," she replied. "Do you know what his name means? It's from the Greek. It means 'noble old man.' " I couldn't tell if there was irony in her voice or not. For a while she concentrated on the driving, and then she asked me, "What will you do now? When you're back in Castell'alto, I mean."

"I suppose all we can do is wait. I have a few more days of my vacation left, and I can't leave Jay there alone. Besides, I'd like to make sure that Hugo really is all right."

This was almost a question, but Clio ignored it. "And after that?"

"I'll go back to Germany, and my job."

There was a silence. Clio gave me a long look. "Alison, I have to tell you—" She faltered, then said abruptly, "What I said earlier, about how Hugo and I met, well, it wasn't the truth. Actually, we first met years ago. We—we were very close for a while. But your father cast such a shadow . . . I felt overwhelmed. Unable to be myself." Her mouth tightened. "As I told you before, I spent a lot of time when I was young running away from things. Hugo was one of the things."

I waited for her to go on; I felt she wanted to say more, and after a moment she continued. "Well, I made a real mess of my life. And then, after years of drifting, I decided to give my original love, archaeology, one last try. I wrote a piece for a journal. Someone who had known both of us sent it on to Hugo. He wrote to me, and we began to correspond. Eventually, he told me about Casteddu, asked me if I'd be interested in working with him there. And so I came to Sicily."

I remembered the inscription in Hugo's book: To Clio, the muse.

Clio said, "Hugo's not a sentimentalist. If I hadn't shown I was capable of working with him he would never have bothered. He's not like Don Calo—'for old times' sake' means nothing to

him. You have to prove yourself with Hugo. Then he's interested."

I said, "I know."

She smiled at me then, a smile of sympathy, almost of complicity.

For the rest of the drive we spoke of other things, the pleasures
of keeping bees, the beauty of the countryside. She knew a
remarkable amount about traditional Sicilian customs, many of
them taught to her, she said, by Donna Anna—Signora Solina.
We had reached her house now, and as we got out of the
car, she pointed to a small mulberry bush that grew by her gate,
thick with tiny dark berries. "Donna Anna gave me that bush
when I first moved here. Have you ever tasted a mulberry?"
When I shook my head, she plucked a handful of berries and
gave them to me. They were simultaneously sweet and tart. "An
offering of fruit, eating it together, can be a gesture of peace
here, of reconciliation." She said this lightly enough, as though
it were simply a curious fact I should know.

I said, "I'm beginning to think that everything in Sicily, every
word, every act, has some sort of significance. It must make life
here more than a little intense."

Clio laughed. "But always interesting."

As I got into my car, she added, "If there's anything I can
do, let me know, will you? I'll probably come up to Castell'alto
tomorrow, just to make sure everything's okay."

"Fine. It'll be good to see you again." I meant it; despite the
doubts, I found myself liking Clio, wanting to trust her.

The return to Erice was uneventful. Now that some of the
urgency of the past four days had begun to ease, I had time to
think about Luke. It suddenly occurred to me that he might not
be waiting for me in Erice. I could hardly blame him if after our
desertion of him that morning he'd decided to abandon us to our
fate, but the possibility of not finding him there was so painful
that it told me a great deal about feelings I had done my best to
suppress.

When I arrived back at the Hotel Ginestra, I asked Signor
Indelicato whether anyone had left a message for me. He said
he thought so, and turned to the pigeonhole that held my room
key. An envelope was lying angled in the small square of wood.
My name was written across it in Luke's oversized scrawl.

At first, I couldn't bring myself to open it. "Apart from the
person who left this," I asked Signor Indelicato, "has anyone
else been asking for us?" He shook his head, and said not to

his knowledge. With an apology for not letting him know sooner, I told Signor Indelicato that my brother and I were leaving Erice but would of course pay for that night as it was already past the checkout time. He expressed polite regret at our departure, and said that naturally we were free to leave when we chose. After I paid the bill, I put my luggage in the trunk of the BMW. Then I opened Luke's letter. It was very brief.

"Dear Alison," I read, "I've gone into Palermo. Should be back late afternoon. I'm staying at the Albergo Moderno. L."

I opened my guidebook, found the Albergo Moderno marked on the street plan of Erice, and set off in search of Luke.

CHAPTER 18

The Albergo Moderno attractively failed to live up to its name.
It was a small pensione in one of the old houses in the center of
the town, with a leafy courtyard cool with the sound of trickling
water and the rustling of doves in the trees. In the shadowy front
hall, a young woman with grave, Byzantine eyes was on her
knees, washing the colored tiles of the floor. Signor Kenniston
had not yet returned, she told me; I was welcome to wait. I
thanked her and said I would return later. Feeling vaguely let
down, I wandered into the main square, a scrap of open space
on a shelving slope.

As I looked about, debating whether to use the time to play
the tourist or simply to sit in a café watching the miniature world
of Erice literally slide by, I noticed the local museum that lay
on the opposite side of the square.

It occurred to me that here I might find the answer to one of
my questions, the origins of the coin in my medallion. Hugo
had called the figure on the coin a mystery; to me, the medallion
itself symbolized a mystery, that of my relationship with my
father. Uncovering a historical past seemed almost simple compared to understanding an emotional past whose complications
and revelations multiplied as it receded. Hugo had given me
something precious; I might never know what it meant to him,
but at the least I could learn more about the object itself.

I was certain of two things: that Clio's coin and mine were
similar, if not identical, and that Hugo had given Clio hers. If
there were other coins like ours on display in the museum, it
would be proof of a sort that Hugo had found or bought the
coins locally. I could ask Clio herself if she knew where the
coins had come from originally, but would I get a straight answer
from her? On the whole, I doubted it.

But a sign posted by the museum door stated that the museum

was closed. The hours were from eight-thirty to two, and it was now almost five. I was standing there indecisively, wondering what to do next, when the door suddenly opened and a man stepped out. He glanced at me, looked me up and down, clearly summing me up as a tourist, and said in English, with the half-concealed satisfaction of a certain type of bureaucrat at giving bad news, "You are too late, Signora. The museum is closed."

As he pulled some keys from his trousers pocket, I asked him if he could tell me where I might find the curator or director of the museum.

He replied that the director was away. "In his absence, I am responsible for the museum." There was a touch of self-importance in this announcement. He was a dapper little man with hair carefully combed to hide a bald spot, and a small, neatly trimmed mustache. He sorted fussily through his keys until he found the one he wanted and fitted it to the lock. When I still lingered there, he added, "But as I have said, the museum is closed for the day."

I persisted. "I'm sorry to be a nuisance, but I'm trying to find out if a coin I own comes from this area. I thought there might be one like it in the museum. Perhaps you could help me?"

He hesitated, his lips pursed, and at first I thought he was going to tell me to come back when the museum was open. Finally, he relented a little. "It's possible. I know something about coins." He said this almost grudgingly, as if torn between a desire to thwart a troublesome tourist who would not take no for an answer and a simultaneous, contradictory urge to help someone who might actually have a serious question. "Do you have the coin with you?"

Although the medallion was hidden under my blouse, it seemed wiser, until I knew more about it, to say that I did not. "But I can describe it. It's a small coin, about so big." I made a circle with my thumb and forefinger. "There's an odd sort of pattern on one side, and a standing woman with a bee hovering above her on the other. I was told that she's the Goddess of Love. There's some writing, too, that looks a bit like ancient Greek. The first letter is exactly like a capital E, so I thought that maybe the word might mean Eryx."

The look on his face had gradually changed from one of slightly bored superiority to alert interest. "A bee, you say. You're sure it's a bee, not a bird?"

"I suppose it might be a bird. It looked more like a bee to me, though."

He became almost fulsomely polite. "But why are we standing here in the sun? You must come inside. There is an office where we can talk." He opened the door and stood aside to usher me in, then led me up a wide marble staircase and through a series of rooms filled with paintings and objects in glass exhibition cases to a small office, where he invited me to sit down in a chair beside the desk. I glanced around the slightly shabby room, at the old prints and yellowing, curled-edged maps on the walls, the neat rows of books behind the dusty glass of the bookshelf. A newspaper and a greasy, crumpled paper napkin sat on one corner of the desk. The curator pushed them into a wastebasket with an absentminded gesture. From the top drawer of the desk he took out two pieces of paper and a pencil and gave them to me. "If you would be so kind as to draw this coin for me, Signora. The side with the woman first, please."

I did as he asked. As I handed the first drawing to him, I said that I had enlarged the coin four or five times. He looked at it without comment for a minute or so, stroking his bristly mustache with a forefinger. When at last he spoke, there was a suppressed excitement in his voice, and his small brown eyes stared at me fixedly. "You remember the letters correctly? They are as you have drawn them?"

I nodded.

"Where did you get this coin?"

I was prepared with another lie, which I brought out with a certain amount of shame. "I bought it at an antiques fair in Germany. There was an exhibition of coin dealers. It was expensive, but I thought it looked so pretty." I hoped this sounded naive enough. "The dealer told me it was supposed to have come from Erice. I'd never heard of this place before that. When I came to Sicily on vacation I promised myself I'd try to find out more about it."

He placed the drawing flat on the desk in front of him. "And where is the coin now?"

"Oh, I left it at home. I make it a rule not to travel with valuables."

"Very sensible." But I thought he sounded disappointed.

"Do you think the coin dealer was right? Is it from Erice?"

Again, he looked at my drawing. "I cannot say, Signora. But it's possible. I would have to see the coin itself, of course, to know if it were genuine. And even then . . . Coins are often counterfeited.

"But this inscription, the word you say is on the coin, is a legend found on other early coins of Eryx. The letters are Greek, of course, but we have never been able to decipher it. All we know is that it is some Indo-European language probably used by the Elymians, the first civilized people to live in this area. Ancient legends claimed they were the descendents of the Trojans.

"As for the woman with the bird, or bee, it is possible that she is Aphrodite. This is almost exactly as she appears on other coins of Erice, from the late fifth century before Christ. I can show you an example from our own collection. I say that it must be a bird, not a bee, because the white dove was a symbol of the goddess. Each year, from this mountain, her priestesses released a single white dove attended by a flock of red doves. After nine days they returned to the sanctuary—the goddess had come home from her annual visit to her birthplace in ancient Libya." His voice held an affectionate familiarity, as though he were speaking of a good friend, lately back from a holiday trip. "You see, before she was Aphrodite, she was Ashtoreth, or Astarte, the great Phoenician Goddess of Fertility. The bee, too, was associated with her cult, but I know of no local coin that pictures it. In general, the Greeks represented Eryx on coins with Aphrodite, or Heracles leaning on his club—there was also the belief, you see, that Heracles founded Erice—"

As he seemed about to launch on a description of yet another myth, I interrupted. If I hadn't been afraid of missing Luke's return, I might have listened more patiently, for as he talked about the past he lost some of his pompousness and became almost appealing in his enthusiasm for his subject. Firmly, I said that I would draw the other side of the coin for him.

This proved to be more difficult without looking at the coin itself—I couldn't be sure that I was remembering the pattern exactly as it appeared on the coin. This time, when he saw my drawing, the curator was obviously baffled, but excited. He took a pencil and beside the coin drew the single figure which, when multiplied and interlocked, made up the pattern. It was a swastika. "This," he said, "is one of the oldest symbols of mankind. Hitler degraded it, but he understood that it had an ancient power and that is why he chose it. It appears around the border of a coin we have here in the museum. But arranged like this—no. I am reminded of coins that were found at Knossos, with such a pattern." He looked across the desk at me almost expectantly.

"Knossos? Isn't that on Crete, where they found the palace of King Minos? And the labyrinth, of course." Then I understood. "Do you think the pattern on my coin is meant to be a labyrinth?" Was that why Hugo had called Aphrodite the lady of the labyrinth?

He smiled, much as a teacher might at a bright pupil. "Perhaps, if I am not reading too much into it, the very labyrinth of Daedalus himself. Do you know that he is supposed to have built the walls around Erice, and a bridge to the temple site?"

I nodded. "And a golden honeycomb for the goddess."

Tentatively, as if he were trying out on me a theory that he had only now begun to formulate, he said, "A honeycomb in itself is a labyrinth, is it not—for all but the bees?"

We stared at each other. His eyes looked into mine with a yearning that was almost frightening in its intensity, and for an instant I wished I had said nothing to him about the coin. I knew he couldn't see the medallion through the dark purple cotton of my blouse, but I felt the metal hot against my skin, hanging like a lie around my neck. Then the look in his eyes faded, replaced by a wistful regret. "I would give much to hold your coin in my hand, Signora."

I said, "You don't think there might be a coin exactly like it in another museum somewhere in Sicily?"

He shook his head. "If it is genuine, this coin of yours is unique. But I did not ask you . . . Is the coin silver or bronze?"

"Neither. It's gold."

He blinked and sat back in his chair. "We have no gold coins from Erice, Signora. That is not to say there were no gold coins— but none have been discovered. In Sicily, you see, gold was normally used only in times of crisis, when invasion was threatened and the supply of silver cut off. There were no silver mines in Sicily—silver had to be imported. Accumulated treasures of gold were sometimes gathered together and melted down to pay the soldiers or bribe the attackers."

"Couldn't this coin come from a period like that?"

"It's possible. Erice was attacked many times, by Sparta, Carthage, and Rome among others. Perhaps such a coin was minted during a siege. If the coin is very late fifth century, then perhaps when the Carthaginians invaded the island."

A theory of my own occurred to me as I thought about all he had told me. "I read that Erice's treasure has never been found. Maybe the explanation is that it was melted down—and the golden honeycomb with it. Maybe that explains the pattern—as a sort of commemoration of what they had to destroy in order to survive." Perhaps, even as I spoke, a part of that myth lay next to my skin.

"It's possible." Signor Possibile—that was the only possible name for the man—gave a small sigh. "It's a pity I can't see the coin itself. Perhaps you could send me a photograph, a good one, when you return. I would be very interested. The museum might be able to make you an offer for it."

"Supposing it was genuine," I asked, "would it be valuable?"

He pursed his lips, as though the question were slightly distasteful. "Much depends on the condition."

"It's in perfect condition. As if it had never been used."

"If that is so, then yes, it is very valuable. But more than the monetary value would be its value to us, to scholars. There are no other coins from Erice that I know of that represent Daedalus' labyrinth or link the goddess with a bee. There was a cult of bees here, of course. Are you familiar with the Greek myth of Eryx?"

"I've read a bit about it."

This was no deterrent, it seemed, for he proceeded to tell me his own version. "Aphrodite fell in love with Butes, a bee-keeper, one of the Argonauts. Some say she did this to make her lover Adonis jealous. She bore Butes a son, Eryx, who became king here and built a temple in his mother's honor. It was as famous in the ancient world as Delphi, and as mysterious. I am sure that you know that beautiful passage in Aelian, the Greek historian?"

When I shook my head, he looked faintly shocked at my ignorance, then leaned back in his chair, and quoted with closed eyes: " 'Upon Aphrodite's altar the fire burns all the day long and into the night. The dawn brightens, and the altar shows no trace of embers, no ashes, no fragments of half-burned logs, but is covered with dew and fresh grass which comes up again every night.' "

Almost dreamily, he went on, "For a thousand years, men braved the perils of the sea to bring the Goddess gifts. Thucydides wrote that the treasure was so great that the people of Segesta tricked the Athenian envoy into believing it was theirs, in order to persuade the Athenians to become their allies. And now nothing of it remains." He gave a small sigh and looked as mournful as if it were a personal loss. I found myself liking this curious, fussy little man with his passion for the past. "If your coin is genuine,'' he went on, ''I would very much like to know where it came from.''

''I wish I could tell you,'' I replied, this time honestly, ''but I was hoping you would tell me.''

''Have you the address of the man from whom you bought it?''

I shook my head and got to my feet. I was beginning to grow uncomfortable with his questions and my lies. ''It was very kind of you to talk to me, but I'm afraid I've taken up too much of your time.''

''Perhaps you should take your coin to a museum,'' he said, as he rose from his chair with me.

''Maybe I'll do that when I get home. Now, I really must go.''

''If you will give me your name and address, Signora, I will write to you in the event that I learn more about this coin of yours.''

Reluctantly, for by now I liked Signor Possibile, I wrote a false address with my name on the piece of paper he held out to me. As we walked out of the office, he showed me a coin in the museum's collection that was similar to mine, but of a dull silver, with a seated Aphrodite and a dove with spread wings above her. It was unmistakably a bird, not a bee, and I was more than ever certain that the creature on my coin was no bird. I thanked Signor Possibile, whose real name, printed on the card he handed me at the door of the museum, turned out to be far more prosaic, and promised to send him the photograph of the coin.

I left feeling mildly guilty at the deception and, apart from the short local-history lesson and some romantic theories, not much wiser. If the coin had come from this area, as it must have, how was it that someone as well up on local history as Signor Possibile had never seen one like it? Were they unique, Clio's coin and mine?

Although I was eager to look at my medallion in the light of all Signor Possibile had told me, I waited until I was back at the Albergo Moderno. This time the pretty young woman with the Byzantine eyes told me that Luke had just returned. While she went to fetch him, I sat down on a sun-warmed stone bench beside a pot of basil and took out the medallion.

I stared down at the side with Aphrodite. The creature hovering in the air above her hand was unmistakably a bee; the double set of wings convinced me that I was right about that much. I turned the coin over. In my drawing, I had duplicated the pattern almost exactly. Now, thanks to Signor Possibile's suggestion, it was no longer simply a curious pattern of lines etched on the soft metal surface. It was a tiny golden labyrinth. As I stared at it, the sunlight glinting off the gold and the sweet smell of basil heady in the heat of the courtyard, the labyrinth swam and spun like a mandala in front of my eyes.

When I heard footsteps crossing the tiles indoors, I put the medallion back inside my blouse. Luke's face was unreadable as he came out into the courtyard. The white suit and panama hat today were replaced by neatly pressed blue jeans and a tennis shirt. He looked fresh, as if he had just come out of the shower, and his dark hair was shiny in the sunlight.

"You'd think I'd have learned my lesson the first time you gave me the slip," he said, finally smiling a little as he reached me. "But you have such honest eyes, Alison. Or maybe I'm just gullible."

"I'm sorry we tricked you, Luke." I looked away, down at a bird pecking for insects in the grass that grew between the cobblestones.

"Perhaps I asked for it. Whose idea was it? Jay's?"

"I'm not blaming Jay. I could have said no."

"I'm not blaming Jay either, or you. I'm just glad you're okay. Did you find Hugo?"

I shook my head and stood up. "I'll tell you all about it. Is there somewhere we can talk?" The young woman had come out of the house and was sweeping the stone steps that led up to the second-floor arcade, within earshot.

"I know just the place." Luke took my arm. "It's not far, a couple of minutes' walk." As we went out into the street, he asked where Jay was. "You can tell him I don't bite."

"I'm not sure he'd believe me, after last night. But it isn't that. He stayed in Castell'alto. I'm going back there myself. I've already checked out of the hotel." I described our lunch with Don Calo and told Luke about his suggestion that we stay at Lupaia, and Jay's insisting, instead, on staying in the tower. "There's someone else living there. A man named Elliot Carter."

"Here we are," Luke said suddenly, leading me through a small garden to a terrace set out with tables under a striped awning. Flame-colored blossoms of bougainvillaea hung like miniature Japanese lanterns against a white stucco wall. We were the only customers. A waiter brought me a lemonade and Luke a beer, and went back to doze on a chair in the sun.

Luke poured half of his beer into the glass. "I think it's time you told me everything, don't you? You can start with San Teodoro. I did some asking around when I was in Palermo today, so I know there's an American woman living there. I heard she was a friend of Hugo's."

I did as he asked. This time I left nothing out. When I finished, Luke leaned forward, holding the beer bottle between his hands on the tabletop. "Did you find out where Hugo is now?"

"No." I took a deep breath. "But he's coming back. According to Don Calogero, anyway. Of course, we only have his word for it. No one else has seen or heard from Hugo. Not even Clio or Elliot."

"This Elliot, what's he like?"

I described Elliot, adding, "He's a sort of entrepreneurial jack of all trades. Among other things, he was helping Hugo organize his papers so that he could write his memoirs. Hugo hadn't got very far—Libya interrupted. He also had plans for Castell'alto." I told him about the Sicilian version of Taliesin West. "Jay has sworn all along that Hugo never intended to stay in Libya for long, and more and more it looks like he's right."

Luke said, "I did some checking up on Don Calogero while I was in Palermo today."

"What did you find out?"

"That he has what amounts to a private fiefdom up there. He owns a lot of the land and he controls local politics. But in his case, it seems to be a benign dictatorship. He's done a lot of good in Castell'alto."

"Did you find out anything about a nephew named Giudico?" I told him about Giudico's relationship with Clio and Elliot, and about his and Clio's falling out.

But Luke had heard nothing about him in Palermo. "Only about the two sons. They run a large tourist agency in the city, which has a fleet of tour buses, charter boats, that sort of thing. Now, tell me about Clio Hunt."

"I'll tell you what I know. Which isn't much." When I'd finished, I added, "She's an enigma. I can't make her out at all. She's friendly with just about everybody, but she keeps to herself. At a guess, I'd say her relationship with Hugo was romantic as well as professional, but she's very closemouthed about it. She's been helpful to Jay and me—but at the same time it's as if she wants to keep her distance, as if she can't make up her mind about us. I feel the same way about her. She and Hugo were working together on this theory she has about a local cult, an offshoot of the one here at Erice.'' I paused to drink some lemonade. ''You know, it's funny, but bees keep turning up.''

''How do you mean?''

''Well, first with Clio, then this cult. And this.'' I fished the medallion out from under my shirt, took it off, and handed it to him. ''Hugo gave it to me.'' I told him the circumstances, then went on to describe what I had learned from my discussion with Signor Possibile. ''Clio has a medallion that seems to be identical to mine, though I only glimpsed the side with the woman and bee. If there are these two, maybe there are others. . . . ''

There was a gleam of humor in Luke's eyes. ''It sounds as though you've been bitten by the treasure seeker's bug.''

''Clio says it's the Sicilian disease. Looking for treasure under every rock. It must be contagious. Seriously, though, you have to wonder where this coin came from. And more and more, I'm inclined to think Hugo found it somewhere at Casteddu.''

Luke gave me back the medallion. ''Well, in a day or two you may have all your answers.''

''When Hugo returns. Yes, I suppose so.'' I slipped the medallion back over my head and hid it back under my shirt.

''Do you feel safe at the tower?''

I thought that over for a moment. ''Yes,'' I replied at last, ''I do. As you said, it's Don Calogero's fiefdom, and he's Hugo's friend. If anything, I suppose we're safer there than here. Despite your protection.'' I smiled. ''Don Calogero wasn't the monster I expected. In fact, he was quite nice to us. And Elliot . . . well, he's charming,'' I finished lamely.

Luke raised an eyebrow, but said only, ''You're going back there now?''

I nodded. ''What will you do?''

''I've booked a room at the Pensione Bella Vista. In Castell'-alto.''

I gaped. ''Don Calogero told me there was no place to stay there.''

''I have the feeling pensione is too grand a name for it. The man at the tourist board in Palermo who made the reservation for me was dubious. He said it was the lowest possible classification of room. It probably has bugs.''

''I'm sure Don Calogero will be told you're there. You don't think he'll find it suspicious?''

He held up his camera. ''I'm taking photographs of Sicily. For a book.''

''Do we know each other?''

"I think it's better if we don't. Will you tell Jay?"

I said that I would. "Won't you miss Erice?" I added, teasingly. "Giudico Coccalo said that the women in Erice are reputed to be the most beautiful in Sicily. The girl at the Albergo Moderno certainly was lovely."

"I hadn't noticed," Luke said. "A bad sign."

"Why do you say that?"

But he merely scribbled something on a piece of paper, then signaled to the waiter for the bill. "Here's the telephone number of the pensione, and the phone number of the consulate in Palermo. In case you need it. Phone me tomorrow morning at the pensione. If I'm not in, leave a message—but not your name. If I don't hear from you by midday, I'm coming up to Casteddu."

As we rose to leave, I said, "There's something else I should tell you." I described Bernd's warning phone call, and my fear that he might somehow be involved with the Libyan terrorists.

Luke dropped some lire notes onto the tabletop. "Renner undoubtedly knew them. But we don't think his involvement went any deeper than his rhetoric." His smile was ironical. "Of course, hot air is combustible—as Renner may find out someday."

We walked together to my car. As I opened the door, he put his hand on mine. "Be careful, Alison." Then he kissed me gently on the mouth. "That's to tell you that I'm here because of you, not your father. In case you still had doubts."

I looked up at him. Though his voice was light, there was something, the trace of an emotion I couldn't put a name to, that made me falter. "Luke, I—I'm grateful that you're here, but, beyond that, well, I just don't know what I feel. I've had too many unfamiliar feelings stirred up these last few days. It's hard enough to sort those out."

He smiled. "It's all right, Alison. I'm not asking for anything."

I got into the car and drove slowly out of the square. In the rearview mirror I could see Luke standing there, watching me out of sight, and when his image was gone, I felt alone.

CHAPTER 19

When I drove into the little square in Castell'alto, Matteo was sitting on the stone steps that led up to the church. His T-shirt struck a frivolous note against the sober setting of gray stone and crumbling plaster, and emphasized the equally sober expression of his face. As I got out of the car, he stood up and walked slowly over to me.

"I come to give you my hand."

The way he said it, with a grave formality, made the offer to help me with my suitcase sound like a marriage proposal. Amused, but grateful, too, that I wouldn't have to carry the suitcase up to the *castello* by myself, I thanked him and warned him that it was heavy.

"No problem." He swung the suitcase lightly from the crook of one finger, to confirm his words. From his well-muscled arms to his broad, sturdy back, it was fairly evident that Matteo was someone for whom physical burdens would rarely present a problem. He looked as strong as a bull. The words scrawled across the T-shirt were ludicrously inappropriate, and yet I could see why they had appealed to Elliot's malicious sense of humor. There was something inescapably animal about Matteo. Perhaps it was simply that the body was so much more in evidence than the mind. But I wondered if this was a fair assessment. Matteo had spent a winter alone and unprotected in the mountains, Clio had said; at the very least, he had the considerable skills of a survivor.

As we began to walk along the path, I told Matteo that I felt lazy letting him carry the suitcase. "I've seen elderly Sicilian ladies with heavier loads than mine on their heads."

"But you are not Sicilian," he said simply. As though that in itself explained away and excused my weakness.

"Clio told us that you worked with my father," I said, after a few minutes' silence. It occurred to me that this might be my only chance to learn something from Matteo, and that I would have to get started if I was going to overcome his reluctance to talk. "What sort of work did you do?"

"Everything. For Don 'Ugo, I do everything."

I smiled. "Then you must have been a great help to him."

"Yeah, sure. I was top gun."

Startled at first by this description, stated as a simple fact rather than a boast, I remembered the G.I. Joe comic books. "And now you help Elliot?"

"Yeah, sure," he repeated, without visible enthusiasm.

"You used to live in Casteddu, Signora Hunt told me. What made you leave?"

He shrugged. "Don 'Ugo left."

But Elliot had remained, I thought, and wondered whose idea it had been that Matteo move down into Castell'alto, and why. "Were you surprised when my father went to Libya?" I asked him.

As he glanced sideways at me, I saw for the first time a flicker of feeling in his eyes. I was shocked to realize that it looked very like pity. He grunted, and shifted the suitcase to his other hand. "Is not my business." I assumed he meant that it wasn't his place to question what Hugo did, not that he didn't care. I also assumed I wasn't going to get much out of Matteo by indirection. Deciding that I had nothing to lose from a blunt approach—he probably already took me for a typical nosy American female, but might be willing to overlook this as I was Don 'Ugo's daughter—I said, "What do you think of Elliot Carter, Matteo?" A little longer in Sicily might have taught me the uselessness of direct questions like this.

Abruptly, he stopped. He turned his dark, unreadable gaze on me and said quietly, "Be careful, please." Then, almost as an afterthought, he pointed to the path ahead. "Is dangerous here."

I was walking on the outside of the path, close to the cliff edge, attracted by the morning glories that grew in a pink-and-white profusion over the tumbled rock. A few feet to my right, there was a nasty drop to a clump of prickly pear on an outcropping of stone. A fall wouldn't necessarily be fatal, but it would be unpleasant.

Without another word, Matteo turned and plodded on up the path. I followed a short distance behind him, in good Sicilian female fashion, and for the rest of the way to the *castello*, held my tongue. It hadn't sounded like a threat, I told myself, not really, but I was sure that he was doing more than alerting me to the dangers on the path. Letting me know, perhaps, that he didn't like questions. Or did the warning have something to do with Elliot Carter?

As we entered the dead town, there was a gentle whicker of recognition and Orlando's face appeared in the unshuttered window of a house close to the one with the blue-painted door. I assumed it was his stall. Matteo stopped to feed the donkey something from his pocket. There was a gentleness on Matteo's face as he patted the donkey's nose that was difficult to reconcile with the man who a few minutes earlier had seemed so unnerving. I reached out and scratched Orlando behind one hairy ear. Silently, Matteo handed me a chunk of carrot and jerked his head in the direction of the donkey, so that I wouldn't mistake the proper recipient. I fed it to Orlando, who responded by blowing a sudden warm and very moist gust of air against my arm. When I laughed, Matteo gave the sweet smile that redeemed his ugliness and made his bulk less intimidating.

The wide courtyard of the *castello* was empty and silent when we came through the ruined arch. Sea gulls, perched in a row along the waist-high remnants of the encircling wall, watched us approach the tower. The late afternoon sun shone on the tower's western face, picking out the tiny wildflowers that blossomed in the crannies, gleaming on the bright green shutters, turning the windows to gold; it made the solitary mass of stone seem almost welcoming. The arched, ironbound door was shut, but opened easily enough when I put my hand to the latch. "They must be inside," I started to say to Matteo, but when I turned around he was already trudging away, head down. My suitcase was sitting in the dust behind me. I picked it up and went into the tower.

Inside, I called out, but there was no answer, and for that I was grateful. It gave me time to absorb the shock of finding myself so unmistakably in Hugo's domain.

There are personalities so powerful that they leave their stamp on any place they inhabit. Their presence is always there, like a spoor, whether or not they themselves are. Hugo made each place he lived in his own, no matter how resistant, how unlikely, the surroundings. Not so much a "home" as his territory.

I looked around. The whole of the first floor of the tower was a single enormous circular room with a high, beamed ceiling and four windows set in deep embrasures of stone. But the way in which the furniture was placed gave a sense of small rooms composed of sofas, chairs, and tables poised against the large round space, defined and embraced by the Oriental carpets that Hugo used here as both tapestries and rugs.

It was a comfortable room, no small achievement for what was, after all, an uncompromisingly stony space; with simple, well-proportioned furniture softened with cushions. It was also richly decorated, thanks in part to the beautiful rugs, which were hung in an arras around the curving wall, thrown over the backs of the white cotton-covered sofas, or spread across the stone floor. There were electric lights, but old-fashioned brass oil lamps stood on several small, dark wood tables, and a large, branching, black metal candelabrum, studded with fat white candles, hung on a chain from the ceiling. There was no need for either the candles or the lamps yet; the last of the day still streamed in from the western-facing windows that stood open on the far side of the room, their wooden shutters pulled back and caught with metal hasps. The golden light touched small objects, picked out a single blue Islamic tile on a tabletop, glanced off a porcelain bowl in a pale shade of pure, translucent green.

In one corner of the room, near the tower door, there was a kitchen area with an open stone hearth and a bread oven built into the wall, a small modern two-burner stove that ran on bottled gas, a sink, and a scrubbed wooden table, all efficiently combined into an alcove formed by two massive wooden cupboards set at angles to the wall. A pile of oranges was heaped in a white china dish on the table, and dried herbs hung from metal hooks suspended above the wide hearth. The area was scrupulously clean and tidy.

I thought of Clio's living room. In many ways, the two rooms were a study in contrasts, Clio's restrained, almost ascetic, Hugo's verging on the sensual in its richness.

Despite Hugo's nomadic life, possessions clung to him like barnacles on the hull of a ship. He sailed on, oblivious, trailing Chinese screens, African masks, Tanagra figurines, porcelain, carpets, whatever caught his eye or had been given to him by a grateful client. Yet, as far as I knew, all these beautiful things never seemed to weigh him down or worry him. Apart from the carpets, he hadn't made the slightest effort to build a particular collection. Nevertheless, all his ''spoils,'' as he called them, made a harmonious whole, or at the least, lived together comfortably. Perhaps because each reflected some aspect of Hugo's character. No matter how disparate and contradictory these aspects sometimes seemed, they coalesced successfully into a single personality.

Possessions apart, I would have known without being told that Hugo lived here, for the first things that struck my eye on entering the room were some architectural drawings, pinned onto one of the rugs hanging against the wall. Hugo liked to have the rough plans of whatever he happened to be working on at the time enlarged and hanging where he could see them around him. As ideas came to him, he scribbled notes, made changes, added and rejected, later incorporating the ideas into the proper plans. I wondered what these were the drawings for. Whatever it was, it, too, must have been abandoned for Libya.

There were stone steps to a second floor, and I was debating with myself whether to continue exploring when I heard voices outside. A moment later, Jay and Elliot came into the room, carrying groceries.

"So here you are," Elliot said when he saw me, dumping several string bags filled with parcels down onto the kitchen table. "We were wondering. Did Matteo bring you up? That figures. The guy's impossible. I asked him to bring you to the café in Castell'alto, to meet us there."

"Really? He told me he was there to help me with my suitcase. The door wasn't locked when we arrived, so I came on in. I hope that was all right." I wondered why Matteo had brought me straight to the tower. Was it a mild form of rebellion at Elliot's orders? Or was it the desire to give me the chance to see the place for myself, a sensitive assumption on his part that I would want some time alone in the tower?

"Sure, of course it was okay," Elliot was saying as he began to unpack the string bags. "Jay and I saw your car, so we figured you'd come up here. Have you had to wait long for us?"

"I got here just before you did." I watched Elliot unwrap a long, gleaming fish with blue-and-green scales like a mosaic. "What a beautiful fish. What is it?"

"Dinner. I hope you like fish?"

"Yes, I do. But I was really wondering what kind it is."

"Your guess is as good as mine. I just take what looks freshest. Hugo'd be able to tell you. He knows the Sicilian, Italian, and English names for almost everything on this island."

Irritation was plain in his voice, and I glanced at Jay, who was standing behind Elliot. Jay shrugged and raised his eyebrows.

Elliot noticed my suitcase. "You haven't found your room yet?" he asked me. When I repeated that I had only just arrived and hadn't had time to look for it, he seemed to cheer up and replied that in that case he would take me to it at once. He wiped his hands, picked up the suitcase, and led the way up the stone steps that curved along the wall. These were steep and narrow, and I was glad of the smoothly curving handrail of some dark wood that ran along their outer side. The handrail was supported by straight wooden balusters, but when I looked more closely I saw that several of them were like miniature pillars with elaborately carved capitals. Tiny grotesque wooden faces, animal and human, peered out from thick carved foliage, lurking under the overhang of the railing.

"Amazing, aren't they?" Elliot said. "The old man who did the carving came from Castell'alto. Apparently, he was inspired by the gargoyles at Monreale. Originally, there wasn't any railing, but some visitor or other slipped and almost broke his neck, so Hugo had it built about seven years ago. The old man wouldn't take any money for his work, either. For some reason, he was in Hugo's debt."

"Maybe he was one of the men Hugo rescued from the Germans," I suggested.

Jay called from the top of the stairs. "Look at this one, Alison." He was pointing at the last baluster, larger than the others, at the top of the stairs. "Do you recognize him? I did, right away, when Elliot showed me earlier."

Framed by curling vines, a massive male head formed the crown of the last baluster. The face was wonderfully carved, each feature exaggerated yet still realistic, large-boned and gaunt, with a massive prow of a nose, a stubborn, thrusting chin, and high cheekbones below eyes that were deep-set and filled with a fierce intelligence. Only the mouth seemed at odds with the rest, its wide, sensual lips slightly compressed in the beginnings of a mordant smile. It was a compelling face, a face that occasionally appears in stone looking down from some medieval cathedral doorway, the face of an ascetic who knows at first hand the sins of the flesh. Hugo's face.

Elliot smiled at me. "Hugo said that when he first saw it he was tempted to take an axe to it. He said it was like looking into your own soul. But he got used to it. Even grew to like it." Elliot flicked a finger at one cheek of the carved head.

On the landing, a simple flight of open-treaded wooden stairs continued curving up to a third floor. I was putting my hand on

the railing when Elliot said, "This is your room, Alison." He
had opened one of the three doors that led off the landing.

It was a small room shaped like a wedge of pie, with a shuttered window in the outer wall. There was a single iron bedstead
with a white coverlet and a heap of blankets at the foot, a night
table with a light and a thermos, and a wooden chair painted
with flowers, similar to those I had seen at Clio's. A small, rose-
pink Persian carpet was the only bit of luxury in the room.

"Jay's room is next door," Elliot said, as he set my suitcase
down. "I hope you'll be okay. I warned you it was a bit spartan.
I'm sorry the generator's on the blink, but there's a flashlight in
the drawer of the table if you need it in the night."

Everything was fine, I told him. "I hope we haven't turned
you out of your own room?"

"Jay's got that. But it doesn't matter. I'll sleep on one of the
sofas downstairs."

"And upstairs?" I asked. "Is that where Hugo worked?"

He nodded. "It's too bad, but I've lost the key. I've been
looking for it for the past two days. It'll turn up." The words
rolled glibly off his tongue, with only the faintest stutter of *f*'s.
His amiable green eyes held mine, as if challenging me to pursue the matter further.

"It's a pity," he continued, "because the best view is from
the tower top. But you'll see it sooner or later. Now, while you
get settled, I'll go organize dinner. The bathroom's next to Jay's
room, by the way. The plumbing's the pull-chain variety, but
there's running water—and it even runs to hot when the generator is working. There's plenty of cold, though. The water comes
from cisterns, which collect a lot during the rains, so don't worry
about using too much. There's a pile of towels—"

Abruptly, he stopped speaking, his eye caught by something
in the corner of the room. He crossed swiftly over to it and I
saw a long dark green lizard scuttling up the wall. Elliot caught
it by the tail, and before Jay or I could stop him had flung it out
the window.

Turning, he saw our shocked expressions, and gave an apologetic shrug. "Sorry. But I can't stand those things inside. Outdoors, well, they're part of the landscape, but—" He paused.
From below, a man's voice was calling out his name. I thought
I recognized the voice.

Elliot went to the top of the stairs. "*Ciao!* Just a minute,
okay? I'll be right down." He turned to Jay and me. "Excuse
me. Business calls."

He ran lightly down the stairs and we could hear the two men exchange some few words in an undertone. Then they went outside. I looked at Jay. "That was Giudico, wasn't it?"

Jay nodded. "It sounded like him. Do you think he's come to tell Elliot about that scene with Clio this morning?"

"Probably. I'll bet they're busy outside getting their stories straight before Clio asks Elliot about it." I began to unpack, while Jay sat on the bed.

"Do you believe what he said, about losing the key to Hugo's room?" Jay asked me after a moment. His voice was low.

I went over and closed the door. I wasn't sure if our voices could be heard downstairs, but I didn't want to take the chance. "You think he's lying?" I asked Jay. I did myself, but impressions weren't proof, and now that we were in the tower, and would have to spend the night here, I didn't want to start making mysteries out of thin air.

"Well, it just seems a weird coincidence that the key's lost when we show up," Jay said. "I can't help thinking he's got something up there he doesn't want us to see."

Trying to make light of it, I said, "A harem of old girl-friends?"

Jay entered into the spirit of the game. "Or maybe those missing German soldiers have lived up there all these years, thinking that the war's still on. Maybe Elliot's charging them room and board."

I laughed at the grotesque idea. "Maybe so. Elliot strikes me as someone who knows a good thing when he sees it."

"Yeah, and I think he saw it this afternoon," Jay said. He picked up my shampoo bottle, skin lotion, and toothpaste and began juggling them.

"You noticed?" I was surprised. He must have seen the subtable footplay at lunch, too.

"I can usually sense that sort of thing," Jay replied with a man-of-the-world air. "He's got good taste." This was said almost shyly.

"Well, she is pretty," I began. "Those dimples . . ."

Jay looked taken aback. He missed the toothpaste, but grabbed the two bottles in time to avoid a disaster. "Not Benedetta," he said scornfully, setting my things down on the bedside table. "I meant you. Old Elliot fancies you. He asked me a lot of questions about you while we were working on the generator. Wanted to know if you had a boyfriend, that sort of thing."

Now I really was surprised. I think most women have some

sort of antenna that tells them if a man is interested in them, and mine hadn't picked up the slightest signal from Elliot. "What else did he want to know?" I asked casually.

He looked thoughtful. "Let's see. . . . Well, for one, he asked what sort of work you did at the embassy. And he wanted to know if I'd met any of your friends. That sort of thing."

"What did you tell him?"

Jay grinned. "This is Sicily, remember? I'm supposed to protect your honor. I didn't tell him anything."

I laughed, then looked around in vain for somewhere to hang my clothes. "Tower life is romantic, but there's one big drawback. No closets." My clothes would have to stay where they were in the suitcase. As I put my shoes under the chair, I said slowly, "You should know, Jay, that I saw Luke this afternoon, when I went back to Erice. He had already lined up a place to stay in Castell'alto—some sort of pensione—and he's going to be there tonight. I think it's better if we don't tell anyone about him, okay?"

To my relief, Jay accepted this without protest. "I guess it's a good idea. You trust him. And there are so many things that seem weird about this place. . . ." He wandered over to the window and stood looking out.

I wondered if he was regretting the impulse that had set him on this journey. But once again he surprised me. He turned around with a smile on his face, and said, "But I like it here. You know, I'm really glad we came, Alison. For the first time, I feel like we're getting closer to Hugo. He doesn't seem so remote anymore. Maybe it's just hearing everyone talk about him—Clio, Don Calo, Elliot. And seeing the tower. It makes him real again. Do you know what I'm saying?"

I said that I did.

We had just begun to be aware that a delicious smell was drifting up the stairs when Elliot called us down to dinner. The table was already set with Sicilian earthenware plates, a bottle of wine, and a loaf of fresh bread. On the stove, the fish was poaching in white wine with a bay leaf floating on top. Elliot pulled a strand of pasta from a large pot and tested it for doneness. Then he drained the water off, dumped in some chopped-up tomatoes, herbs, and grated cheese, stirred briefly, and put a generous helping on each plate. As we ate, we talked generally about life in Sicily for an American. He made no mention of his visitor.

"I like the kind of mental chess that goes on all the time

here," he told us as he twined the tagliatelle around his fork. "It's a challenge. You almost never see your opponent's moves, so you don't find out until later whether you've won or lost. Sometimes long after the game is over. And in order to do business here, you have to win more than you lose. So you've got to learn a lot of unwritten rules. But once you understand them, it's a very liquid marketplace. Some of these people would do very well on Wall Street.

"Sicilians are pragmatists, and I respect them for it. You know what they say? It's better to be a devil with a pocket full of money than a fool with five cents. And if they call you *tre volte buono*—triply good—they're not telling you what a fine person you are, they're insulting you." He grinned.

I contrasted Elliot's cynicism with Clio's more generous feelings about the Sicilians. And I thought of Rosalia and her grandmother. I wondered if Elliot judged all Sicilians by this harsh measure.

"Where are you from, Elliot?" Jay asked him.

"No place I'd ever want to go back to." He smiled to take the bite from the words. "I grew up in a little town north of San Francisco and I escaped to UCLA when I was eighteen. I should finish up my degree, but school really isn't my thing."

Jay digested this. "So when Hugo comes back, will you stay here?"

"Probably not for long. I've got plans. What about you two?"

Jay glanced at me. I said, "That'll depend on Hugo. If the past is anything to go by, we'll spend a couple of days together, then get on with our lives. Jay will go back to school and I'll go back to my job."

"You two don't know how lucky you are," Elliot said. "My old man was always around when I was growing up. Always."

Jay took this literally. "Did he work at home?"

"You might say so." Elliot gave a small smile. "He was a captain, but the navy gave him early retirement. For overindulging a taste for discipline. Nothing they could court-martial him for, just enough to make them nervous. But that meant he didn't have anyone but his wife and his youngest kid—me—to order around. And he loved giving orders. But what he really enjoyed was finding out you hadn't followed them. That meant he could enforce Discipline. With a capital D." Elliot's face was mildly amused at the memory. "He was into punishment, my old man. You could even say he had a gift for it."

As he pushed back his chair and got to his feet, he added,

"Some people can't understand how I can live up here alone. You know what I tell them? Up here, no one gives me orders." He gathered up our plates. "I'm going to take the fish out now. In one piece, I hope."

Elliot hadn't sounded in the least bitter as he told us of his father; his voice was cool, remote, as though he was describing someone else's childhood. I felt a small shiver of pity.

"Did you know that the tower is supposed to be haunted?" Elliot asked as he brought the fish to the table.

"What haunts it?" Jay asked eagerly, as relieved, perhaps, as I was at this change of subject.

"A beautiful woman. I'm sorry to say she's never bothered to haunt me. But night fishermen claim to have seen lights up here when no one's in the tower." When I asked him if anyone knew who the ghost was, he replied that she was the wife of the French count who lived in the *castello* in the thirteenth century, when the French ruled the island. "The countess was gorgeous and her husband was insanely jealous. Count Jean had the habit of locking his wife up in the tower room whenever he went away on one of his expeditions around the countryside oppressing the locals. He put water and food in the room with her, then locked the door and took the only key and the servants away with him.

"Unfortunately for the countess, Jean was in Palermo during the Sicilian Vespers. Do you know about that?" Jay and I shook our heads. "The French weren't popular, mainly because of men like Jean. Anyway, on Easter Tuesday in 1282 at the hour of Vespers, a French soldier stopped a bride on her way into church to be married. He insisted on searching her for concealed weapons. Well, even in those days the Sicilians weren't too crazy about other men touching their women, so this was the final straw. They went on a rampage and murdered every Frenchman they could find in Palermo. Including Count Jean.

"When someone finally thought of the countess, and broke the door down, she had starved to death. They found her by the battlements, with the half-chewed sole of her shoe clamped between her teeth. The locals say she walks the battlements when the moon is full."

Jay's eyes were wide. "Maybe she's the lady of the labyrinth! The one Hugo said would be angry if they killed the German soldiers."

"Maybe." Elliot stood up, and held out his hand for our plates. "Why labyrinth, though?" But none of us could answer that.

After dinner, we did the dishes together, talking about the States and what we missed about them. Elliot said he missed Sunday afternoon football. "Real football, the way Americans play the game." He made his voice deep and mock-tough. "You know, the kind of game where you can enjoy a little brain damage and spinal injury along with the touchdowns."

Jay laughed, and the laugh turned into a wide yawn. He apologized, but I said that I was tired, too, and that I at least was going to have an early night. We thanked Elliot for supper, and said good night.

Upstairs, before Jay went into his room, I told him, "Lock your door, Jay, okay?"

He promised that he would. He gave me a brief, bone-crushing hug, then turned and went into his room.

CHAPTER 20

I closed the door to my room and went over to the window. The shutters stood wide open to the night. The warm, languid air was rich with the smell of the sea, thick with insect noises that somehow underlined a profound silence, the deep, elemental isolation of water and rock and darkness. Without the light of day, it seemed as if only the thin veil of tower stone remained to separate me from all that was primitive, unknown, mysterious.

Sicily, the dead town of Casteddu, the tower within the ruined walls, each was enclosed within itself like concentric rings in a maze of solitude. They were islands of stone, with the secret loneliness that all islands hold at their hearts—this island of earthquakes more than most, perhaps, where even the solid rock was not to be trusted.

Rosalia's words came back to me: "Sicilians say, 'You play alone, you never lose.' " Was this why Hugo loved it here? Hugo, who never lost because he cast off the wives and lovers, the children, the countries, all that threatened to hold him down, tethered to the ordinary, to dull routine. That isolation, that threat of quaking rock, might give a shiver of excitement to a man for whom all other pleasures had grown stale. And working for Qaddafi, the unpredictable, an earthquake in human form— did that offer an even greater stimulant?

The wine at dinner, I told myself, combined with the hour and the atmosphere of the place, were making me fanciful. Like an antidote to the poison of my imaginings, the words of Donne's famous meditation whispered in my ear, and I repeated them softly to myself as I undressed. "No man is an island . . ."

I stood for a while leaning against the windowsill, to watch the full moon rise like a great molten globe out of Africa. As it spilled its silver across the water, the image of the countess in her prison room above came into my mind. How many African moons had swelled and dwindled while she waited at her window, how many ships had she watched sail past, before she abandoned hope? When I thought of her, it was easy to understand why threats and danger failed to persuade Jay into giving up his search for Hugo. Anything was better than mere waiting.

I slept badly when I finally went to bed. Perhaps it was the moon, flowing like a white river into the tower room, that made me restless, that tossed me on waves of choppy dreams. A strange flotsam of doves and bees and golden coins strung on an endless necklace drifted in and out of these dreams, until I found myself climbing a steep slope in a misty darkness, some great weight on my back. When the dream shifted, I was standing before a desolate, ruined tower, its door shut and barred. As I hammered desperately to be let in, the bars gave way and the door swung open onto a void. Suddenly, a veiled figure rose from the emptiness, its hands reaching out for me.

Terrified, I sat bolt upright in the bed, clutching the sheet. I had no idea where I was, and this frightened me almost more than the dream itself. Everything seemed bathed in a coldly surreal white light. Only when I saw my dusty sandals lying on the floor, reassuringly prosaic, did I take in the rest—the clothes heaped on the painted chair, the opened suitcase—and remember. Gradually, my heart stopped hammering and the dream receded, with a small backwash of fear. I looked at my wristwatch; it was one in the morning, and I was wide awake.

While I sat there staring at the pattern of shadows cast by the moonlight on the wall opposite the bed, I heard a small noise outside my door. The faintest creak of wood.

I held my breath, listening, but there was only the sigh of water on stone as the sea lapped gently against the rocks far below, a softer sibilant echoing the sleepless rasp of the cicadas.

The lonely spirit of the count's lady walked the battlements when her soul was restless, Elliot had said, pacing out the bounds of her prison; fishermen at sea had seen the glow of her aura, a small flicker of light, like a candle's flame teased by the wind. I don't happen to believe in ghosts myself, but disbelief is easier when the lights are on. As I stretched out my hand to the bedside lamp, however, I remembered that the generator wasn't working.

I fumbled for the flashlight Elliot had said was kept in the drawer of the nightstand. And as I did, I heard the noise again, this time overhead. It was followed almost at once by a whispery protest of hinges.

Someone was opening the door to Hugo's room.

Any ghost worth its salt should be able to walk through walls, I told myself; it would hardly need to open doors. Whoever was up there was no ghost, and had, moreover, the "missing" key; it could only be Elliot. Either he had found it, or he had deliberately lied to us.

With the flashlight pointed at the floor, I snapped the switch on. Nothing happening. I unscrewed the cap to discover that there were no batteries inside. Elliot, I thought angrily, clearly wanted to make very sure that I would not go creeping around after dark. For a wild moment, I was tempted to rush upstairs and confront him, to see just what he was hiding from us. But as I swung my legs over the side of the bed, the thought came to me that perhaps it would be wiser to spy on him instead. I rejected this almost at once, however; it would be almost impossible to escape being seen if Elliot should come out of Hugo's room before I had time to get downstairs and into my own room again.

In the end, a mixture of fear and caution held me back. Elliot, for all his easy charm, was an enigma, and I had no idea how he might react if I surprised him at something he wanted kept a secret. Isolated as we were on the promontory, cut off by the sea and the night, Jay and I were defenseless. Our only protection was our ignorance.

Still, I was curious. As quietly as I could, I slipped out of bed and pulled on a T-shirt and my jeans, feeling less vulnerable once I was dressed. I eased the latch off my door, but left it shut while I debated with myself.

I could wait for him to come back downstairs, then pretend to run into him on my way to the bathroom. He would have no choice but to admit that he had the key; this would force him to give it up to us in the morning, without risking the dangerous reaction that might be provoked if I surprised him in Hugo's room. But it would also warn him, giving him time to tidy away whatever he had hidden upstairs.

So what? I asked myself. Maybe he was simply ashamed to show us the mess he had made working with Hugo's papers. Maybe his guilty secret was some venial sin: cribbing ideas from Hugo's work against the day when he would return to his university studies, instant projects in hand. Perhaps he simply wanted time to clean up the evidence of this. Elliot might be nothing more sinister than a young man on the make, using people, in the nicest possible way, to get ahead. Some slant of harsh Sicilian sun, or the effect of the island's layered, twisted history, colored the man, made me see him in a false light. He was out of place here, suspicious in a way he would never be in California.

I was about to go back to bed, when the door above softly closed. In a moment, there were stealthy footsteps on the wooden stairs. Elliot came down so quietly that only the occasional squeak of a step gave him away, and when he reached the stone stairs, where no loose floorboards could betray him, there was silence. I let a minute elapse, to give him time to descend before I moved myself. I did not want him to hear me in turn.

But while I waited, leaning my head wearily against the wood, another door creaked open—the main tower door downstairs. At once, my senses were on the alert again, all my suspicions resurrected. Where on earth could he be going at this hour, and why?

There was a window on the landing outside my room that overlooked the courtyard. Remembering this, I left my room and leaned forward from the window until I had a view over the whole area below, careful to stand in a shadow so as not to be visible if Elliot chanced to look up.

The moonlight, shining down onto chalk-white dust and pale rock like a giant, silvery floodlamp, picked out Elliot's dark figure with fierce clarity as he moved swiftly out of the long shadow of the tower toward the ruined gate. In a long-sleeved dark shirt and blue jeans, with his blond hair covered by a flat Sicilian cap, he was made into a giant by his own shadow, which seemed to run before him, urging him on. One arm was crooked up against his chest, as if he were cradling something, but his back was to the tower and it was impossible to be sure.

I turned away from the window and ran up the wooden stairs to the third floor. But I twisted on the handle of the door to Hugo's room in vain; Elliot had locked it behind him. I was suddenly filled with a violent curiosity to know what it was that took Elliot out so secretly in the middle of the night.

There was no point in going back to bed; I would never sleep now. I decided, instead, to satisfy my curiosity. As I hurried downstairs past Jay's doorway I felt a momentary qualm. He might be angry and hurt that I had left him to sleep away an adventure, might argue with some justice that it was his urging that had brought us here. The thought held me wavering on the landing, but for an instant only, before I plunged ahead down the stairs. If there was any chance that Elliot's midnight expedition had some sinister purpose . . .

Before I left the tower, I looked out of a window that stood open onto the courtyard. But Elliot was now nowhere in sight.

Outdoors, I kept to the north side of the courtyard, where I hoped the deep, uneven shadows cast by the half-toppled walls would hide me. I crept slowly along, carefully picking my way through the tumbled stones that littered the ground, until I reached the pile of rock fallen from the gate's broken arch. Cautiously, I peered around it into the silent streets of Casteddu.

The three short streets of the dead town extended before me like the ribs of an open fan, but the angle of the outer two meant I could get no clear view down them from where I stood and the center street was in such deep shadow that little was visible. Intently, I listened for a sound that might tell me which of the three streets Elliot had taken.

Even the cicadas were quiet now. It was so silent, too silent, as if the insects knew that something dangerous stirred in the night. Gooseflesh crawled along my bare arms where the cool stone touched the skin. What if Elliot had not left the courtyard after all? What if he was even now creeping up behind me to stop me from following him? I jerked my head around to stare wildly back. But nothing disturbed the perfect stillness of that wide, ghostly whiteness.

When my breathing was peaceful again, I turned to peer once more into the gloomy little street. Halfway along it, something moved. It was Elliot. I pressed back into the shadows, although I was sure he hadn't seen me.

In his dark clothing he had blended so perfectly with the shadows thrown down by the double row of houses that when he materialized suddenly in a patch of moonlight it seemed at first as if one of those shadows had come alive. Like a cat secure on its own terrain, he moved with a certain wary assurance, not quite so furtive now that he was safely away from the tower. He never once looked back over his shoulder, or stopped to listen.

As I watched him from behind the heap of rock, it occurred to me that perhaps Elliot simply had a rendezvous with Benedetta. If he knew of Don Calo's suspicions, it would explain the hour and his stealth.

When Elliot was almost at the end of the short street, he stopped in front of the house with the padlocked blue door and boarded-up window, two houses up from Orlando's stall. As he turned, the side toward me was visible in the moonlight, and I could see now that, as I had guessed, he did have a small package tucked under his left arm. With his right, he must have taken a key from his trouser pocket, for in a moment I heard the grating of the metal hasp, then the squeak of unoiled hinges as he opened the door and went inside, shutting the door once more behind him. Soon there was a pale flare of light, very faint and ghostly, showing through the cracks in the boards over the window.

I wondered if I dared risk going any closer. But I couldn't be sure that I would find a hiding place as secure as the one I was in, and I was reluctant to risk making a noise. In the end, I decided to stay put. The decision was wise, for almost at once the light went out and Elliot reappeared. In his arms, he held something large and bulky, but the street was too shadowy, and he was too far away, for me to make out what it was. It was obviously heavy, though, because his back bent a little under its weight. With the toe of his shoe, he pulled the door to, then carried the object to the end of the street, setting it down on the cobblestones outside the house that held Orlando's stall. I could see now that it was some sort of large wooden box, about the size of an orange crate. The small package was lying on top of it.

Orlando gave a soft whinny of greeting as Elliot opened the two halves of the Dutch door and, picking up the box, stepped inside the stall. In ten minutes, he emerged again, leading the donkey by the bridle. He must have transferred the heavy box to Orlando, for there was something large tied onto the donkey's back, covered up with a blanket.

Elliot and the donkey set off across the metal footbridge. It was a moment before my mind registered an absence—what should have been the sharp clip-clop of the donkey's hooves on metal was instead a soft thud. Elliot had muffled the hooves.

On the other side of the bridge, they came to the stony clearing where the path split, the two figures of man and donkey clearly visible despite the distance. I expected Elliot to take the fork to the left, down toward the village, but to my surprise he turned right, up along the path that Matteo had said eventually led to Don Calo's meadow, the *prato di Venere*, where Clio kept her bees. The moon was so bright that he did not need any light to see the way; still, he was going slowly, carefully picking his way over fallen stones, the donkey following obediently behind.

I gave up the idea that he had a romantic assignation; I couldn't imagine he would take a donkey to a rendezvous with someone like Benedetta. Besides, I very much doubted if Benedetta would wait patiently alone at night in the countryside for her lover, when she could just as easily meet him in Palermo.

However, I couldn't follow Elliot now. The track was unfamiliar and almost certainly difficult, and I was wearing open-toed sandals, which wouldn't be much use in scrambling over rock. Besides, somewhere along the way I was bound to stumble or trip, and it would take only one loose pebble bouncing off rock, as loud as a rifle shot in the silence of the night, to warn Elliot that someone was on his trail. And I didn't much relish the idea that I might run up against him on some cliffside.

But here in Casteddu I felt safe for the first time since waking from my nightmare. Elliot seemed likely to be gone for what might be a long time, more than enough time to discover what lay inside the house with the blue door. I left my hiding place by the gate and went over to it. As I'd hoped, Elliot had merely pulled the door shut with his foot, and the padlock dangled unlocked from the hasp.

Inside, the single room was pitch-dark at first, but when my eyes adjusted I saw that on a wooden table close to the door there was a lantern, with a book of matches lying beside it—the same brand of matches, I noted with interest when I picked them up, as those I had found on the path that led down from the meadow to the little bay. I shut the door, then lit the lantern and looked around.

There was disappointingly little to see: three wooden crates sitting on the dirt floor, a heap of empty feed sacks in one corner, a rickety-looking chair with a small, empty plastic bag on its seat. I took the lantern over to the crates. There was some sort of lettering stamped on their sides: MIELE D'ERICE, the letters said, the name of Clio's honey. The cover was off one of the crates, propped against its side, and inside the crate were jars of chunk comb honey like those Jay and I had watched Clio prepare.

I had expected more than this innocuous evidence of Elliot's business with Clio. Disappointed, I prodded idly at the pile of sacks with my toe, and felt the hard edge of something underneath. When I stopped and pulled away several of the sacks, I saw another wooden crate, its slatted cover nailed shut. A few of the slats were less securely nailed than the rest; it seemed as if they might have been prized up, then sealed again. It was easy enough to lift them open, so that I could get a look inside.

But the crate was almost empty. At the bottom there were only a few pieces of something pale and plastic, like small, peculiar bowls. When I lifted one of them out, to get a better look, I was surprised to find that its outer surface imitated a white-capped honeycomb, while the inner surface was smooth. It was an irregular shape, roughly oval, about four inches long, two inches wide, and an inch and a half deep. I fished out another piece. It was identical to the first in shape and size, but flatter, with a grooved inner edge. On an impulse, I put it together with the first. The two fitted neatly, like a plastic food storage container, their outer sides rough with mock honeycomb. Puzzled, I separated the two pieces and dropped them back in the crate and closed it up again. In her honey house the day before, Clio had said that some beekeepers used plastic foundation for the bees to build their comb on—perhaps this was some form of it. I pulled the sacks back over the crate, wondering why Elliot bothered to hide it. And why he was transporting honey in the middle of the night.

Whatever he was doing might take hours, but by now I wanted very much to know exactly what it was. There were too many peculiar aspects to Elliot's life in Castell'alto, too many secrets, and if Hugo was somehow involved . . . The more I knew, the easier it would be to persuade Jay that it was time to take Luke's advice.

Looking for a hiding place where I could see, but not be seen, when Elliot returned, I went across the narrow street to the houses opposite. The second door I tried was unlocked, opening with only a small resistance when I forced it with my shoulder. Once inside, I left a crack open wide enough to squeeze through, so that, if I needed to, I could get out again without making a sound. The shadows, I hoped, would prevent Elliot from seeing that the door wasn't shut.

The house was filthy and smelled of damp and worse, as if something unpleasant had crawled in and died there, but the boards across the window had wide cracks that gave a clear view of the house with the blue door. There was nowhere to sit, so I leaned against the crumbling plaster wall and settled down to wait.

The time dragged slowly along, and only the small rustlings and occasional slither, which told me that I was not alone, kept me from falling asleep. Every now and then, when the noises seemed to venture close to me, I scraped my feet on the ground, to frighten whatever it was away. I tried not to think about the exotic varieties of snakes and spiders that I was sure Sicily must glory in.

Sometime after three-thirty, I heard the soft thudding of Orlando's muffled hooves on the bridge. I edged close to the window and peered through the crack in the board. In a moment, Elliot came up the street, leading Orlando. The donkey seemed weary; its head was bowed, and it stumbled once over a cobblestone. It was still carrying the load on its back. Elliot pulled Orlando across the threshold into the house with the blue door.

When they came out again, the load was gone from the donkey's back. It must have balked at something, for Elliot swore and jerked savagely on the bridle. As he pulled the donkey around, his face turned briefly in my direction, illuminated by the moonlight, livid with a terrible anger that distorted his handsome features. Whatever sins the donkey might have committed, it seemed hardly likely that they were the cause of such rage. Elliot looked so angry that I was suddenly frightened of what he might do if he caught me spying on him. All at once, I wanted desperately to get away. Stupidly, I hadn't once considered the fact that Elliot slept downstairs in the tower; that meant I had to get back there before he did. I slipped off my sandals—bare feet would move more quietly over the cobblestones—and cursed myself for not wearing running shoes. The dirt floor felt clammy and rough, and I prayed there was no broken glass.

Elliot led the donkey into its stall. I had to move fast. It wouldn't take him long to remove whatever was muffling Orlando's hooves. I squeezed through the door's narrow opening, and ran barefoot and silently down the middle of the street. If Elliot came out of the house, he would certainly see me, but that was a chance I would have to take. I couldn't risk stumbling now, or time lost in navigating the shadows.

I made it to the ruined gate unseen. Only there did luck desert me briefly, as I foolishly turned to look back for Elliot and ran up against a block of stone that projected out from the others in the large pile that had been my former hiding place. One rough edge caught me squarely on my left shin. The pain was instantaneous and horrible as a wave of nausea swept over me, and I bit down hard on my lower lip to keep from crying out.

But I had to keep going. I raced across the bright expanse of courtyard and gained the tower door with an overwhelming sense of refuge. Upstairs, in my bedroom, I took off my jeans and examined my leg. But the skin was unbroken, and apart from the promise of a beautiful bruise in the morning, it seemed I had gotten off lightly.

I lay down on my bed and waited, mystified by all that I had seen and unnerved by the memory of Elliot's inexplicable anger. In ten minutes or so, I heard the same soft click of the main door below, and after that only the sound of the cicadas and the sea.

CHAPTER 21

I overslept the next morning, waking groggily in a twisted tumble of sheets. Through the open window came the wheedling cries of sea swallows, and the sudden white flash of a gull as it sheered past the tower. The sun shone high and brilliant in a hard blue sky. I put on a cotton blouse and my blue jeans, wincing as the rough cloth moved over my bruised shin, where the flesh was plum-colored and softly puffy. The bruise was the painfully tangible evidence that I had not dreamed last night's adventure, but it was also the only evidence, all I had to show for my amateurish sleuthing, apart from a clutch of questions.

Two facts were clear, however. Not only did our presence in the tower inconvenience Elliot in his affair with Benedetta, but it was interfering with some other illicit, less romantic, activity. I wasn't looking forward to facing Elliot over the breakfast table now that I knew he had another reason to resent his houseguests.

The door to Jay's room was open, his bed made, and when I went downstairs, he was sitting at the scrubbed wooden table in the kitchen area, peeling an orange. Elliot was nowhere in sight.

Jay let out an exaggerated sigh of relief. "Finally! I thought you'd never wake up."

"Why do early risers always take that self-righteous tone? If you knew what sort of night I had, you wouldn't be so hard on me." I wandered over to the stove. "Coffee! And it's hot. You've just redeemed yourself." I ladled a generous helping of sugar into my cup, hoping that it and the caffeine combined would clear my muzzy head. On the counter beside the stove, there was an uncut melon and a loaf of bread on a board with a bottle of Clio's honey next to it.

"It's not that," Jay said impatiently. "Look what I've got. . . ." He held up a large, old-fashioned iron key. "Elliot gave it to me. It's the key to Hugo's room. Do you know how hard it's been to wait for you, instead of just going straight up there?''

"I am grateful, Jay, really. Where is Elliot, by the way?''

"He went to see Clio. He left first thing. Said to say he was sorry not to be here when you got up, and that he might not be back until after lunch." Jay pushed back his chair. "Now, let's go up and—''

I put a hand on his arm. "I've got to eat something first. And I don't think there's much reason to rush up there anyway, now that Elliot's got rid of whatever he didn't want us to see. He had a very busy night, and if you'll go on being patient, I'll tell you about it.''

Somewhat reluctantly, Jay sank back down onto his chair and picked up the orange again, tossing it from one hand to the other while I cut a slice of the melon and spread the honey thickly on a large chunk of bread. The sweet smell of melon and honey mingled deliciously, and I found I was suddenly ravenous. As I ate, I told Jay everything that I had seen and heard the night before, wondering if he would be able to make any more sense of it than I had. He sat with his chair tilted back on two legs as he listened, the orange forgotten.

But his reaction, when I had finished, was at first only what mine had been. "But it sounds so pointless . . . What's in the meadow, after all—'' Then he gave a start, and the front legs of the chair dropped forward with a small bang onto the flagstones. "Smuggling! That's what he's doing. Remember Clio told us that the bay was used by smugglers?''

"But not anymore. She said there were easier places.''

"Unless you lived up here. Then it would be perfect. No one would notice comings and goings at night, the way they might if you went through Castell'alto.''

"But why smuggle honey, for heaven's sake?''

Jay shrugged his shoulders as he pulled the orange apart into sections; it was a blood orange, with the bright red flesh that makes all other oranges look anemic. "Maybe it wasn't honey in that box Orlando was carrying for him.''

Another thought came to me. Slowly, I said, "Maybe you're right about the smuggling. Hugo owns so many valuable things. Maybe Elliot has been selling them off, thinking he'd get away before Hugo returned. Maybe that's why he doesn't want us to see the tower room—maybe he's afraid of what we won't see, not what we will. . . .''

"But neither of us has been here before this, so how would we know what's missing?"

"Yes, but Elliot can't be sure we wouldn't know. Hugo might have written to us, or sent us photos."

"What about Clio? She'd notice, wouldn't she?"

"Clio said that yesterday was the first time she'd been to the tower since Hugo left. Matteo might notice, I suppose, but look how Elliot seems to have forced him into moving down into Castell'alto. I'll bet he doesn't allow Matteo into this place. Just lets him work outside. So he's free to do whatever he likes at night, when no one is here."

Jay sat with his elbows propped on the tabletop, resting his head in his hands, his brow furrowed as he thought this over. "Wouldn't it be easier just to tell us that he'd put Hugo's things away somewhere, where they would be safe? Besides, he's given us the key now, so he obviously isn't worried any longer about what we might not see. And he couldn't have replaced the stuff. It must be that he got rid of something instead."

This made sense. Wearily, I rubbed my forehead; the coffee and food had helped, but traces of the headache lingered.

Jay said, "I'd like to get a look in that box you said Elliot locked away last night in the little house."

I dabbed at the last crumbs of sticky bread with a fingertip. "The padlock on the door looked pretty strong, but there might be another way in, I suppose," I said halfheartedly. "We could try to prize the boards off the window. . . ."

Jay pounced on this proposal. "Then I vote we try as soon as we've had a look at Hugo's room."

It might have been simply the combination of caffeine and a full stomach, or the contagious effect of Jay's energy—whatever the reason, my head was suddenly clear, the headache vanished. It would be a relief, I thought, to do something. I put my cup down in its saucer with a small clatter. "All right, why not? Maybe we'll find that parcel Elliot was carrying, too."

But as we crossed the room toward the stone stairs, it occurred to me that Elliot could easily have taken both the parcel and the box from their hiding place when he left this morning.

When I suggested as much to Jay, he shook his head. "I don't think so. I was up before he was, and I walked to the Jeep with him. So he never had a chance to go into the house. And he wasn't carrying anything."

"What sort of mood was he in?"

"Sort of subdued, I guess. He didn't seem mad or anything, just quiet."

Upstairs, on the small third-floor half-landing, Jay unlocked the heavy wooden door that led to Hugo's room. Opening, it swung wide on a large, almost-circular space striped with bars of light that filtered through the shuttered windows. A rich, dim silence hung over the room, spiced with a grain of what might have been incense, and that indefinable library smell of the bindings of old books. Jay and I went to each of the four windows, raising the shutters, opening the windows, until light and air flooded in. We looked around then, without speaking.

At last, Jay said quietly, "Hugo's ivory tower."

It was, I thought; and it was something more.

The stylite's isolation, with a fabulous view. Ancient texts, architectural drawings, a typewriter—and a Turkish narghile. Stone and silk. It was an ivory tower for a scholar gypsy with an aesthete's tastes. Nowhere else had I seen the contradiction in Hugo's nature, the struggle between the ascetic and the sensualist, so apparent as in this room.

Along the only flat wall, the one with the door, were floor-to-ceiling bookshelves crammed full of books; the shelves were metal, as were the filing cabinet and the architect's drafting table beside the window that looked out across Casteddu to the mountain. The typewriter that sat on the desk in the center of the room was an old portable Remington, functional, ugly, but the desk itself was a graceful antique. On the floor beside it were two open cardboard boxes.

A tall wooden folding screen, intricately carved with birds and flowers, separated the bed from the rest of the room. The bed was narrow, a simple iron bedstead, but across it lay a silk rug as delicate as a spiderweb. The narghile sat on a small brass table next to the bed, the long flexible tube with its ivory mouthpiece coiled around the water jar like a snake. Hugo smoked the occasional pipe—I wondered if the narghile provided inspiration, or was merely decoration. But when I looked more closely, I saw that a little water remained in the bottom of the jar. Elliot, then, must have used it, and recently. It would account for the incense smell.

Another rug in bold shades of blue and red covered much of the floor. On the gentle curve of the stone wall hung three etchings of classical ruins and an old map of ancient Sicily. Architectural plans and drawings were pinned to several large easels. Behind one of the easels was a steep flight of wooden steps up to a small door, which opened, presumably, onto the tower's battlements. Where that pitiful creature who had slowly starved to death still walked. But if her spirit inhabited this room, it was no match for Hugo's. His vitality, his personality triumphed here.

What must have been the original of the bowl Clio had showed us in the cave sat on the desk. Elliot would surely know that it was valuable, and no thief would pass it up. Behind the type-writer four ledgers sat between bookends, each with a different-colored cover. I picked one out at random and opened it to the first page. At the head of the page was written, in pen, MIELE D'ERICE: C. HUNT. I did not recognize the handwriting, but assumed it was Elliot's. I riffled through the book; on each page the ruled columns were filled with figures, and each had a different date in the top right-hand corner. It was obviously a record for the sales of Clio's honey. I looked at the other ledgers. Each was in a different person's name, but they all seemed to be business accounts of some sort—Elliot's "irons in the fire," I assumed. Apart from the stack of typing paper beside the type-writer, there were no overt signs of Elliot's work on Hugo's papers, and the typing paper was unused.

Meanwhile, Jay was browsing along the shelves. I went over to join him. There were collections of poetry, a few novels, some philosophical works, but for the most part the books were a mixture of architecture, history, archaeology, and the history of religions, grouped by subject and within that by author. Hugo's own books were there.

Laid flat on the bottom shelf of the far left-hand bookcase was a heap of wine-colored portfolios, the kind in which artists and photographers carry their work. Each portfolio was tied with a black ribbon and labeled with the name of a place and a date. Some of the labels were peeling off, the glue long since dried out. The top portfolio was covered with a thin film of dust, as though it hadn't been touched in some time; the label said TEH-RAN, 1977. Jay untied it. Inside were drawings for a project Hugo had undertaken for the Shah. "Never completed" was penciled in Hugo's handwriting on the top drawing.

Without opening them, Jay lifted each of the others in the pile and passed them to me. I recognized some of the projects, names I had heard Hugo mention. But the last portfolio was unnamed—instead, Hugo had written some words in classical Greek on the label. The date was 1938.

I remembered that Jay had boarding-school Greek. "Do you know what this says?" I asked him.

Jay leaned over my shoulder. "The lady of the labyrinth," he translated, then looked at me wonderingly. "That's what Hugo said that night, the night he rescued Don Calo and the others."

"I remember."

I untied the black ribbon and opened the portfolio. A small heap of pencil drawings lay inside. There were seven, and they seemed to be drawings of archaeological sites, ground plans, or maps, but there was nothing written on them to indicate where or what the sites were, or why they were labeled as they were. Some were carefully drawn and detailed, while others seemed to be hastily sketched and left unfinished. They were of different sizes, and oddly shaped; some had been neatly torn along one side, as if from a sketchbook. Jay glanced at them in my lap, lost interest, and went back to scanning the bookshelves.

If it hadn't been for the epigraph, I would have put the drawings back in the portfolio and thought no more about them. But I felt that they were significant in some way, if only I could puzzle it out. Scraps that they seemed, Hugo had kept them; they meant something to him. I found an empty manilla folder and put the drawings inside it, then slipped the folder into my shoulder bag.

Uneasily, feeling that I was prying despite the fact that Hugo had asked Elliot to go through his papers, I pulled open the three drawers of the filing cabinet and examined the hanging files. Each file was labeled. Most of them contained records relating to the tower—work done, work planned, bills.

The folders in the boxes beside the desk held Hugo's personal papers, and were roughly sorted by type: letters he had received, copies of letters he had sent, notes for each book he had written, reviews, miscellaneous scraps of paper that wouldn't fit neatly into any other category. There were a number of letters that seemed personal and unrelated to his work, but when I scanned the few that were dated from the months before Libya, I saw nothing that could be taken as a motive for abandoning everything.

At the bottom of the heap there were two bundles of small notebooks, the kind that I had seen Hugo write in when something struck him and he wanted to remember it. Each bundle contained ten notebooks. I opened one, and gave one of the others to Jay. Like everything else, each notebook was dated, and I was holding the one that covered the six months before he went to Libya.

The year started with random jottings, sometimes only a single word; most seemed to center on projects he was working on or planning, or thoughts for a book. There was nothing more personal than that. I flipped through the pages. Near the end, something caught my eye. Hugo had written the name of Libya's main city, Tripoli, and beside it a man's name, Salim. A large question mark punctuated the margin of the page. This was the last entry in the notebook, followed by a dozen or so empty pages.

Apart from that single cryptic jotting in the notebook, there was nothing else in the room that linked Hugo with Libya. For all our searching, we were no closer to knowing why Hugo had chosen the path he had. Or what it was that Elliot had seemed to want to hide from us.

I looked around the room. "Elliot must have done his tidying last night," I told Jay resignedly. Then I remembered my theory that Elliot might be stealing ideas from Hugo.

"I don't see how that would fit in with whatever he was doing last night," Jay pointed out when I told him about it. "I've been thinking, and I'll bet instead it's tied up with Clio's honey business. After all, Clio thinks Giudico's up to something, and Elliot is Giudico's partner. Maybe last night he was trying to fix the problem before he talked to Clio today." Jay gave a last look around the room. "So now let's find out what Elliot's got hidden in that house. After that, we could go to the meadow—there might be something there. . . ."

I thought of the tiny bay with its shining crescent of sand. "I wouldn't mind a swim. Why don't we take a picnic? You can buy the food in Castell'alto while I telephone Luke. I promised I'd get in touch with him this morning."

"What will you tell him?"

"Everything."

Jay did not protest.

We tried to leave Hugo's room as we had found it, closing and shuttering the windows once more, locking the door. "Now for a little housebreaking!" Jay said. His face was pink with excitement as he pocketed the key.

But as we approached the house with the blue door, we saw Matteo outside Orlando's stall; he was kneeling down, examining the donkey's right foreleg. The face he turned toward us was angry, and Matteo angry was a disconcerting sight.

I asked him if something was wrong with the donkey.

"He is hurt. Here." Gently, he touched the donkey's leg.

There was a deep gash just below the knee, crusted over with dried blood.

"What happened?" asked Jay.

Matteo ignored Jay's question. "He should not leave an animal this way. Is bad." It was clear whom he meant by the masculine pronoun.

I remembered the donkey's stumbling steps as he followed Elliot back into the little house. It seemed likely that Orlando's injury had happened somewhere on the mountain, and that in the darkness Elliot had not been aware of it. Otherwise, he almost certainly would have tended to it—if only to spare himself precisely this reaction. But I was surprised that Matteo seemed so positive that Elliot was responsible, and I wondered how much else he knew of Elliot's nocturnal activities.

"Matteo," I said on an impulse, "you don't happen to have keys to any of these houses, do you? Some of them are locked, and well . . . we're curious to see inside. Elliot told us Hugo was planning to fix them up."

Matteo regarded me unblinkingly. I had the uncomfortable feeling he saw this explanation for what it was. But all he said was "Elliot has keys." After gently sponging water onto the donkey's wound, he dried it, then plucked some leaves from a small sage-green plant with tiny yellow flowers that grew in the dust beside the wall of the house. He crushed the leaves between his fingers, then placed them against the cut, wrapping a clean rag around it.

I persevered. "I know Elliot has keys, but I thought you might have extras." I met his eyes. Then I turned and pointed to the padlocked house. "That, for instance. Do you have a key for that lock?"

He shook his head. "Only Elliot. He make that lock after Don 'Ugo go away."

"I see. Do you know why?" When he only shrugged, I said, somewhat desperately, "Have you ever noticed things going on at night here, something to worry about?"

He stood up, the damp piece of cloth he had used to wash the donkey's leg with hanging from one hand. He said simply, "The people say the lady walks at night. They say there are lights moving on the water. Evil spirits, they say."

"Do you believe that?"

"I think the only evil spirits are in men."

While we were talking, Jay had walked over to the house with the blue door. "A good crowbar would get this off." He fingered the padlock.

"But then Elliot would know." I watched Matteo's face as I spoke. A trace of surprise appeared on the impassive features.

"Who cares?" Jay replied. "At least we'll know what's in that box." He leaned dejectedly against the wall of the house. To no one in particular, he added, "Everyone here says how much Hugo did for them, how much they owe him, but no one seems willing to help us because of it." I was sure he knew how unjust the accusation was, but it was as if the frustrations of the last few days had suddenly become too much for him. His voice was rough with anger and unshed tears. Abruptly, he turned away and savagely kicked a stone down the street.

Matteo, who had been watching him, seemed to have made up his mind about something. He said suddenly, "You are wrong to think this. If you want help, you must ask."

Jay turned to him, his eyes intent. "And would you help us?" Matteo inclined his head.

"Then help us get in here." Jay jerked his thumb at the padlocked door.

"Is easy," Matteo said, surprisingly.

"You know how to get the lock off?" I asked him.

He shook his head. "Is another way. But dirty."

"That's all right," I told him. "We don't mind a little dirt."

For the first time, Matteo smiled. "Is not little dirt."

He turned and walked over to the neighbor of the house with the padlocked door. With no visible effort, he took hold of its door and simply lifted it aside. We could see then that there were no hinges—it had been wedged into place in the door frame. Matteo set the door against the outer wall and stood back, motioning us to follow him inside.

The hard-packed earth floor of the small single room was littered with refuse—broken crates, bits of rusted machinery, an ancient mattress with its stuffing oozing damply from it, a heap of dusty wine bottles. The wall it shared with the padlocked house had no common door, nothing that would make entry into the padlocked house a possibility. But Matteo pointed to the ceiling, which virtually grazed his head. Much of the plaster had fallen away in a corner next to the back wall, as though a giant fist had punched a large hole, exposing ancient, rotting beams thick with dust and cobwebs.

"One moment." Matteo disappeared, to return almost at once with a short wooden ladder that looked as unsafe as the ceiling, propping it against the wall beneath the hole. He climbed up it and hauled himself into the black hole. For an instant, he disappeared, then his head emerged, looking down at us. "Come."

"Ladies first," Jay said, grinning.

"Thanks very much." I was glad I was wearing blue jeans.

When I got my head up through the hole in the ceiling, Matteo was squatting on the wide beam that ran along the length of the house against the wall. "Is okay, this one," he reassured me. "Very strong."

He began to crawl forward along it and I realized, when my eyes adjusted to the darkness, that the attic or whatever it was extended far beyond the single room below, that in fact it probably ran the entire length of the row of houses, common to all. It was in this attic, or another like it, I remembered that Don Calo and the others had hidden Luzzu from the Germans.

In a few yards we were over the padlocked house. Matteo was wrestling with a large square of flat wood, a kind of trapdoor. He pulled it aside, then dropped through the opening into the house below. Quickly, Jay and I crawled after him and followed suit.

Last night the table in the padlocked house had only a lantern and a book of matches lying on it. This morning the large box that I'd seen Elliot carrying sat in the middle. Beside it was a ledger like those we'd seen on Hugo's desk.

Carefully wiping my filthy hands on my jeans, I picked up the ledger and opened it. There was no label on the cover, and nothing to indicate what account it kept. As with the others, there were pages of figures, but this time the figures were much larger. Whatever business this was, it seemed far more profitable for Elliot than the others. The figures were so large, in fact, that they resurrected my suspicions that Elliot had been selling off Hugo's treasures. But there was no description of what was being sold, only a number assigned to each transaction, and a date. I couldn't see any pattern to the dates, either; sometimes a week elapsed between dates, sometimes as much as a month.

"Creative bookkeeping?" Jay asked, looking over my shoulder. "Is he cheating Clio?"

"I don't know." I handed him the ledger. "But he's making a lot of money at something. Watch that you don't get dirty finger marks on the pages." I turned to the crate on the table. "Do you think we can get this crate open without breaking anything?" I asked Matteo, who was standing with his hands in his pockets, watching us.

"No problem." With his bare fingers, he prized the slatted cover loose from its nails. But inside the crate were only jars of honey. I took one out. It was no different from all the others—a large bottle with a big chunk of honeycomb surrounded by liquid honey. A label was pasted across the glass. It wasn't Clio's label, however. This one read: MIELE DI CARINI.

I thought that there might be a false bottom to the crate, but the jars of honey went all the way to the bottom. Although Jay and I carefully examined the crate all over, we weren't able to find anything that seemed the least bit suspicious.

Jay said, "I don't see what the big deal is. Why all the secrecy?"

"I don't know," I confessed, equally frustrated. I was about to put the bottle back in the crate when it occurred to me that the plastic honeycomb I had found the night before could be used to conceal something. Surrounded by amber honey, it might very well be impossible to distinguish it from genuine honeycomb. The chunk of honey inside the jar I was holding looked real enough, but the dark honey surrounding it might easily give it that appearance. With Matteo present, I was hesitant to mention this theory to Jay; Matteo seemed to be friendly, but . . .

Jay took another bottle of honey from the crate. "You know," he said softly, turning the bottle around in his hands, "if there's anything weird about this honey, maybe some sort of chemical examination might turn it up. Why don't we keep one of these bottles, and replace it with one of the others in those crates over there? You said Elliot didn't seem so concerned about them. That way maybe we can find out if Clio's honey is being tampered with."

We chose a bottle from a bottom row in one of the crates, hoping Elliot would not notice immediately that it was missing, and placed it in the empty section of the crate on the table. Matteo, who had watched us all the while without comment, sealed the crate back up again.

I looked around the room, but saw nothing else that had not been there the night before. "Let's go," I said. "If Elliot decides to come back early . . ."

Returning wasn't quite as easy as coming across had been. We didn't have the ladder. But Matteo hoisted himself up and reached down for Jay, hauling him up by the arms, while Jay did a sort of spider walk with his legs against the wall. I handed Jay the honey, then mimicked Jay's actions while Matteo held my forearms and pulled. Matteo replaced the trapdoor and we crawled slowly back along the beam and down into the room next door. By the time we were through, my bruised leg was aching.

When we thanked Matteo, he only ducked his head. Then he gave his rare smile. "Is secret, okay?" We agreed that it was a secret. It did not need saying from whom.

We went back to the tower to wash up before going down into Castell'alto. I changed from my jeans, the knees of which were filthy from the crawl, into my only other pair of trousers, then brushed the cobwebs and dust from my hair. I didn't know where to hide the jar of honey, so in the end I simply took it with me in my shoulder bag.

As we walked down the track toward the village, I told Jay firmly that we were not going to spend another night in the tower. "When Clio comes up this afternoon, I'm going to ask her if we can stay with her. Right now, even Don Calo's hospitality is beginning to look good."

Jay must have been feeling much as I was, for he agreed that one night in the tower had been enough. "Elliot seems a nice-enough guy, but if he's got something going on he doesn't want us to know about . . ."

"Then better for us not to know about it." It was, I reflected, an appropriately Sicilian sentiment.

I called Luke from a telephone in the first bar we reached. It took me a moment to understand what the female voice on the other end of the line was saying, and then another moment for her to understand what it was I wanted, but eventually I managed to make it clear that I wanted to speak to the American gentleman staying there. After a few minutes, Luke came on the line.

"Everything okay?" he asked, when he heard my voice.

"I'm not sure. There's something peculiar going on."

"Like what?"

"There's so much to explain, Luke, and it's complicated. It would be better if we could meet, say in an hour from now. There's a place about a mile outside Castell'alto. . . ." I described the meadow and how to reach it.

"In an hour, then."

Afterward I joined Jay in the small grocery store next to the bar. We bought a bottle of *acqua minerale*, rolls, some cheese, and a large bag of cherries. Back at the tower, we loaded Jay's knapsack with our swimsuits, towels, and the food. I put the manilla envelope with Hugo's drawings down the side of the backpack. But as we were about to set off, we heard footsteps outside in the courtyard. And then Elliot came into the room.

CHAPTER 22

This morning Elliot did not look quite so much like the popular image of a Californian whose dreams are troubled by nothing worse than the less than perfect wave. His eyelids were heavy and puckered at the edges with sleeplessness, and under the tan his skin had lost some of its color. But there wasn't a trace of last night's anger to cloud the disarming smile that made it so impossible not to smile back at him.

In the shadowy streets of Casteddu, Elliot had been a man without definition, frightening. But now, as the morning sun sharpened him into focus again, I could see only the attractive, capable man who was both Clio's and Hugo's friend. What real evidence did we have, after all, to persuade us he was anything but what he seemed at this moment?

As he made coffee, Elliot said that he had visited Clio that morning. "She knows how to handle bees, but she still hasn't figured out Sicilian business practices. And Giudico's methods aren't exactly sophisticated. He thinks if a woman's upset about something, you tell her she's beautiful. And if that doesn't work, you threaten to bash her face in." He poured the steaming coffee into a cup. "So I get called in to arbitrate."

He must have succeeded, I thought, to be this good-humored, when not eight hours earlier he had seemed so grimly angry. Either that, or he was a very convincing actor. Hoping there was only casual interest in my voice, I asked him what the problem was.

"Nothing major. We export Clio's honey to a couple of luxury food stores in New York, the kind that cater to homesick rich Italians. But our market in the American bases here was growing, so Giudico diverted the last couple of shipments. He should have told her, but he thought she wouldn't like it. Don't complicate things with unnecessary explanations, that's his philosophy. A simple man, Giudico. By the way, Clio said to tell you she'll come up to visit this afternoon.''

With a glance at Jay, I said, "We were thinking . . . well, that when she gets here we might ask her if we could stay with her tonight. We'd like to do some sightseeing while we wait for Hugo—and to be honest, while it's beautiful here, it isn't exactly convenient. You did warn us. I hope you won't think it's very rude of us.''

Elliot's smile was charming. It managed to be both understanding and regretful, without showing anything of the relief he must be feeling. "I'll be sorry to see you go. But it makes better sense, especially with the generator out. Speaking of which, I'm going to do some more work on it for a while, and then, thank God, it's siesta time. The one civilized custom on this island. And after last night, I need it. I don't think I got to bed until way past three." The pale green eyes looked steadily and candidly into mine. "I hope I didn't disturb you?''

Startled by the admission, it was all I could do not to look at Jay, to keep my eyes meeting Elliot's. As lightly as I could, I said, "I thought I heard you moving around sometime during the night. What kept you up so late?''

"Another Sicilian custom, but not so nice this time. There's an old scoundrel called Leporino who lives over in Custonaci. He's a shepherd who got rich smuggling heroin past the eyes of the *carabinieri*. Under the pelts of his sheep, supposedly. That's what I've heard, anyway.

"Leporino claims he's the rightful owner of the meadow where Clio keeps her bees. He used to graze his sheep all over the side of Monte Castello, so he thinks the meadow belongs to him by some sort of natural law. He says Don Calo cheated him out of it. Which, as far as I know, is a lie. Don Calo ignores Leporino, so the shepherd takes it out on more vulnerable victims. Clio thinks her beehives survive because the locals are superstitious, or else because they're afraid to trespass on Don Calo's land. That's partly true, but old Leporino doesn't give a damn for superstition or for Don Calo. He'd burn up the hives, if I didn't pay him off—and blame it on the evil eye if Clio complained.''

"How much do you have to give him?" Jay asked. He had turned one of the chairs at the table around and was straddling the seat, his hands resting on its back.

"Maybe a hundred thousand lire a year, plus the occasional case of honey. He's not in it for the money so much as for the kick it probably gives him to think he's pushing me around.

What he really likes is to get me out in the middle of the night. He insists that I meet him in the meadow, but doesn't want me to come with the Jeep, he says, because people would hear the sound of the engine. So I bring the donkey, and he waits in his Mercedes. Symbol is very important here," he added dryly, "as all the anthropologists will tell you."

"And you had to do this last night?" I asked him.

Elliot nodded. "But when I got there he never showed. I've just about had it with Leporino and his games."

"What does Clio think about it?"

"I haven't told her. It's part of my job, running interference."

"Why don't you just tell Don Calo?" Jay asked. "I mean, if he's the boss around here . . ."

"There's always a price for that kind of favor. I'd rather deal with it myself and save the favors for stuff that matters."

It explained everything, I thought, the box on Orlando's back, the package under Elliot's arm, which must have been a bundle of lire in an envelope, and the fury on Elliot's face when he returned. As bizarre as the story sounded, it was believable. Nothing, I was coming to accept, was too improbable to be true on an island where television and the evil eye existed side by side, where people found no contradiction in their simultaneous prayers to the Madonna and the "ladies of the outside." But what happened to a foreigner, to an American, who lived too long here? How did you reconcile the contradictions, and yet remain untouched by them?

Jay was asking Elliot if Hugo had to pay protection, too.

"I doubt it. Hugo had more authority around here than I do. I'm a natural target, I guess." He gave a rueful laugh. "The ignorant American who can't even be bothered to learn the language. Maybe it serves me right."

Elliot was so frank about his failings that, for the moment, I liked him very much. More, I wanted to believe him, I wanted to trust him. But a grain of doubt persisted. Perhaps self-deprecation was simply a tool Elliot used to defuse the envy his looks were bound to arouse, and he was using it now to allay any suspicions that Jay and I might have. Elliot was a "fixer," Clio had said; maybe he "fixed" emotions, too.

Despite her reservations, though, Clio was his friend; and Hugo apparently had trusted and liked him well enough to let him stay on in the tower. Only Don Calo's opinion of Elliot was ambiguous. No more ambiguous, however, than Don Calo himself.

Elliot drained off the last of the coffee and set the cup down in the sink. "Have you been up to see the tower room yet?"

We said that we had, and there was a moment's awkward pause while I wondered whether to ask Elliot how much headway he had actually made toward the organizing of Hugo's papers. Before I could speak, however, he went on hurriedly, "Well, then, if you two have nothing better to do, how about giving me a hand with the generator? Matteo's nowhere around, and there's something I can't manage alone."

Jay glanced at me; I knew he was thinking of our appointment with Luke. "Do you need both of us? I don't mind staying, but Alison really wanted to hike over to the meadow and have a swim. It's okay to go over there, isn't it?"

"Sure," said Elliot. "I never do during the day because of Clio's bees." I was relieved to hear him say this; for one nervous moment I thought he was going to propose joining Jay and me.

"You wouldn't want me here, anyway," I added quickly. "Machines tend to fall apart at my touch."

"I thought women never admitted that sort of thing to men these days," Elliot said with a smile. "Go on and have your hike, then. But I wouldn't swim alone along this coast. The currents can be pretty bad sometimes."

"Thanks for the warning." As I picked up my shoulder bag, something occurred to me. "Do you think Leporino will be hanging around the meadow today?"

Elliot shook his head. "When I drove through the main square of Custonaci a half hour ago, Leporino was sitting in his pajamas on his balcony, pretending not to see me."

"In his pajamas?"

"It's how you show the world you're a big shot. You don't have to get up early like other poor jerks, so you slop around in your pj's as late as possible."

"Sounds just like the prefects at my boarding school," Jay said, as he gave me the picnic supplies from his backpack.

Carefully, I cushioned the bottle of honey hidden in my shoulder bag with the rolls and cheese before I added the *acqua minerale*; the cherries went on top. The bag was heavy, but it would be lighter coming back. I told Jay and Elliot to expect me back in two hours or less.

As I left the dead town behind and started up the track, I was surprised to find myself missing Jay. Ordinarily I craved solitude as the anchorite yearns for his cell, and on this trip I'd had precious little of it. Even when Bernd stayed weekends with me in Bonn, he had spent part of that time looking up old friends and making useful new ones, which suited me fine. But with Jay it was different. I liked having him there beside me.

In some ways, however, it would be easier without Jay along. I wouldn't have to appease his resentment of Luke, wouldn't have to play the mediator between them. And, I confessed to myself, I was looking forward to being alone with Luke.

The track to the meadow rose steeply up the mountainside, rough with jagged, chalk-white stones that littered the dusty ground, a reminder of the rock slides that made the mountain perilous. Casteddu and the tower were soon left far below, out of sight around the curve of the mountain's flank. The threadlike track ran between the sheer rock above and a steep slope on my right covered with loose shale and boulders. An unchecked fall here would carry a body down and down until at last it fell like Icarus into a sea that seemed as distant as the sky.

The burning midday sun struck hard against the stone; its rays seemed to vibrate off the rock, pulsing in counterpoint to the rhythmic throbbing of the cicadas, waves of sound and heat. A smoky limestone dust covered everything, the flat, paddle-shaped hands of the prickly pear, the razor-sharp blades of esparto grass, even the little gray lizards that ran among the boulders, giving them all the pallor of death. High overhead, some bird of prey made endless, monotonous circles in the sky, searching for a victim. And far above the bird, the mountain's peak loomed like a hunched and threatening god.

Once, as I scrambled around a boulder, I almost put my foot down on a snake sunbathing in the dust. I froze, while he uncoiled his black length and slid lazily away under a rock, his thin tongue flickering in protest at the intruder. After that, I looked before I stepped.

Another few minutes of strenuous hiking brought me around onto Monte Castello's southeast face, the face that towered above the meadow. Here the track finally leveled out before its descent. Panting hard from the climb, I stopped for a moment to catch my breath. Inland to the east was the lonely, sunburnt heart of the countryside, a vast panorama of bare rolling hills cradled by other mountains; below, the uninhabited rocky coast stretched away to the south, a dark curving border laid like the edge of a sword against a sea as pure and shining as the sky.

Seen like this, with the giant's eye, the colors of the wild and desolate landscape seemed separate and distinct from each other, like the colors in a child's painting: blue above gray, a blot of green, then gray, and finally blue again—the sky, mountain, meadow, cliffs, and sea. Only a closer look, down at my feet, revealed the scarlet, bright purple, yellow, orange that lay hidden among the rocks, the tiny wildflowers whose blossoms only emphasized the greater barrenness.

Less steeply than it had risen, the path descended in a series of switchbacks treacherous with loose stones. I could see the bamboo canopies that covered Clio's beehives, straw-colored oblongs against grass that was a shade more yellow today, as the sun's power steadily leached away moisture from the meadow.

At a point where the track turned to zigzag back on itself one last time before the final hundred feet of descent, there was a flat overhang of rock, a natural shelf of stone some twenty feet above the meadow. I paused there by the overhang, to look for Luke. But the meadow was empty.

Then, above the sound of the cicadas, rose the burr of a car's engine. I hurried down to the large boulders that screened the last few yards of the track to wait hidden in the rocks, just in case the car belonged to someone other than Luke. I did not much want to discuss property rights with old Leporino. A car door slammed, and in a moment Luke appeared, dressed in a navy polo shirt and khaki trousers, with his camera slung across one shoulder.

My foot knocked some loose shale as I came out from behind the boulders. He looked around, surprised.

"Hello, Persephone. Where have you sprung from?"

"From above." I pointed to the narrow stone ribbon that wound up the mountainside above us. "Not from below, thank heaven. Ten minutes in Clio's cave yesterday gave me some idea of what Persephone had to suffer. Didn't someone say that it's better to serve on earth than reign in hell?"

"That's not quite it. But never mind, I know what you mean. Where's Jay?"

I explained. "He sends his love."

"Liar."

We sat down on the grass. With a sigh of relief, I slipped off the heavy shoulder bag and rubbed the place where the strap had cut into the flesh.

"You sounded mysterious on the phone," Luke said, as I unscrewed the cap from the *acqua minerale* and took a long drink. "What's happened?"

I passed the bottle to him. "Several things. But I'm still not sure if I know what they were exactly. Maybe you can help me make up my mind.''

I followed the account of Elliot's midnight expedition with a description of all that Jay and I had done that morning. When I reached the part where we had crawled with Matteo into the house with the padlocked door, I took out the bottle of honey that we had filched. ''This is what we found in the crate,'' I said as I handed it to Luke.

He held the jar up to the sun, turning it slowly in his hand. The light shone through the liquid and around the chunk of honeycomb. Then he unscrewed the cap, dipped a finger into the honey, and put it to his lips. ''It certainly tastes like honey.'' He took a red Swiss army knife from his pocket.

''What's funny?'' he asked, when he saw me smiling.

''Nothing really. Only that you and Jay have more in common than you think.''

He slid a look at me. ''I'm beginning to realize that.''

He bent his head back over the jar of honey, poking at the comb with the point of the small knife, which only succeeded in pushing the comb to the bottom. Some honey flowed stickily over the top of the jar and down the sides. ''That's strange,'' Luke said. ''The knife is sharp enough—you wouldn't think it would have any trouble piercing honeycomb. But this stuff resists it.''

''I think I know why.'' I told him about the plastic comb I had found in the crate under the sacks.

While I talked, Luke got a grip on the comb with the knife and dragged it up out of the liquid honey. ''You're right,'' he said. ''It's plastic.'' He held the comb over the grass, turning it over and over so that the excess honey dripped off it. Some of Clio's bees flew across to investigate. After a minute, he took his other hand and pulled on opposite sides of the comb. It came apart easily. But the hollow space inside was empty.

''Curiouser and curiouser,'' Luke said.

''It gets more so. Wait till you hear Elliot's explanation of what it all meant.''

''You asked him?''

''I didn't need to. He volunteered it.'' When I finished, I added, ''It might explain the plastic comb. Maybe Elliot was playing a trick on Leporino. To teach him that he wasn't such a pushover after all.''

''Maybe.'' But Luke sounded dubious. He held the two pieces and stared at them for a moment, then put them together again and dropped the imitation comb back into the bottle. Slowly, the clear golden liquid oozed around the plastic. "I'd like to take this honey down to Palermo and get it analyzed. Someone at the consulate should know where that can be done quickly. It doesn't taste like anything but honey to me, but who knows?"

"You remember I told you about that quarrel Clio had yesterday with Giudico? Well, Elliot had an explanation for that, too."

"Elliot seems to have an explanation for everything," Luke said when I had finished. With a sideways look, and almost as if he expected an argument, he added, "You know, Alison, I really think it would be a good idea not to spend another night in the tower. God forbid that I should tell you or Jay what to do, but—"

I smiled. "I agree. With both propositions. It's not Elliot so much—in many ways, he's very likable—but the place is just too isolated. I made up my mind last night that Jay and I would ask Clio to take us in, and Jay agrees. Clio's coming up to Castell'alto later this afternoon. If she says no—and I can't imagine that she would—we'll go back to Erice."

"Good girl."

A small swarm of bees had collected around the honey in the grass, so we moved farther off. I began to unpack the picnic food. "And will you be completely honest with me now, about Hugo?"

"I have been honest, Alison. I just haven't told you everything. But you might as well know . . ."

"Good boy," I said sweetly. I handed him a round roll filled with a slab of some local white cheese whose name, when Jay had asked the grocer, was incomprehensible, then made one for myself. Despite being slightly flattened with the journey, the roll's light brown crust was crisp, its inside freshly soft, and the cheese had a sharp, salty flavor. The combination was delicious.

While we ate, Luke told me the little he knew. "In 1983 there was a coup attempt against Qaddafi by some disaffected army officers. It was quelled, with some savagery, apparently. Our information is that somehow Raphael was connected to the aborted coup. He was close to one of the imprisoned officers, a man named Salim."

Salim. The name in the notebook.

Luke saw my reaction. "Do you know about this, Alison?"

"Remember those appointment diaries I told you that Jay and

I found in Hugo's room? Well, that name, Salim, appears in the last one, the one he kept just before he went to Libya.''

''What else?''

''That's it. Just the name. And it appears only once. But it was the last entry in the diary.''

Luke looked faintly disappointed. He said, ''It's just a theory, but there's a possibility that somehow Hugo's connection to this man Salim was the reason he stayed in Libya. Qaddafi may have used Salim to blackmail Hugo into working for him. At any rate, as soon as Salim escaped from prison, Hugo left Libya.''

''What happened to Salim?''

''We don't know.''

''So all the while that my father was being reviled for working for Qaddafi, he may have secretly been working against him?''

''That's not certain. If he was, it was without the knowledge of the American government.''

''As far as you know.''

He conceded this.

I found it incredible that Hugo would be mixed up in a coup attempt, and said as much to Luke. ''Hugo was never political, Luke. I just can't imagine him taking it into his head to overthrow Qaddafi. It doesn't make any kind of sense at all.'' I was confused, and angry for no reason that I could understand; in fact, I understood nothing. Perhaps that was why I was so angry. The more I learned about my father, the greater an enigma he became. But when had I ever thought he was a simple man? I handed Luke the bag of cherries and lay back in the grass, my eyes shut against the glare of the sun, one arm across my face.

After a while, Luke took a cherry by its stem and held it against my mouth. It was warm and ripe, and when I bit into it, a sweet dark juice ran down my chin onto my neck. I sat up then, wiping the juice away with the back of my hand. Slowly, we took turns feeding each other cherries until the bag was empty. The hot air was heavy with the scent of thyme and wild mint, Demeter's perfume.

At last Luke got to his feet, holding out his hand to me. ''Where's this cave you told me about?''

I took him into the cave, lit one of the lanterns, and showed him the little bowl. We searched for any sign that Elliot had used the cave the previous night, but if he had, he left no trace behind him. Afterward we clambered down the path that led to the cove. The empty shells of tiny snails crunched dryly underfoot, and gray and yellow thistles with blown, puffy heads rustled around our legs. Each step we took sent a plague of grasshoppers leapfrogging into the air. The rocks crawled with insects and reptiles, fat-bodied spiders, the ants that were everywhere, and a lizard like a nightmare, with a pale, balloon-shaped head and wide-splayed legs. Bees and hornets and dragonflies flew past, and once a butterfly as big as a bird fluttered down the cliff, a miniature orange kite bobbing on some imperceptible updraft.

As we descended, the heat increased, and when finally we came to the beach the sun seemed to be everywhere at once, dizzying, intense, penetrating even the narrowest crack of rock. It skipped like a round-edged stone off the sea straight into our eyes, dazzling, blinding. The pale limestone cliffs towering above cradled the tiny beach in a white-hot glare, focusing the sun on the sand like a magnifying glass, so that its rays burned hotter here than they had in the meadow. The twin rock towers that rose from the sea gleamed and shimmered like geysers of steam. Down here, the heat was a living presence.

A streaky green lizard lay flattened by the sun, too stunned to move from its rock. Far above us, a bird with widespread wings hung suspended in the quivering air, a drop of ink flicked against the blue blotting-paper sky.

It was a curious sensation, this feeling that everything was more intense: the heat, the light, the silence. Luke and I stood on the sand without speaking, gazing out at the sea, so close to each other that I could feel the heat like a thin membrane vibrating between us. A bead of sweat formed and broke at his hairline, trickling down across his forehead. Automatically, I reached one hand up to smooth it away before it ran into his eyes. His flesh was hot, and the look he turned on me seemed dazed from the sun, feverish.

"Alison."

The way he said my name made it a confession of emotions that I knew at once were also my own. But it was too hot; I couldn't think clearly, or else too much had happened that I didn't understand, and somehow Luke was too close now, too much a part of it. I walked to the water's edge, where the sand shelved gently out toward a rocky bottom. The sea rippled like a spilled bolt of Thai silk, sapphire and jade shot with amethyst, a shimmer of constantly changing color. On its surface, a thick weed floated in a mass of purple color, trailing long tentacles down into the water. A stippled shoal of some small fish flickered through the weed, broad then narrow bands of silver-blue that changed direction in the blink of an eye.

My bathing suit was back at the tower, in Jay's knapsack, but if I couldn't swim, I would wade. I took off my running shoes, rolling my trousers up to the knee.

Luke saw the bruise on my leg. "How did you do that?" His voice was harsh.

"I ran into a stone, last night when I was following Elliot. It's nothing."

He ignored this and knelt down on the sand in front of me, at the water's edge, lightly touching the skin around the bruise with the tip of his forefinger. His head was bent, exposing the nape of his neck, which was smooth and already dark from the sun. Sunlight rainbowed against his hair, shiny like the pelt of some sleek animal. The urge to stroke it was almost irresistible.

When I shivered, he stood up. "Did I hurt you?" The hazel eyes looked down at me, intent.

I couldn't speak; my throat felt dry, as if it were filled with the thin white dust of the crumbling rock around us.

He put his hands on my shoulders, running them down along the bare flesh of my arms. Unresisting, I moved toward him, urged forward by something I had never felt before and had no name for. A beat went by; time hung suspended like the hawk above us. Then Luke caught his breath and bent his head to mine.

His mouth was sweet with honey and cherries, salt with the sweat on his upper lip. I put my hand on the back of his neck, smoothing the hair that lay in the hollow at the base of his head, silk against the hard, hot skin. Like an answer at once miraculous and obvious, his kiss, and the sure way our bodies moved together, delivered me from all uncertainties. There was nothing, no one, I wanted so much at that moment.

When we finally drew apart, I felt lightheaded, my heart pounding, as though I had climbed too far too quickly. I reached out and put my hand against Luke's chest. Through the thin cloth, I could feel his own heart racing.

I looked at the sea. "It's so beautiful," I said, and my voice sounded strange to my ears. "I wish we could swim."

"Why can't we?"

"I don't have a suit."

"I don't see why that should stop us."

"No? Then I don't suppose it should."

"Good."

We half turned our backs to each other, and stripped off our clothes. In a moment I heard a splash behind me, and looked around in time to see Luke make a barebacked dolphin's dive into the sea, a crescent of biscuit-colored skin arcing over the water. He surfaced once, then sank slowly into the water again and swam away, his naked body sinuous and pale, moving like a current through the changing colors of the sea.

I folded my clothes and left them on a rock by the water, then waded out and dove in after him. Underwater, the golden light of the sun changed, became milky, piercing the thin veils of dark red seaweed that moved gently to and fro, anchored to the sea floor. The water was simultaneously cool and warm on my skin; its heat seemed to shift with its color, emerald, apple-green, blue. . . .

I came up for air to find Luke behind me. "I'll race you to the other side of the bay," he said. "You can have a head start."

"I don't need it." I was a good swimmer, made better by practice in the excellent German public pools that had helped me survive the long dank winter in Bonn.

But I wasn't quite as good, it turned out, as Luke. He beat me easily. I crowned him with a piece of yellow kelp, and gave him the kiss of victory on each cheek, which turned inevitably into something else as we clung together, treading water. Together, we sank down through the water, our mouths and bodies joined, twisting like fish under a net of desire.

Then came up spluttering, out of breath. I opened my eyes to see a gull perched on a rock overhead, watching us with a quizzical eye as though we were some species of exotic sea life, possibly edible. "Voyeur," Luke said, and splashed water at him. The gull flapped off with a loud affronted squawk.

I wriggled out of Luke's arms and looked up at the cliffs above us. "Anyone could be up there watching, not just the gulls. Besides, I should be going."

While I dressed, Luke floated on his back in the water. "A gentleman would close his eyes," I told him.

"And miss the beauties of nature? You should be grateful my camera's out of reach. But I will do one thing to spare your sensibilities . . ." He pulled a fringe of weed across his groin, reminding me of the Priapus in Clio's garden.

The climb back up to the meadow was steep and hot. Conscious of Luke behind me, of his breathing, the movement of his body, I felt heavy-limbed, clumsy. Once I stopped to catch my breath and he came up behind me, holding me gently against him, wordless. The way his hand moved along my body made me ache. I wondered why I had taken such a long time to recognize feelings that must surely have been there from the beginning, they seemed so familiar, so inevitable. Love must be like this, I thought, a longing for more than the body, a sense of communion.

As we said good-bye at the foot of the *trazzera*, I asked Luke what he would do that afternoon.

"I'm going to drive into Palermo, to have the honey tested. I'll find a way to get in touch with you later at Clio Hunt's."

"There's a bar in San Teodoro. In the main piazza . . ." I described the one Jay and I had been to with Clio. "I'll find some way to meet you there this evening. Around eight?"

"Good." Luke moved a finger lightly down my cheek. "Be careful, Alison. Okay?"

The hike back around the mountainside seemed endless. The air hung limp, sullen with the heat, and I felt as if I were the only living creature that moved across the face of the burning rock. Even the lizards had gone to find a bit of shade. The sky had a curious cast to it, too, as though a thin yellow gauze filtered the blue.

When the track reached the northwest face, I saw a dark gray line of cloud on the horizon, resting like a heavy blanket on the rounded peaks of a far range of northern mountains. The line thickened perceptibly as I watched; that meant the clouds were moving south, and very quickly. A small wind began to blow in my face, the sirocco stirring.

I quickened my pace. I could imagine only too well what it would be like to be caught in a storm on this exposed face of rock.

Casteddu and the ruined castle came into view, a toy town, a child's tower, growing larger as the path descended toward them. Suddenly, farther down the track, Elliot appeared, with Jay close behind him. Even at this distance I could see relief on their faces as they hailed me, waving. When I got closer, Jay shouted, "We saw the storm coming. We were afraid you wouldn't make it back in time."

"It looks bad," Elliot added as I reached them. "And the mountain is no place to be when it breaks."

They turned, and together we went swiftly down the track.

CHAPTER 23

The storm swept in from the north on a current of cold air. The sky became as yellow as a lemon, then a deep, angry gray with the massed ranks of clouds. The seabirds were flying inland, away from the storm. Their harsh, urgent cries plucked at my nerves; even the birds were leaving, I thought, and I wished we were going with them.

Inside the tower, it was soon as dark as early evening. Elliot lit the oil lamps, then moved restlessly around the room. He seemed preoccupied, edgy with more than the electricity of the storm. He stutter was worse, too, as we made desultory conversation while Jay sat reading on the other side of the room. After a while, as the rain and wind increased, Elliot and I gave up the effort at polite small talk. Idly, I flipped through an old magazine, thinking of Luke. I hoped he had seen the storm in time and abandoned the idea of going to Palermo.

I found myself worrying about Clio, too, and it occurred to me that if the bad weather lasted too long, she might decide against coming to Castell'alto that afternoon. No matter; we had the car, and when the storm was over, I swore to myself, nothing would stop us from leaving.

Elliot seemed so on edge, so unlike his usual calm self, that it came as a relief when he finally excused himself to go up to the third floor, saying that he would try to get some work done on Hugo's papers. When he was safely upstairs, out of hearing, I told Jay about my meeting with Luke—most of it, anyway. Jay said he had spent an uneventful couple of hours working on the generator with Elliot, who had seemed comparatively relaxed at that point. "But when he saw we were in for a storm, he got sort of nervous. He said he was worried about you."

"I'll bet."

The sound of the rain slashing against the stone outside began to wear me down. I started across to the stove with the thought of making tea, but in the gloom almost stumbled over Jay's backpack on the floor. For the first time since finding them, I remembered the strange assortment of Hugo's drawings that we'd taken from the portfolio. They might not signify anything at all, might be merely the equivalent of idle sketches—I had seen Hugo almost absentmindedly sketching out plans while he talked about something quite different, his equivalent of doodling—but if that was so, why, then, had he kept them? And why was the folder marked in such a curious way? The lady of the labyrinth: it had to mean something.

I picked up the backpack and went over to Jay. In a low voice, I told him I wanted to have a good look at the drawings. "Upstairs in my room, where I won't be interrupted by Elliot."

Jay pulled the folder out of the backpack and handed it to me. "Shall I come with you?"

"Not right away. I'll think better alone." I took one of the lamps and went upstairs.

In my room, with the door shut, I spread the seven drawings out on the floor. For a long time I simply sat staring at them, trying to pin down a faint niggling memory of something else, something familiar.

Each drawing was on the same-size sheet of European standard graph paper, but the shapes of the drawings on the paper were odd. They were rough geometrical shapes, a rectangle, a sort of parallelogram, and triangles of various sizes. Each seemed almost to be the plan of some small labyrinthine medieval town full of little alleys, short streets, odd-shaped blocks and squares. I picked up the drawings in turn and studied them. I must have been sitting there for at least half an hour, while the wind and the rain lashed the tower, when at last there was a tap on the door and Jay called my name out softly. I told him to come in.

"Any luck?" he asked, as he closed the door quietly behind him.

I shook my head. "There's something familiar, but I can't put my finger on it." I was sitting cross-legged on the floor, with the drawings spread out around me. "I've been trying to figure out why they're all different shapes."

"Like a puzzle," Jay said.

When he said that, I knew. It was so childishly simple I felt a fool for taking so long.

"Pass me that pink plastic bag, will you?" I asked Jay. "The one on top of my suitcase." The pink bag held my makeup, and from it I took out a small pair of scissors. Quickly, I cut out each drawing, making straight lines out of the rough shapes, careful to stay close to the penciled edges of the drawing. Jay watched silently. In a few minutes, I had cut out each of the seven shapes. I arranged them so that they fit together neatly in a large square.

Jay looked nonplussed. "I still don't see," he said. "Even when you put them together like that, the drawings themselves don't make any sense as a unit."

"Don't you see? It's a tangram." His face was still mystified. "Haven't you ever played with one?"

"Uh-uh. What's a tangram?"

I explained. "It's a puzzle with seven pieces—a square, a parallelogram and five triangles of different sizes. You're supposed to connect all seven shapes to make up a figure of some sort. Hugo gave me an antique tangram when I was about eight or nine. It was made in the nineteenth century, when there was a real craze for tangrams. I remember it was hand-painted wood and very beautiful. I spent my entire weekend visit with him playing with it. He told me you could make over six hundred figures, and I was determined to make every single one."

Jay was quick. "You think if we arranged these pieces in the right way, we'd see a pattern?"

"I'm sure of it."

"Great. Now we only have to think of six hundred shapes."

"Not so many." It was falling into place. "Remember what he wrote on the portfolio? 'The lady of the labyrinth'? I think if we can make some sort of female figure out of the pieces, we'll have the answer."

We spread the shapes out once more on the floor, and I began to arrange them. "The important thing about a tangram is that it suggests a figure more than it accurately represents it. Your mind is tricked into turning the shape into something specific. All we have to do is arrange these until we have something vaguely resembling a female. The tangram came from China originally, so when the pieces are arranged to suggest a female, she usually seems to be wearing some sort of Oriental dress."

As I shuffled the pieces, I tried to visualize the figures I had made in my childhood. Finally, after a number of false starts and several figures that looked reasonably female but made no sense as a whole map or diagram, I found the one that fit. To my surprise, it also vaguely resembled the figure in profile on the coin in my medallion, the standing woman in a long tunic, her hand upraised. The two largest triangles formed the base, or the skirt of the long dress or kimono, the parallelogram was a kind of bustle at the back, and three smaller triangles were the bust, shoulders, and upraised arm, and the square set on one of its angles onto the shoulder was the head. Now the lines of the various maps flowed into each other, connecting and clearly making a single map.

Almost before I finished, Jay, who was squatting beside me, exclaimed, "But that's got to be a map of some sort of cave system connected to Clio's cave! See, that's Clio's cave there!" He reached forward and touched the lower right-hand angle of the bottom shape, one of the large triangles that formed the base of the figure. "Here's the entrance, and this must be the tunnel. . . ."

"Are you sure?"

"Yes, now that I see it all together like this. I read cave maps all the time—you have to be able to if you go caving. I know this is Clio's cave. And here's the tunnel. Let's orient the figure to the points of the compass, like this." He moved the pieces carefully around. "Clio's cave is at the southwest, then obviously the rest of the system runs under Monte Castello, and this—" he pointed at the square that made up the head of the figure—"look how this is almost separated from the rest of the figure, so it has to be Casteddu. That long tunnel there might be another entrance leading up under the plateau. If everything is in scale, it has to come out—"

"Under the *castello*," I finished for him.

Jay picked up the square drawing and studied its details for a minute. Excitedly, he said, "That place where weapons were stored, the arsenal or armaments room or whatever it's called, with the locked door that Elliot said only Hugo had the key to? The entrance has to be under that. It's the right place on this map. If only we could check—"

"No," I said firmly, for I knew what he was about to propose. "No more exploring. You can ask Hugo for a guided tour when he comes back. But when this storm is over, we're leaving. I've had enough of ruined castles and towers and caves. The thrill of the gothic never had much appeal for me anyway."

Jay looked disappointed, but he was a good sport. "I guess you're right." Then, "Why do you think Hugo went to all this trouble?"

"The date on the portfolio was 1938, remember? I think it's

safe to assume he drew the map on that first visit to Castell'alto. He was eighteen—maybe he was just having fun, making a game of it. Hugo always liked puzzles and mysteries. And I suppose using the tangram was a way of ensuring that no one else would understand it.''

''What was he trying to hide?''

''The same thing he hid when he rescued Don Calo and the others. A cave system that must have been used as a secret way up to Casteddu from the meadow.''

''But why keep it secret?''

''Because he hoped to find something down there.'' I thought about this for a moment, and it began to make a kind of sense to me. ''If he had found something, I don't think Hugo would have kept it a secret. He was an archaeologist, after all. And he always said it was important to publish findings right away. So it has to be something he hadn't found, but hoped to someday. Most likely something to do with the cult of the goddess that Clio said existed once at Casteddu. Maybe that's why he didn't get along with Giudico, because Giudico knew something was down there, too, and was trying to find it first. Only his friend got killed in the process and he was half blinded.''

At that moment we heard Elliot coming down the stairs from Hugo's room. In our concentration I had forgotten all about him. I realized now, too, that I couldn't hear the wind anymore. When I went over to the window and opened my shutters, we saw that the rain had stopped. The sky to the north was clear, the cloudy sky above already streaked with blue. Below the tower the sea still heaved with choppy, white-capped waves, but the storm had passed on.

Downstairs, Elliot was calling our names. Hastily, I stuffed the drawings back into Jay's knapsack. ''Come on. We'd better go.''

When he saw us, Elliot said, ''I don't know what sort of shape the road will be in after this. Do you still want to try?'' I thought I saw relief in his eyes when we said yes. I went to fetch my suitcase.

''What if Clio decides to visit after all?'' Jay asked me as we climbed into the Jeep.

''We're bound to run into her on the way,'' I said. ''We'll flag her down.''

The track down the mountain was soupy with mud in places, but the Jeep managed it without too much difficulty. In the slanting rays of the late afternoon sun the wet rocks glistened like crystal, and the scent of warm damp earth and jasmine drifted from the garden plots. When we reached the square in Castell'-alto where I'd left the car, there was still no sign of Clio.

As we were saying good-bye to Elliot, Matteo suddenly appeared on the other side of the square, coming toward us. "You are going?" he asked. When we said yes, he shook his head. "No way. I was coming to tell you this. The road is no good now. Much mud has come down on it. Tomorrow, perhaps, it will be clear, but now . . . no way."

I looked bleakly at Jay. "The sightseeing will have to wait." Then, to Elliot, "I'm afraid you're stuck with us one more night."

To his credit, Elliot managed a smile. "That's fine with me." But his voice lacked conviction.

While Elliot questioned Matteo about the mudslide, Jay swung my suitcase back into the Jeep. Under his breath, he muttered to me, "We could always hike it to Don Calo's if you don't want to stay in the tower tonight."

The idea was almost appealing, but I shook my head. It seemed to me that there was little to choose between the tower and Lupaia; they were equally isolated and the men who occupied them equally unfathomable. Besides, we really had no legitimate reason to fear another night spent at Casteddu. If Elliot felt an urge to wander the mountain after dark, he was welcome to do it in private this time. Jay and I would keep to our rooms.

Matteo said good-bye and went off to help with the digging out. Before we climbed back into the Jeep, I told Elliot that I wanted to leave a message for Clio. "She gave me a number to call if I needed to get in touch." If I could manage to use the phone in the bar alone while Jay somehow distracted Elliot, I would also call Luke.

"I'm afraid you can't," Elliot replied. "Matteo's just been telling me that the mudslide brought the phone lines down, too."

I told myself that if Luke had seen the storm coming and decided to wait it out in Castell'alto, he would be here now, and would know we were forced to spend another night at the tower. If he had gone to Palermo, he would be unable to return to Castell'alto. Somehow or other, whether he talked to Clio or not, he was bound to realize that we were trapped in Casteddu. But I wanted to be sure. I said, "You know, Elliot, Jay and I wouldn't mind seeing something of Castell'alto now that we're here. You don't need to wait for us. We can walk back up later.'' We could find the Pensione Bella Vista, and with a little luck, Luke.

"Let me show you around, then," Elliot said.

"No, really, you don't have to bother—"

"It's no bother. Besides, the track up really isn't fit for walking until the mud dries. You'll be better off in the Jeep."

At that moment I hated Elliot. "All right, then. Thank you."

We must have explored every alley, every cranny of Castell'-alto, but I remember very little of the tour. "That looks interesting," I would say as we came to one more dismal, dark lane. Or, with desperate enthusiasm, "Oh, let's look down there. I've never seen that sort of stonework before." Elliot seemed tolerantly amused by my appetite for Sicilian domestic architecture; perhaps he put it down to Hugo's genes. But Luke and the Pensione Bella Vista remained elusive. Finally, weary and hungry, I conceded defeat. It was growing dark anyway.

We said almost nothing on the ride back up to Casteddu. Elliot seemed disinclined to talk, and neither Jay nor I had much desire to break the silence. After a quiet dinner of anchovies, bread, and salad, Elliot excused himself to go back to work. I wondered if he was trying now to make up for lost time before Hugo returned. Or was he getting rid of whatever evidence remained of his other activities, evidence Jay and I had overlooked?

Jay and I went outside to watch the sunset, a spectacular fireworks that lit up the undersides of the clouds with orange and pink. The sea was still now, with the flat, exhausted calm that comes after a storm. "Lock your door again tonight, okay?" I told Jay as we leaned on the stone wall, looking out at the water. "We'll leave first thing tomorrow, even if we have to dig our way out."

"In a way, I'll be sorry to go," Jay said wistfully. "It's almost like he's here sometimes. Hugo, I mean. Like he's going to walk in the door any moment . . ."

We went to bed early. I waited outside Jay's door until I heard the bolt snick home and then, still dressed, settled down in my room with a book and the flashlight, lit now by batteries I had found in a drawer downstairs. I intended to read for a while before bed, but I was so tired from the previous night, the hike back and forth from the meadow, and our tour of Castell'alto that my eyes closed once, twice, and before I knew it I was asleep.

When the flashlight fell off the bed onto the floor with a thud, I woke up. My wristwatch showed just after eleven.

Stiff from lying at an awkward angle, I got up and stretched. My mouth was dry, but I had forgotten to fill the thermos by my bed. Softly, I opened my door and went across the landing to the bathroom, where there was a carafe of water for toothbrushing. On the way back, I noticed that Jay's door was pulled to, but not shut. Anxiously, I tapped once, then opened it and looked in.

Jay's room was empty, his bed not even slept in.

I ran downstairs.

Elliot, too, was gone.

CHAPTER 24

I tried not to panic. Remembering the wistful look on Jay's face that afternoon when he said how much he wished he could find Hugo's secret entrance to the cave system, I thought perhaps the temptation to explore might have been too strong for him. But when I ran outside to the sunken door that led to the underground armory, I found the lock undisturbed.

Standing in the middle of the courtyard, I shouted out Jay's name, not caring now how much noise I made. The only answer was a rustling somewhere near my feet as some small night creature slithered away through the dust to safety. Fearfully, I stared up at Monte Castello; the moon hung above the mountain like a single baleful eye, glaring back at me. If Jay had followed Elliot on another of his expeditions to the meadow . . . The terrible thought was enough to send me running through the dead town to the house with the blue door. At the touch of my hand, the door swung open onto emptiness, the padlock dangling from the hasp. Two houses down, the upper half of the Dutch door stood open; Orlando was gone from his stall. It was all the proof I needed. I raced to the bridge, searching the great dark face of the mountain for the invisible line of the path, straining to make out a shape, some sign of movement.

And then, far above, I saw the figures of a man and a donkey.

Elliot and Orlando were just at the point where the track began to disappear around the curve of the mountain. I was watching them start around it when, thirty feet or so behind, a smudge of darkness moved on the track, briefly took human shape, then blended into the rocks again. The shout to come back died in my throat, barely a whisper, choked off by the instinctive conviction that Elliot must not know Jay was following him. Something was forcing the man out on the mountain tonight, but it was a pressure more real, I was sure, than his story of black-

mailing shepherds. All afternoon he had seemed like a man
close to some inner edge. Now the edge was real, a fifteen-
hundred-foot drop at his feet.

And at Jay's.

Halfway across the footbridge, I looked up again. At that
outer curve of the track, a stealthy dark figure paused for a
heartbeat, alone against the night sky.

I crossed the bridge running and started up the track, which
was storm-marked with mud and debris, small landslides of
stone that slipped treacherously underfoot. In places, Orlando's
muffled hooves had stamped the thin layer of wet earth with
wide blurry prints, but the muffling cloth must have grown uselessly heavy with mud, for shortly afterward I saw several large
pieces of burlap cast off on the rocks near the track, and the
outline of the hoofprints sharpened.

My fear for Jay made me careless. I was hurrying, almost
running, when I stepped sideways off some loose shale and went
stumbling forward. Desperately fighting to keep my balance, I
put my right foot down hard in the cleft of a rock—so hard that
the rubber sole of my shoe wedged tight in the crack. When I
tried to yank my leg back, the shoe wouldn't budge. Worse, my
foot was twisted at such an awkward angle that I couldn't sit
down or stand up straight. Cursing myself, I bent over to try to
free the foot from the trapped shoe. But the shoe closed with
Velcro straps, instead of laces, and they were fastened on the
side that was wedged most securely against the rough rock. It
took me several sweaty minutes of patient struggle to work the
top strap loose enough to release my foot from the shoe. I ro-
tated my ankle gingerly, relieved to find I could move it without
pain.

I pulled the shoe loose and put it back on. Then I set off up
the path again, more cautiously this time, consoling myself with
the thought that the snakes, at least, were in bed.

It seemed to go on forever, that slow journey up the high and
empty moonscape of white rock. The arms of the prickly pears
stood palely aghast as I climbed past them, frozen in attitudes
of shock. Intruder, go back, the upflung limbs seemed to say.
Far below, the black sea glittered with a cold brilliance. Only
the thought of Jay somewhere ahead kept me moving forward
across the face of that vast, terrifying indifference.

At last I saw them, close to the summit of the track on a short
stretch of open ground free of tumbled boulders, Elliot and the
donkey, two small figures in silhouette against the shining rock.

They were climbing quickly, Elliot forging ahead, his body straining forward up the slope, Orlando following with a large bulky load on his back. Expecting to see Jay in pursuit soon after, I tried to distinguish between the boulders and what might be a human figure.

But although I waited until Elliot and the donkey had climbed the final yards to the top of the track and vanished onto the southeast face, no one followed them.

I could have missed him, if he were keeping low and close to the rock; it was difficult enough to make out a man with a donkey at that distance, let alone someone doing his best to keep from being seen. Wearily, I rubbed my eyes, which ached from the combined strain of searching the distances and staring down at the ground below my feet in an effort to keep from stumbling again. What if Jay had had an accident somewhere along the way? An almost overpowering urge to shout his name took hold of me, to call out his name until the whole mountain rang with it.

Then it struck me that Jay might have realized the risk he was running and given up the chase, and was even now making his way back down the mountain toward me. Spurred by sudden hope, I toiled on up the track. Around every turning, every boulder, I believed I would see him.

Some ten minutes later I was high on Monte Castello's southeast flank—and there was still no sign of Jay. Far away to the east, small pinpricks of light marked villages invisible during the day, too distant to be comforting now. Below, on the length of the track's long descent, all was a dark, empty silence. The warm night wind gusted around me, plucking at my clothes like some restless soul searching for shelter.

The descent was in some ways the most dangerous part of the journey. Anyone might look up from the meadow and catch sight of me when the track passed through a stretch of moonlight. As much as I could, I kept close to the rock and stayed in the shadows, terrified all the while that the slightest misstep would start off a warning landslide of shale. After endless minutes of cautiously picking my way from hiding place to hiding place, I reached the wide shelf of rock that overhung the meadow. Part of the cliff reared up next to it, casting a broad shadow across half of its width. Keeping well in the shadow, I crawled out onto the rock on my hands and knees. Near the edge, I lay down on my stomach and inched my way slowly forward. The jagged limestone dug into my body through the thick cloth of my jeans and cotton shirt. The stone smelled of some sharp, peppery herb growing in the crannies of the rock. Its surface was dry, despite the storm, as if the arid rock had sucked up every bit of the rain that had fallen.

Somewhere out at sea there was the distant *phut-phut* of an engine, night fishermen perhaps, although I couldn't see the lights of a boat. Then, from almost directly below in the meadow, came Orlando's soft whicker. Startled, I pressed myself flat on the rock, one cheek resting against the stone. After a moment, I cautiously raised my head until I could see over the edge down onto the meadow.

Elliot was leading the donkey behind the boulders that screened the entrance to Clio's cave. After he disappeared, I briefly contemplated moving closer but chose in the end to keep to the relative safety of the ledge, where I had a bird's-eye view. The moon shone down onto the little meadow like a powerful arc light. It gave everything a sharper edge, outlining the angles of stone, deepening the shadows. But there was still no sign of Jay. I knew I needed to stay calm for his sake, but I could feel worry working away at my fragile self-control like the jaws of some persistent, burrowing insect, widening the cracks where fear crept in.

Elliot emerged without the donkey a few minutes later. He walked to the cliff edge above the beach. He must have been carrying a flashlight, for as he raised his right hand a powerful beam of light speared the darkness ahead of him. He flicked the light on and off three times. After a moment, an answering light pulse flashed out from the vast blackness of the sea. Elliot turned and walked back across the meadow. "They're ready," he said. His voice was loud, jarring the stillness of the night.

For a nerve-tingling instant I thought he was talking to me. But he was looking straight ahead, not up.

Footsteps crunched on shale. Like some small wicked spirit, Giudico Coccalo stepped out from behind the boulders at the cave entrance. His misshapen face was more terrible now than in daylight; it seemed a leering satyr's mask, inhuman. He and Elliot stood talking intently in the middle of the meadow, too far off for me to be able to hear what they were saying.

But their voices grew louder, and it soon became clear they were arguing. With a curse, Giudico pounded his fist into his palm. "No!" he shouted. "Do you think I am a fool?"

"For Christ's sake, Giudico, calm down." Elliot was shouting, too, but his voice did not sound angry. "Just do as I say and everything'll be okay. No one will connect you with any of this anyway. Later, when things have settled down, I'll get word to you."

"I tell you it's crazy to leave the girl behind. She'll just make trouble."

"Damn it, Giudico. Don't mess things up by interfering now—"

I stopped listening. Something had stirred in the thick clump of boulders at the bottom of the track, where I had hidden that morning, waiting for Luke. It had to be Jay. He made no sound, but the slight movement alone was enough to catch my eye as I watched from above. Somehow I had to warn him to stay out of sight.

His dark figure crept forward, drifting like a silent wraith from rock to rock, using the boulders as shields to make his way slowly closer to Elliot and Giudico. He kept to the edge of the meadow, next to the mountain. When he paused behind a boulder, he was well hidden from the two men but clearly visible now to me as I looked down on him. Shocked, I realized that it wasn't Jay at all. It was Luke.

We weren't much more than twenty yards apart, but I had no way to let him know I was there. I didn't dare risk a thrown pebble, a whisper, some sign, for any sound I made would carry clearly to Elliot and Giudico. I could only watch, frightened and helpless. A sickening thought gripped me: If Luke had been trailing Elliot, where then was Jay?

By now, Giudico and Elliot seemed to have reached an agreement; Giudico nodded as Elliot tapped him approvingly on the side of the shoulder with his fist. When they separated, Elliot returned to the cave, while Giudico walked toward the cliff edge. He was wearing a light jacket, which he took off and laid carefully over a stone some ten feet from the edge after removing what looked like a pack of cigarettes from one pocket. For a few moments he stood there, staring out to sea, watching perhaps for the boat that had signaled earlier. Then he sat down on the stone. He sat slightly hunched over, his head bowed, as if he were trying to light his cigarette.

Meanwhile, Luke had come out of hiding and was silently crossing the meadow, approaching Giudico from behind. But the wind must have blown out Giudico's match for he suddenly turned, to put his back to the wind, and saw Luke not five feet behind him. As he opened his mouth to shout, Luke lunged at him. The shout died to a grunt when Luke's fist struck his face.

The two men crashed sideways to the ground, Luke half on top of Giudico, who managed to twist partly free as they fell. Scrabbling at the ground to pull himself away, his hand found a large stone. He grabbed it, raised it up, and was about to smash it into the side of Luke's head as I screamed.

The scream startled Giudico into an instant's hesitation so that Luke was able to clutch at his wrist, slamming it down on the ground. Giudico grunted with pain, and the stone fell from his grasp.

My scream brought Elliot running from the cave. He must have realized where the sound came from, for he looked up, scanning the slope above. By now I was on my feet and halfway down the track, in plain sight. Our eyes met, held, and then he ran swiftly up the track at me like a tiger toward its prey. Breathless, I stood my ground. I couldn't outrun Elliot, and I couldn't abandon Luke. Or Jay, wherever he was. I prayed he would have the sense to stay hidden until he could go for help.

When he saw I wasn't trying to run away, Elliot slowed to a walk. As I came toward him, he said, "You should have stayed in bed, Alison. This really doesn't concern you."

Warily, I tried to edge past him. "We've got to stop them—" I began.

"You want to be peacemaker?" His voice was amused. "Come on, then. We'll get them to kiss and make up." With that, he turned and went ahead of me down to the meadow.

Luke and Giudico were locked together in a horrible embrace at the far side of the meadow, near the cliff. Giudico was smaller than Luke, but he twisted and squirmed like a weasel, flailing away as if possessed. When Luke flinched back from a wild sideways punch to his head, Giudico broke free and scrambled to his feet. But as he leveled a badly aimed kick at Luke's head, Luke rolled over out of the way, grabbing his leg. Giudico staggered back, lost his balance, and fell. Luke threw himself at him. Each movement was bringing them closer to the edge of the cliff.

"Make them stop!" I screamed, grabbing at Elliot's arm. "For God's sake . . ."

In an utterly calm voice, Elliot said, "Wait."

I looked at him, shocked. He was watching the fight with a detached interest, much as Nero must have watched two gladiators while he made up his mind which was to die.

I started forward, but Elliot threw one arm up in front of me. In his hand was a small and very lethal-looking gun. "I said wait. I'll take care of this." His gaze as he stared down at me held a faint glint of amusement more chilling than any threat.

Luke was on top of Giudico now, pinning him down. Giudico screamed at Elliot for help.

Elliot gave a small sigh. "Shit," he muttered. Before I could stop him, he moved swiftly across the grass toward the two men and brought the butt of his gun down hard on the back of Luke's skull. Luke slumped forward. With a curse, Giudico heaved Luke's unconscious body off him and struggled to his feet. *"Porca miseria!"* he said furiously to Elliot. "Were you waiting for him to kill me?" He put the back of his hand to his face, to stanch the blood that streamed from his nose.

Elliot gestured at me with the gun as I ran past him to Luke. "A small problem to deal with first."

Sick with fear, I knelt down beside Luke. He lay sprawled on his side with his face hidden in the long grass. As gently as I could, I turned him over. His eyes were shut, and his head sagged heavily against my arm. I felt for his pulse, relieved to feel it beating under my fingers, but when I touched the place where I thought Elliot's blow had landed something sticky and wet clung to my fingers. Blood was trickling down his neck. "We've got to get him to a doctor!" I said frantically, looking up at Elliot. "If he has a concussion . . ."

Elliot ignored this. "Who the hell is he, anyway?"

"He's a friend—"

Giudico did not let me finish. Grabbing my arm, he jerked me roughly to my feet. I cried out as Luke's head fell back onto the grass. "What's he doing here?" Giudico said angrily. "Sightseeing—like you?"

"Let me go!" I pulled free from Giudico's grip and turned to Elliot. "I don't care what you and Giudico are up to. I promise I won't say anything about this to anyone. I swear it! If only you'll help me get Luke to a doctor." Even as I begged him I recognized the idiocy of expecting a man who had cold-bloodedly knocked someone unconscious to help his victim.

Elliot paid no attention to my pleading; he and Giudico were quarreling again. I thanked God that Jay at least had the sense to stay hidden. He might even have gone for help, back along the path to the village, or to Don Calo's. If he had, it would take at least a good half hour, and probably far longer, before he managed to reach anyone, whichever way he went. And another ten minutes before they could make it back to the meadow by car. More than enough time for whatever Elliot and Giudico had in store for us.

That was when I took in what Elliot and Giudico were arguing about. Horrified, I heard Giudico say that they should push Luke's unconscious body over the cliff, to kill him and make his death look accidental. Elliot, mercifully, was reluctant. "We can't do that, Giudico. It would only complicate things. Besides, our friends will arrive soon, and then we'd have to explain. It might frighten them off."

Giudico was insistent; he wasn't going to take the chance, he said angrily, that Luke would survive. "You are leaving Sicily, perhaps. I cannot. It is better always to make certain your enemy is dead." Without waiting for Elliot to agree, Giudico put his hands under Luke's arms and began dragging him toward the cliff. I threw myself at Giudico, screaming at him for God's sake to stop, but he struck at me with one hand, knocking me back onto the grass.

Elliot looked down at me, then reached out and helped me to my feet. "I warned you that this was how Giudico resolved his problems." Incredibly, he sounded amused.

"If you don't stop him, Elliot," I said desperately, "I'll tell him you were having an affair with his wife."

"What do you—" he began.

I didn't let him finish. There wasn't time. "Make him stop!" I said fiercely. Then, loudly, "Giudico, do you know that—"

Elliot's voice overrode mine. "For Christ's sake, Giudico, you don't have to kill him. Look, I have an idea . . ."

But Giudico ignored him. Leaving Luke several feet from the edge, he took a few steps forward, possibly to make certain that the drop was enough to finish Luke off. But the heavy rain must have softened the unstable earth at the very edge of the cliff, and now Giudico's weight did the rest. He was turning around, so we plainly saw the shock on his face as he realized what was happening, the way fear filled his one good eye. His arms flailed out frantically, but there was nothing to catch hold of, no way of keeping his balance. And then he was gone, as the earth gave way under him. There was a short desperate cry, and silence.

I gasped. Beside me, Elliot swore softly, a stream of profanity that continued as he grabbed my arm, and began to pull me toward the cliff edge with him. Terrified, I resisted him with all my strength, struggling against his grip.

"Don't be so stupid!" he said impatiently. "Do you think I'm going to push you over after Giudico? I just wanted to have a look, that's all."

"Then do it by yourself. I'm not going any closer."

With a small exasperated sigh, he let me go. I knelt down again beside Luke and pulled him as gently as I could back to safer ground. I checked his pulse and breathing; as far as I could tell, they seemed stable. The blood was oozing from his wound, but more slowly now. I pulled my shirttail out from my jeans and ripped a strip off from the bottom, then bound it around Luke's head.

Elliot walked slowly back to me. His face was hard, fixed—not with anger so much as with a grim concentration. He nodded when I asked him if Giudico was dead. "No one could survive a f . . . fall like that." He raised the little gun, which had been held almost casually down at his side, and told me to get up. "You're going to have to keep me company now. Until things get sorted out."

"What about Luke? He needs help—"

"I didn't hit him hard enough to kill him." Elliot motioned me to go ahead of him, toward the cave entrance. "He'll come around eventually, so I'm going to have to tie him up. There's some rope in the cave." Although he never threatened me directly with the gun, its presence was unequivocal. Every bit of me rebelled at the thought of leaving Luke alone and unconscious in the middle of the meadow, of entering the cave with Elliot. But I had no choice.

Both the lanterns were lit, each sitting in a niche along the cave wall. The donkey stood motionless near the center of the cave, his head down, a large blanket-covered burden on his back. A little distance from the donkey, on the cave floor, was the same crate from which Jay and I had stolen the bottle of honey that morning.

When Elliot approached the donkey, the blanket stirred slightly. And then from under it came a muffled groan.

Horrified, I ran over and pulled the blanket off. Underneath, Jay was tied facedown across the donkey's back, a gag covering his mouth. His knapsack was strapped to his back. "Jay," I whispered. "Oh, Jay." With trembling fingers, I unknotted the gag and pulled it away. He ran his tongue across his lips, but his eyes were closed. I put my head close to his and gently touched his cheek. "Are you all right? Did he hurt you?"

To my relief, his eyes fluttered open. "Alison." It was more a breath than a word.

"He'll live," Elliot said. "He's just a little stiff from the ride. You can untie him now."

A rope ran under the donkey's belly linking Jay's hands and feet. My fingers felt hopelessly clumsy as I struggled to work the coarse rope loose from the thick, difficult knots. "Why in God's name did you do this to him?" I asked Elliot, trying to read some emotion in his face. "He's only a boy . . ."

"What did you say!" For the first time that night Elliot looked angry.

"I said he's only a boy. It's a cowardly act, to hurt someone smaller—"

"Shut up!" His face murderous, Elliot took a step toward me, holding the gun as though he would hit me with it, while I tried to shield Jay with my body. But he stopped suddenly, and the anger in his face drained away as swiftly as it had risen. "Listen," he said, "in a way, you know, it's your own fault— you had to insist on staying at the tower. You just never gave me the chance to tidy things up properly before Hugo comes back. Now Giudico's dead, and I'm going to have to do something about you two."

My throat was dry; for a moment I couldn't speak. Finally, I managed to ask what he meant.

"Don't worry. I'm not going to hurt you—unless you make me. Violence isn't the way I like to get things done." He leaned back against the cave wall by the entrance, at his ease. "The Sicilians never learn that there are more efficient ways to achieve your goals. Just look at Giudico—the dead proof that I'm right. So if you and your brother do as I say, you'll be fine. You're only going to take a little trip with some friends of mine. They'll reunite you with Hugo. Eventually. It's what you want, after all."

"What friends?" I asked him, remembering the signal from the water. By now I had undone half the knots. Jay lay without stirring, but at least his eyes were open and his breathing was regular.

"Libyan friends." He smiled then, amused at my reaction. "I met some Libyans through my business contacts here soon after I came to live at the tower. While I was working on Hugo's papers, I stumbled on one fact I thought might interest them. It did. It interested Qaddafi even more. He was quite generous in his appreciation of the information."

I stopped in the middle of wrestling with a stubborn knot and stared at Elliot. "You're the reason Hugo had to go to Libya?"

"I can't take all the credit. Let's say I'm part of it. You'll find out the rest soon enough. But I won't spoil the surprise." He smiled genially. "Hurry up with that rope. Your friend outside won't stay unconscious forever. And you don't want me to have to hit him again."

As another knot gave way, the rope that bound Jay loosened sufficiently so that I was able to free his feet. One end of the rope still tied his hands, but the other dropped to the cave floor. With an arm around his waist, I helped Jay off the donkey's back, feeling his thin body trembling against mine. He was stiff, and held on to me for support. "I'm okay," he said in a weak voice, "but I'm sorry—"

I hugged him softly. "I'm so thankful you're not hurt, Jay. That's all that matters." That and Luke. I bent my head over Jay's wrists so he wouldn't see my face, and began to work on the rope that bound them. Fiercely, I swore to myself that I would allow nothing and no one to hurt these two people I loved.

"You know," I said to Elliot, "people will look for us."

"Of course people will look for you. Clio, for a start. She knows that Jay likes to go caving, so it won't surprise her that the three of us decided to explore this cave. They won't find our bodies, of course, just some evidence we entered the cave. The rain was useful—we've left some nice footprints outside. Meanwhile you'll be safe in Libya. And I'll be . . . well, never mind where I'll be."

"It'll never work," I told him. "The American government will insist that we're freed."

Elliot smiled cynically. "And Islamic extremists are so eager to do as the American government tells them, aren't they? I'm sure Qaddafi would deny all knowledge of the kidnapping. And you could be held somewhere else, if necessary—in Lebanon, for instance."

"What do you get out of all this?"

"A chance to expand my business. Come on, Alison, you're wasting time. My associates won't be as patient as I am."

As I struggled to undo the last knot, I heard a faint humming sound in the silence. I knew immediately what it was. The small swarm of bees, fanning their wings to keep warm in the coolness of the cave. They were in the shadows, so Elliot hadn't seen them, and he hadn't heard them because he'd been too busy talking, first to Giudico and then to me. Given his allergy, he would never have come into the cave if he had realized the bees were there.

"I can't untie this," I said to Elliot, letting a tearful whine creep into my voice. "It's just too tight."

"All right, then, I'll do it. Stand back, way back. If you do anything stupid, Jay will be sorry."

I did as he said, moving back into the cave against the wall where I remembered the swarm was hanging. The soft humming came from just behind my head. Elliot rested the gun on Orlando's rump while he ordered Jay to stretch his arms out in front of him. As he worked on the last knot, he kept an eye on me.

I had to keep talking, so that he wouldn't hear the bees. I told him I had followed him as far as the bridge the previous night, had seen him return."You were angry about something, but it wasn't Leporino, was it?"

"So you were watching, were you?" He seemed to find this entertaining. "No, it wasn't Leporino. I had another kind of meeting. I wanted my friends to know about you and Jay—Hugo, too. But they never made it. They're here tonight, though." With these words, he pulled the rope free from around Jay's wrists and picked up the gun again. He draped the rope over one arm. "Go stand over there beside Alison," he told Jay.

I took a deep breath, then turned around and slid my hand up the stone until I felt the honeycomb, which hung like a stalactite from the jutting piece of rock. I was sure I'd be stung, but, remembering Clio's advice, I made all my movements deliberate and slow. I couldn't afford to rush this, and I counted on the shadows and surprise to keep Elliot from knowing for a crucial few seconds what it was I was doing. I pulled hard with a twisting motion at the crown of the comb where it joined the rock. It broke off in my hand.

"What the hell are you—" Elliot began.

Holding the sleepy mass of bees in front of me like a burning brand, I turned and took a step toward him, putting myself directly in front of Jay. When Elliot saw what it was I had, his face blanched in fear. Behind me, I heard Jay's gasp of surprise.

Backing away, Elliot stretched one hand out imploringly toward me; in his other hand the gun was visibly shaking. "F . . . f . . . for God's sake, Alison, don't—"

"Put the gun down!"

He was still backing away toward the entrance of the cave as I advanced on him. Terror distorted his face. He was about to speak but then he stumbled over something, falling backwards, and his arm jerked up. He fired the gun, but the shot went high and wild. Desperately, I threw the swarm at him. It caught him full in the chest, the bees exploding against him like a child's piñata filled with candy. He screamed and fired again and again, wild shots that hit stone. Jay and I threw ourselves onto the floor of the cave. Then Elliot turned and ran crazily into the night, arms flailing, while the bees swarmed after him. His screams were terrible. I felt sick to my stomach. Somewhere overhead, in an ominous echo of Elliot's screams, there was a strange rumbling sound.

"We've got to get out of here," I told Jay as we scrambled to our feet. "Luke's outside. And Elliot was waiting for someone else. . . ."

The rumbling sound grew louder. And all at once I knew what it must be. I grabbed Jay's arm and pulled him toward the entrance. "Hurry! Hurry!"

But it was too late. With a great roaring and crashing, a flood of rock and earth fell across the entrance and a blinding, choking cloud of dust filled the cave.

CHAPTER 25

An invisible hand slammed me back, knocked Jay to the ground, snuffed out the lanterns. Like a giant in torment, the mountain groaned and shook in a hideous rumbling fury of stone grating and smashing on stone, while I cowered there on the cave floor with no thought in my head but death. On and on it went for endless, mindless, terrible seconds until at last the roaring faded into intermittent muffled crashings as the last moments of the landslide died away. A faint trickling sound followed, like the hopeless scratching of some trapped creature growing steadily weaker. Finally there was only silence, the black silence of the tomb.

Frantically, I whispered Jay's name into the darkness, choking on the dust that hung in the air, not daring to call out for fear of what a loud noise might do to still-precarious rock, all that rock, those thousands of tons of rock, just above my head.

A harsh coughing came from my left. "I'm here," Jay said at last, his voice rough but free from any sign of pain.

I said a silent prayer of thanksgiving. "Are you all right?"

"Yes. You?"

"Yes."

"Hold on," Jay said, and I laughed, because it was so absurd to think that I could be going anywhere. His voice came back worried. "Are you sure you're okay?"

I got a grip on myself then. "Yes, I really am."

"The flashlight's in my backpack. We'll have some light in just a second." There was a pause and the sound of rustling, and then a blessed beam of light shone out through the blackness, Jay's face floating pale above it as his body gradually came into focus. He was kneeling like a penitent beside the altar stone. Brushing the dust from our hair and clothes, we got to our feet. Slowly, Jay shone the flashlight over the walls of the cave.

Nothing had fallen in, nothing had collapsed. Only the entrance was gone, plugged with the landslide of rock and dirt set off by the ricochet of Elliot's gunshots. I remembered the long slanting rise of shale and boulders that covered the slope above the cave entrance. If it had all come down . . .

I fell on my knees and began pulling away the small stones and loose earth. Jay propped the flashlight on a rock, directing the beam at the blocked entrance, and dug with me. The first layer of earth and rock came away easily enough, and after half an hour we had burrowed through most of it, but behind the loose shale and dirt were large boulders so tightly wedged against each other that no effort of ours would budge them. After another half hour of useless effort, we sat back exhausted, our hands cut and bleeding from the effort.

While I slumped wearily against the cave wall, Jay found the fallen lanterns. The glass mantle and globe of one were broken, so it was useless, but the other was intact, and when Jay shook it gently we could hear the fuel sloshing around in the tank. Jay asked me if I had any matches. I shook my head. "But Clio kept some sort of flint, didn't she?"

Jay felt in the niche closest to the lantern hook beside him. "Here it is." He struck a spark off the cave rock and lit the lantern. "There's only enough fuel in this for a couple of hours."

"How long do you think the flashlight batteries are good for?"

"They're new. With luck, maybe eight to ten hours."

I wondered if that was long enough. Morning was six hours off, and it might be hours after that before anyone wondered where we were and began to look for us. Surely though, Luke would recover, would know where we were. . . . But he was unconscious when Elliot forced me into the cave. And before Elliot hit him with the gun he must have seen the signal from the sea, from Elliot's "associates." What if he assumed they had kidnapped us?

A stray bee flew into the lantern light. It made me think of what I had done to Elliot, and I didn't want to think about that, didn't want to wonder if the bee stings had killed him by now. Or how he had died.

But there were worse thoughts, much worse. If the men on the boat found Giudico and Elliot both dead and assumed Luke had killed them, Luke who was unconscious, vulnerable . . . At this point, I slammed down a mental shutter in my mind, closing out everything but our survival, Jay's and mine. For Jay's sake, I must not think about Luke.

Jay was on his knees, prizing the cover off the wooden crate. "We should eat some of this honey," he said. "It gives you energy." He held one of the jars out to me and twisted the cap off another for himself.

Dubiously, I dipped one finger into the liquid to taste it, remembering Luke's suspicions; but it seemed to be simply honey. I was about to tilt the jar up to my mouth when it occurred to me that we had no water and that it might be a mistake to eat something as sweet as honey without it. While I was saying as much to Jay, I set the jar carelessly down on a rock beside me. The jar tottered, then fell with a crash onto another rock, the honey spilling out as the glass cracked apart, flowing around the chunk of honeycomb, which proved to be, when I touched it, another artificial comb. Carefully lifting it free from the glass shards, I pulled the two halves apart. As they separated, a small plastic bag filled with white powder fell onto the cave floor.

"What's that?" Jay picked up the little bag and held it close to the lantern light. His face, at first merely puzzled, grew amazed. "Alison! This has got to be—"

"Heroin," I finished for him. It didn't matter that I had never seen the real thing; television had shown me what it looked like. "So you were right, Jay—Elliot was a smuggler after all."

He had sold Hugo to Qaddafi for drugs, for the freedom to use Casteddu, the perfect smuggler's lair.

"Do you think Clio knew? It's her honey."

But I couldn't believe she was involved. "I'm sure they were using her, Jay. She must have been getting suspicious, though. That run-in with Giudico . . ." I rubbed my forehead. "Look, none of this matters much right now. All we should be thinking about is how to get out of here. What else do you have in your backpack?"

Jay handed me the small plastic bag of heroin, which I dropped back into the crate of honey, then pulled out the contents of his knapsack. A few clothes, a large chocolate bar, his Swiss army knife, his passport, that was all it contained. And the manilla folder with Hugo's drawings.

"We forgot about this!" he said excitedly, waving the folder in the air. "If we're right, if the drawings really are a map of this cave system, we might be able to find our way to the entrance under the *castello*." While I held the lantern over his shoulder, he hunkered down on the cave floor and arranged the drawings to compose the map. "Hugo obviously got into Casteddu somehow through the cave. If he could do it, so can we."

He rubbed the back of his neck, then, and grimaced as though it hurt him. When I asked him anxiously if he really was all right, he shrugged it off. "Just a little stiff, that's all. Orlando's back isn't the most comfortable place I've been." Suddenly remembering, he looked around. "Where is he, anyway?"

We listened, and in the utter silence heard the donkey's heavy breathing. It seemed to come from somewhere along the tunnel. When Jay shone the flashlight down the pitch-black passage, the beam of light picked out Orlando's flank. The donkey was standing only a few yards away, motionless. Speaking in a quiet voice so as not to startle him, Jay went slowly down the tunnel. Obligingly, Orlando allowed Jay to grab his bridle and lead him back into the cave. When I ran my hand along the donkey's side, I could feel him trembling, but he appeared to be unhurt. I found the rough blanket which had covered Jay, and draped it over Orlando's back. It seemed to calm him, perhaps because it had a familiar smell, but he stood with his head hanging down dejectedly, as though he sensed the trouble we were in.

Jay and I went back to studying the map. Eventually he said, "I think I have it figured out." Tracing his forefinger through the maze of passages, he showed me the route he thought we should take. "This is obviously the main tunnel. These unfinished lines must be passages Hugo never explored, and these must be dead ends. We'll have to be careful not to wander down one by mistake. But if we go slowly and check the map wherever the tunnel branches, we should be okay."

He spoke so bravely that I had to match his courage. "Of course we'll be okay. We have the map, you're a caver, and I was a Girl Scout once upon a time." For six months, anyway. Remembering one small lesson scouting had managed to teach me, I suggested that we mark our way. "So that we can come back if we have to. If we don't find Hugo's route out."

"We'll scratch a mark onto the rock at every fork," Jay agreed. "Just the way you do in a maze. You know, when you go down one branch you put an arrow on the side you go in, and if it's a dead end, you put another on the other side as you come out. That way you won't keep going down the same dead end." Then Jay noticed what Orlando was doing at that moment, and added, "As long as he keeps that up every hundred feet or so, we won't have any problem."

"But can we take him with us?"

Orlando looked mournfully up at us, as though he knew we were talking about him. Jay said, "I wish we could. But there'll probably be places where the tunnel will be too narrow or the roof too low. Where there won't be room for him." He gazed at the donkey, who looked steadily back at him, almost imploringly. "But I guess that's a risk Orlando's willing to take."

I agreed. Besides, there was something comforting about the donkey's sheer animal presence, his warmth. The cave was beginning to seem cold, and a small current of air blew chilly against the skin. When I mentioned this to Jay, he replied that it was a good sign. "It has to be coming from somewhere. That means another entrance. With luck, one we can use to get out."

We gathered up our belongings and tied them onto Orlando's back, then set off down the tunnel, Jay leading the way with the lantern in one hand, the map in the other; we would use the lantern as our main light for as long as the fuel held out, to save the flashlight batteries. I followed close behind him with Orlando's reins in one hand.

We were forced to go very slowly, watching for places where there might be passages branching off from the tunnel. Wherever this happened, we paused to consult the map, and I marked the place with a long arrow scratched at eye level onto the surface of the rock. At that point, too, we looked back at the way we had come. "So we'll recognize the route if we have to return," Jay told me. "Things look different from the other direction."

The tunnel was very like a large tube of smooth stone, with rounded walls curving up to a ceiling some three or four feet over our heads, sloping at a gentle incline that took us deeper and deeper into the mountain. Curious scallopings decorated the stone, caused perhaps, Jay said, by the high-speed floodwaters of a river during the formation of the cave system hundreds of thousands of years ago. But although it was very damp in the cave, we found no water at first, only the evidence of past water when, from time to time, the tunnel widened into small chambers with ribbons of glistening limestone, stalactites and stalagmites like pale fingers forever pointing but never touching, and thin and twisty trunk channels clogged with stony debris. The air stayed fresh, and this gave me hope that Jay was right: somewhere there had to be an exit.

After half an hour, we stopped to rest and to swallow a few squares of chocolate. We didn't dare eat much, for the chocolate was all we had with us apart from a couple of jars of the honey, which we would eat only if we became desperate. We couldn't be sure it wasn't tainted with the heroin.

"Ten minutes, that's all," Jay warned me. "It's better to take a couple of short breaks than one long one. So we don't chill down." While we sat with our backs against the smooth flowstone of the tunnel wall, I told him my part of the story. His face was agonized as I described what had happened to Luke.

When I finished, there was a short silence. Jay sat with his hands dangling loosely between his upraised knees, his head bowed. Then he looked sideways at me. "You could have been killed. Because of me. Might still be if we . . ." He couldn't finish.

"Please don't kill me off quite yet, okay?"

Mock indignation did the trick where any show of real emotion might have undone him. He managed a sheepish smile. "Sorry."

"Tell me," I said, "how did Elliot get you out of your room so quietly?"

"He didn't have to. I couldn't sleep, so I was at the window, trying to figure out the constellations. That's when I saw somebody crossing the courtyard. But I couldn't tell who it was, so I unlocked my door and went out onto the landing, to listen. I heard Elliot go to the door, and then it sounded like he went outside. I thought maybe downstairs I could hear what they were talking about." He shifted slightly, as though he was uncomfortable. "I know it was a stupid thing to do. But I was sort of hoping whoever it was might have brought news about Hugo."

I pointed to the backpack. "Do you wear that when you stargaze?"

"What? Oh, I see. You mean how come I had it with me." Once again, he looked abashed. "Yeah, well to be honest, I guess I thought if it turned out they knew where Hugo was, I might follow them. I know, I know, it was dumb. . . .

"Anyway, I got all the way to the front door and then I bumped against the corner of a table. They must have been right outside, because they heard me. Elliot came running in and Giudico was just behind him. Giudico had a gun in his hand. Elliot told me to go back to bed, but Giudico was angry. He told Elliot I must have heard what they were talking about, and anyway I'd seen the gun. I said I didn't hear anything and I didn't care if he had a gun. But he didn't believe me. He grabbed me, and told Elliot they couldn't afford to let me go back to bed. By this time I was really scared. Then Elliot told Giudico to give him the gun. He said he'd take care of things, that Giudico should go ahead to the meadow to wait for their friends.

"Giudico wasn't too keen on the idea at first. But he finally agreed. After he left, Elliot told me he wasn't going to hurt me, but that I'd have to do as he said. If I didn't he'd have to wake you up and . . . well, he made it pretty clear what he'd do. He got some rope to tie my hands up, and made a gag for me out of a dishtowel. Then he took me to Orlando's stall. That's when Matteo tried to stop him—"

"Matteo! What was he doing there?"

"I don't know. He jumped Elliot, but I guess Elliot heard him or something, because he hit Matteo with the gun on the side of his face and Matteo sort of staggered back. I tried to stop Elliot, but I couldn't—he just pushed me away. Then he hit Matteo again. It was awful, Alison. . . ."

I reached out for Jay's hand and held it tightly. After a moment he continued. "Elliot made me lie across Orlando's back and he tied me on. Then he tied Matteo up and gagged him, and dragged him into the stall." I remembered that the bottom half of the Dutch door had been shut when I glanced into the stall; Matteo must have been lying on the floor, out of sight.

"Elliot put the blanket over me so I couldn't see anything. But I could tell we were crossing the mountain, so I knew where we were going. When we got to the meadow, Giudico was waiting inside the cave. He was furious when he saw Elliot had brought me with him. He said they should kill me. But Elliot wouldn't let him. He said he had a better idea. I heard him telling you what that was. . . ." He raised his head and looked at me, "I'm sorry, Alison. It's all my fault we're stuck here in this cave. It's my fault Luke—"

"Jay. Elliot and Giudico are to blame for what's happened, not you. All you did was come downstairs at the wrong moment."

"Yeah, but if I'd—"

I put my finger against his lips. "Come on. Our ten minutes are long since up. You see, I remembered. I'll turn into a caver yet. . . ."

But this was a hollow boast. With each downward step, I began to feel that an utterly alien and malignant world of stone had me in its grasp, pressing down on me, pressing in, while the long, cold fingers of claustrophobia curled around my spine, working their silent way toward my heart and lungs, squeezing them softly, relaxing their grip, squeezing again, so that my blood pulsed in my head and each breath came in a painful, ragged sob. Desperately, I tried to stem the rising flood of terror, concentrating so hard on calming myself that I walked blindly into Jay's outstretched arm.

"Wait!" he said. "Do you hear it . . . ?"

Somewhere, but far off, there was the sound of rushing water. Jay set the lantern down and switched on the flashlight. He swept the beam back and forth across the passage floor ahead. "There!" He held the beam focused on what seemed to be some sort of hole, about two feet in diameter, on the left side. Turning, he asked me to give him the rope we'd brought with us, which was coiled up in his knapsack on Orlando's back. He tied it under his arms, then looped the other end around the donkey's middle and knotted it securely. "Just in case I'm wrong," he told me. "Now you hold on tight to Orlando's bridle, okay?"

I grabbed his arm. "What are you going to do?"

"Don't worry, it's perfectly safe. But one thing I've learned in caving is always to be two hundred percent sure." As I watched, he moved cautiously along one side of the tunnel, keeping to the wall. Before each step, he stretched out one foot and pounded down on the stone ahead. Finally, he knelt down, shining the beam of the flashlight into the hole. "Just as I thought," he called back to me after a moment. "It's a shaft. There must be an underground river down there. Way down." He got up and came back along the tunnel, walking this time in the center. "I had to be certain there wasn't a false floor. Sometimes there's just a thin layer of stone over an underground river. But I could see there's solid rock for a long way down on all sides of the shaft."

Despite his reassurance, I went down that passage as though I were walking on thin ice; each step seemed treacherous. Oddly enough, however, the immediate danger had cured my claustrophobia.

Not long afterward the tunnel finally leveled off, opening suddenly into a series of large chambers. Each was clearly marked on Hugo's map, so we knew we were on the right track. It was here, in the first of the chambers, that the air current suddenly seemed much stronger. Jay used the flashlight to scan the walls around us; if his calculations were right, he said, we were now at sea level. Already, I was imagining how we would scramble out through the air passage, drop down to the water and swim ashore to safety.

When the light finally found the source of the current, we saw a narrow chimney high overhead, too high to reach even standing on Orlando's back, and too narrow for either of us to fit into even if we could reach it. Jay and I looked at each other, trying to hide our bitter disappointment. "There'll be other chances," I said. I almost believed it.

A minute or two later we reached the second chamber, which smelled powerfully of ammonia. Something soft and unpleasantly squishy seemed to carpet the stone, and as we entered, a rustling, chirruping sound whispered above our heads. Jay raised the lantern and we looked up. Like a fat pulpy fungus, large clusters of bats clung to the ceiling, from which individual bats broke loose to swoop down with a quick flittering of wings in protest at the light.

That was all the warning we needed. Heads bent, we crossed the chamber as quickly as Orlando would let us, Jay shielding the lantern with one arm to dim its light. When we were safe, Jay said, "We're lucky it's night. Most of the bats were probably gone. They must use that chimney to get out." For an irrational moment I hated the bats, free to come and go as they pleased, free as we were not.

We continued through the third and into the fourth chamber, which was larger than the others and littered with tumbled rock and boulders. All this time Orlando had followed patiently and without complaint, but now he balked, putting his head down and pulling back against me. I tried unsuccessfully to get him to budge. "Tell him we'll leave him here if he doesn't get a move on," Jay said.

"It's obvious you know nothing about donkey psychology. Threats don't work. But a piece of chocolate might." I took one of our precious squares and held it in front of Orlando's nose. The donkey raised his upper lip—and I moved the chocolate just out of reach. In this manner, I got him to start up again. After several dozen yards he seemed to have forgotten his stubbornness and followed along obediently once more.

But, in the end, we might as well have sat down with Orlando. We weren't going any further anyway. Ahead, where there should have been tunnel, there was only fallen rock, great chunks of it wedged into the tunnel like a cork into the neck of a bottle. Jay climbed over it but found no way through. On the map, the tunnel continued frustratingly free and unobstructed.

We stared at each other. I said, "This must have been the rock fall Clio told us about. The one that injured Giudico and killed his friend."

Jay nodded mutely. For the first time, he looked as though he realized what our fate might be. It was a disheartened, frightened look.

"I'll bet there are other tunnels we could take. Let's check the map again." The too-loud optimism in my voice echoed hollowly in the tunnel.

But the map showed no other possible route.

"Well, we'll just have to go back and wait by the entrance," I said, trying to inject into my voice a calm I was far from feeling. "Eventually someone will come. Luke will bring help. Benedetta will make a fuss when Giudico doesn't come home. Clio will visit the tower first thing this morning. . . ."

We turned around to start the long dismal trek back. But, once again, Orlando balked in the same chamber. Too tired to argue with him, I capitulated, and sat down on a rock. "We might as well rest here a moment anyway," I told Jay.

But when I dropped the halter, Orlando trotted over to the far side of the chamber, and then abruptly vanished behind an enormous boulder.

"Hey!" Jay and I jumped to our feet and ran over to where the donkey had been just a moment before. From a distance the cluster of boulders looked impenetrable, tumbled in front of the flat wall of rock that rose sheer to the ceiling of the chamber fifteen feet above. When we reached the spot where Orlando had vanished, however, we saw that there was in fact a narrow defile between the boulders, more than enough space for the donkey to slip through. Jay shone the flashlight into the crack. We could see then that it wound behind another boulder. We went around the second boulder and to our amazement saw that what had appeared from the middle of the chamber to be solid wall was in fact a curtain of rock masking an enormous fissure about three feet wide and six feet high.

"Orlando!" I called. A hollow, booming echo answered me from somewhere beyond the fissure.

Jay stared at me excitedly. "There's got to be a really big room through there, Alison! You'd never get an echo like that otherwise." It was clear that, for the moment at least, the balance had shifted and he was a caver again, the adventure far outweighing the dangers.

Then we heard Orlando. He was making an odd lapping noise. "Why, he's drinking!" I said. "He must have found water. That's why he wouldn't budge back there—he could smell it." An image flashed into my mind, a pond in a bright green meadow, sunshine sparkling on water, air and light and freedom. . . . All at once I was achingly, desperately thirsty, as though the dust from the landslide still lay thick on my tongue.

We passed through the fissure and entered an enormous cavern longer than it was wide, with a high vaulting roof that dwarfed us and swallowed up the lantern light. Like some subterranean basilica, domed and apsed, arched and pillared, it seemed a place rich with silence and shadows and the undeniable presence of mystery. Only incense was lacking. In the center, about ten feet from the cavern wall, lay a long black lake like a pool of spilled ink, lipped by shining flowstone smooth as glass. Orlando stood drinking at the margin, his tail swishing back and forth contentedly.

After Jay and I had knelt down and drunk our fill of the icily delicious water, we walked cautiously along the edge of the lake toward the far end of the cavern. And then, where the little lake narrowed almost to a point, our light picked out a vision like a miracle.

Above the water there was a kind of natural dais of rock where two flying buttresses met in an arch, framing a small grotto. The stone of the grotto gleamed like crystal in the light. It seemed to pour out of the limestone above it, flowing down the cavern wall like a frozen waterfall into the flat black waters of the lake.

But it was not the natural beauty of the grotto that caught at the throat, so that Jay and I cried out in unison. It was the figure in the grotto. A figure carved by a human hand. A smooth, rounded statue three feet high of some dark polished stone, all breasts and hips, with a tiny featureless head. The ancient image of the female.

"The lady of the labyrinth," I whispered.

Below her, at the base of the stone waterfall, like a priestess in attendance, was a slightly smaller terra-cotta statuette. It was a woman standing with her arm partly raised against her breast, the other hidden in the folds of her long pleated dress. The head was covered with a drapery and the features of her face were almost worn away, as though she had at one time stood outdoors, exposed to the wind and rain. But the expression on her face lingered despite the near obliteration of her features, the archaic smile, cold and wise, here transmuted to something gentler by the weathered terra-cotta. In front of her sat a bowl very like the one Clio used for her offerings, and on her far side was a clay pot with a long thin neck and a wide base.

I shone the flashlight down into the bowl, and on the bottom we could see the crude shapes of human figures dancing with lifted arms around the outline of a bee. I moved the light over to the clay pot, which had concentric circles incised on its side and curious handles crudely shaped like human faces; something glittered deep inside it. The neck was just wide enough to allow a hand in. Carefully, I reached down and felt coins hard and cold under my fingers. When I took one out, the tiny golden figure of a goddess with her arm raised up to a tiny golden bee lay in my palm. The coin was identical to my medallion.

"All that stuff in Hugo's letter, the stuff Clio told us about—the treasure, the priestesses, the bee dance—it was all real!" When Jay looked at me, his eyes were wonderstruck, the eyes of a child who has seen fairy tales come true. But the look faded fast. "Maybe nobody but us will ever know that if . . ." His voice trailed off.

I slipped the coin gently back into the clay pot, where it fell with a soft chink onto the pile. "You wait," I told him, "someday we'll bring Hugo here and show him ourselves."

"Promise?"

"Promise."

He smiled then. "Let's take some of these with us, so that when we're rescued—" He was about to reach down into the pot for a handful of coins when, instinctively, I stopped his hand. He looked startled. "Why not?"

But I had no reason, only a feeling. "I'm not sure. Just that it's hers." The Mother Goddess, source of all life, that small potent figure who had sat in perfect darkness for thousands of years while the world that worshiped her turned away to other gods. Jay must have understood, for he only nodded and walked back to Orlando. On an impulse, I lifted the medallion from around my neck and laid it in front of the goddess. "Help us," I whispered. "Help Luke."

Jay had the map out again and spread over a boulder. The cavern wasn't marked, he told me, and that in itself seemed to indicate that Hugo hadn't known about it, but if we searched along the wall that separated the cavern from the tunnel we might find another fissure, a way back to the tunnel past the point where it was blocked by the rock fall.

Slowly, methodically, we shone the flashlight over every bit of the cavern wall, working our way forward from the place where we had entered. Each boulder, each slab of fallen stone, might mask a tunnel that could save us. It was tedious, eye-straining work. The fantastical shapes of water-tortured rock that crusted the cavern wall seemed at times grotesquely human, like gargoyles brought to malevolent life by the light that danced over them, jeering at our feeble, hopeless efforts to save ourselves.

When we heard the splashing, we thought at first it must be Orlando drinking again, but he was standing a little distance from the lake, simply watching us. The sound, we realized after a moment, was coming from above, but muffled, as though it was behind the stone. Then we saw it, a natural staircase in the rock, very narrow, very steep, which led to a ledge some four feet overhead. Flashlight in hand, Jay carefully climbed up to the ledge.

"There's a tunnel!" he called down to me just before he disappeared from view. "I'm just going to—" His words ended in a choked-off scream.

"Jay! Jay, what's happened!" I set the lantern down on the ground and began frantically to scramble up the rock, but before I was even halfway to the ledge, he reappeared, white-faced but unharmed. "Thank God!" I said, as I grasped the hand he held out to help me up the rest of the way. "I thought you'd fallen down a shaft. What in—" And then I saw it, too. A large skeleton, like some guardian monster at the entrance to the tunnel, its head almost at my feet.

It lay facedown, arms outstretched, the finger bones splayed so that they seemed to clutch at the stone beneath them. The skull was on its side, the mouth wide in a scream or a prayer, the eye socket huge and black and empty. A jagged crack ran across the white surface of the skull. Next to the skull was a large stone, like a second head sprouting from the collarbone.

A little way inside the tunnel there was another skeleton, curled up in a sort of fetal position, the bones all collapsed together. In its embrace it held a pot, the twin of the one with the gold coins. But the neck of this pot was broken off, and gold coins lay scattered across the stone.

"The other two German soldiers." Jay's voice was sober.

"Maybe." Or thieves from some earlier age. The grisly tableau was like some medieval morality woodcut, white bones on black stone, the wages of sin. Or a mystery writ small: All the clues are here, you figure out what happened. But I had no stomach for this puzzle.

All the while I'd been vaguely aware of the splashing sound grown louder, like heavy rain falling in gusty sheets, and now by the light from the lantern we saw its source. At the end of the short tunnel was a waterfall, a real one this time. Over ten feet high, it poured down in a liquid curtain that frothed and sparkled in the light, disappearing into the wide crevasse that, along with the waterfall, marked the tunnel's end. A narrow stone ledge, perhaps two feet wide, wet and slippery with water, bordered the crevasse on the right for about five feet before disappearing under the waterfall; on the left, the water fell unobstructed into the abyss.

"I wonder what's on the other side." Jay's voice was curious, speculative, rather than frightened. "We'll have to find out. It's our only chance. Do you think Orlando could make it up here?"

"Orlando's a Sicilian donkey," I replied, quoting Matteo. "He can go anywhere."

The drink seemed to have restored Orlando's innate good temper, and when I gathered up his lead he followed obediently. Matteo was right—Orlando loved to climb, and he mounted the steep incline easily, ignoring the skeletons but shying just a little at the sight of the waterfall. I wondered if he would go through it willingly.

"Let me go first," Jay said. When I protested, he told me that he knew what to do. "I've been in caves with water before. I'll be careful, don't worry. Besides, I have a theory, and I'd like to know if I'm right. I'll come right back again, I promise."

He wrapped the flashlight in the sweater and stripped off his shirt and jeans, then stuffed them all in his backpack, which he slipped over his shoulders. While I held the lantern up, he traversed the rock ledge, shuffling slowly forward with his hands gripping the rock wall. I caught my breath as he disappeared through the water, willing him to be safe. After what seemed an eternity but must have been at most six or seven seconds, he shouted that he was returning.

When he reappeared, dripping, shivering, his eyes were full of hope. "Alison! The tunnel on the other side, it's the main one, I'm sure of it! The ledge does a sort of zigzag when you come out of the waterfall. Around some really huge stalactites, as big as columns. But then you're in the tunnel again. The water's really cold, so it's a shock. But you'll be through it almost at once. Just take it slowly and carefully." His teeth were chattering, but he refused Matteo's blanket when I held it out to him, saying that he would dry off on the other side, where he'd left his clothes.

Jay had brought the now-empty knapsack back for me. I jammed my shirt and trousers and the blanket into it. Before I set off, I told Jay firmly, "Orlando has got to do this on his own.

Don't try to bring him with you. That ledge is just too narrow to have an argument with a donkey on if he decides he doesn't want to get wet. If he stays here, we'll be back to get him one way or another." Reluctantly, Jay agreed.

I followed his example then, moving crabwise along the ledge, my face to the rock, until I reached the waterfall. The icy water hit me like a jolt of electricity, but I forced myself forward. And almost banged into the rough pillar of rock that suddenly appeared on the other side of the waterfall. Not daring to look down at the chasm below the ledge, I inched my way around the huge stalactite and found myself in a large tunnel partly lit by the flashlight, which Jay had left behind. Here, screened by a cluster of enormous stalactites, the waterfall was all but invisible.

Almost at once Jay appeared behind me, shielding the lantern from the water. But no Orlando.

We each took one end of the rough blanket and dried ourselves off as best we could. After we had dressed, Jay said, "If I'm right, we're in the main tunnel again, but on the other side of the rock slide." He shone the flashlight back down the tunnel and we saw the proof that he was right, fallen slabs of rock blocking the tunnel. We grabbed each other and jumped up and down in a wild dance of celebration. Never mind that there might be other obstacles, other dangers, I felt crazy with relief.

At that moment Orlando appeared, snorting and shaking himself vigorously. Perhaps he was proud of his courage, perhaps he wanted to join in the celebration—whatever the reason, he suddenly let loose a loud, trumpeting bray that ricocheted off the walls of the tunnel, echoing like the trumpet that wakes the dead.

Something answered him. At first I thought it was just a weird echo, distance transforming the animal to a human sound, but then it came again, and this time there was no mistaking. It was a man's shout.

Jay and I screamed together, shouting with every bit of strength left to us. Orlando joined in, braying at the top of his lungs—a cacophony so terrible that I was suddenly afraid we might bring the mountain down on us. I shoved the last of the chocolate into his open jaws and he subsided. We listened. And the voice came again, closer, multiplied by the tunnel so that it seemed to be more than one. Men's voices calling our names.

"Here we are!" I screamed. "Here we are!"

Suddenly a beam of light snaked along the far wall of the

tunnel. Footsteps sounded, coming fast. I had time for one last terrible thought: What if Elliot . . . ? Before a man appeared.

The light was so powerful that it dazzled our eyes, blinding us. Jay saw him first.

He flung himself at the man who was standing there, into his open arms. "Daddy!" he cried, "Oh, Daddy!"

For a moment they simply stood there, Hugo's bent head resting on Jay's as he held him. Then Hugo raised his head and looked at me. "Alison. Thank God!" And he reached out one hand to me.

I ran to him then and put my arms around the two of them.

CHAPTER 26

As I reached out to Hugo, the journey of my life seemed to unroll before me, like a ball of twine. All its convolutions, the roads traveled and turnings taken, became the straight and simple line that led me to this moment. I held on fiercely to the two beings now so precious to me, aware with a terrible clarity of what I had nearly lost. "My children," I heard Hugo whisper, one hand touching my hair, touching Jay's, and when at last I raised my head to look into his face, the deep blue eyes gazing down at me held everything I had once longed to see in them.

Behind Hugo, a man stepped out of the shadows, a man with a makeshift bandage wound around his head. I broke away from Hugo, not trusting my eyes until I could touch him, could know with my body that he was real, that it was Luke. He caught and held me against him, and I thought of that small black figure in her grotto and of Luke's laughing words now become true. "Sent by the goddess herself . . ." For the first time, I believed in answered prayers.

"How—" I began, but before I or any of us could ask a single one of the countless questions we had, Orlando reminded us that the journey was not over yet. With an impatient grunt, he pushed his nose into the small of my back, trying to get past Luke and me as we stood blocking the way up the narrow tunnel.

"I think Orlando wants out of here," said Jay, laughing and crying both. He leaned against Hugo, cradled in his father's arm, rubbing at his eyes with the back of one hand.

"Sensible creature," Hugo said briskly. "We've been lucky, but the waterfall is a warning. It wasn't there three years ago. Runoff from the storm may be feeding some underground river, and if it's still rising, the sooner we climb onto higher ground, the better." With his arm around Jay's shoulders, as though afraid to let him go, he took command. "Jay, you follow behind me, Alison after Jay, Luke last, if you will. Keep your ears open, would you, Luke, for anything that sounds like water. You take Orlando's bridle, Jay." He spoke with the voice I knew from my childhood, energetic, powerful, assured. I smiled to hear it again.

"I see a definite family resemblance," Luke said quietly, as we all meekly did as we were told. He kept one hand resting lightly on my shoulder while we walked single file, following Hugo. The tunnel, he told me, would come out under the *castello*, in the armaments room, just as Jay and I had thought.

As we set off, Jay was telling Hugo how afraid he had been that we, he and I, would find flooding somewhere in the tunnel. A sinuous current of cool air carried his words back to me in echoing snatches. "We were lucky, though. It was clear all the way. Until we came to the part that was blocked off by the rock fall . . ." I watched that thin figure ahead of me, the boy old beyond his years, who seemed more than ever his father's son, and I was struck once again by his courage. The flooding had been one more threat to frighten him, and yet he hadn't said a word to me about it, had kept the fear to himself. Just as he had gone with Elliot while I slept, to keep me safe. But now that he was free to be his age again, he fairly danced along, glorying in his father's return.

The next few minutes are a blur of images in my memory. Now that I no longer had to memorize every turning, the markings on the way, I simply followed, oblivious to my surroundings, content. Jay was safe, Luke was alive, Hugo was home. All danger was past. Ahead, Hugo strode up the tunnel with a confidence that could only be born of familiarity, a confidence I found almost miraculously reassuring in its implied promise that he would lead us safely from the cave. When he turned every now and then to glance back down the passage at us, the light from the lantern he was carrying flowed upward, underlighting the planes and angles of his face from below, exaggerating the nose, so that he looked uncannily like the carving in the tower. Once he looked past Jay, at me, and said quietly, "Each time I turn around I'm afraid I'll find you gone." I told him I was no Eurydice, and he smiled.

Talking virtually nonstop, Jay told Hugo our story from beginning to end, pausing only when Hugo or Luke asked a question, and once when I interjected to stop him blaming himself. Even by the lantern light his flush of pleasure and embarrassment was plain when I told the others that if it weren't for Jay I would have succumbed early on to fear and claustrophobia.

"Orlando deserves some credit, too," he protested, describing how Orlando had saved us by sniffing out the water. He did not tell Hugo what lay in the large cavern Orlando had found, but there was something in the way Hugo listened, an alert interest on his face when he looked back once at Jay, that made me think he might suspect.

However, Hugo said only, "Orlando has earned himself a place in the legends of Casteddu. Luke and I were already heading back when he bellowed—"

"Matteo!" Jay interrupted, suddenly remembering, clutching at Hugo's sleeve to stop him. "I forgot! He's—"

Hugo turned to reassure him, the expression on his face very gentle. "Matteo's fine, Jay. He's waiting for us at the tunnel entrance. He'd managed to get the gag free and was making such a racket that Luke and I heard him when we got to Casteddu. He told us what had happened to you. Until then, we had hoped that you at least would be safe in the tower."

"What was he doing there," I asked Hugo, "when he tackled Elliot?"

"Doing his best to look after you. The poor fellow feels a failure, of course. But he never knew Elliot had a gun."

"I don't understand," said Jay. "Why did Matteo feel he had to look after us? Did he suspect Elliot?"

"Calogero suspected. When you insisted on staying in the tower, he asked Matteo to keep an eye on you, and on Elliot." So Don Calo had been a friend, after all, I thought, and was sorry for my doubts. Hugo told us that Don Calo had been sure that Elliot was up to something, but Elliot always managed to hide his tracks. In a voice harsh with anger, he added, "Of course Calogero had no idea Elliot would try to harm you. The cold-blooded bastard! When I think of what might have happened . . ."

And he did not know the full extent of Elliot's duplicity, I thought, did not know that Elliot had betrayed him to Qaddafi, had betrayed Clio. I wondered if there was anyone that Elliot had not betrayed?

The lake and shrine must have been at the lowest level of the cave, for we climbed steadily upward. The tunnel was narrow but high enough to let us stand upright. We had been walking like this for some twenty minutes when I noticed that the tunnel walls had changed. Almost imperceptibly, the natural stone had given way to roughly carved blocks. And then abruptly the tunnel ended in a door, which was standing open. Through the door we could see a large room, some sort of storage room, filled with bits and pieces of old furniture and broken wooden boxes and lit by a single lantern hanging on a hook at the bottom of a flight of stone steps along the far wall. It was the armaments room, Luke said.

When we had all filed through, Hugo closed the door behind us. On this side, the wooden door was faced with stone, and when it swung back into place it was impossible to know it existed at all. One stone, more roughly carved than those around it, gave a purchase to the hand. Across the room, Orlando was already mounting the steps to the courtyard as though he smelled water again, but it was Matteo he wanted, Matteo who was standing at the top of the stairs, a broad smile on his face.

The night sky seemed wonderfully vast, blazing with bright white stars, the air sweet and warm and so delicious that I took greedy breaths, filling my lungs. Each noise was vividly distinct, the sea gulping and sucking at the rocks below, the cicadas, an owl's cry, all the small sounds of life. I felt like Persephone fresh from Hades, her senses quiveringly alive to a world reborn and newly beautiful. Jay spun like a top, his arms flung out, rejoicing.

Hugo, Luke, and Matteo talked together intently for a few moments and then, after shyly telling Jay and me that he was happy we were safe and listening reluctantly to our words of thanks, Matteo led Orlando away to give him food and water. He would hike across the mountain, Hugo told us, to let the rescuers working in the meadow know that Jay and I had been found.

In the tower, when the lamps were lit, Hugo located a first-aid kit, and cleaned and dressed the wound on Luke's head where Elliot had struck him. Until now, Hugo said, Luke had refused all attention to it; with mock irritation, Hugo added that I seemed to have chosen a singularly determined young man. I looked up from the soup I was stirring, and smiled at him. "Someone must have set me a bad example, then." Luke said nothing, but his own smile as his eyes met mine was a mixture of amusement and simple happiness.

While we ate the soup and sandwiches Jay and I had made, we took it in turns to fill in the gaps in the night's events. I began. The others heard me out in silence as I described the journey across the mountain, the scene in the meadow, and Giudico's accidental death. Luke looked thoughtful as I described how narrowly he had escaped being murdered. Finally, reluctantly, I came to that moment in the cave when Elliot announced that he had sold Hugo to Qaddafi. Uneasily, I looked at Hugo. "He . . . he said he found out something when he was working on your papers, something that interested Qaddafi. He didn't say what it was."

Shock, disbelief, fury, all these emotions passed swiftly across Hugo's face while he sat without speaking, his eyes fixed on me but seeing something else, something invisible to the rest of us. At last he said wearily, "Why in God's name did he do it? Do you know?"

Quietly, Luke said, "He did it to get you out of the way. And for a large share in the local heroin industry. Am I right, Alison?"

Before I could ask him how he knew that, Jay said excitedly, "Tell them about the honey!"

Luke listened intently. When I finished, he nodded and said, "That's pretty much what I thought. He and Giudico must have had quite an operation going. I called the consulate this afternoon, before the lines went down. They were very interested when I told them about the plastic honeycomb. Apparently an American soldier was picked up yesterday from the base at Comiso. They found heroin packed in plastic combs in the four jars of honey he was trying to take back to the States."

"You don't think Clio . . ." I began.

Hugo said flatly, "Clio won't have known a thing about it."

Luke agreed. "Elliot and Giudico probably used her honey as a cover. She wouldn't have to know anything about it because they handled her distribution for her. In any case, there are signs it was a fairly large operation. The likelihood is that other beekeepers were innocent fronts as well. But it looks like things were beginning to come apart for Elliot and Giudico. I'd say the odds were good that Elliot was getting out, with—or more likely without—Giudico. Maybe he was setting Giudico up to take the fall while he disappeared. One way or another, Giudico's death was probably convenient."

"Don Calo won't blame Luke for Giudico's death, will he?" I asked Hugo. I knew enough by now to understand that accident or not the death might have unpleasant repercussions for Luke if Don Calo subscribed to the Sicilian version of Old Testament revenge.

To my relief, Hugo shook his head. "Calogero had no illusions about Giudico's character. He felt responsible for his dead brother's son, but the two never got on very well. He always said Giudico was pigheaded. And Calogero had strong feelings about drug trafficking. He made it clear he didn't want anyone in his family mixed up in it.''

I asked Luke about the Libyans. "Elliot called them his 'associates.' ''

"It's a given that Libyans are involved in the drug trade in Sicily,'' he replied. "There's an island off the south coast—Pantelleria, it's called—used by drug dealers and a variety of terrorists, including Libyans, as a kind of trading post.''

Jay was looking puzzled. "It seems like a lot of work to me. Bothering to bring the heroin all the way up here to stick it in plastic honeycombs, then lugging it back over the mountain to the meadow.''

"It would be,'' Luke agreed. "It's more likely that the Libyans or someone else provided Elliot with the raw material. Then he manufactured the heroin here.''

"Here!'' Hugo said explosively.

Luke nodded, his face grave. "I'm afraid it's a good possibility. If you search the houses in Casteddu, you'll probably find a lab in one of them. Do-it-yourself labs are dangerous—there's always the risk of explosions—but the appeal is that you don't need much to get going and the profits are huge. There are homemade heroin labs all over this island.''

"That must be why Elliot didn't want Matteo living up here,'' Jay said. "So he could do all this stuff in secret.''

As I ladled more soup into the bowls, I asked Luke if he had followed Elliot to the meadow because he knew he was smuggling drugs.

"Suspected,'' he replied. "Look, why don't I start from the beginning . . . ? After I left you yesterday afternoon, I saw we were in for a storm so I went back to the pensione. That's when I called the consulate. From the moment they told me about the heroin, I knew I was going to keep an eye on Elliot until you were out of the tower. After the storm was over, I was heading up to Casteddu when I saw the three of you arriving in the Jeep. So I followed you around town—why do you smile?'' When I explained how all the time he'd been tracking us, we'd been fruitlessly searching for him, he laughed, too, and said, "It did strike me that there was something compulsive about the way you wanted to look at every last house in Castell'alto. . . . Anyway, after you went back with Elliot to Casteddu, I found a place on the mountain side of the bridge, where I was fairly well hidden, and settled down for the night. It wasn't comfortable, but I figured that would keep me from falling asleep.

"Matteo must have got into Casteddu before I arrived, because I never saw him. I did see Giudico—heard him coming down the track, luckily, before he saw me." He recognized Giudico, he said, from my description. "I gave him a few minutes' head start and was going to follow him to the tower, but then figured he and Elliot would probably come back together. Well, Giudico came back alone. So I let him go and waited some more.

It was around eleven when Elliot came over the bridge with the donkey. I saw the crate on the donkey's back but had no idea the other bundle was Jay. When Elliot met Giudico in the meadow, I overheard enough to realize they were expecting the Libyans. At that point I decided to go back to the tower and get you two out of there. But then the bundle on the donkey's back moved. I just assumed it was you, Alison. I'd heard Elliot say your name, and Giudico arguing with him about you. So now I had to figure out how, without a gun, I was going to be able to rescue you before the Libyans got there. At first I thought of jumping Elliot after he'd signaled, but then he called Giudico. . . . The rest you know up till the landslide." He told us that he was just coming to consciousness again when Elliot ran screaming from the cave, firing the gun. "Then the side of the mountain seemed to fall down. Elliot disappeared. Later, I figured either he got covered in the landslide, though it had looked like he was beyond its range, or else he and Giudico got down to the beach where the Libyans were waiting for them."

I told Luke about Elliot's allergy to bee stings. "Is that why he was screaming?" Luke asked, surprised. "I thought it was because of the landslide. I never really took in the bees. You think the stings might have killed him?"

"The bees were all over him," I said. "He told me how violently he reacted to bee stings. He couldn't possibly have got down the cliff."

Luke glanced at Hugo. "Maybe he went up into the mountain."

I had a vision of Elliot lying in some rocky crevice, curled up, in shock. Despite the things he had done, I couldn't wish that fate on him. "If they don't find him soon," I said, "he'll die."

Neither Luke nor Hugo looked as though the idea bothered

him much. Hugo said, "If he's still there, he'll be found. If he isn't, we have to assume the Libyans came in and picked him up."

"My greatest fear," Luke continued, "apart from your being killed in the landslide, Alison, was that you were trapped in the cave with Giudico." Luke had dug furiously at the rock that covered the entrance to the cave, as uselessly as Jay and I were doing on the other side. He gave up sooner than we had, however, because he realized how little he could do without help of some sort. Immediately, he set off to Don Calo's. "I couldn't be sure Don Calo wasn't somehow mixed up in it all. But I had no other choice. I decided I'd tell him his nephew was trapped along with Alison, so he'd have to do something. It took me about half an hour to reach the place and when I arrived . . . well, there was Hugo."

Hugo smiled grimly. "I had just recovered from the considerable shock of learning my children were up at Casteddu, when in comes Luke with his nightmarish tale."

Luckily, the telephone lines were working again, and while Assunta called for help, the men—Luke, Hugo, and Don Calo and his sons—got picks and shovels and drove back to the meadow. Looking for Elliot, they found Giudico's body on the track down to the beach. "We thought Elliot had killed him," Luke said, "or the Libyans. I thanked God he wasn't in the cave with Alison. We wanted to make sure you were back at the tower, Jay, but the road to Castell'alto was still blocked. So while the others dug, Hugo and I went across the mountain to Casteddu. We found Matteo, and he told us you were gone. We had to assume you were trapped with Alison. That's when we decided to try working from this end . . ."

Hugo said, "I had told Luke about the tunnel. And about the rock fall blocking it. We decided to give it a shot anyway, hoping to hell something had happened in the three years I had been gone. But it hadn't. All we could do then was turn around and start back to help the others. That's when we heard the donkey. And there you were." He looked at Jay and me in turn. "Thank God."

Luke pushed his bowl away and got to his feet. "I'd better go now. If I hurry, I'll reach the meadow before Don Calo and the others leave. After that, I'm going to Don Calo's to call the consulate and let them know about Elliot and the Libyans. I probably won't get back here until morning. By then maybe the road'll be clear."

Before Luke left, Hugo scribbled a note for Don Calo. "So that you won't have any difficulties with him," he told Luke as he gave him the folded piece of paper. "Although you seem to be a man more than capable of looking after himself."

"But this is Sicily after all," Luke said, and grinned.

"Precisely." Hugo's face grew serious. "Luke, I'm more grateful than I can say. You risked your life for Alison and Jay. If it weren't for you, they might be . . . well, it doesn't bear thinking about. Although"—and here he looked from Luke to me—"I imagine you have all the thanks you want."

"Yes," Luke said and his arm tightened around my shoulders. "I have." As he shook hands with Hugo, I saw with delight the obvious respect and liking the two men had for each other. Then Luke stretched out his hand to Jay. "Friends now?" he asked him with a smile.

"Friends," Jay agreed, flushing, as he pumped Luke's hand.

Outside, as I walked with Luke to the bridge, he said, "I didn't want to shock your father, but I could think of one or two tangible ways you could show your appreciation. This, for example . . ." He stopped, and showed me.

When the kiss ended, I said, "Nothing would shock Hugo. That least of all."

"Is that a challenge? Let me try harder."

Afterward, I watched Luke out of sight and then went back to the tower. Hugo was alone at the kitchen table, his head bowed. He looked up when he heard my footsteps. "I packed your brother off to bed," he said, as I sat down across from him. "His eyes were closing."

Hugo looked weary, too, his face drawn, almost gray. I thought of what he had been through that night, the long climb around the mountain, the search through the cave, the fear for us he would have felt. . . . I reached across the table for his hand and put mine on top of it. It was the first time in years that we had touched that way. He gave me an affectionate, searching look. "Luke's a remarkable fellow. He came into Calogero's house looking like a wild man and had us convinced and moving in under two minutes. I like him."

"I'm glad. I do, too."

"I could see that."

There was a comfortable silence. How amazing it was, I thought, that we should be here together like this, a father and daughter again. Softly, Hugo said, "There is so much I must tell you, Alison."

"You don't have to explain—"

"Ah, but I do. I want you to understand. . . . I was going to wait until the morning. But while you were outside with Luke, Jay asked me why I had never written to him. I want you to know the answer I gave him." His face changed, a sadness passed over it, and I began to be afraid of what he would say. "You and Jay must have found it very difficult when I went to Libya without a word to either of you. These past three years . . . they have cost us all." He sat for a moment without moving, without speaking. Then, gradually, in a low, weary voice, he said, "You knew, didn't you, that I was married once to a Libyan? When I was a young man."

"Moroccan" was my startled response. "I always thought she was Moroccan. And I thought, well, that you weren't really married."

Surprised, he shook his head. "We met in Morocco, Yasmin and I, but she was Libyan. And we really were married. If for less than a year. She died in childbirth. I was away at war, here in Sicily, and I couldn't be with her. I was told the baby died, too. But many years later I learned that the child had survived. It was a boy. Yasmin's family wanted him to be raised a Moslem, and they were afraid I would take him away from them. So they lied to me. But Yasmin's mother and I had liked each other, and the lie was on her conscience. She wrote to me before she died. And she told Salim the truth. That was your brother's name, Salim."

Almost before he spoke the name, I knew it.

"By then he was a man of thirty-seven, safely Moslem. He was in the army, an officer, a follower of Qaddafi. We met, and agreed it would be better for him if it was not known that he was the son of an American. I told almost no one. I wanted to tell you and Jay, but I waited too long for the right moment.

"Salim and a number of other officers became disenchanted with Qaddafi. Tragically, they attempted a coup. It failed, of course, and Salim was caught and imprisoned. I knew nothing of any of this. But it must have been about this time that Elliot found out about Salim, because several months after Salim was put in prison I was contacted by a representative of the Libyan government and asked to consult with them over a project. I agreed to come to Libya—I was glad of the chance to visit Salim. Before I left, however, I got my business affairs in order and asked Elliot to look after the tower. There was always the possibility in the back of my mind that there might be trouble.

"When I reached Libya, I had an interview with Qaddafi. He was charming—he can be very charming—and he explained what he had in mind. A city in the desert, he said. And he wanted me to design it. Before I could respond, he went on to tell me what Salim had done. He said my decision could affect Salim's fate. If I refused . . . well, Qaddafi said, the penalty for treason was severe. If I accepted the commission, Salim would be released from prison on the completion of my part of the project. I was to tell no one of the terms of the agreement and during my work on the project I must not leave Libya.

"I had no choice but to agree. But if Salim was in danger, I thought, then so were you, so was Jay. It seemed wiser not to write to you. The less contact I had with you, the safer you might be.

"I was Qaddafi's tame American for three years. He was pleased with my work, and gradually Salim's prison conditions improved. A year, year and a half, he said, and Salim would be free. Then, last month, we bombed Tripoli. The prison where Salim was held was hit in the raid.

"For two terrible weeks, I couldn't find out if Salim was alive or dead. At last, word came through a mutual friend that he had escaped and was in hiding. He would stay where he was until he heard from me. I promised to get him out of Libya, but I knew I couldn't do it alone. Through this same friend, I sent a message that Salim was to meet me in three days' time at a certain place on the coast. That night I made my way to Tunisia. I flew back to Sicily and came to Calogero for help. I knew I could count on him."

"He told us why," I said.

"Yes?" A faint smile. "Exaggerating my part, no doubt. Calogero has a great loyalty to his friends. And he did not fail me. His son Gaetano owns a fishing boat, and he and Tommaso, the other son, took me to the place on the coast where I was to meet Salim. We waited there, but—" Abruptly, his voice sank into silence. He sat slumped in his chair now, as if the story he was telling exhausted him in a way that all the rigors of the night had not. Wearily, he rubbed his face. "I was too late. Salim had been wounded when the prison was hit. They hadn't told me that. He died while he was in hiding."

Salim. A brother I had never known, would never know. The brother Jay had wanted. He did not seem real to me, not yet. Only Hugo's suffering was real.

A slant of light fell cruelly on him, and I saw how his face

had narrowed, how time and pain had carved away the flesh at
his temples, under his eyes. The last three years had turned my
father into an old man. I rose and put my arms around his neck,
resting my cheek on his bowed head where the once-dark hair
lay gray and thin across his sunburnt scalp. For so many years
I had thought of Hugo as invulnerable, someone almost mythic,
and now I saw that he was mortal. I yearned to comfort him,
but I was frightened by the change. A father who needed
me . . . Suddenly, I wanted the old Hugo, the one I never had
to worry about, never had to think about; I had grown used to
that man, used to the distance between us.

But what I felt was a child's fear of a new order. While words
of consolation and affection reached out like tentative fingers
across a steadily narrowing gap, the fear gradually passed away
into a tender love for the real father I was at last beginning to
know.

CHAPTER 27

Sunrise and a sea gull's cry woke me early the next morning. Filled with an odd, melancholic contentment, I lay half asleep in the tower's silence as the band of sunlight falling on the bedclothes widened. Then I dressed and went quietly downstairs, taking an orange from the bowl on the kitchen table. Outside, I sat on the stone wall watching the colors of the sea far below, immersed in a luxurious sense of light and space and the infinite possibilities that freedom and the open air can offer. But the dark, sad shadow of Salim passed across my mind's eye, and I thought of all that might have been, and all that would remain unknown.

At last the smell of coffee drifting from the open tower door lured me inside again. Hugo was standing by the stove, his back to me. "Would you like some, too, Alison?" he asked, without turning around.

"Thanks. How did you know it was me?"

"I saw you out there. You've been sitting there a long time." It was more a question than a statement.

"Trying to absorb it all. I can't quite, not yet." I looked around. "Where's Jay? Still asleep?"

"Still asleep."

"How did he take it last night, when you told him about Salim?"

Hugo turned and handed me my cup. Rested, the blue eyes vivid in the morning light, he was a younger man, still powerful. He wore an open-necked white shirt, crisp against his tanned skin, and he looked strong and handsome and vital in the way that I remembered. The pain and sadness that had darkened his eyes last night still lingered, but were tempered now by the same wistful happiness I recognized in myself.

"He said he wished he'd known Salim. He said Salim must

have been very brave." Hugo gave a faint smile. "I told Jay that he and his brother were alike in that. And in other ways."

I smiled back. "Their inheritance."

We carried our cups over to a pair of chairs next to an open window, and as he sat drinking his coffee, with his back to the great expanse of the room, I thought how he belonged here, how curiously he completed and yet diminished his surroundings. His "spoils," the remarkable room itself, seemed a natural backdrop for a man who had always been, still was, larger than life—and yet you hardly noticed them, such was the force of his presence. There was a time when I could not see beyond the presence to the man himself, but no longer. With a shock of pleasure I realized that Hugo had become at last simply my father.

He had his pipe and a pouch of tobacco with him. As he tamped the tobacco into the bowl of the pipe, he asked quietly, "Do you blame me, Alison?"

I shook my head. "Not now. What else could you do?"

"I wasn't choosing Salim over you and Jay, you must believe that. He needed me. You were independent, and as for Jay, well, Charlotte may not be an ideal mother, but she does love him. And he has always been a supremely self-sufficient child. As you were." He struck a match and lit the pipe, drawing the flame into the tobacco with deep breaths. "Both of you seemed to do very well without too much paternal interference in your life. Perhaps that was simply a way of justifying to myself my neglect of you, but I don't think so."

"In Jay's eyes you can do no wrong."

Hugo gave a wry smile. "I'll enjoy that while it lasts. I think you were younger when light broke."

"Puberty has a lot to answer for. Maybe I just spent too long outgrowing it."

Musingly, he said, "You were so much like your mother, as you got older. I know I didn't handle that well. I found it difficult sometimes." His head was turned away, toward the window; his profile carved the air, lit by the sunlight that silvered his hair. The pipe sat motionless in his hand, forgotten.

I waited. When the silence lengthened, I put my cup down on the table by the chair. "Shall I make us some breakfast?" I asked him. My voice sounded unnaturally loud in my ears. "There's some fruit, and rolls from yesterday that aren't too stale. And Clio's honey . . ." I stopped, and her name hung in the air between us.

Hugo was looking at me now. Slowly, he said, "I don't want to burdén you with too much, Alison. But there is one more thing you have to know. . . ." An odd expression passed across his face, one I could not remember ever seeing there, something close to an embarrassed awkwardness, a sense of inadequacy.

To make it easier for him, I said quickly, "If it's anything to do with Clio and you, I'm glad. I like her."

But the look remained. "In a way it has everything to do with Clio and me. But as much to do with you."

"With me?" It seemed late in the day for Hugo to start worrying about my reactions to his taste in women. "Honestly, it really doesn't matter what I—"

One hand moved impatiently on the armrest of his chair. "I'm doing this badly." He laid the pipe aside and got to his feet, looking down at me. His face was grave. "Maybe the best thing is simply to say it. Alison, Clio is your mother."

I couldn't speak, could only stare at him, amazed. But that first shocked impulse of denial gave way almost instantly to belief. It explained so much. It was as though a veil had been lifted from a shape wholly mysterious yet always, inexplicably, familiar.

Hugo rested one hand on my shoulder. "Before Libya, I meant to bring you here, to tell you. Clio was afraid. She thought you would not forgive her for all those years—"

I twisted around to look up at him. "She never wrote, not once." The words came out so baldly, in a rush, spoken by the child who remembered the hurt, not the adult who supposed she had long ago come to terms with it.

Hugo seemed surprised at this. "She said she did, for years, but you never answered. Constance always wrote back for you. Finally, when you were about twelve, Constance wrote to say that you didn't want to hear from her anymore."

I believed that. Aunt Constance had been so angry with her sister. She had found a way to punish her. A sudden bitterness swept over me as I thought of those unseen letters.

Quietly, Hugo said, "Clio knows how you must have suffered. But she has suffered, too."

I bit my lip. "I might have been glad to hear that, once. But last night, in the cave . . ." Lamely, I finished, "I learned something. What matters, and what doesn't." To escape Hugo's gaze, I stood up and carried my empty cup over to the sink, taking refuge from my confused emotions in questions. "Why is she called Clio? My mother's name was Amelia."

"She never liked the name Amelia. Clio was my name for her. She adopted it." Hugo was wandering slowly around the room, picking up objects and examining them as if he only now recognized them as his. "Clio was the muse of history. Your mother was, in some ways, my muse."

I remembered Clio saying that she and Hugo had come together again because he'd read an article of hers; I asked him if this was true. He replied that it was. "We wrote back and forth for a while, and eventually I suggested we meet here, at Castell'alto. She had been here once before, when we first knew each other. She was happy here. She always had an extraordinary sense of place, a feeling for the way the past endures." He placed the tips of his fingers against the glazed surface of the blue Islamic tile, almost in a caress. After a moment, he added, "We found our own past wasn't as remote as we had thought it was."

"When you went to Libya, did you tell her—"

"She knew about Salim." He put the tile down. "When I didn't come back I expect she drew her own conclusions. I couldn't write to her, any more than I could write to you. It was too dangerous. Pointless restraint, of course," he added bitterly.

At that moment we heard footsteps outside, and then Luke appeared in the open doorway, with Matteo behind him. Both men looked exhausted. While I gave them coffee and rolls, Luke told us that Elliot had not been found alive or dead, only his shoes, left behind on the little beach below the meadow. After pausing to wolf down a roll, he added, "It looks as if he might have been able to swim out to a boat despite the bee stings. We have to assume his Libyan friends picked him up after all. The Italian coast guard will be watching for them, but they've had a good head start. . . ." He stifled a yawn, and when I asked him if he'd slept at all shook his head. "I waited for the consulate people to arrive. Then gave them a hand."

"When you've eaten, why don't you go on up and get some sleep? You can have my bed." I asked him if he knew whether the road out of Castell'alto was clear again. He said that it was, that he and Matteo had just driven along it with one of Don Calo's sons. "Then we could go and see Clio now, couldn't we?" I said to Hugo. "While Luke and Matteo stay here with Jay."

"Of course we could." His pleased surprise was touched with anxiety. "But are you sure this is what you want? You've been through so much. Clio will understand if you don't come at once."

"I want to see her." But even as I spoke, a frightening thought occurred to me. "I don't want to leave Jay, though, if there's the slightest chance that the Libyans might come back here, with or without Elliot."

Luke was drinking the last of his coffee. "I meant to tell you," he said now, setting his cup down, "that Don Calo sent a couple of men up here last night, when he heard you'd been found. They're still here, by the bridge, and they have guns. So Jay will be perfectly safe. Though I think the Libyans are long gone anyway." Through a mouthful of honey and roll, Matteo added firmly that he would be awake while Luke slept.

Reassured, I told Hugo that we would leave as soon as I had got Luke settled. Luke looked so weary that once we were upstairs, I made him stretch out on my bed. While I sat beside him, I told him who Salim was and why Hugo had spent the years in Libya. Luke rose up on one elbow, taken completely by surprise; in all the speculation, he said, no one had ever suggested this as a possible explanation for Hugo's thralldom to Quaddafi.

He linked the fingers of his right hand with mine, and said gently, "I'm so sorry, Alison. To lose a brother you've never known. . . ." He kissed my hand and held it against his cheek. The words were simple, the gesture undramatic, but I thought how unaccountable and strange it was that this voice, of all voices, this body next to me, of all bodies, should have such power to soothe me. And unsettle me.

Through the open window came a dove's plaintive notes, soft as the morning air, the mournful "cucurucu" of the bird without its mate. "Salim died before he even existed for me," I said. "I don't really know yet what I've lost. It's Hugo I'm sad for."

"He did his best for Salim. And it sounds as though Salim was someone who made his own choices."

"Yes, I know. And at least Hugo's safe." Struck by a sudden hope, I asked Luke if he thought Qaddafi would leave Hugo alone now that he could no longer use Salim as a weapon against him.

Luke lay back, one arm under his head. "My sources in Palermo think it's more likely he'll back off because we know of Elliot's involvement in the affair. I doubt Qaddafi would want his link with the drug trade publicized."

Then, haltingly, I told him about Clio Hunt. Although he must have found it a strange story, he heard me out in sympathetic silence. "If I had learned she was my mother before all this happened, three years ago when Hugo planned to tell me, I wouldn't have been able to accept it. But now the anger's gone. I have more than I dreamed of when Jay and I set out on this journey. I have a family." I leaned over him, smoothing the dark hair back from his brow where it fell across the bandage. "I have you."

"Yes." The hazel eyes looked back into mine, amused and tender. "You have me."

He drew me down and kissed me with slow sweet kisses, his lips moving softly across my face, down along my throat, his hands restlessly touching the bare skin on my arms and on my neck, touching my hair. Our bodies curved and joined until I felt his body not as something separate but almost as a part of me. I pulled away a little then, to look down at him. Unshaven, tousled, his eyes ringed with weariness, he seemed so beautiful, and infinitely desirable. A lover who was both friend and mystery, a mystery that promised revelations of an undiscovered happiness.

"Do you know what would help me sleep?" he murmured, his breath warm against my cheek.

"I can guess." I traced the outline of his mouth, and said half teasingly, "But you can't possibly have the energy."

Under my fingers, the sleepy smile grew mischievous. "You'd be surprised." He began slowly to undo the buttons of my blouse.

"Not now," I said, stopping his hand. "Not when my brother's in the next room, and my father's downstairs waiting for me. Besides, you need to sleep." Gently, I disengaged myself and got to my feet, doing up the buttons. With a dramatic groan of disappointment, Luke collapsed back on the bed. But his eyes were closing before I was out the door.

Matteo walked with Hugo and me as far as Orlando's stall. He had brought the donkey sugar lumps, a reward, he said, for saving Jay and me. On the opposite side of the bridge, the two men sent by Don Calo stood smoking cigarettes, rifles slung across their shoulders. They were big, formidable-looking men. After Hugo spoke briefly with them in Sicilian, we took the Jeep down to Castell'alto, then switched to my car. Hugo offered to drive. "I know the road. And I'd be glad of the chance to drive it after all these years." I accepted, smiling to myself because I knew very well that Hugo hated to be driven; he made a bad passenger, impatient when anyone but himself was at the wheel.

As we drove, we talked about the last three years, about Salim, about Clio. "Salim taught me what my children mean to me," Hugo said at one point, his voice reflective. "I always loved you and Jay, Alison. But until Salim I don't think I ever realized just how much." His sideways glance at me was shy. " 'The owl of Minerva flies at dusk,' someone once wrote. A way of saying that wisdom comes when it's almost too late."

"I learned the same lesson from Jay," I said, hearing the roughness in my voice. "He showed me how to love you."

Hugo took my hand and gave it a gentle squeeze. "Bless you for that." He told me then that he had loved my mother, too. When they learned that she was pregnant, he asked her to marry him. "But she refused. She said I'd be marrying her only because of you. She was right—I knew it and she knew it. I loved her, but I was caught up in my career. I knew I'd make a bad father and a worse husband." He shrugged. "I'm not trying to excuse myself, but for good and ill, work is my life. Even had I known the cost then, my choices might not have been different."

The storm had washed rivers of mud and debris across the road, tearing away large chunks from the crumbling asphalt verge and widening already lethal potholes. While Hugo maneuvered the car around the worst of the hazards, I thought about what he had told me. I accepted his words as one version of the truth, as the way he saw it, aware that my mother might have a different truth. I didn't want to judge Hugo, I didn't want to judge my mother. I was tired of judging. But there was a question I had asked myself from the moment I was old enough to understand that a pregnancy did not necessarily have to result in a baby. I had never been able to ask Aunt Constance, or Hugo—then. But I asked him now.

"Why have me, after all, if she didn't want me?"

"Ah, but she did want you" was Hugo's reply. "Clio was, is, a romantic. She had a vision of herself meeting all obstacles and triumphing. Reality proved more intractable. She had a difficult pregnancy and a worse birth. She was very ill for some time afterward. Later she found out she couldn't have any more children, but that was long after she'd given you up. From the first, Constance took care of you. When Clio felt strong again, you seemed settled and happy there, and her own life was turbulent. She went through a long bitter period when she seemed to cast off everything that once had mattered to her. Her scholarship, her family, me. And, finally, you—although she genuinely believed that you'd be better off with Constance and Harold. I was partly to blame, but there was more to it than that. Clio wanted to punish herself. I've never known why. She was too young to understand the implications when she allowed Constance to adopt you. And she did not know then how much Constance hated her.''

''Why did Aunt Constance hate her?''

''I can only guess. Clio was beautiful, intelligent, a little spoiled. She was the child of her father's old age, and he made no secret that she was his favorite. He divorced Constance's mother to marry Clio's. Perhaps there were other reasons, but I doubt we'll ever know them. Despite that, Constance was a kind woman in many ways.'' He turned his head to look at me. ''But you know that.''

I did know it. She might have hated my mother, but she had loved me. Perhaps that was why, now, I could forgive them both.

After Clio gave permission for the adoption, Hugo said, she traveled from country to country, settling finally in Australia, where she married a man named Hunt. They lived on a farm and it was there she began raising bees. Eventually, after the marriage failed, she went back to the university in Sydney, where she at last completed the degree in archaeology begun twenty years before. ''And gradually,'' Hugo said, ''she began to find some peace of mind.''

Without thinking, I reached up to the place where the medallion had hung around my neck. Reminded by its absence, I asked Hugo if he had given Clio hers.

He said that he had, that he had found the two coins, Clio's and mine, lying in a small crevice on the tunnel floor of the cave not far from the waterfall where Jay and I had appeared last night. ''There were only the two, but I've always felt certain that others were hidden somewhere in the cave. The map you and Jay used—it was the beginning of my treasure hunting.''

The urge to tell him about the sanctuary was almost irresistible, but I couldn't, not without Jay. All I said was ''Your map saved us.''

''Thank God I was that absurd boy who liked to make mysteries. And thank God you had a taste for puzzles.''

I remembered another of his mysteries. ''The lady of the labyrinth—who did you mean by that? The goddess on the coin?''

He nodded. ''She had other names, of course, but I thought

of her that way. It was the name the Minoans gave to their Great Goddess, and it seemed right, somehow, for Casteddu's goddess. There's an inscription from Knossos that reads, 'To the Lady of the Labyrinth, a jar of honey.' Clio was delighted by that, of course.'' He smiled at the memory.

We were entering San Teodoro. Hugo suggested that I leave him at the bar in the main square; he would have an espresso and then walk to Clio's in half an hour or so. ''You and she should have some time alone together,'' he told me.

Now that the moment was so near, I found I was frightened. ''Maybe you should go first. She'd probably much rather see you. After all this time.''

''Nonsense.'' Hugo's voice was brisk. Abruptly, he pulled over by the fountain and we both climbed out. I came around to the driver's side and got in behind the steering wheel while he held the door open for me. He was about to shut the door when he seemed to hesitate. After a moment he said softly, ''There was always another lady of the labyrinth, Alison. Your mother. I don't mean that I thought of her as a goddess or an Ariadne—I'm not such a fool as that. And God knows she never wanted a Theseus, or needed a Dionysus. But during all the years of our separation she was there, waiting at the heart of things. She was, is, more to me than any other woman I have known. And she knows that.'' His blue eyes held mine. ''But it's you she needs to see now.'' And then he closed the door, turned, and strode away across the square.

And he had called Clio a romantic.

I thought about all the women who had passed through his life after they parted—had he been searching for her, restlessly seeking someone who offered the same enigma, the same challenge, flint to his steel?

During the short drive to Clio's house, I tried not to think of that moment when I would at last confront my mother. I wanted whatever I said or did to come from my heart, not from some preconceived notion of how I ought to behave. Perhaps when I saw her, talked to her, I would find it difficult, after all, to forgive her. But I hoped the spirit that had guided our journey, Jay's and mine, would see me through its final meeting.

The Land Rover was parked in front of the house. But there was no sign of anyone, including Argo, and no response to my knock on the door. I called out Clio's name, watching a butterfly hover uncertainly above the stone bee amid the geraniums. When there was no answer to my call, I decided to try the honey house and the hives. Muffled barking greeted me as I went around the back, and when I opened the honey house door Argo bounded out, jumping up and licking my face joyfully.

"Where's Clio?" I asked him, as if he could tell me.

I never heard the back door open, but when I lifted my head she was suddenly there on the concrete terrace. She stood with her arms crossed, gripping her elbows, her hair uncombed, her blouse only partly tucked into her skirt. Around her neck was a long blue scarf, very wrinkled, as though it had been tightly knotted. I was shocked by the way she looked, gray and old, almost ill. Her smile was peculiar; it seemed both surprised and joyful, and yet she was, I was sure, distressed to see me. "Alison," she said, and her voice cracked slightly.

"Clio! Are you all right?"

"I . . . I don't feel well. A bad headache." When she made an effort to smooth her hair, I saw that her hand was trembling. Argo trotted to her side, but she ignored him.

"I'm sorry." I took a few steps closer to her. "I wanted to talk to you. Can I come in?"

"No!" This was said so sharply, with one hand held out as if to stop me, that it brought me to a halt at the edge of the terrace. "Not now, Alison. This isn't a good time."

"Later, then? Maybe this afternoon?"

She nodded. "Yes. That would be better." Her fingers played restlessly with the ends of the scarf.

"Good. Well, I'll . . . I'll see you then." Disturbed, I turned and started to walk away, but paused, reluctant somehow to leave her. An indefinable menace seemed to hang in the air, an uncomfortable sense of oppression, of something out of joint. It was then, as I hesitated, that I noticed the window of Clio's garage standing slightly open. Inside the garage was a black Alfa Romeo. A black Alfa Romeo just like Giudico's. But Giudico was dead. Elliot, I thought, instinctively, irrationally, somehow Elliot was alive, was here. Thoughts tumbled through my brain. The car must have been hidden near the meadow, the keys would have been in Giudico's jacket pocket, of course he'd come in a car, why didn't we think . . .

And then: I must get out of here.

But it was too late.

Behind me, on the terrace, a familiar voice said hoarsely, "You persistent, nosy bitch! I should kill you right now."

I turned around. Elliot stood in the open back door, the gun in one hand. He was virtually unrecognizable, transformed into a nightmare creature with a blotched and swollen face and bloodshot eyes buried deep in soft, sickly flesh that shone with a thin film of sweat. The smooth blond hair, now lank and dark, hung in greasy strands over his forehead. His shirt and trousers were torn and filthy.

"That's right, take a good look," he said venomously. "It's your doing."

I didn't reply. I was thinking that if he was here, hiding at Clio's, she must be involved in the drug smuggling after all. The knowledge sickened me.

Clio was ashen-faced. "Why," she said, and her voice was thin and strained, "why didn't you go when you had the chance?"

"Shut up." Elliot motioned once more with the gun. "Go on, both of you. Inside."

I wasn't going anywhere with Elliot, that much I knew. I shook my head. "I'm staying here."

"Then I'll have to shoot Clio. Before I shoot you." His smile was a travesty of handsome Elliot's amiable smile. He took a step forward. "How I'd love to shoot you, you—"

"He won't," interrupted Clio, surprisingly. Her face had changed, become urgent. "He needs us. He doesn't dare drive now that it's daylight." The words tumbled out before Elliot could stop her. "He told me you were trapped in the cave. That no one knew you were there so if he killed me no one would ever know. I had to do as he said." She winced when Elliot pushed the gun hard into her back.

"I said shut up!" Then, to me, "She's right. I do need you. But only one of you. And I'll happily kill the other if you don't do as I say." He wiped the sweat off his face with the back of one hand.

We did as he said. I followed Clio into the house, almost lightheaded with relief now that I knew she wasn't Elliot's accomplice. But terror overwhelmed that frail emotion when Elliot shut and locked the door behind the three of us. He was more than physically unrecognizable; the last shred of that amused, controlled persona was gone. He seemed to be breaking up, bits of some buried self baring its teeth through the shards of the former man.

"Jay?" Clio half whispered. "Is he—"

"He's safe," I told her.

Argo had pushed through the door with Clio and me, evading Elliot's attempt to shut him out. Now he followed us into the living room and lay curled up on the rug, his head on his paws, watching us. He looked puzzled, but he obviously thought of Elliot as a friend. The daybed was rumpled, a pillow and blanket tumbled together at one end of it. Clio's papers were strewn across the floor, the remains of breakfast, a half-eaten loaf of bread, a bowl of mulberries, a dirty cup and plate, in their place on the table. Over the back of a chair hung a length of clothesline, with several clothespins still attached.

"Clio was about to drive me into Palermo," he told me. "But you can do it now that you're here." He threw the length of clothesline at me. "Tie her to the chair." When I hesitated, he knocked everything on the table to the floor with one sweep of his arm, shouting, "Now!" Then he sat down on the daybed, slightly hunched over, with the gun held in both hands between his knees, its muzzle pointing at us. He looked like some sick wild animal, all the more dangerous for its wounds.

At the crash of china, Argo raised his head and gave a low growl, but Clio spoke gently to him and he settled down again.

Silently, I removed the clothespins from the line and began to wind the rope around Clio.

"How did you get out?" Elliot asked me.

"There was another entrance. Jay found it." Then, "How did you survive the stings?"

"Sorry I disappointed you." The voice came through the thickened lips in a sneer.

Clio said, "He always carries medication with him. He told me he injected himself and hid in some rocks while the epinephrine took effect. Then he managed to drive down here. God knows how. I keep medication here, too."

I noticed that Elliot's feet were bare and swollen. "They found your shoes on the beach," I told him.

A grunt was his only response.

Desperately, I thought of Hugo. Half an hour, he had said, and then he would join us. How long had I been here already? Ten minutes, fifteen? Let him wait, I prayed desperately, let him not come now. I tried to work faster, thinking that if I could just get Elliot out of here before Hugo arrived, while Clio and Hugo were still safe . . . "I guess you were waiting for your Libyan friends, weren't you?" I said, making an effort to keep my voice steady. "Your gunshots must have scared them off."

"Why don't you just shut up?" Elliot said. "It won't be long before you can tell them your interesting theories in person. Make sure those knots are tight. If they aren't, I'm not going to bother tightening them. It'll be easier just to kill her." When I finished, Elliot told me to take the cloth napkin from the table and stuff it in Clio's mouth. "Then use her scarf to gag her." He got up to watch as I did it.

When Elliot was satisfied that Clio was securely tied and gagged, he told me we were going outside to my car. "You'll walk right in f . . . front of me. My gun will be pointed at your back. Remember that, if you're tempted to try anything. It isn't going to take much to make me kill you."

I bent over to hug Clio. "Everything will be all right," I told her while she watched me mutely. In case everything wasn't, I whispered softly in her ear, "Hugo is back. I know who you are." Our eyes met. Hers were wide with shock; in mine I hoped she read everything I could not say. I hugged her once more, before Elliot jerked me away. His puffy fingers felt like fat sausages on the bare skin of my arm.

Argo padded after us to the front door. Before Elliot opened it, he glanced through the window that looked out to the road. His eyes left me only for the instant it took him to check that there was no car driving by, no one walking down the road.

I was calculating frantically: If Hugo arrived soon after Elliot and I had left, then he would surely find Clio, and they would call the police, and maybe, just maybe, Elliot and I would be stopped in time. But if Hugo was on his way here now, if Elliot saw him . . .

Mercifully, the road was empty. "Open the door," Elliot ordered. "And remember, this is right behind you." He waved the little gun in my face. Then he stepped back, gripping my arm hard. Argo was right by the door, whimpering oddly, begging to go out. "Get back!" Elliot said viciously, shoving Argo away with his foot.

I opened the door.

Hugo was standing there on the stoop. He was holding the stone bee in his hands, gazing at it, his expression bemused. When he looked up and saw us, his face blanched. I opened my mouth to warn him, and behind me Elliot swore savagely, but before any of us could move, Argo gave a great yelp of joy, pushing violently past Elliot and me to get to the man who had saved his life, the master who had come back to him at last. In his bounding rush forward, he knocked the gun from Elliot's grasp. It fell to the tiles with a clatter. Both Elliot and I dove for it, but Elliot got there first. The puffy fingers closed over the gun. Before Elliot could roll over and raise it to shoot, Hugo slammed the stone bee down on his head. Elliot grunted and collapsed like a sack on the floor.

"Clio?" Hugo said desperately. All the blood had drained from his face.

"She's all right. In there—"

He was already past me, with Argo right on his heels. We untied Clio and I left them to their own reunion while I used the rope on Elliot. When I stood up, they were behind me, his arm around her shoulders. Clio's face was twisted with a kind of anxious happiness. In answer to our questions, Hugo's and mine, she said that Elliot had arrived before dawn. After she had given him more medicine, he told her his own version of what had occurred. Disbelieving, she had pressed him, and he took out his gun and told her the truth, enough of it anyway to terrify her. Then he tied her up, saying he needed to sleep. Only when I called out Clio's name did he wake up. He untied Clio, then, and told her to go out and get rid of me. "It seemed a miracle that you were safe, Alison. . . . But I was so frightened that Elliot would change his mind, would decide not to let you go. And then you saw Giudico's car."

Shortly after this, Hugo—accompanied by Argo, who refused to be separated from him—walked down the road to use a neighbor's telephone. Clio and I were alone. Silently, we picked up the mess of papers, broken china, and food from the tiles. The mulberries had rolled everywhere; a few were crushed, their dark pulp like drops of blood on the floor. I gathered them up, heaping them into a little pile on a napkin.

When we were finished, Clio turned to me. "Alison," she began, and the way she said my name, hesitantly, almost beseechingly, moved me. Her hands hung by her sides, the palms upturned, like a supplicant's. She had suffered, Hugo had said, and I could see that it was true. All the angry, vengeful words I had once imagined myself saying to her were forgotten. "I was a fool," she said, her large gray eyes clouded with pain. "I threw away my chance to be your mother. I failed you in so many ways. All those things I should have done for you, and didn't. So much you needed, so much I never gave you . . ." She looked away from me then, down at the pile of broken china on the table.

The pretty yellow earthenware plate had cracked neatly in half. I reached out and picked up the two pieces, fitting them together. "This could be mended," I said. But I wasn't thinking of the plate; I was thinking of what she had seemed to me from the beginning, a strong and independent woman, someone who had made a good life for herself out of little. The quality in myself that I had taken for a colorless prudence might be something else, the self-sufficiency Hugo had seen, her gift to me.

I said, "You gave me things that matter. I know that now."

She told me then that she had been badly shocked when she saw Jay and me standing in her garden that first day. "For one insane moment I thought maybe you'd come because you knew. . . . Then, when I realized you were looking for Hugo, I was afraid for you. There was so much here to hurt you. The truth about Hugo. The truth about me." She gave a bitter smile. "And I never knew that Elliot was a far more terrible danger."

She said that she had contemplated telling me who she was, but her courage failed her. "Without Hugo's support I thought I would do it badly, might alienate you forever."

Deliberately, I picked up a mulberry. I ate it, and then I picked up another and held it out to her. It took her a moment to understand the gesture for what it was. When she did, the puzzled look on her face changed to an astonished happiness. Hugo found us eating mulberries together, in tears.

Hugo's return was soon followed by a seemingly endless stream of officials. We had to answer questions from the police, more questions from a special drug unit, still more questions put by a pair of Americans from the consulate in Palermo. Elliot, still unconscious, disappeared in an ambulance soon after the police arrived, and somewhere in the middle of all these questions, Luke and Jay and Don Calo arrived.

Eventually, Don Calo persuaded the Sicilian questioners that still more questions could wait, while Luke convinced the two Americans that we had told them all we knew about Elliot and his associates. Astonishingly, or perhaps not so, Hugo announced that he intended to give Luke a full account of his time with Qaddafi, and the Americans left, reasonably content. When the last of the questioners had departed, Don Calo carried us all away with him to Lupaia. He had not known that Clio was my mother, but he seemed unsurprised by the news. I suspected that nothing would surprise Don Calo.

That night, after the others had gone to bed, I stood on the terrace at Lupaia with Luke, the first time we had been alone together since the morning. The air had the soft warmth of black velvet, thick with a hundred small sounds. Against the night sky, Monte Castello was a great dark shadow outlined by stars. Teasing Luke, I said, "You've won Hugo over. So it seems you have what you came for. But I warn you, I'm going to ask him to tell you his story very, very slowly. It will take years. . . ."

"I hope, my darling," he replied, just before he kissed me, "that it takes a lifetime."

EPILOGUE

There was a final journey yet to make, one last trip into the labyrinth. I dreaded that dark subterranean silence, but I had a promise to keep and a debt of gratitude to pay.

Myth is someone else's religion. Hugo's words came back to me again. I was no convert, but I could not dismiss the impulse that had prompted me to petition that small stone figure, laying the medallion at her feet, as simply a superstitious weighting of the odds. If I owed it to Jay to go back with him and Hugo, as I had promised I would, I also owed it to the lady of the labyrinth.

Jay, naturally, did not have the slightest qualm about returning to the cave. Never mind that we might have died there, he talked about our grim experience as though it were the most wonderful adventure any boy could have. As I suppose it was—if the boy lived through it. He declared firmly that we couldn't just tell Hugo and Clio about the grotto; we had to show them ourselves. Besides, once Hugo learned of its existence he would immediately insist on seeing it for himself, and then we'd have to go with him anyway. Wasn't that true? I had to admit that it was.

"It won't be so bad this time, Alison," Jay told me kindly, perhaps noticing my lack of enthusiasm for the expedition. "And just wait till you see Hugo's face when we show him. That'll make it all worthwhile."

Hugo and Clio both suspected something was up, of course. They could hardly avoid it, given Jay's excitement and the hints he dropped. But they were good sports, and refused to spoil the surprise with educated guessing. In any case, the reality would, I knew, far exceed anything they could imagine.

I insisted to Jay on certain precautions, however, before we set off, and Luke backed me up. He and Matteo reconnoitered the tunnel to make sure that no flooding had occurred since we were last in it. They came back to report that not only was the tunnel still dry, but the waterfall had vanished. I was relieved—pneumonia, at least, would not be one of the risks.

In proper caving fashion, each of us carried three separate sources of light and wore hard hats that Hugo dug out of some storage locker. All this made me feel a little better, but it took every ounce of my courage to leave the warm sunlit courtyard and go down the stone steps into the armory. Matteo stayed behind, a final precaution, while the five of us—Hugo and Clio, Luke, Jay, and I—descended into the tunnel.

Ultimately, as Jay predicted, I found that the journey back was not the test of my bravery I had thought it would be. This time I knew what lay at the heart of the labyrinth, I knew how to reach it, and I knew how to escape. Moreover, I was fed, rested, happy, and secure—everything, in short, that before I was not. Even the ledge that ran along the little passage connecting the tunnel with the cavern, the ledge that bordered the seemingly bottomless chasm, wasn't quite so daunting now that the thunderous, pounding waterfall had disappeared, leaving behind it only a steady rivulet trickling down the rock and a few pools of water cupped in the crevices.

Before we crossed the chasm, Jay and I warned the others about the skeletons and the coins scattered on the ground. Proudly, Jay told Hugo that he and I had remembered not to disturb anything. Then he turned and led us through into the cavern, past the skeletons, and in silent single file along the edge of the lake. Hugo and Clio showed remarkable self-restraint; they must have badly wanted to stop for a moment to concentrate on the treasure strewn across the rock, but they confined themselves to a quick examination of the coins and then followed Jay obediently to the end of the cavern.

Now that the moment had come, I was trembling. I reached out for Luke's hand, steadied by his warmth. Then, at Jay's signal, I raised my lantern in unison with his, lighting the grotto.

No one stirred, no one spoke. We stood together in a semi-circle, pilgrims who had reached their different meccas, united now. Jay was right. The sight of Hugo's face when he saw what lay beyond us in the soft light from the lanterns was the reward for our ordeal. He looked like someone who sees a long-held dream become reality, dazzled, gratified, with the boy's sense of wonder shining from his eyes. He looked exactly as Jay had at the same moment.

Clio broke the silence. "The Lady of the Labyrinth," she whispered. "She's been found at last."

"Yes," Hugo said. "She's been found at last." He turned and took my mother in his arms.